Love, marriage...

The Rinucci Brothers

Three glitzy, glamorous romances from one beloved Mills & Boon author!

The Rinucci Brothers

LUCY GORDON

> **DID YOU PURCHASE THIS BOOK WITHOUT A COVER?**
> If you did, you should be aware it is **stolen property** as it was reported *unsold and destroyed* by a retailer. Neither the author nor the publisher has received any payment for this book.

All the characters in this book have no existence outside the imagination of the author, and have no relation whatsoever to anyone bearing the same name or names. They are not even distantly inspired by any individual known or unknown to the author, and all the incidents are pure invention.

All Rights Reserved including the right of reproduction in whole or in part in any form. This edition is published by arrangement with Harlequin Enterprises II B.V./S.à.r.l. The text of this publication or any part thereof may not be reproduced or transmitted in any form or by any means, electronic or mechanical, including photocopying, recording, storage in an information retrieval system, or otherwise, without the written permission of the publisher.

This book is sold subject to the condition that it shall not, by way of trade or otherwise, be lent, resold, hired out or otherwise circulated without the prior consent of the publisher in any form of binding or cover other than that in which it is published and without a similar condition including this condition being imposed on the subsequent purchaser.

® and ™ are trademarks owned and used by the trademark owner and/or its licensee. Trademarks marked with ® are registered with the United Kingdom Patent Office and/or the Office for Harmonisation in the Internal Market and in other countries.

First published in Great Britain 2010
Harlequin Mills & Boon Limited,
Eton House, 18-24 Paradise Road, Richmond, Surrey TW9 1SR

THE RINUCCI BROTHERS © by Harlequin Enterprises II B.V./S.à.r.l 2010

Wife and Mother Forever, Her Italian Boss's Agenda and *The Wedding Arrangement* were first published in Great Britain by Harlequin Mills & Boon Limited in separate, single volumes.

Wife and Mother Forever © Lucy Gordon 2005
Her Italian Boss's Agenda © Lucy Gordon 2005
Wedding Arrangement © Lucy Gordon 2006

ISBN: 978 0 263 88117 2

05-1210

Printed and bound in Spain
by Litografia Rosés S.A., Barcelona

Lucy Gordon cut her writing teeth on magazine journalism, interviewing many of the world's most interesting men, including Warren Beatty, Richard Chamberlain, Sir Roger Moore, Sir Alec Guinness and Sir John Gielgud. She also camped out with lions in Africa and has many other unusual experiences which have often provided the background for her books. She is married to a Venetian, whom she met while on holiday in Venice. They got engaged within two days.

Two of her books have won the Romance Writers of America RITA® award, *Song of the Lorelei* in 1990 and *His Brother's Child* in 1998, in the Best Traditional Romance category. You can visit her website at www.lucy-gordon.com.

WIFE AND
MOTHER FOREVER

PROLOGUE

IT WAS four o'clock and almost time for Signora Rinucci's birthday celebration to begin. Gleaming black limousines were gliding up the hill to the Villa Rinucci in its place of eminence, overlooking the Bay of Naples.

The food and wine were laid out on the great terrace of the villa, best Neapolitan spaghetti and clams, fruit grown in the rich volcanic soil of Vesuvius, wine from the same place. A feast for the gods.

High above, the sky was the deepest blue. Far below, the blue was reflected in the bay, sparkling in the afternoon sun.

'A perfect day.' Toni Rinucci joined his wife on the terrace where she was looking down the hill, and laid his arm gently around her shoulder. 'Everything as it should be.'

He was a stocky man of sixty with grey hair and a heavy face that broke easily into a grin. As always, his eyes were tender as he gazed at his wife.

She was fifty-four but could have passed for her late forties. Her figure was still as slim as a girl's. Everything about her spoke of grace and elegance, not to mention marriage to a rich man who delighted in spending money on her.

Despite some inevitable lines, her face was still beautiful. Not pretty; it was too strong for that.

Her nose was large for a woman, slightly flattened at the bridge, dominating her features, speaking of character and decision.

Her mouth was wide and generous, and could break into a smile that many men had found breathtaking. She offered that smile to her husband now, her fingers caressing the diamonds at her throat.

'And your gift to me is the best ever,' she told him, 'as it is every year.'

'But it's not the gift you really want, is it?' he said softly. 'Do you think I don't know that?'

She seemed to give herself a little shake.

'That's all in the past, *caro* Toni. I don't dwell on it.'

He knew she didn't speak the truth. The secret that had lain between them for the thirty years of their marriage was as potent now as always. But, as always, she would not hurt him by saying that her happiness was incomplete. And, as always, he pretended to believe her.

Two men appeared in the doorway that led from the house to the terrace, and stopped at the sight of the couple holding each other tenderly.

Luke, the more heavily built of the two, grinned at the sight.

'There's no time for that, you two,' he said fondly. 'You have guests arriving in a minute.'

'Send them away,' Toni said, his eyes on his wife.

Primo, tall, with brilliant eyes and a laid-back air that proclaimed his Neapolitan ancestry, shook his head in mock despair.

'Incorrigible,' he told his brother. 'Maybe we should leave them alone and take everyone off to a nightclub.'

'You already spend too much time in nightclubs, my son,' Hope said, coming over to kiss Primo's cheek.

'A man needs a little innocent fun,' he said, giving her a beguiling smile.

'Hm!' She stood back and surveyed him tenderly. 'My

opinion of your 'innocence' is best not expressed at this moment.'

'No need,' he said wickedly. 'Not when you've expressed it so often before. I'm a lost case. Give up on me.'

'I never give up on any of my sons,' she said, adding softly, 'None of them.'

In the brief silence that followed Primo and Luke exchanged glances, each understanding the hidden meaning of those words.

'One day, Mamma,' Primo said gently.

'Yes, one day. One day he will be here. I know it in my heart, although I cannot tell how or when it will happen. But I will not die until he has come to me. Of that I am certain.'

Toni had drawn close to his wife in time to hear her last words.

'*Cara*,' he said gently, 'no sad thoughts today.'

'But I am not sad. I know that one day my son will find me. That can only make me happy. *Ah, there you are!*'

With a bright smile she turned away to greet the first guests. The newcomers had been ushered out on to the terrace by three young men whose facial resemblance proclaimed them kin.

'Mamma,' the tallest of the three called to her, indicating the guests, 'look who's here.'

This was Francesco, who might have been his mother's secret favourite, or might not. It was marvellous how many of her sons thought he alone was the possessor of the talisman.

The other two were Ruggiero and Carlo, the twin sons she had borne to Toni. At twenty-eight they were the youngest. Although not identical, they were much alike, both ridiculously handsome, with the same air of being ready for anything. Especially if it was a party.

And this was going to be the party of parties. As the light faded and the dark red sun plunged into the bay the lights came on in the Villa Rinucci and the guests streamed up the hill, bearing gifts for Hope Rinucci's fifty-fourth birthday.

Those present included everybody who was anybody in Naples, with a fair sprinkling of guests who had made the journey from Rome, or even as far away as Milan, for the Rinucci family was one of the more notable in Italy, with extensive connections in business and politics.

The woman at the centre of it was English, even after thirty years in Italy. Yet nobody would have mistaken her for an outsider. She was the heart of the family, not only to her husband but to the five men who called themselves her sons. Only three of them had actually been born to her, but, if challenged, the other two would have fiercely claimed her as their mother.

They were the best-looking men there: all in their prime, all strolling about with grace and unconscious arrogance. They were Rinuccis, even those who did not bear the name.

Throughout the evening Hope moved among her guests, receiving gifts and tributes with great charm, an undisputed queen among her admirers.

Not all the guests would have called themselves admirers. For each one who spoke of charm and generosity another could tell of ruthlessness. Yet even her enemies had not spurned her invitation.

The enemies were easy to spot, as Luke remarked wryly to Primo. They brought the most lavish gifts, showered her with the greatest praise and lingered the longest to say what a wonderful evening it had been.

But finally the last one departed, the staff had cleared the tables on the terrace and the family were free to relax with their various choice of nightcap.

'That's better,' Primo said, pouring himself a whisky. 'Shall I bring you something, Mamma? Mamma?'

She was looking out over the sea, and although her fingers touched the diamonds about her neck it was clear that she was oblivious to her surroundings.

'Couldn't she have forgotten him even today?' Primo sighed.

'Less today than at any other time,' Luke said. 'Don't forget that this was his birthday too.'

'Why can her five sons not be enough for her?' Carlo asked with a touch of wistfulness.

'Because she does not have five sons,' Toni said quietly. 'She has six, and even now she grieves for the one who was lost. She believes with all her heart that one day she will find him again.'

'Do you believe she'll get her wish?' Ruggiero asked.

Toni sighed helplessly. He had no answer.

CHAPTER ONE

'OK, FOLKS, that's it.'

The bell for the end of school sounded as Evie finished talking. Fifteen twelve-year-olds did a more or less controlled scramble, and in seconds the classroom was empty.

Evie rubbed her neck and stretched it a little to relieve the tension.

'Hard week?' asked a voice from the door. It was Debra, Deputy Head of the school, and the friend who'd asked her to help out for a term.

'Yup,' she replied. 'Mind you, I'm not complaining. They're good kids.'

'Do you have time for a drink?'

'Lead me to it.'

Later, as they sat on a pleasant terrace by the river, feeding scraps to the swans, Debra said in a carefully casual voice, 'You really like those youngsters, don't you?'

'Mm, some of them are smart, especially Mark Dane. He's got a true feel for languages. By the way, I didn't see him today.'

Debra groaned. 'That means he slipped away again. His truancy is getting serious.'

'Have you told his parents?'

'I've spoken to his father, who said very grimly that he'd 'deal with it'.'

Evie made a face. 'I don't like the sound of him.'

'No, I didn't take to him either. Too much assurance.

I gather he's a big man in industry, built it up himself, finger on a dozen pulses, everything under control.'

'And that includes his son?' Evie said sympathetically.

'I think it includes everything—you, me, Mark—'

'And the little mouse in the corner,' Evie said whimsically.

'Justin Dane wouldn't have a mouse,' Debra said at once. 'He'd hire a tiger to catch it. But enough of him.' She took a deep breath and said with an air of someone taking the plunge, 'Look, Evie, I had an ulterior motive in asking you out.'

'I was afraid you might,' Evie murmured. 'But don't spoil the moment. Seize it. Relish it.'

She leaned back on the wooden seat, one elegantly booted ankle crossed over the other knee. Her eyes were closed and she threw her head back, letting the late afternoon sun play on her face, where there was a blissful smile. With her boots and jeans, her slim figure and dark cropped hair, she might have been a boy. Or an urchin. Or anything but a twenty-nine-year-old schoolteacher.

'Evie,' Debra tried again in the special patient voice she kept for coping with her wayward friend.

'Skip it, Deb. I know what you're going to say, and I'm afraid the answer's no. One term I promised, because that's all I can do. It'll be over soon and then you won't see me for dust.'

'But the Head's knocked out by the way you've clicked with the pupils. He really wants you to stay.'

'Nope. I just filled in while the language teacher had her baby. She's had him now, a bonny, bouncing boy, which means it's time for me to go bouncing off into the sunset.'

'But she doesn't really want to return, and I have strict instructions to persuade you to stay on, full time.'

Evie's response to this was to back away along the bench with an alarmed little cry, like somebody fending off an evil spirit.

'What's up with you?' Debra demanded.

'You said the fatal words,' Evie accused her, wild-eyed.

'What fatal words?'

'Full time.'

'Stop fooling around,' Debra said, trying not to laugh.

Evie resumed her normal manner. 'I never do anything full time, you know that. I need change and variety.'

'But you said you like teaching.'

'I do—in small doses.'

'Yes, that's the story of your life, isn't it? Everything in small doses. A job here, a job there.'

Evie gave a grin that was wicked and delightful in equal measure.

'You mean I'm immature, don't you? At my age I ought to be ready to settle down to a nine-to-five job, one offspring and two-point-five husbands.'

'I think you mean that the other way around.'

'Do I? Well, whatever. The point is, you think I should be heading for a settled life, suitable for a woman approaching the big "three". Well, nuts to it! I live the way I want. Why can't people accept that?'

'Because we're all jealous,' Debra admitted with a grin. 'You've managed to stay free. No mortgage. No ties.'

'No husband.' Evie sighed with profound gratitude.

'I'm not sure that's something you should rejoice about.'

'It is from where I'm standing,' Evie assured her.

'Anyway, the point is that you just up and go when the mood suits you. I suppose that might be nice.'

'It *is* nice,' Evie said with a happy sigh. 'But as for no mortgage—what I pay on that motorbike is practically a mortgage.'

'Yes, but that was your choice. Nobody made you. I bet nobody's ever made you do anything in your life.'

Evie gave a chuckle. 'Some have tried. Not with much success, and never a second time, but they've tried.'

'Alec, David, Martin—' Debra recited.

'Who were they?' Evie asked innocently.

'Shame on you! How unkind to forget your lovers so soon!'

'They weren't lovers, they were jailers. They tried to trick me up the aisle, or soft soap me up the aisle, or haul me up the aisle. One of them even dared to set the date and tell me after.'

'Well, you made him regret it. The poor man was desperate because you'd kept him wondering long enough.'

'I didn't keep him wondering. I was trying to let him down gently. It just turned out to be a long way down. I never even wanted him to fall in love with me. I thought we were simply having a good time.'

'Is that what you're doing with Andrew?' Debra asked mischievously.

'I'm very fond of Andrew,' Evie said, looking up into the sky. 'He's nice.'

'I thought maybe you were in love with him.'

'I am—I think—sort of—maybe.'

'Any other woman would think he was a catch—good job, sweet nature, sense of humour. Plus you're in love with him, sort of, maybe.'

'But he's an accountant.' Evie sighed. 'Figures, books, tax returns—'

'That's not a crime.'

'He believes in *the proper way of doing things*,' Evie said in a tone of deepest gloom.

'You mean about—everything?'

Evie gave her a speaking look.

'One day,' Debra said, exasperated, 'I hope you'll fall hook, line and sinker for a man you can't have.'

'Why?' Evie asked, honestly baffled.

'It'll be a new experience for you.'

Evie chuckled. It was the happy, confident laugh of someone who had life 'sussed'. She had her job, translating books from French and Italian into English. She was free to travel and did so, often. She had all the male company she wanted, and female company too for, unlike many women who attracted love easily, she also had a gift for friendship with her own sex.

It wasn't immediately clear why people were drawn to her. Her face was charming but not outstandingly beautiful. Her nose tilted a little too much and her eyebrows were rather too heavy, adding a touch of drama to her otherwise perky features.

Perhaps it was something in the richness of her laugh, the way her face could light up as though the sun had risen, her air of having discovered a secret that she would gladly share with anyone who would laugh with her.

'Time I was going,' she said now. 'Sorry I couldn't help you, Deb.'

They strolled to the car park, where Debra got into her sedate saloon and Evie hopped on to her gleaming motorbike, settling the helmet on her head. A wave of her hand, and she was away.

She enjoyed riding through this pleasant suburb of outer London. Speed was fun, but dawdling through leafy roads was also fun.

Then she saw Mark Dane.

She recognised him from behind. It wasn't just the dark brown hair with the hint of russet. It was the fact that he was walking with his head down in a kind of dispirited slouch that, she now realised, she'd seen often before.

Mark had a bright, quick intelligence that pleased her. In class he was often the first to answer, the words tumbling over each other, sometimes at the expense of accuracy.

'Take it a bit slower and get it right,' she often told him, although she was pleased by his eagerness.

But out of class he seemed to collapse back into himself, often becoming surly.

No, she thought now. Unhappy.

She slowed down and tooted her horn. The boy turned swiftly, glaring, but then smiling as he recognised the goggled, helmeted figure pulling up beside him.

''lo, Miss Wharton.'

She uncovered her head. 'Hallo, Mark. Had a busy day?'

'Yes, I've been—' He stopped, reading the irony in her eyes and gave up. 'I didn't exactly come to school.'

'What did you do—exactly?'

He shrugged, implying that he neither remembered nor cared.

'It's not the first time you've played truant,' she said, trying not to sound like a nag.

Again the shrug.

'Where do you live?'

'Hanfield Avenue.'

'You've wandered quite a way. How are you going to get home?'

Shrug.

'Wanna lift?' She indicated the bike.

He beamed. 'Really?'

'As long as you wear this,' she said, removing her helmet.

He donned it eagerly and she checked that it was secure.

'But now you don't have a helmet,' he said.

'That's why I'm going to go very slowly and carefully. Now, get up behind and hold on to me tightly.'

When she felt him grip her she eased away from the kerb. It took half an hour to reach his home, which was in a prosperous, tree-lined street, full of detached houses that exuded wealth. She swung through the gates and up the drive to the front door, mentally preparing what she would say to Mark's parents, who would be home by now, and worried.

But the woman who opened the door looked too old to be his mother. Her eyes were like saucers as she saw his mode of transport.

'What on earth—?'

'Hallo, Lily,' Mark said, climbing off the bike.

'What do you mean, coming home at this hour? And on this thing?' She glanced sharply at Evie. 'And who are you?'

'This is Miss Wharton, a teacher from school,' Mark said quickly. 'Miss Wharton, this is Lily, my dad's housekeeper.'

'You'd better come in,' Lily said, eyeing Evie dubiously. 'Mark, your supper's in the kitchen.'

When she was in the hall Evie said quietly, 'Can I talk to Mark's parents?'

Lily waited until Mark was out of sight before saying, 'His mother's dead. His father won't be home for a while yet.'

'I'd like to wait for him.'

'It could be a very long wait. Mr Dane comes home at all hours, if he comes home at all.'

'What does he do that takes so long?'

'He takes over.'

'He does what?'

'He's in industry. Or rather, he owns an industry, and his industry owns other industries, and if he doesn't own them he takes them over. If he can't take them over he puts them out of business. That's his way. Get them before they get you. I've heard him say so.'

'So that's why he's not here,' Evie mused. 'After all, if you're busy taking over the world it wouldn't leave much time for other things.'

'That's right. I'm usually all that poor kid has, and I'm not enough. I do my best, but I'm no substitute for parents.' She checked herself, adding hastily, 'Don't tell Mr Dane that I said that.'

'I'm glad you did. But I won't tell him, I promise.'

'I'll make you some tea. The living room's through there.'

While she waited for the tea Evie looked around and understood what Debra had told her about Justin Dane, plus what Lily had just revealed. This was the home of a wealthy man. He could give his son everything, except the warmth of a welcome.

It dawned on her that there was something missing in the living room. She began to look more closely, but without success. She started again, examining every ledge and bookshelf, searching for some sign of Mark's mother. But there wasn't a single photograph, either of her or her and her husband together: nothing to remind her child that she had ever lived.

'Who the hell are you?'

The outraged voice from the doorway made her jump.

There was no doubt of the identity of the man standing there. If the hint of russet in his dark brown hair hadn't proclaimed him Mark's father she would still have known him from Debra's description.

Pride and assurance personified, she thought. Everything under control. And when it wasn't he hit the roof.

His lean face was set in harsh lines that looked dangerously permanent and there was a ferocity in his eyes that she refused to let intimidate her.

'I'm Miss Wharton,' she said, determinedly pleasant. 'I teach languages at Mark's school.'

He made a wry face. 'Really!'

'Yes, really,' she said, nettled.

'Dressed like that?'

She looked down at her colourful outfit and shrugged.

'A verb conjugates exactly the same, however I'm dressed, Mr Dane.'

'You look like some crazy student.'

'Thank you,' she said, giving him her best smile. She knew he hadn't meant a compliment but she couldn't resist riling him. 'At my age that's a really nice thing to hear.'

'I wasn't flattering you.'

'You amaze me. I'd assumed you went through life winning hearts with your diplomacy.'

There was a flicker in his eyes that suggested uncertainty. Was she, or wasn't she, daring to mock him?

Let him wonder, she thought.

'How old are you?' he demanded.

'Old enough not to tolerate being barked at.'

'All right, all right,' he said in the voice of a man making a concession. 'Maybe I was hasty. We'll start again.'

She stared at him in fascination. This man was so lacking in social skills that he was almost entertaining.

'I suppose that's as much of an apology as I'm going to get,' she observed.

'It wasn't meant as an apology. I'm not used to coming home and finding myself under investigation by strangers.'

'Investigation?'

'It's a politer word than spying. Are you here to report back to the social services? If so, tell them that my son has a good home and doesn't need anyone's interference.'

'I'm not sure I could say that,' she replied quietly.

'What?'

'Is this a good home? You tell me. What I've seen so far looks pretty bleak. Oh, it's comfortable enough, plenty of money spent. But after all, what's money?'

Now it was his turn to be fascinated. 'Some people think money amounts to quite a lot.'

'Not if it's all you have.'

'And you feel entitled to make that judgement, do you?'

'Why not? At least I looked at the whole room. You judged me on the basis of my clothes and my age.'

'I told you, I've drawn a line under that,' he said impatiently.

'But maybe I haven't,' she said, incensed again. 'And maybe I stand on my right to jump to conclusions, just like you.'

She knew she was treading on thin ice, but what the

hell? She was usually slow to anger, but there was something about this man that made her want to be unreasonable. In fact, there was something about him that made her want to jump up and down on his head.

He gave an exasperated sigh. 'This is getting us nowhere. What are you doing in my house?'

House, she noticed. Not home. Well, he was right about that.

'I gave Mark a lift.'

'Riding that contraption outside?'

'No,' she shot back. 'I rode it while he ran behind—' She checked herself. This was no time for sarcasm. 'Of course. He rode pillion.'

'Did he have a helmet?'

'Yes, I gave him mine.'

'So you rode without one?'

'Yes.'

'Which is against the law.'

'I'm aware of that, but what else could I do? Leave him there? The point is, his head was safe.'

'But yours wasn't.'

'I'm overwhelmed by your concern,' she snapped.

'My concern,' he snapped back, 'is for my son if you'd been stopped by the police while in breach of the law.'

Evie ground her teeth but wouldn't risk answering. He had a point. An unfair point, but still a point.

'And why were you giving him a lift anyway? Do you normally bring your pupils home from school?'

'I didn't bring him home from school. He played truant today, not for the first time.'

'Yes, I've heard about his behaviour before this.'

'What did you do?'

'I went to the school and talked with the Deputy Head.'

'No, I mean what did you do when you got home? Did you talk to Mark?'

'Of course I did. I told him to behave himself or there'd be trouble. I gather he didn't listen. All right, leave it to me. I'll deal with him.'

She stared, aghast.

'And just what do you mean by that?' she demanded.

'I mean I'll make sure he knows the consequences of disobeying me again. Isn't that what you came here for?'

'*No!*'

Evie spoke so loudly and emphatically that he was actually startled.

'That is *not* what I came here for,' she said firmly. 'That boy is very unhappy, and I'm trying to find out why. I hadn't been here five minutes before I could see the reason. Heavens, what a place!'

'What's the matter with it?' he demanded.

'It's like a museum. Full of things, but actually empty.'

He looked around at the expensive furnishing, then back at her. He was totally baffled.

'You call this empty?'

'It's empty of everything that matters—warmth, parents to greet him when he comes home.'

'His mother is dead,' Justin Dane said in a hard voice.

'She's worse than dead, Mr Dane. She's missing. Where are the pictures of her?'

'After what she did, I saw no need to keep them, much less put them on display.'

'But what about Mark? What would he have liked?'

She heard his sharp intake of breath before he said, 'You're trespassing on matters that do not concern you.'

'You're wrong,' she said firmly. 'I am Mark's teacher and I'm concerned about his welfare. Anything about him concerns me, especially his suffering.'

'What do you know about his suffering?'

'Only what he's trying to tell me without words. I rely on you to tell me the rest. What exactly did she do that entitles you to airbrush her out of existence?'

But he wouldn't explain, she could see. His face had closed against her.

It was her own fault, she realised. What had she been thinking of to have lost her temper?

She took some deep breaths and tried to calm down. He seemed to be doing much the same for there was a silence. Turning, she saw that he was at the window with his back to her.

He was a tall man, well over six foot, and leanly built with broad shoulders which were emphasised by the way he was standing. When he left the window and began to stride about the room she was struck by how graceless he was. There was strength there, muscle, power, but nothing gentle or yielding.

Heaven help the person who really gets on his wrong side, Evie thought. *He'd be pitiless. What kind of life does that poor child have?*

When he spoke it was with an exasperated sigh, suggesting that he was doing his best with this awkward woman, but it was very difficult.

'This is getting us nowhere,' he said. 'I accept that you came here with the best of intentions, and I'm glad to know about his misbehaviour. But your job is done now, and I suggest you leave it there.'

She lost her temper again. She couldn't help it. This man was a machine for making her angry.

'My job is not done as long as you're talking about

Mark's "misbehaviour". He is not misbehaving. His mother's dead, his father's trying to pretend she never existed. He is miserable, unhappy, wretched, lonely, and *that* should be your priority. Am I getting through?'

'Now look—'

A sound from the doorway made them both look, and see Mark. She wondered how long he'd been standing there, and how much he'd heard.

'Hallo, Dad.'

'Hallo, Mark. Has anyone offered Miss Wharton any tea?'

'Yes, Lily's made some.'

'Then I suggest you take it upstairs and show Miss Wharton your room. She'd like to see some of your interests.'

She guessed that he would really have liked to throw her out, but he would not do so in front of his son.

'Thank you,' she said. 'I appreciate your being so helpful.'

That annoyed him, she was glad to notice.

Mark's room turned out to contain all the gadgets any boy could want, including a music centre and computer. Evie guessed she was supposed to admire, and conclude that Mark had everything. Instead, she shivered.

Such a profusion of mechanical things, and nothing human. Even here, no pictures of the child's mother were on show.

'How powerful is your computer?' she asked.

He switched on and showed her. As she'd expected it was state of the art, linked to a high-speed Internet connection.

'It's the next generation,' he said. 'They aren't even in the shops yet, but Dad brought it home for me. He makes sure my machine is always ahead of the other kids' machines.'

'I'll bet your school loves him for that,' Evie observed wryly.

'At my last school they told him he was throwing everything out of kilter by making their computers look outdated. He replaced every machine in the entire school with the newest thing on the market. Then he turned to the headmistress and said, 'Not out of kilter now.' And he winked.'

'He *what*? Mark, I don't believe it. I shouldn't think your father knows how to wink.'

'He can sometimes. He says there are things any man can do if he has to.'

So, Evie reflected, winking was Justin Dane's idea of putting on the charm, something a man could do when he had to, but which was otherwise a waste of time. But she felt she was getting to know him now, and ventured to say, 'I'll bet he bought you a new computer too, and it was one step ahead of the school's.'

Mark grinned and nodded.

'What do you want to do when you leave school, Mark?'

'I'd like to do something with languages. Dad doesn't like it, but it's what I want.'

'Why isn't your father keen?'

'He says there's no money in it.'

'Well, that's true,' she agreed with a rueful grin.

'But I don't care about that,' he said eagerly. 'Languages take you into other people's minds, and different worlds, so you're not trapped any more, and—'

This was the boy she knew in class, words tumbling over each other in his joy at the glorious flame he'd discovered. Evie smiled encouragement.

'I like Italian best,' he said. 'One day I want to go to Italy—hang on.'

A knock at the door had signalled Lily's arrival with tea. While Mark was letting her in Evie looked at the shelf behind her chair and saw, with pleasure, how many books it contained. She took down the nearest volume and jumped as a photograph fell out from between the pages.

Picking it up, she saw that it was of a young woman with a little boy, plainly a much younger Mark. They were laughing directly into each other's eyes.

His mother, she thought.

Something caught in her throat at the feeling that blazed from that picture. If ever two people had loved each other it was these two. But she was dead, and now his life was lived with a harsh father in a house whose luxury couldn't hide its bleakness.

Suddenly she became aware of the silence and looked up to find Mark watching her, his face pale.

'Oh, that's what became of it,' he said. 'I was afraid I'd lost it.'

He held out his hand and she gave him the photograph.

'Is that—?'

'Shall I pour you some tea?' he asked, almost too politely.

His face was implacable, setting her at a distance. At that moment his likeness to his father was alarming.

'Thank you, I'd like some,' she said, recognising that she must back off.

He put the picture away and poured her tea, taking up their previous conversation about Italy, a country that he'd evidently studied closely.

'You've got the makings of a scholar,' she said at last.

'Don't let Dad hear you say that,' he warned. 'He'd hit the roof.'

'Yes, I suppose he would. I guess you need to be a bit older before you can stand up to him.'

'People can't often stand up to Dad. He just flattens them. Except you.' He gave a sigh of delight. 'You flattened him.'

'Mark,' she said, laughing, 'life is about a lot more than who flattens whom.' She couldn't resist adding, 'Whatever your father thinks.'

'Yeah, right,' he said, unconvinced. 'But it helps. And you're the only one who's ever flattened Dad.'

'Stop saying that,' she begged. 'And how much did you overhear, anyway?'

'Enough to know that you fla—'

'All right, all right,' she said hastily.

'Wish I could do it.'

Diplomatically she decided not to answer this.

'I have to be going,' she said.

'I wish you wouldn't. It's nice with you here.'

'I'll see you at school tomorrow. That is—' she added casually, 'if you're there.'

'I will be.'

'No more truanting?'

'Promise.'

They shook hands.

'Good,' said Justin from the door. 'The best deals are made over a handshake.'

There was nothing but calm approval in his voice, and she had no way of knowing if he'd heard his son's words.

'We've made a very good deal,' Evie assured him. 'Mark has promised me that he'll attend school every day from now on, and since I know he's a man of his word I consider the matter closed.'

Her eyes told Justin that if he was wise he'd better consider the matter closed too. She thought she detected a flicker of surprise in his expression, but all he said was, 'Mark, perhaps you'll show our guest out? Goodbye, Miss Wharton.'

He gave her a brief nod and walked away, depriving her of the chance to talk to him again. Which, she thought, had probably been the idea.

CHAPTER TWO

EVIE didn't teach Mark the next day, but she saw him at a distance and knew he was in school. On the following morning he was there in her class, quiet but attentive. As he left she drew him briefly aside.

'All right?' she asked briefly.

'Fine.'

'He didn't give you a hard time after I left?'

'He never said a word about my playing truant, but he asked a lot of questions about you.'

'What sort of questions?'

'About who you were, how much did I know about you, how were you different to the other teachers?' There was a touch of mischief in his voice as he added, 'I said you were no different from the others, and he said, 'You mean they *all* go around on motorbikes?''

She tried to suppress a chuckle and failed.

'You'd better run along,' she said hastily.

The rest of the week passed uneventfully. Mark attended every day, as he'd promised, and Evie was able to feel mildly satisfied for a job well done.

Her personal life was less tidy. Andrew was growing disgruntled at the feeling that he didn't come first with Evie. She knew she could save the relationship with a huge effort. But then what? Marriage, which she'd always avoided? Just how hard did she really want to try? She wished she knew the answer.

Tonight he was taking her to dinner and she had discarded jeans and boots in favour of an elegant blue dress and a necklace of filigree silver. She stayed at her desk for a couple of hours after school, catching up on paperwork until Andrew called for her. She was just finishing when Justin Dane walked into the classroom.

She could feel his anger before she saw it. It was like watching a volcano preparing to erupt.

'So much for deals,' were his first words.

'I beg your pardon?'

'You made a deal with my son, a young man of his word, according to you. He was to stop playing truant.'

'And he has. He's been here every day since. I've seen him.'

'Today?'

'Yes, this afternoon. In fact, he did a particularly good piece of translation. I've just finished marking it—here.'

She pulled the book out and showed him.

'Then where is Mark now?' he asked in a tight voice.

'He didn't come home?'

'No.'

'Perhaps he went out with friends?'

'He isn't allowed to just go off like that. Either Lily or I must know in advance.'

'Are you saying that he's wandering around alone?' she asked, horrified.

'I don't know. I wish I did. Where did you find him last time?'

She scratched her head. 'I know where it is but I didn't notice the name of the road.'

'OK, you can take me there.'

His casual way of giving her orders made her grind her teeth and say, 'Since you seem not to have noticed, I am about to go out on a date.'

'How could I have noticed?' he asked, puzzled.

'Because I'm dolled up,' she said, indicating her dress

and make-up. Unwisely, she added, 'I don't dress like this unless I have to.'

Incredibly his lips twitched. 'I believe you.'

'Mr Dane, I'm sure this will come as news to you, but I do have a life. I don't just sit here waiting for you to give me orders.'

'So you won't help me?'

'I didn't say that, but "please" would be good.'

'All right. Please. Now can we get going?'

She looked at her watch. Andrew would be here soon. She guessed how he'd feel if she put him off, but she couldn't shut out the memory of Mark's unhappy face and the miserable hunch of his shoulders.

'All right,' she said. 'But I don't have long, and I must make a call first.'

She dialled Andrew on her cellphone and was relieved when he answered.

'Darling, I'm going to be a little late,' she said. 'Can you leave it for an hour?'

She heard him sigh. 'An hour then.'

Justin's luxurious car was waiting in the school yard. For a while, on the journey, neither of them spoke. Evie remembered Mark saying that his father had asked a lot of questions about her. He'd described some of the questions, but how many others had there been?

She took a cautious look at Justin's profile, which was set and hard, otherwise she would have called it attractive, with a sharply defined nose and a firm chin. A good man to have on your side in a fight. Otherwise, steer clear.

'So, tell me everything that happened,' she said at last.

'I called home and asked to speak to Mark. Lily said he wasn't there and she didn't know where he was. Just like last time.'

'So you immediately blamed me.'

'I thought you might have some ideas.'

'I don't know why we're going back to this road,' she said. 'He's hardly likely to be there a second time.'

'Unless there's something nearby that attracts him. A cinema, a shop?'

'It's a tree-lined street. And so are all the others near it. What's the matter?'

She had noticed him grow suddenly alert, slowing the car and looking around him at the passing streets.

'I know this part,' he said. 'We used to live here.'

'When?'

'About three years ago. Is this where you saw him?'

'In the next road.'

He turned into the street where she had seen Mark slouching along, but, as she had feared, there was no sign of him.

'Where was your house?'

'Another five minutes,' he said tensely. 'The next turning, then the first on the right.' He was turning the car as he spoke.

'There he is,' Evie said quickly. 'In the cemetery.'

Of course, she thought. His mother must be buried here.

Justin was drawing over to the kerb and getting out. She hurried to catch up with him and together they climbed the few stone steps to the raised ground where the graves were laid out.

Something made the boy look round as they approached and it was Evie he saw first. His face brightened and he took a step towards her.

'Hallo, son,' Justin said.

The child checked himself before turning obediently to his father and there was nothing in his face but blankness. It was enough to stop Justin in his tracks. Evie clenched her hands, hoping he wouldn't berate his son, but he only turned away with a shrug that would have suggested helplessness in anyone else.

Evie took her chance, walking up to Mark and speaking quietly so that Justin couldn't hear.

'You know,' she said, trying not to sound too heavy, 'this isn't playing fair. You promised me, no more playing truant.'

'But I've been at school,' he said quickly.

'Don't split hairs. No truancy means no vanishing after school either. No forcing us to chase around after you, and sending your father grey-haired with worry.'

She thought she saw a smile of disbelief flicker across the child's face.

'I just like being here,' he said.

'Had you been here the other night, when I caught up with you?'

'Yes. It's beautiful.'

'Show me.'

He took her hand and led her deep into the cemetery, which was old-fashioned with elaborate Victorian graves and mausoleums. Grass and trees made the effect charming rather than bleak.

Once she looked over her shoulder and saw Justin standing where they had left him, at a distance, watching them, motionless, isolated.

They wandered on for a while.

'Your mother's dead, isn't she?' she asked.

A nod.

'And is she buried here?'

A shake of the head. Then, 'But she ought to be,' he said so quietly that she wondered if she had heard properly.

'What do you mean, Mark?'

'Nothing. I suppose we'd better go back to Dad.'

Justin was still standing in the same place, watching for their return. For a moment Evie had an impression of uncertainty, but that must be an illusion caused by the distance.

'Are you ready to come home?' he asked Mark as they neared.

Quickly he looked up at Evie. 'Are you coming with us?'

'I can't. I'm going out tonight and I'm late already.'

'Please,' he said.

Beside her she could sense Justin turn to stone, waiting for her reply.

'All right,' she said. 'But I can't stay for long.'

Mark's face broke into a smile of relief. Justin relaxed slightly.

'Let's go,' he said briefly, indicating the way back to the car.

Mark grabbed hold of her hand and almost dragged her along, making sure that she got into the back seat with him. Justin started up the car without a glance at them.

Nobody spoke during the journey. Mark kept hold of her hand and seemed content simply to have her there. Evie was glad of anything she could do for him, but she was beginning to be alarmed. This child barely knew her, except in class, yet he clung to her as though she were his saviour.

She didn't know what he wanted to be saved from, but the glimpse she'd had of his lonely life had filled her with dismay. And something told her there was worse to come.

Lily opened the front door for them.

'Miss Wharton's really hungry,' Mark said quickly.

'I'll go and see to supper,' she said, and vanished.

Mark gave a violent sneeze.

'I hope you haven't caught cold,' Evie said.

'I'm all right,' he said quickly, and vanished after Lily.

'I hope you can stay with us long enough for supper at least,' Justin murmured.

'I'd better make a phone call.'

Andrew's voice, when he answered, was revealing. It had a subdued exasperation that told her he'd been expecting this.

'I've got a situation here that I can't walk away from,' she pleaded.

'Another one?'

'Darling, that's not fair,' she said, and sensed Justin looking quickly at her. 'I didn't ask for this to happen—'

'You never do. Things just happen to you. Evie, did it ever occur to you that your life is too crowded? Maybe you need to junk a few things, starting with me.'

'You mean break up?' she asked, aghast.

'Isn't that where we're heading?'

'No, no,' she said frantically. 'I don't want to do that. Please, Andrew, it's too important to decide like this—'

'Sure, let's put it off for a while so that you can keep me dangling at your pleasure.'

'Is that really what I do?' she asked penitently.

'I can't believe that you really don't see it. C'mon, Evie, be brave. Say you don't care about me—'

'But I *do* care about you. It's just that tonight—please be patient. I'll call you again tomorrow, and maybe we can fix something—'

'Yes, sure we will. Anything you say.' The line clicked.

'Andrew—Andrew?'

She stared at the phone, trying to understand that dear, gentle Andrew had hung up on her.

'Did he give you a hard time?' Justin Dane asked.

'I can hardly blame him,' she said edgily. 'Wouldn't you be annoyed?'

'Probably. You sound as though you're leading him a merry dance.'

'You'd have hung up long ago,' she said.

But he surprised her by giving her an odd look and saying, 'Maybe not.'

She wasn't sure what he meant by that, but she had no time to brood on her own problems now. Only Mark mattered. She couldn't forget how he'd brightened at the sight of her, or how quickly he'd said she was hungry, an excuse to keep her here.

'All right,' Justin resumed in a businesslike tone. 'You're entitled to an explanation, so I'll make things clear.'

'Not now.'

He stared. 'What?'

'What Mark needs now is for us all to sit down to supper and be friendly—or at least act friendly. Explanations can come later. Then I'll tell you what I want to know.'

From his frown she guessed that this wasn't how people usually treated him. And she seemed to have the gift of reading his thoughts, for she could follow the lightning process by which he worked out how to turn this to advantage.

'Fine,' he said. 'Then if you'll have supper with Mark I can do some work.'

'No, you can have supper with us,' she said firmly. 'How often do you and he eat together?'

'Not often, but I have things to do.'

'Indeed you have, some more important than others. The most important is to be with your son.'

His lips tightened. 'Miss Wharton, I'm grateful for the trouble you're taking for Mark, but this is not your decision—'

'Oh, but it is. Let me make it clear to you how much my decision it is. If I can give up my evening for your son, so can you. Either you agree to be there for supper, or I'm leaving, right now. And you can explain my absence any way you like.'

Now he was really angry. 'I'm not in the habit of being dictated to, in my own home or anywhere else.'

She was too wise to answer. She merely followed her instincts and met his eyes. Anger met anger. Defiance met defiance. Mark, returning, found them like that.

'Lily says she's laid supper on the terrace,' he said. 'Shall I tell her you're coming?'

For a moment she thought Justin would refuse and walk out. But at last he smiled at his son.

'Fine,' he said. 'Lead the way.'

Mark instantly took Evie's hand and almost dragged her out on to the terrace overlooking the garden. It was a pleasant place with red flagstones and wooden railings, expensively designed to look rustic. Here a wooden table had been set for supper.

The meal was excellent—spaghetti, well cooked, expertly served; fish, coffee made to perfection.

'So, let's hear it,' Justin said to his son when Lily had left them. 'Why did you vanish tonight and worry everyone?'

'Oh, leave that until later,' Evie said before the boy could reply. 'Mark's the thoughtful type, like me.

Sometimes we like to have a little time on our own, away from the crowd. There's nothing wrong with that.'

'I only—' Justin began.

'I said "enough",' Evie interrupted him. She spoke lightly, determined to keep the atmosphere pleasant, but she knew Justin understood her meaning.

'I was telling your father about the last piece of work you did for me,' she told Mark. 'A really good translation.' She turned to Justin. 'He's one of my best students. You should be proud of him.'

'If you say he works hard, I am proud of him,' he replied.

She wanted to yell at him, *Try to sound as though you mean it. Say something nice without freezing, or sounding as though every word has to be wrung out of you.*

Instead, she said, 'According to his regular teachers there are other things to be proud of. They say Mark is always the first to volunteer, to help out. He's a good team player.'

Justin seemed a little taken aback by this, and Evie realised that being a good team player probably didn't rank high in his list of priorities. She was sure of it when he grunted, 'Well, I guess that can be useful too. What do you mean, his regular teachers? Aren't you regular?'

'No, I'm just a fill-in for one term. Then I'm back to my real job, translating books.'

'You're not staying?' Mark was crestfallen.

'I never stay long anywhere,' she admitted. 'I like to take off into the wide blue yonder. There's always new places to travel. I'll be going back to Italy before the end of the year.'

'Where?' he asked at once.

'Travelling all over, studying dialects.'

'But I thought they all spoke Italian.'

'They do, but the regions have their dialects which are almost like different languages.'

'How different?' he wanted to know.

'Well, if you wanted to say, "Strike while the iron's hot" in Italian, it would be, *"Battere il ferro quando 'e caldo"*. If you were Venetian you'd say, *"Bati fin chel fero xe caldo"*, and if you came from Naples you'd say, *"Vatte 'o 'fierro quann' 'e ccavero"*.'

'That's great!' Mark said, thrilled. 'All those different ways to say one thing.'

'But what's the point?' Justin asked. 'Why don't they all just speak Italian?'

'Because a regional dialect springs from the people,' Evie explained. 'It's part of their history, their personality. It's their heritage. Don't you care about your heritage?'

His reaction startled her. His face seemed to close, like the door of a tomb, she later thought. After a moment's black silence he said, 'I just think one language is more efficient.'

'Of course it's more efficient,' she conceded. 'But who wants to be efficient all the time? Sometimes it's more fun to be colourful.'

'I wouldn't get far running a business on that theory.'

'The Italians aren't a businesslike people, thank goodness,' she said, trying to lighten the atmosphere. 'They're delightful, and full of life and music. All those things matter too. Who wants to be efficient all the time?'

'I do,' he said simply.

Evie and Mark exchanged glances. Justin saw them but said nothing.

'Will you send me postcards from Italy?' Mark asked wistfully.

'Lots and lots of them, from everywhere.'

He began bombarding her with questions which she answered willingly. Justin seemed content to sit there and listen, except once when he said, 'Take a break from talking, Mark, and eat something.'

His tone was pleasant enough and Mark stopped to take a few mouthfuls. Evie took advantage of the moment to look around the garden, and saw a dog walking towards them, followed by five puppies, who seemed about six weeks old.

'That's Cindy,' Mark told her. 'She belongs to Lily. They all do. And there's Hank. He's their father.'

A large dog, part Alsatian and part something else, had appeared around the side of the house, accompanied by Lily bearing food bowls. She set them down on the terrace, returned to the kitchen and came back with more bowls. Under Evie's fascinated eyes the family converged on their supper, the five pups diving in vigorously.

They finished quickly, then looked around for more to eat. Cindy, evidently knowing the danger, had cleared her bowl fast. Hank seemed less well prepared, for some of his food was still there and the smallest pup advanced on him purposefully.

The huge dog began to snarl horribly, revealing terrible great teeth. Undeterred, the pup went on towards the bowl, while his father hurled warning after warning.

'Shouldn't we rescue that little creature?' Evie said, beginning to rise.

But Justin laid a hand on her arm, detaining her.

'Leave them,' he said. 'It's all right.'

'But Hank will devour the pup in one mouthful,' she protested.

'Nothing will happen,' he said. 'It never does.'

Reluctantly, she sat down and watched as the puppy, unimpressed by his father's belligerence, reached the bowl and tucked in.

At once the snarls stopped. Hank was left looking around with a puzzled expression as if asking what he was expected to do now.

Something in the huge animal's air of baffled pathos struck Evie as irresistibly funny and she began to laugh.

'That poor dog,' she choked. 'Beneath all the aggro he's just an old softy. Oh, dear—'

Waves of laughter swept her again.

'Come here, boy,' she said, holding out her hand. Hank came at once and sat gazing up at her, silently seeking sympathy.

'Poor fellow, you hardly had any supper,' she said, taking his face between her hands. 'Here, let's see if you like spaghetti. Yes, you do, don't you?'

She wrapped her arms around him, chuckling and kissing his forehead at the same time. Lily joined in her amusement, and so did Mark.

She glanced up at Justin, hoping that he too might be laughing. But he wasn't.

He was staring at her with a stunned expression on his face, like a man who'd been struck by lightning.

Lily intervened and hustled her little 'family' out of sight. Evie went to wash her hands where Hank had licked them, and returned to find Lily serving gateau and cream.

'You look ever so pretty tonight,' Mark ventured. 'You don't usually dress like that.'

'I was going out,' she told him.

'On a date?'

'Yes.'

'Have you got a boyfriend?'

'Yes,' she said, laughing.

'Mark,' Justin muttered through gritted teeth.

'Will he be mad at you?' Mark asked, undeterred.

'Nothing I can't handle,' she said cheerfully.

'I bet you could handle anyone. I bet you'd really tell him off.'

'If I did that he wouldn't be my boyfriend for very long,' she pointed out.

'Are you nuts about him?'

'Mark!' This time Justin covered his eyes and his voice betrayed only an agony of embarrassment. Evie almost liked him.

'That's a secret,' she said.

She was aware of Justin uncovering his eyes and looking at her, but she kept her attention on Mark.

'Is he nuts about you?' Mark persisted.

'He probably won't be after the way I stood him up tonight,' she said lightly.

'But if he's really nuts about—'

'Mark, that's enough,' Justin said edgily.

She noticed that the boy fell silent at once, as though a light had gone out inside him.

'I honestly don't mind,' she said. 'We're just joking.'

She gave Mark a reassuring smile and followed it with a broad wink. After a moment he winked back, then cast an uncertain glance at his father, as though worried about his reaction. Evie followed his look and was startled by Justin's expression. It vanished at once, and she supposed she might have been mistaken. But for a brief moment he'd looked almost forlorn, like a child excluded from a charmed circle.

Absurd. Whatever this harsh man was, he wasn't forlorn.

CHAPTER THREE

AS THE meal ended Lily came to say that Justin was wanted on the phone. Guessing that he would now be gone for some time, Evie agreed to Mark's suggestion that they go to his room and, with a sudden burst of inspiration, she signalled a question to Lily. Receiving a nod in return, she scooped up a couple of puppies and followed Mark upstairs.

Now he was more relaxed, chatting about the dogs and what fun he had taking photographs of them.

'Can I see?' Evie asked at once.

Of course he owned the very latest state-of-the-art digital camera, and handled it like an expert.

'I'm green with envy.' She sighed. 'I can't work mine and it's much simpler than yours.'

'It's easy,' he said innocently.

'Yeah, for some people!'

He giggled. 'Dad can't understand this one either. He gets so mad.'

Mark switched on the computer and called up pictures of the dogs. He had, apparently, taken dozens every day, almost obsessively, reinforcing Evie's feeling that this child lived inside himself far too much.

'Don't you have any pics of your friends?' she asked.

He shrugged uneasily. 'I haven't lived here long. I don't know many people.'

'But you had a house nearby.'

'We moved when Mum left. Dad bought this place.

He said he never wanted to see that house again. And I changed schools.'

'Your mother left?'

'Yes, she went away and didn't come back. I've got some more pictures here—'

He opened another file of pictures of the puppies and she let the matter go, guessing this was his way of describing his mother's death.

There were so many pictures that it was hard to take in details of any one, but suddenly a collection of them caught her eye. Mark seemed to have taken them at the rate of one per second, so that it was like looking at a film strip.

He had caught his father at the moment when one of the pups had approached him and was ordered off. Undeterred, the little creature had scrambled up on to a sofa and made his way determinedly on to the desk.

Almost as though it was happening now, Evie found herself holding her breath against the moment when Justin angrily swept him off. But it hadn't happened. Instead he'd picked the puppy up in one hand, holding him before his face with a look of gentle resignation. It was the gentleness that particularly struck her.

Then he'd turned his head, seeming to become aware of his son and the camera. He'd held his captive out, clearly ordering that he be removed, and he'd almost been smiling.

She took a moment to study Justin's face. It wasn't handsome. The features were too irregular for that, the nose too large. Even in a milder mood he still gave the impression of power, and his dark eyes radiated an intensity that, she guessed, would put other men in the shade.

And women would be attracted to him, she knew. Not

herself, because he wasn't the kind of man that had ever appealed to her. Too impatient, too sure of himself, too unwilling to listen. She could imagine having some interesting fights with him, but not warming to him.

'Hey!' Mark said suddenly.

Startled, she glanced his way with a smile, and heard the click of the camera.

'Gotcha!' he said.

'Oi, cheeky!' she said, laughing outright, and he promptly snapped her again.

'Now look,' he said, opening the back of the camera and extracting a tiny card. He plugged this directly into the computer and the two pictures of Evie came up side by side on the screen.

'That's brilliant,' she breathed. 'Why doesn't it happen like that when I do it?'

Mark just grinned.

'Yes, I know,' she said ruefully. 'Some of us can, and some of us can't. They're beautiful, Mark.'

He took a small memory stick from a drawer, connected it to the back, copied the pictures on to it, and gave it to her.

'Just plug it into your machine when you get home,' he said.

'Thank you. I'll give you this back at school.'

This wasn't how she'd meant the conversation to go. She should be asking him why he kept vanishing and trying to understand him. But she felt that the key to understanding lay elsewhere. The friendly feeling they'd achieved would do him more good than all the talk in the world.

'Will your father cut up rough about tonight?' she asked gently. 'I imagine he's not easy to live with.'

'He's not so bad,' Mark said unexpectedly. 'He gets angry, but he's always sorry afterwards.'

This was the last thing she had expected to hear.

'He shouldn't get mad at all,' she said. 'Why can't he see that you're unhappy?'

He considered this with an oddly adult expression.

'He's unhappy too,' he said at last.

'About your mother?'

'I think so, but—there's lots of other stuff that he can't talk about. I used to hear him and Mum rowing—terrible things—she said he had something dark inside him, and why couldn't he talk about it? But he said talking wouldn't change anything, and walked out. I was watching from the stairs and I saw his face. I thought it would look angry, but it didn't. Just terribly sad.'

'Did he know you saw him?'

Mark shook his head. 'He'd have hated that. He doesn't like people to know how he feels.'

He fell silent. Then he said unexpectedly, 'I keep wishing I could help him.'

She gave him a quick look of surprise, asking, 'Shouldn't he be helping you?'

'We help each other. Well, that's what I wish. I want to be—it's just that—if only—'

His shoulders sagged and she saw the glint of tears on his cheeks. Evie abandoned words and took him in her arms, holding him while his shoulders shook.

'I'm sorry,' he sobbed.

'You've nothing to be sorry about. If you're sad you need to cry, and tell someone.'

'There isn't anyone,' he sobbed. 'Nobody understands.'

She did the only thing she could—tightened her arms and rocked back and forth, trying to comfort him.

A sound made her look up to see Justin standing in the open door. He stood dead still as though amazement had stopped him in his tracks, and she was reminded of the way he had looked at her on the terrace.

Quietly she shook her head, and he retreated without a word.

Mark seemed unaware. He freed himself and straightened up, wiping his eyes and managing a smile.

'Sorry,' he said again.

'Don't be,' she told him.

He was obviously embarrassed, as though feeling he'd given way to an unmanly display.

Sweet heaven! she thought. He's only twelve years old.

'It's getting late,' she said. 'Why don't you go to bed?'

'Will you come and say goodnight before you go?'

'Yes, I promise.'

She gave him another hug, then went downstairs, feeling thoughtful.

Through the open door of the front room she could see Justin, and walked in.

'Is he all right?' Justin asked gruffly.

'Not really. But he's calmed down, and he's going to bed. I promised to look in and say goodnight before I leave, but I think you should go up to him now.'

'There's no point,' he said wearily. 'This has happened before. He won't talk to me. He hates me.'

'He doesn't,' she said at once.

He looked at her sharply. 'You know that? What did he say?'

'I can't tell you what he said. It's confidential between him and me—'

'That's nonsense,' he said impatiently. 'I'm his father—'

'And I'm the person you had to bring in to help you. I'm the one he talks to, although he said very little even to me. I'll tell you that he doesn't hate you. Far from it. But I won't break his confidence. Please understand that that is final.'

'Like hell it is!'

'OK, throw me out!'

'Don't tempt me.'

For answer she pulled out her cellphone and dialled. 'Andrew?'

Justin's hand closed over hers, gripping her so tightly that it hurt. 'It's better if you stay.'

'Really?' she said, freeing her hand and flexing the fingers. 'I'm glad you made your mind up about that. I can't stand a man who dithers.'

He drew a deep breath. 'Now Andrew will be wondering what happened. You'd better call him back.'

'No need. I wasn't really connected.'

'Playing games?'

'No, just warning you not to try to push me around. I'll help all I can, for the sake of that poor child. But it has to be on my terms, because they're the only ones I can use.'

'I'm the same way myself,' he said grimly.

'Then one of us is going to have to give in.'

She realised then how far she had travelled in a short time. Once she'd feared to antagonise Justin in case it rebounded on Mark. But now her instincts were telling her that he only respected people who stood up to him.

Deference equalled disaster.

Besides, she didn't do deference. She didn't know how.

From the thunderous silence she guessed he was assessing his options, realising that they were limited, but not knowing how to admit the fact.

'Don't you think you should tell me what's really happening?' she said. 'Why did Mark go to that cemetery? You said his mother was dead, so I thought she must be buried there, but he says not.'

'No, she's not. Did he say anything else? Or can't you tell me?'

'He said she ought to be there.'

'Hell!' he said softly.

'What did he mean?'

'My wife left us two years ago.'

'Us?'

'She left us both. There was another man. She went to live with him in Switzerland.'

'She didn't take her son with her?' Evie asked, aghast. 'Or did you stop her?'

'I wouldn't have stopped her if she'd wanted him, but I don't think she even thought of it,' he said in a soft voice that had a hint of savagery.

Evie rubbed her hand over her eyes.

'I just don't understand how any mother can do that,' she said distractedly. 'To leave a man—well, it happens if the relationship isn't working. But to abandon a defenceless child—'

'It's the crime of crimes,' Justin said sombrely. 'It's unnatural, unforgivable—'

He stopped. Evie stared at him, alerted by something in his voice that went beyond anger. Hatred.

'That poor kid,' Evie breathed. 'Did she stay in touch?'

'She wrote to him, telephoned sometimes. There were presents at Christmas and birthdays. But he wasn't invited to visit her. The new boyfriend didn't want him, you see, and he was much more important to her than her son.'

Again there was that bitter edge of something that was more than anger. More like pain.

'It must have devastated him,' she murmured. 'How does he cope?'

'He's brave and strong,' Justin said unexpectedly. 'And he knows what the world is like now.'

'He's too young to learn that side of the world,' Evie said quickly.

He gave a mirthless laugh.

'Is there a proper age for a boy to learn that his mother doesn't want him?'

'No, of course not,' she agreed.

'Any age is too young, but it happens when it happens, ten, nine—seven.'

As he said 'seven' his voice changed, making her look at him. But he didn't seem to notice her. He was talking almost to himself.

'And then the whole world becomes unreal, because it can't have happened, yet it has happened. All the reference points are gone and there's only chaos. Disbelief becomes a refuge when there's nothing else.'

'Yes,' she agreed. 'That's how it must be.'

'But it isn't a reliable refuge,' he said in a low voice. 'The world blows it apart again and again, and it becomes harder to find excuses to believe the thing that's least painful.'

'Mr Dane—what are you telling me?'

'I'd have done anything to save my son from the knowledge that his mother rejected him. I stalled on the divorce, went out to Switzerland to see her, begged her to return to us. I hated her by then but I'd have taken her back for his sake.

'I even bought this house for her. It's bigger, better than the one we had. She liked nice things. I thought—'

'You thought you could get her back by spending money?' Evie said, speaking cautiously.

'She wouldn't even come home for a while, even to look at it. She was besotted by her lover. She cared about nothing else.'

'What happened?'

'She died. They died together when his car crashed. I was over there at the time, and since she was still legally my wife it fell to me to oversee her funeral. I suppose it should have occurred to me to bring her home, but it didn't. She's buried in Switzerland.'

'But—Mark—you were willing to do so much to get her back for him—'

'When she was alive, yes. But when she was dead, what difference could it make?'

She stared at him, nonplussed by a man who could be so sensitively generous on the one hand, and so dully oblivious on the other.

'I think it would have made a difference to Mark to have her nearby, even if she was dead,' she tried to explain. 'People need a focus for their grief, somewhere where they can feel closer to the person they've lost. That's what graves are really for.

'And Mark feels it more because you sold the house where she used to be and made him live in a place where she never was. So he can't go around and remember that this was where they shared a joke, and that was where she used to make his tea.

'He needs those memories, but where does he go for

them now? This great mausoleum, which is empty when he comes home every day?'

'Not empty. Lily's here, and he wouldn't want me. You seem to see everything, surely you've seen that?'

'I've seen that the two of you aren't as close as you ought to be. There has to be something you can do about that. I'm guessing you don't spend very much time with him.'

'I have to work all hours. The business doesn't run itself. I created it and I need to keep my eye on it all the time.'

'And it's more important than your son?'

'I do the best I can for my son,' he snapped.

'Then your best is lousy.'

'I'm trying to make a good life for him—'

'Yes, I've seen that ''good life'' upstairs. The latest computer, the latest printer, the latest digital camera—'

'All right, you think I put too much emphasis on money,' he broke in, 'but you can rely on money. It doesn't betray you. And what you've bought really belongs to you.'

'So then you control it?'

'Right,' he agreed, not seeing the trap she'd opened up at his feet.

'And that's what really matters, isn't it?' she challenged him. 'Control.'

'Sometimes it's important to be in control of things. In fact, it's always important.'

'Just things? Or people. Why did your wife *really* leave you?'

He flashed her a look of pure hatred. 'I guess I didn't pay enough,' he snapped.

Before she could answer he walked out of the room and slammed the door.

Evie was left silently cursing herself.

I had no right to say that about his wife. She sighed. *Why do I keep losing my temper? Now I'll have to find him and apologise. Oh, hell! Why don't I grow up?*

Hearing him outside the door, she braced herself for the worst, but his manner, when he entered, was quieter.

'Shall we start again?' he asked mildly.

'That would be a good idea. Please forget that last question. I had no right—'

'It's over,' he said hastily. 'Besides, all the worst you think of me is probably true, and you'd be the first person to say so if you hadn't decided it was wiser to be tactful.'

She let out a long breath at his insight. *'Touché,'* she said at last.

He gave her an ironic look. 'It's good for my pride if I win the odd point or two.'

'I don't think the worst of you,' she said. 'I think you're just floundering.'

'That's true. I don't know what to say to Mark, what to do for him. We don't speak the same language. What you say about moving house may be right, but I meant it for the best.'

'I wish I could help—' she sighed '—but I'm not even going to be here much longer. I leave when term's over. But I'll stay in touch with Mark, if you like, from anywhere in the world.'

'I'd appreciate that.'

'Now I'll go up and see him, because I promised.'

'Thank you. Then I'll take you home.'

'There's no need. I can call a cab.'

'Miss Wharton, I will take you home,' he said firmly. He came upstairs with her and they stopped outside

Mark's door. Evie raised her hand to knock, then thought better of it and opened the door a crack.

'I'm awake,' came Mark's voice at once.

Laughing, she slipped inside and went to sit on the bed, giving him a hug.

'I'm going now,' she said. 'I just came to say goodnight. And thank you for the pictures. I'll give you back the memory stick at school.'

'You will be there?'

'For a bit longer.' She kissed his cheek. 'Bye!'

He flung his arms about her neck. 'Bye!'

Then he saw his father standing in the doorway and removed his arms.

'Hallo, Dad,' he said politely.

'I'm going to drive Miss Wharton home, son.'

'Goodnight.'

If only he would smile at his father, Evie thought. Or at least stop being so woodenly polite. But Mark didn't say another word as she and Justin left the room.

Downstairs, Justin stopped for a word with Lily before leading Evie out to his car.

'Where to?'

She gave him her address and he swung out on to the road. As he drove he said, 'I'm sorry about your ruined evening with your boyfriend.'

'I'll call him when I get in.'

'What will you tell him?'

'The truth. What else?'

'Might he not misunderstand?'

'He won't, as long as I stick to the facts.'

'Are you one of those terrifyingly honest people who always tell the truth about everything?'

She laughed. 'No, I'm not as bad as that. And honesty really has nothing to do with it. It's just that lies have a habit of backfiring on you. I learned that when I was ten.'

In the darkness of the car she just sensed him grinning.

'I learned a lot earlier than that,' he said.

'I even think that honesty can sometimes be an overrated virtue.'

'Heresy!'

'No, just that sometimes you have to choose between honesty and kindness, and kindness is usually better. My home is just up ahead, in that apartment block.'

'How do you manage with the motorbike?'

'I park it in the basement garage. If you drop me on the kerb here—'

'Actually, I was hoping to come in and talk to you for a while.'

Before she could answer her mobile phone rang.

'I guess that's Andrew,' Justin said. 'You might still save your evening with him. OK, I'll drop you here. Goodnight.'

It wasn't the moment she would have chosen for Andrew to call, but she had no choice but to get out of the car. Justin closed the door behind her and sped away into the darkness, leaving her to answer the phone call, which turned out to be a wrong number.

Evie looked for Mark at school on the following Monday, but there was no sign of him, and Debra said that his father had called to say he had a cold and would be off for a few days.

She'd brought the memory stick in to return to him, but now she wrote him a little note saying that the pictures were lovely, and including her email address and sent the whole thing off in a package.

The following evening his reply was waiting on her computer, with some attached pictures of the puppies. She thanked him, and they settled into an amiable gossip that lasted for the next few days until she wrote at last:

If I don't see you before I go, I promise to email you from all over the place. I'm off to my seaside cottage now. I'll send you some pics of it, taken with my digital camera. If you can work yours I'm sure I can learn to work mine.

She had briefly considered calling at the house to see him, but decided against it. She was leaving soon, and it wasn't kind to encourage Mark to cling to her.

She wondered if Justin would ask her to visit the child, but there was no word from him. Obviously he reckoned that she had outlived her usefulness.

Grumpy but curious, she looked him up on the Internet and what she found there confirmed what Lily had said. Justin Dane took over—people, firms, the world. Starting with nothing fifteen years earlier, he had created an empire out of hard work, genius and ruthlessness.

Before that fifteen years there were gaps in the information. Reading between the lines, all carefully worded to avoid the libel laws, Evie picked up an impression of a wild man, coldly indifferent to the feelings of others, who might even have done a spell in jail.

'A nasty piece of work,' she mused. 'Perhaps it's just as well I won't come into contact with him again.'

CHAPTER FOUR

ON THE last day of term the pupils were due to leave immediately after lunch. Evie skipped lunch and prepared to go quickly. She had a long journey ahead.

'Making your escape?' Debra said, looking in while she was clearing up her things.

'It's not exactly an escape.'

'That's all you know. The Head is talking about kidnapping you and locking you up in a cupboard until next term.'

Evie laughed. 'Then I'd better make a run for it.'

'Is this from the kids?' Debra indicated a large card with many signatures scrawled on it.

'Yes, isn't it sweet of them?'

'I don't see Mark's name. He didn't manage to get back in time then?'

'No, and I'm sorry not to have the chance to say goodbye to him. On the other hand, he might have come to rely on me too much, so maybe it's best as it is. I just wish I didn't have this niggly feeling that I've let him down.'

'You haven't. You did all you could. Now, forget about this place and have a great summer. Are you going anywhere nice?'

'A little seaside cottage for a few weeks.'

'Lovely. With Andrew?'

'He'll join me in a day or two, but it's a bit iffy at the moment. He's very fed up with me and I don't blame him.'

'Never mind. Once you've got him down there you'll bring him round—moonlight on the sea, romantic atmosphere. He won't stand a chance.'

'I hope not.'

Now that she was on the verge of losing Andrew, Evie found herself remembering how sweet-tempered and kind he was, and what a fool she would be to let him go. But all would be well. He would join her, they would spend quality time together, and all their troubles would be forgotten.

What she hadn't told Debra was that she was clearing her things out of the cottage for the last time. It had belonged to an elderly great-uncle, who had recently died and left it to her. But he had also left a mountain of debts and the cottage had to be sold to pay them.

It was time to remove the possessions she'd left there over the years, and she had rented a van to take them. When she'd finished her goodbyes, she went out to where it was parked in the school yard.

It was a relief to head out of noisy, crowded London and south to Cornwall, and Penzance. The sun shone, the countryside soon enveloped her, and her spirits rose.

She had a three hundred mile trip and it was late at night as the van bumped and shuddered down the track to the place where the cottage stood close to the sea.

It was an old-fashioned building, the ground floor taken up by one large room. At one end was a tiny kitchen and at the other end a staircase rose directly to the upper floor.

Her body ached from sitting in one position for so long, and she walked up and down, stretching and rotating her shoulders until she felt human again. After preparing a quick snack she decided to go to bed at once.

The house was a little chilly and would be more cheerful in the morning.

Or perhaps it would be more cheerful when Andrew arrived. Of course he was coming, she assured herself. He'd left a question mark over his arrival, but that was because he was annoyed about her cavalier treatment. It couldn't end like this, and if it did it was Justin Dane's fault for making her stand him up.

Her mind resisted the idea that it was Mark's fault. That vulnerable boy carried enough burdens already without her piling more on him. Perhaps she'd already done so, by leaving without a proper goodbye. She wasn't sure what else she could have done, but the thought troubled her.

She thought about the way she'd fought with Justin. She hadn't meant to fight him, but there didn't seem any other way to communicate with this man. At least he listened while she was insulting him, even if only out of surprise.

If he'd had any decency he'd have come to the school and invited her home to say goodbye to Mark. But it clearly hadn't occurred to him to consider his son's feelings.

She must have been lonelier for Andrew than she realised, because she was suddenly swept by despondency. It would be better in the morning, she promised herself. On that thought she fell asleep.

Next day she went into the village and bought groceries. On her return she started spring-cleaning so that the cottage should be at its best for potential buyers. By keeping busy she could ignore the fact that the telephone didn't ring and there was no sign of Andrew.

She made sandwiches and ate them sitting outside,

watching the sunset again, feeling suddenly very much alone.

But then she heard it. The sound of a car horn followed by crunching as wheels came down the gravel track.

Andrew! she thought, delighted.

She was surprised too, because it was not his way to arrive without calling first, but obviously his feelings had carried him away. In a moment she'd jumped up and raced around the cottage to where a car had just drawn up. Then she saw that the driver was not Andrew.

'You!' she cried, aghast, as Justin Dane climbed out. 'What on earth—?'

Her voice faded as she saw Mark emerging too, smiling when he saw her. She smiled back and made her voice sound pleased as she greeted him.

'We were in the area and thought we'd look you up,' Justin said.

'You just happened to be in this remote part of the world?' She couldn't keep the scepticism out of her voice.

'Well—it's a little more complicated than that,' he said, sounding as though he were choosing his words carefully.

'Let's go inside and you can tell me how complicated it is,' she said, trying to sound agreeable, although inwardly she was cross.

Once before he'd spoiled things for her and Andrew. Now he was going to do it again.

Mark darted away around the side of the house, calling, 'Hey, look how close we are to the sea!'

'I know what you're thinking,' Justin said.

'I wonder if you do,' she mused wryly.

'I shouldn't have just come here without warning, I know.'

'Mark has my email address. You could have used it.'

'But you might have said no.'

She threw up her hands in despair.

'In that case, you were probably right not to take the risk,' she said with ironic appreciation of his methods.

'I did it for Mark. He was upset at not seeing you again. We came to the school yesterday; you'd already gone. In fact, I'm in Mark's bad books because he wanted to go sooner and I promised to get home early from work, but I got held up and then—'

'So it was your fault that you missed me,' she said, amused despite herself.

'Yes, and then the caretaker told me you'd left in a van, but didn't know where.'

'Otherwise you'd have come chasing after me like we were in some Grand Prix.'

'Mark was upset. And may I remind you who it was told me that I should listen more to him?'

'Oh, very clever!' But what could she say? It was true. 'So how did you know how to find me?'

'You told Mark you had a cottage by the sea.'

'I didn't tell him where.'

'Well, I just—' reading wrath in her eyes again he became deliberately vague '—I just asked around.'

'Where?' she asked implacably.

'I went to your flat. One of the neighbours was very helpful—'

'You mean you had me investigated like a criminal?'

'I had to find out where you were.'

They glared, each baffled to find the other so unreasonable. Justin wondered why she couldn't understand that he'd done whatever was necessary to get what he wanted. That was what he always did, and it seemed simple enough to him.

To Evie it was also simple. She disliked being treated like prey to be hunted down for his convenience. But she wouldn't say so while Mark might be within earshot. The real quarrel could wait until later.

'Dad,' Mark called, reappearing around the side of the building. 'It's a wonderful place. Is it really yours?' This was to Evie.

'Sort of,' she said. 'Come in and have something to eat.'

But Justin said, 'It's getting late. Mark's tired and needs to go to bed soon, so I guess we'll find a hotel, if you'll tell us where the nearest one is.'

It was a direct challenge, and thoroughly unscrupulous.

'You know I won't turn you out at this hour,' she said.

He gave her a smile that was suddenly charming.

'But you can't just put us up without warning. I don't suppose you have the room, and I don't want to inconvenience you—'

'That is not true,' she said, speaking lightly but with a glitter in her eyes that gave him fair warning. 'You do not care if you inconvenience me. You don't care about anything as long as you get your own way. Now shut up and get in there before I stamp hard on your feet.'

The smile changed into a grin. He'd won again.

Mark was also grinning, Evie was glad to notice. For his sake she forgave his father everything.

Well, almost everything.

From the amount of luggage he hauled into the cottage it was clear that he'd come prepared to stay for a while.

But it would just be until Andrew arrived, and not a moment longer.

'It's not what you're used to,' she warned. 'No luxury. Just basic.'

'You wouldn't be trying to put me off?' he said, regarding her ironically.

'Would I do that?'

Again he gave that grin. This was Justin Dane in holiday mood. The grin was surprisingly attractive with a blazing quality that could lift a woman's spirits unless she was on her guard against him. Which she was.

Mark dashed in and looked around at the large downstairs room with its big open fireplace.

'It's great!' he enthused. 'Just like a picture book.'

'I didn't think modern boys read that sort of picture book,' she said.

'Not now,' he agreed, 'but when I was a kid.' He looked round and found something else to please him. 'No central heating,' he said ecstatically.

'That's a plus?' Justin queried.

'Radiators would have spoiled it,' Mark explained.

'That's what Uncle Joe used to say.' Evie chuckled. 'He said he didn't want to spoil the place with a lot of ''new-fangled rubbish''. We used to put electric fires on in winter.'

'If there's somewhere to lay our heads,' Justin said, 'that's all we ask.'

'You can have the guest room. It's got two single beds.'

She'd just finished cleaning the room. Now she found linen and dumped it on the beds.

'It won't take you long to make them up,' she said, smiling at Justin. 'Mark, why don't we leave your father to it, while you and I go into the kitchen and we'll see what there is for supper?'

She departed, throwing a challenging look over her shoulder. He regarded her with his eyebrows raised, but did not seem disconcerted.

When they were in the kitchen Evie muttered to Mark, 'What is your father playing at?'

Mark's shrug was eloquent. 'Dad sets his heart on something and he has to have it. He promised me I could talk to you again.'

'Even if it means chasing me halfway across the country *and missing a whole day's work*?'

Mark gave a snort of delighted laughter.

'Actually he won't be missing that much,' he said. 'He's brought his laptop computer. He can send and read emails at any hour. And he's got his mobile phone so that all his calls won't go on to your phone—'

'*All* his calls? How many calls will there be, and how long is he planning to stay?'

'The actual time doesn't matter,' Mark said wisely. 'Dad can get through more business in five minutes than anyone he knows. That's what he says, anyway. And he always calls America in the evening because they're five hours behind us, and he says that's really useful—'

'In other words, he isn't actually planning to take any time off at all. It'll be business as usual, just in a different setting.'

Mark nodded.

'Until I tell him to leave.'

'You wouldn't,' Mark said, awed by this reckless courage.

'I would. I'll be straight with you, Mark. At the right time, I'll square up to your father and order him off my premises.'

'Wow!' he said, impressed. He moved closer and spoke like a conspirator. 'Will you promise me something?'

She too leaned close. 'What?' she whispered dramatically.

'That when you order Dad off your premises I can be there to see. *Promise* me.'

She laughed. 'You wretched boy. All right, I promise you can be there to enjoy it.'

They jumped apart as Justin appeared with air of suppressed triumph.

'Everything is done upstairs,' he said. 'If you'd care to look.'

'Why are you looking so pleased with yourself?' she asked.

'Come and see.'

She was beginning to suspect the truth, but it was still a surprise to find the beds made perfectly and all the clothes neatly hung up in the wardrobe.

She realised that he was watching her closely, enjoying her expression.

'Well done,' she said. 'Can you cook as well?'

'Try me.'

'I intend to,' she said incredulously.

But again he proved himself better than her doubts. His egg and chips might not have been haute cuisine but they were properly cooked, even if both father and son drenched everything in tomato ketchup. She had to smile at the sight of them acting in unison, wiping their plates with bread, fearful of losing the last smidgen of ketchup.

When the meal was over she leaned back, watching him, her arms folded.

'Well?' she said.

'Well?'

She inclined her head slightly towards the sink.

'I did the cooking,' he said indignantly.

'Yeah, but we invited ourselves, Dad,' Mark muttered.

'Fine. I'll wash, you dry.' He rose. 'Where's the washing-up liquid?'

'I'll do it,' she said, laughing.

In the end they all did it together in an atmosphere that was more pleasant than she would have dared to hope. Afterwards Mark asked to watch the television, and was amazed to discover that the set only received four terrestrial channels and had no teletext. Nor was there a video.

'Gosh, it's like history!' he gasped.

'Mark!' Justin said sharply.

'It's all right.' Evie chuckled. 'He didn't mean it rudely. It must be like something out of the Dark Ages to a modern child.'

In the end they settled down to watch the news, until they heard an ominous sound outside. Evie turned down the sound and they all listened in alarm.

'It's raining!' Mark whispered in horror.

They went outside, where it was pelting down.

'It'll be all right in the morning,' Evie said.

Mark looked at her. 'Promise?'

'Promise,' she said recklessly. 'And now I think you should go to bed. It's late and tomorrow's a big day.'

'Can we go swimming?'

'What about your cold?'

'It's better, honestly. Isn't it, Dad?'

'I wouldn't have brought him here otherwise,' Justin assured her. 'Mark, you heard what Miss Wharton said. Up to bed.'

Mark took her hand. 'Miss Wharton—can I call you Evie?'

'*Mark!*'

'Well, I'm not his teacher any more,' she said. 'Evie it is.'

Mark departed, satisfied.

'I apologise,' Justin groaned.

'Don't. He's just being friendly.'

'How friendly do you think he'll be tomorrow when it rains?'

'It won't rain.'

'How can you be sure?'

'Because I promised him. You heard me.'

'Yes, but—'

'It won't rain. I promised.' She yawned. 'I think I'll go to bed too. Sea air makes me sleepy. 'G'night.'

'Goodnight.'

In her room she undressed and went to bed, listening for the sound of him coming upstairs. She was still listening when she fell asleep.

She didn't know what roused her, but she awoke suddenly in the darkness. The clock by her bed showed two o'clock. She listened and thought she could hear a voice talking in the distance.

Pulling a dressing gown on over her pyjamas, she crept out into the corridor and went to the top of the stairs, from where she could see down into the main room.

Just as Mark had predicted, Justin had set up a laptop computer and was staring at the screen at the same time as talking into his cellphone. He spoke softly, but Evie could pick up the tense note in his voice.

'I'm sorry but I just couldn't take the call this afternoon—I know what I said but I had important business—'

She went quietly downstairs and into the kitchen. By

the time she returned with two large mugs of tea he was off the phone.

'Thanks,' he said, taking one. 'Sorry if I disturbed you, but I had to catch up with my work somehow.'

'Yes, you've obviously come prepared. I'm surprised you could put work aside long enough to drive down here. All those hours not at the computer, not on the phone, not making contacts.'

'I don't bother to make contacts any more. I don't need to. People contact me.'

'You arrogant so-and-so,' she said, amused. 'Anyway, it isn't true. There's always someone bigger you can be doing business with.'

'That's true,' he reflected. 'Why don't you say outright that you're just surprised that I put Mark first?'

'Well—'

'Don't worry, you've already made your poor opinion of me pretty plain, and I'm not arguing with it.'

'Hey, I didn't exactly—'

'Are you saying you don't have a poor opinion of me?'

'Well, it improved when you took the trouble to drive down here for Mark's sake. Although it takes a dive at your way of moving people around like pieces on your own private chessboard.'

'Do I do that? Well, maybe sometimes.'

'You know quite well that you do.'

'Miss Wharton—' he began in a patient voice, but she stopped him.

'What did you say?'

'Nothing.'

'You did, you called me something.'

'I called you Miss Wharton.'

'But why?'

'I thought it was your name.'

'But why aren't you calling me Evie?'

'Because you haven't given me your permission.'

She tore her hair. 'I gave it to Mark.'

'Yes, to Mark. Not to me.'

He was serious, she realised. Was it possible for a modern man to be so old-fashioned? Against her will she realised that there was something charming about it.

'Why are you smiling?' he asked suspiciously.

'It's nothing.' It wouldn't do to tell him she found him charming. He would hate it. 'Call me Evie. And look, you can stay for a short time, but I'll have to ask you to leave without warning. I'm expecting someone.'

'Andrew?'

'Yes, not that it's any of your business.'

'When's he coming?'

'I'm not sure, but when I know he's on his way you really do have to go. He and I have a lot of ground to make up.'

'You mean because of the other evening?'

'Among other things.'

'But surely you made it up when he called you?'

She made a face. 'That wasn't him. It was someone trying to sell me insurance.'

A tremor passed over his face as he tried to suppress his grin and didn't quite manage it.

'Oh, go on, laugh,' she said. 'The poor man who called me didn't think it was so funny when I'd finished giving him a piece of my mind.'

'Having been on the receiving end of a piece of your mind, he has my sympathy.'

'Well, I apologised to him in the end.'

'Did Andrew ever call you?'

'I called him. Same thing.'

He didn't comment on this, but asked thoughtfully, 'Are you in love with him?'

She drew a sharp breath. 'That is none of your business.'

'I suppose not, but I've asked it now, so why not tell me? Either you love him or you're not sure, and the reason you dump him so easily is because you're actually trying to tell him to get lost.'

Since Andrew himself had said something of the kind she was briefly at a loss for words. She decided that she preferred Justin Dane when she could regard him with outright hostility, simple and uncomplicated.

'Yes, I am in love with Andrew,' she said firmly.

He was silent for a moment. 'I see,' he said at last. 'So you want us to leave tomorrow?'

'I didn't say that.'

'But if he finds me here he might think you're playing around. Yes, I know, you'll tell him the truth, but will he believe you?'

'Of course. We trust each other completely. And he won't turn up without warning, he'll call me first.'

'He might do it differently this time.'

'Not Andrew.'

'Solid and reliable?'

'Yes.'

'Doesn't that make life a bit repetitive?'

She regarded him with smouldering eyes. It was simply unforgivable that he should echo her own thoughts. Her own *previous* thoughts, she corrected hastily, dating from before she'd realised how foolish she would be to lose him.

'I will not discuss Andrew with you,' she said.

'You know, I think that's probably a very wise decision.'

They eyed each other and she realised that her previous impression had been correct. He really could be charming.

'I was very impressed by your domestic skills,' she said. 'All that cooking and bed-making. Your mother did a really good job on you.'

He didn't answer, and when she looked at him she found him staring into the distance.

'Hey, I was just paying a compliment to your mother.'

'No need. I never knew her.'

'You mean she died early?'

'Something like that. I'm going to pack up for the night now.' He began switching off his computer.

'Did I say something wrong?' she asked, puzzled at the way he had suddenly closed a door on her in a manner that was uncannily similar to his son's.

'Not at all.'

'Did I offend you, mentioning your mother?'

'Of course not. There, everything's switched off. By the way, I think it's stopped raining.'

'Of course. What did I tell you?'

He regarded her for a moment, taking in the impish gleam in her eyes, and unable to stop smiling at her.

'Any minute now you'll almost have me believing that you cast a magic spell,' he said.

'Maybe I did. I think I'll just leave you to wonder about that. By the way, what about swimming trunks? I mean, if you weren't expecting to stay—'

'We do have them. I thought I might, just possibly, prevail on you.'

'Hogwash!' she said sternly. 'Has anyone ever managed to turn you away at the door?'

'The last man who tried was fending off my takeover bid.'

'No guesses who won.'

'Well,' he said, considering, 'I took him over, but he made me pay more than I'd meant to.'

She threw up her hands in mock horror. 'Disaster!'

'No, just something you have to be prepared for in business. You have to start out knowing what a thing is worth to you and how high you're prepared to go. Winning at a cost is still winning.'

'At *any* cost?'

'That depends what you're aiming to win. Only a few things are worth any cost.'

'What are you aiming to win now?'

'My son's confidence—his trust—his love—at any cost.'

That surprised and silenced her. She had suspected it, but hearing him say it warned her that she had partly misread him. There was more to him than she had believed. It was becoming possible to like him.

Then he said, 'But I need your help; that's why I'm here. You're vital if I'm to have any chance.'

And suddenly she was a pawn on his chessboard again, irritated into saying, 'So you worked out the cost of working at half-speed for a few days and decided it was affordable. But where do I figure in your equation?'

'I told you—vital.'

'But supposing I come with a heavy cost?' she fenced. She was beginning to find fencing with this man strangely exhilarating.

He raised an eyebrow.

'If you do,' he said with soft irony, 'perhaps you should tell me now, so that I can make the necessary arrangements.'

'Oh, get lost!' she said, cheated of her victory. 'I'm going to bed.'

CHAPTER FIVE

LOOKING out of her window next morning, Evie gave thanks that her reckless promise to Mark had been kept. It was a perfect day; the sun was riding high and making the waves glitter almost blindingly.

Mark was leaning out from the next window, beaming and making ecstatic thumbs up signs. She raised her own thumbs in return, laughing and enjoying his happiness.

Downstairs, she put on the kettle and began preparing breakfast. After a few minutes they both joined her. Evie stared at the sight of Justin in shorts and casual shirt.

She stared even more when he gave her a solemn bow, then glanced at his son, as if asking if he'd done it right. But Mark wasn't satisfied.

'Oh, mighty one!' he cried, bowing low.

'Mark insists that we do this,' Justin explained. 'He says you're magic because you made the rain stop and the sun come out. So we must propitiate you, mighty one.'

To her delight he bowed again.

'All right,' she chuckled. 'That's enough grovelling—for today, anyway. Come and have breakfast.'

'Can't we go to the beach now?' Mark begged.

'Later, when the water's had a chance to warm up a bit,' she told him. 'You've just recovered from a cold.'

'And we should go out and buy some food first,' Justin said.

Going around the local supermarket gave her another glimpse of his many facets. Not only could he cook but he also knew what to buy.

He had good legs too, she thought distractedly.

After filling the trolley Justin stopped by the wine shelves. 'White or red?'

'White, please,' she said.

'Can we go to the beach *now*?' Mark asked plaintively as they drove home. 'It's ever so hot.'

'We could make some sandwiches and take them with us,' Evie said.

They agreed on that, packing up a picnic basket before setting off.

The road from the cottage to the beach was strewn with large rocks that had to be negotiated on foot. At the far end the sand spread out into an area of pure gold, stretching away to the sea. It was a small area, flanked on two sides by more rocks, which made it almost like a private beach.

Other holiday makers had been known to brave the rocks for a while, but the trouble of having to climb back over them to get an ice cream was a deterrent. Today they had the place to themselves.

Evie had changed, putting on her swimsuit beneath her clothes. She was a little troubled by that swimsuit. It was a bikini, chosen with Andrew in mind, and ideally she would not have worn it now. But she hadn't thought of it until too late.

Well, it might be worse, she told herself. *As bikinis go it's fairly modest. Even the top is respectable, and I haven't got much to display anyway. First time I've ever been glad of that.*

They tucked into sandwiches and orange squash, but Mark ate very little.

'You need more than that,' Evie protested.

'Nope,' he said, shaking his head firmly. ''Cos otherwise you'll say I mustn't go swimming after a big meal. So I've only eaten a little meal, and I'm going now.'

Before they could stop him he jumped to his feet and shot away across the sands to plunge into the sea.

'Let's go,' Justin said, pulling off his clothes and haring after his son.

Now there was no time to worry about revealing too much. Evie tore off her own clothes and sped after them, rejoicing in the wind whipping past her, the sun on her bare skin, and then the glorious moment of diving in.

She came up, looking around, then saw the two of them preparing to scoop up water and douse her with spray. She screamed and backed away, trying to fend them off. But they splashed her without mercy until she had to sink right under the surface to escape them.

'I give in, I give in,' she cried at last as they roared with laughter.

They splashed around together for a while, with Evie keeping in the background so that father and son could be together. At last Mark declared he was hungry.

'Come and finish your lunch,' Evie said.

'OK.'

'I'll have a longer swim first,' Justin said, and turned to head out to sea.

Back at base Evie and Mark dried themselves off and settled down on large towels.

'I'm ever so glad we came,' Mark confided. 'So's Dad.'

'Did he tell you that?'

He shook his head, spraying crumbs.

'Dad doesn't say things like that,' he said, when he

could speak again. 'But he's cheerful. 'Spect it's 'cos of you.'

'No, it's 'cos of you,' she said. 'He likes being with you. But I'm glad he's cheerful. He's much nicer to be around when you can get a smile out of him.'

'Yes,' Mark said with feeling.

She looked out to sea. 'Where's he gone?'

Mark produced binoculars from his bag. 'There,' he said, handing them to her. 'He's a long way out.'

After a moment she saw Justin's dark head and the movements of his muscular arms, pounding through the waves. As she watched, he turned back towards the rocks where they stretched out into the sea. Reaching them, he hauled himself up and stood for a moment, his wet body gleaming in the sun. Then he dived back in, swam in a wide circle and climbed back on to the rocks.

He stood there long enough for Evie to study him and realise how conventional clothes failed to do him justice. She had known that he was tall, broad-shouldered and long-limbed, but, seeing him almost naked, she suddenly understood many things. His air of walking through the world like a prince was not based on his wealth, but on the proud angle at which he carried his head.

There was the shape of his body, lean and taut, not an ounce of fat, despite his muscular build. He might have been an athlete, or a man doing heavy manual labour. But a silk-suited tycoon flying the world and making deals—that wouldn't have occurred to her.

'Evie!' Mark touched her arm.

With a start she came back to reality, lowering the binoculars.

'Sorry—what?'

'I kept calling and calling you, and you didn't hear.'

'I got distracted by the scenery,' she said vaguely.

'I've poured you some more orange juice.'

She tried to concentrate on the snack, but the sun had dazzled her and she couldn't blot it out, even with her eyes closed. He was there behind her eyelids, diving in and out of the glare, his body shining in the spray.

When she opened her eyes again she saw him walking up the beach.

'That's better,' he said, dropping down beside them. 'I've been too long without exercise.'

'Somehow I pictured you working out in the gym,' she said.

'In theory I do, but the work piles up and it's always tomorrow.'

'Domani, domani, sempre domani!' she declaimed, with a knowing look at Mark.

Justin stared from one to the other.

'Tomorrow, tomorrow, always tomorrow,' Mark translated.

'There, I told you he was one of my best pupils,' Evie said triumphantly.

Mark got to his feet. 'I'm going to explore.'

'Don't go too far,' Justin said quickly.

'Promise.' Mark sped off before he could be asked for any further promises.

'I've never seen him have such a good time,' Justin said, watching the slight figure scampering away. 'Thank you.'

'Didn't you two ever go on seaside holidays before?'

'We went away while his mother was alive, but it was always somewhere like Disneyland. That's what kids seem to want these days, but this—' He made a gesture indicating their surroundings. 'He's happy.'

'Did your family ever take you to the seaside when you were a child?'

She wondered if he had heard her, because he stared straight ahead without answering. At last she realised that he had simply blanked out the question.

If she knew the reason for that, she mused, she might understand more about Mark's inner turmoil.

'Whatever is he doing now?' Justin asked, his eyes on his son.

They could see Mark on the rocks, staring down into a pool, evidently fascinated by something he saw there.

'It's probably a crab, or a starfish,' Evie said. 'I used to look at them in that same pool when I was a kid.'

'Did your family own this place?'

'My Great-Uncle Joe. He was a wonderful old boy, and he virtually brought me up after my parents died, when I was twelve. But it was more than giving me a home. I loved my parents, but they were very conventional people. They reckoned there was only one right way to do everything. It was stifling.

'Joe was just the opposite. He thought there was no right way to do anything, you just had to choose the wrong one that suited you. His motto was "To blazes with the lot of 'em!"'

He grinned and rolled over on his back, propping himself up on one elbow to look up at her.

'I'll bet a twelve-year-old loved it.'

'It was great,' she said, sighing in happy remembrance, 'like having a light come on in the world. Joe reckoned the only crime was to do what other people expected. And he thought it was a virtue to offend at least one person every day.'

'Oh, that's where you—'

'No, I never quite went that far,' she told him repressively.

'Just me, huh?' he asked with a raised eyebrow.

'Just people who deserve it. Shall I continue?'

'Please do.'

'I was really sad when I had to leave here to go to college. I even thought of not going, but Joe lost his temper and nearly threw me out. He said if I didn't seize my chance, I needn't show my face here again. So I went, but I always came back in summer. To me it was the most wonderful place in the world.'

She sighed happily, looking around her at the beauty. But then her face grew sad.

'He died recently and left it to me, but then I found he had huge debts. I'd had no idea. I used to send him money to help out, but apparently it all went into betting shops.

'I never knew about his problem, and I have a horrid feeling it only developed after I left, because he was lonely. Now the cottage has to be sold to pay the debts. I'm just here to clear out my stuff and take a last look.'

'You're going to lose this place?' he asked, sitting up and speaking sharply.

'Just as soon as there's a decent offer. I thought of trying to keep it by paying off the debts—I just can't afford it. I even thought—'

She was interrupted by the sound of her cellphone. Justin didn't miss her sudden alertness, or the eager way she scrabbled in her bag for the phone. He saw the sudden sagging of her shoulders as she said, 'Oh, hi, Sally.'

There followed a conversation about proofs, galleys and corrections, and it was no surprise when she hung up and said, 'That was my editor, about a book I have coming out next month.'

'Not Andrew, then? Has he called you at all?'

'I've only been here two days.'

'And in those two days,' Justin said relentlessly, 'has he called you?'

'Please don't interrogate me, Mr Dane.'

'I'll take that as a no. If I were in love with a woman I wouldn't forget to call her.'

'Well, maybe he doesn't want to seem too anxious. We've been having a few problems. That's why he's coming here.'

'But *is* he coming here?'

She ignored this. 'We'll spend some time together sorting things out.'

'It's a bit early in the relationship for that, isn't it?'

'I don't know what you mean,' she said, wishing he'd drop the subject. But he wouldn't, almost as if he knew how uneasy it made her.

'Sorting things out is what happens when people have been together a while,' he said, 'and things have turned sour, but they want to recapture the magic. If you're "sorting out" in the courtship stage, he's the wrong guy.'

'I'll decide about that, thank you.'

'You can decide what you like, but he's the wrong guy. Why pick on him? Unless you're afraid of being an old maid.'

'Get lost!' she said amiably.

'Well, it has to be said. You're no spring chicken. You must be pushing—what? Forty?'

'Thirty!'

He roared with laughter. 'I had a bet with myself that you'd tell me your age by the end of the day.'

She made a face at him and he laughed again. 'So, thirty, and he's your last chance. Life has passed you by. Men have passed you by. You're pretty enough in a dim light, but nobody's offered you lifetime commitment.'

His eyes were wicked and she smiled back, disconcerted by the sudden reappearance of his charm.

'So, my guess is that you put up with any amount of awkward behaviour on his part, for fear of losing him.'

'No way,' she said. 'It's my awkward behaviour that's caused the problems.'

'Just because you stood him up that night, he's throwing a wobbly?'

'Don't you throw a wobbly if you get stood up?'

'I don't get stood up,' he said with an assurance that was so complete she almost admired it.

'You are the most arrogant, conceited man I've ever met.'

'I'm just recording facts. He can't take it that you put him second that night.'

'It's not the only time—other things happen, and get in the way. But that's over now.'

'Because he's your hero? The one and only whose voice makes your heart beat? The man who—?'

'All right!' she said, trying not to laugh. 'It's a bit more prosaic than that, but, like you said, old age is creeping up on me.'

'Yeah, sure,' he said in a tone of disbelief. Added to the way he looked her figure up and down, it amounted to a definite compliment.

It was the first time he'd even hinted that he admired her as a woman, and it threw her off balance. Suddenly the 'modest' bikini wasn't modest any more. Her bosom was more generous than she'd realised, and the bra was cut low enough to display the fact.

It was like discovering that she'd been naked under his gaze all the time, and had never known it. She could feel herself beginning to blush.

But, just in time, she saw what he was really up to.

He wanted her to think only of Mark, and if that meant fighting off other interests, then he'd do just that.

Well, forewarned was forearmed she thought, amused. It wouldn't hurt to torment him a little.

'The truth is that I'm at a crossroads in my life.' She sighed. 'Freedom's all very well up to a point, but sooner or later a woman wants to settle down with a good man. And then there's security. When I've paid off Joe's debts there won't be much left and I should be looking to the future.'

'You mean you'd marry him for money?'

'Not just that. You said it yourself, he's my hero. His voice makes my heart beat with anticipation—'

She stopped. He was looking at her.

'Well, something like that, anyway.' She laughed.

'You're playing a very cool game. Why aren't you in London, knocking on his door, making sure of him?'

'Because that would send him running in the opposite direction. How would you feel about a woman who threw herself at you? Silly me, I suppose they already do.'

He regarded her satirically. 'Think so?'

'With your money?' she asked airily. 'Of course they do.'

It was a gross slander, she thought, looking at him stretched out on the sand in negligent ease. She had seen him from a distance, but close up he was even more impressive.

She considered this matter entirely dispassionately. Her own preference was for a man like Andrew, built on less spectacular lines, but with a mind that met hers.

And a man's mind was important, she mused. Andrew was intelligent, literary, with fine, sensitive fibres. Justin Dane was undoubtedly intelligent. Or rather, where his own interests were concerned he was shrewd and cunning. He certainly wasn't literary, and she suspected that his fibres resembled thick canvas.

It was just annoying that he had a body designed to send an easily provoked female into a frenzy. Luckily for her, she wasn't easily provoked.

Mark came running up the beach with a little crab which he displayed proudly.

'Look what I've got.'

'Very nice,' Justin said, regarding the object askance.

'Isn't he beautiful?' Evie said, taking the little crab in her hand. 'I used to look for these on this beach when I was a child.'

'What did you do with them?' Mark wanted to know.

'I used to look for someone whose shirt I could drop it down.'

'Really!' Justin said in a voice heavy with significance. 'Let me advise both of you to forget any such idea.'

Then Mark delighted her by asking, 'Not scared, are you, Dad?'

And Justin pleased her even more by grinning and saying, 'Terrified. So remember that, and beware!'

They all laughed. It was the happiest and most relaxed moment that the three of them had shared.

Her phone rang again. Her heart leapt at the thought that it might be Andrew, yet she knew a brief flash of regret that the moment was over.

But it wasn't Andrew. An unfamiliar female voice asked if that was Miss Wharton, then went on to explain that a couple would like to look over the cottage.

'This afternoon, if possible.'

'Yes—yes, of course,' Evie said. 'Do you need directions?'

As she described the way, Justin began to pack up their things, quietly explaining to Mark what was happening. When Evie hung up they were ready to go.

'That was the estate agent,' she said. 'A Mr and Mrs Nicholson will be here to view the cottage in a couple of hours.'

Then she turned away quickly so that her face shouldn't betray how wretched she suddenly felt.

'I suppose a potential buyer is good news,' Justin mused.

'Yes,' she said, trying to convince herself. 'I should go and tidy up.'

They had all left early that morning, not stopping to make beds and do washing-up, in their eagerness to get to the beach. Now they helped her, going around the cottage at speed, shoving things into drawers and hurrying dusters over every spare surface.

The Nicholsons arrived half an hour early and walked in as though they already owned the place. They were rich, middle-aged and insensitive.

'Isn't this just wonderful?' Mrs Nicholson demanded of her husband, standing in the middle of the downstairs room. 'Look at those flagstones. How romantic! And a real open fire! How beautiful! Of course, it'll have to come out.'

'But why, if it's beautiful?' Evie couldn't help asking.

'Unhygienic. All that smoke.'

'It goes up the chimney,' Justin observed.

'But it's still unhygienic,' Mrs Nicholson said firmly. She was plainly a woman who grabbed an idea and hung on to it.

She and her mostly silent husband went through the whole cottage like that, criticising while pronouncing everything beautiful, wonderful, magnificent.

Justin's brow was getting darker, as though this behaviour upset him too, and at last he came up behind Evie, putting his warm hands firmly on her shoulders and murmuring into her ear, 'It's perfect, but it's all got to be changed. To hell with them!'

She growled agreement. His hands vanished from her shoulders, leaving behind a warm imprint that stayed with her for several minutes.

'We just love it,' Mrs Nicholson proclaimed at last. Mr Nicholson nodded without speaking.

'Of course, it's very over-priced,' she charged on. 'We'd expect you to come down.'

'I'm afraid that's not possible.'

For a moment Evie wondered who had spoken. All she knew for certain was that it wasn't herself. Then she saw Justin's face. He was giving Mrs Nicholson the kind of resolute look that she imagined he'd used to close profitable deals in the past. Evie stared at him, past speech.

'You see,' he went on, 'Miss Wharton can't make any agreement. You have to deal with her uncle's executor, who is obliged, by law, to get the best possible deal. So I'm afraid he won't be in favour of an "agreement"—'

'But I'm sure you realise—'

'And I'm sure that you realise that he would be very displeased with her if she agreed a lower price with you.'

'But surely a private arrangement first—'

'Miss Wharton will give you the executor's number, and he'll expect your call.'

Sulkily the woman took the number and made a grand exit, her husband trailing meekly in her wake. Through the window, the three of them watched the couple get into a car whose size and luxury left no doubt of their ability to meet the price.

Evie turned awed eyes on Justin, and found him regarding her with less than his usual confidence.

'Did I go too far?' he asked.

'No,' she said. 'You were terrific. But how—?'

'She was trying to steamroller you and I wasn't going to let it happen. I'm an old hand in the art of not getting steamrollered.'

'I'll bet you are. Thank you.' Then she sighed. 'But I'll have to sell in the end.'

'Yes, but you've got a little more time.'

'Don't you want to sell?' Mark asked her. He'd been listening intently.

She could only shake her head.

The call from the lawyer came an hour later. The Nicholsons had made an offer, but it was below the market price.

'I've refused and we're playing a waiting game,' he said. 'I think they'll go higher if we wait. Or do you think I should make the deal now?'

'No,' she said quickly. 'We should wait.'

'What happened?' Justin asked as soon as she hung up.

'They've made an offer below the price. I'm not taking it.'

'Good for you.'

'Does that mean we can stay here?' Mark asked eagerly.

'Yes, we don't have to go for a bit,' she told him, smiling.

'Yippee!' he crowed. 'We're going to have a wonderful time.'

She hugged him. 'That's right. We're going to have a wonderful time.'

CHAPTER SIX

EVIE had expected Mark to grow quickly bored with an old-fashioned seaside holiday, but it didn't happen. He was eager for even the simplest experiences, and she could almost imagine that she saw herself again in him.

For the next few days they all enjoyed themselves so much that she nearly forgot about her problems. Nobody else came to view the place, and she was able to relish her temporary reprieve.

They went exploring, and Mark listened, entranced, to the tales of pirates. When they actually found a pirate museum he was in seventh heaven. Evie bought him a book called *Black Simeon's Revenge*, which he read in the car all the way home. After supper he fell asleep over it.

The next day Justin found a fisherman with a boat big enough for them all, and they went out to sea. After a day in the salty air they were all sleepy, and Mark actually made the journey back fast asleep with a smile on his face.

Evie watched all this with delight, but she was also puzzled by Justin. He was pleasant, and on the surface all was well between him and his son. But sometimes she happened to glance at him when he thought nobody was looking, and then his smile would be replaced by a look that was distant, almost haggard.

Mark had spoken of a darkness inside his father, and Evie began to sense an air of unreality. Justin was doing his best, but he was following rules that he didn't understand.

Once or twice he came close to losing his temper—about nothing, as far as she could see. He controlled himself quickly and apologised, but she was disturbed by how trivial were the things that triggered his outbursts. He was living on his nerves, and the strain was pulling him apart. She often caught him watching her with Mark, as though desperately trying to discover something.

Then she told herself that she was being fanciful. He worked long hours at night to keep up with his business, and he was simply very tired. When she found Mark asleep over his book, Justin was also fighting not to nod off.

'Go to bed,' she told him, laughing and yawning.

She was about to say that she too fancied an early night, when the cottage telephone rang.

The other two watched her pick up the receiver and announce herself cheerfully. Then they saw the smile fade from her face. After that she said very little before hanging up and turning to face them.

'That was Uncle Joe's executor,' she said. 'The Nicholsons have upped their offer, and he's accepted it. They want to push the deal through fast, so that they can take possession as soon as possible.'

Dawn was just beginning to glow across the sea when Justin came quietly downstairs, meaning to slip out for an early swim. He was dressed in shorts and his shirt was open, for the day was already growing warm.

He headed for the door, eager to get outside and plunge into the water, but then he stopped, realising that he was not alone.

The figure on the couch was so still and silent that at first he hadn't seen her. Now he moved closer, uncertain what to do next. He supposed he ought to leave and not invade her privacy. Instead he dropped to his knees beside her.

She looked as though she'd been crying, but that might have been a trick of the poor light. Last night she'd been near to tears, following the phone call, but she had brightened up at once, insisting that everything was fine.

But it wasn't fine, he thought, as he leaned a little closer, noticing how her usual elfin cheekiness had drained away. Now he saw the tension beneath the laughter, and realised that she no more let the world see inside her heart than he did himself.

Without warning she opened her eyes, looking straight at him. For a moment he was transfixed, more startled than she.

'I'm sorry,' he said at last, softly. 'I was worried about you.'

'Why?'

'You're not happy.'

'I'm all right.'

'*Are* you?'

She shook her head. Then she rubbed her eyes.

'What am I doing down here?' she asked, looking around.

'You don't remember?'

'Oh, yes, I stayed up late and fell asleep. I started looking around, and remembering everything about this place. It still looks almost exactly as it did when I first came here.'

She rose to her feet, but her limbs were cramped and

she moved awkwardly. He put out both hands to help her and she clung to him.

'What was it like then?' he asked.

'I thought it was magic—flagstones, open fireplace, little old-fashioned windows. When Mark walked into this room for the first time, it was like seeing myself again, full of a child's wonder.

'And it went on being wonderful when I grew up. I loved coming back here and being with Uncle Joe—all the happiest times of my life—and I wanted to keep it for ever, just as he kept it—'

Her voice had grown more and more husky until at last it ran out, and she passed a hand over her eyes.

'Look, we'll do something about it,' he said. 'Don't cry—'

'I'm not crying,' she flashed. 'I never cry.'

'So I see,' he murmured.

'It's just that—that dreadful woman will change everything. I don't want her to, but I can't stop her because it'll be hers and—it's all wrong.'

This time she buried her face in her hands, and her shoulders shook.

'I think perhaps you're crying,' he said kindly.

'No, I'm not—yes, I am—*oh, hell!*'

'Yes, that's usually the best thing to do,' he said, putting his arms about her so that her head fell naturally against his shoulder.

She left it there. She didn't want to argue any more. She just wanted to release all the tears she'd been holding back ever since she'd understood the extent of her loss.

He surprised her by being the perfect comforter, holding her patiently against the warm, strong column of his body while she wept. And she, a woman who prized her independence and detachment, clung to him as though he were her last hope.

But at last she began to feel self-conscious, and moved to disengage herself.

'I don't know what came over me,' she said awkwardly. 'I don't usually do that.'

'Perhaps you should do it more often.'

'Not me. I'm not the type,' she said firmly.

'Of course you're not. But you shouldn't try to do everything alone. Isn't there someone to help you?'

'I don't have any other family.'

'Then what about Andrew? Isn't he an accountant?'

'Yes, but—'

'Then why can't he think up some brilliant financial scheme—a tax dodge or something? What's the point of knowing an accountant if he can't fiddle the books for you?'

'I don't want him to fiddle anything.'

'But he should at least have offered.'

She remembered telling Andrew about the cottage. He'd advised her to hold out for the best price, but he hadn't thought of a way to help her keep it.

'Why not ask him?' Justin urged.

'I suppose I could. He'll be here any day.'

'Any day? How much time do you have?'

'None. You're right. I'll call him now. At this hour he'll be asleep.'

And it was the perfect excuse to call him and ask him when he was coming down. Seizing the phone, she dialled Andrew's London apartment. It rang for some time before he answered, sounding slightly muffled.

'Hallo, sleepyhead,' she teased.

She heard the moment of shocked silence but refused to understand it.

'Evie,' he said at last.

'Who did you think it was?' she asked, trying to laugh, although there was something inside her that wasn't laughing at all.

'I—well—I don't know.'

'I've been at the cottage a few days now. You're going to love it here, really.'

'Well—actually, I wanted to talk about that—I mean, the way things have been recently—'

He let his voice die away awkwardly, and in the silence Evie heard a sound that froze her blood.

A giggle.

It was definitely a giggle, not a laugh, or even a chuckle, but the giggle of a young woman who had been put in a very good mood by something or other.

'Come on, darling,' she cooed from close to Andrew. 'Don't stay on that phone for ever.'

Andrew spoke in a low, hurried voice.

'Evie, are you still there?'

'Oh, yes. I wouldn't miss this for anything.'

'I hope you're not going to be unreasonable. After all, it's usually you apologising to me—'

'Not for being caught out in bed with someone else.'

'Well—things haven't been going well for us, and I don't really think you mind about this—'

'Don't tell me what I mind and don't mind,' she said tensely.

'I'm sorry, but it's just a nice change to be with someone who puts me first. You never did that, and if you think over *why* you didn't, you'll realise that this isn't really such a big deal.'

She opened her mouth to put him right on this point, then closed it again. While she was choosing her words the line went dead. He'd hung up on her.

'Andrew? *Andrew!*'

She hung up, dazed by shock. Justin, coming out of the kitchen, where he'd retired to give her some privacy, saw her staring into space.

'No?' he asked gently.

'No.'

'He can't help you?'

'I didn't even ask him. It's over. He isn't coming here.' She gave a jerky laugh. 'I suppose he never really was, was he?'

'I don't think so,' Justin agreed gently.

'I'm a fool. I should have seen it all before. He was in bed with someone else.'

He came beside her. 'You really never suspected?'

'No,' she said with self-mockery. 'I've been so full of myself. I just saw it from my own point of view. We were going to have an idyllic time here, and I was going to tell him that I really did love him, and everything was going to be all right. But things don't work like that, do they?'

'No, I guess they don't.'

He touched her face, brushing her untidy hair back. 'Come on, Evie, you're not broken-hearted. You're not madly in love with him. You never were.'

'You're as bad as he is,' she said, incensed. 'Telling me how I feel.'

He made a wry face. 'When a woman's really in love it's pretty obvious. She never forgets the man for an instant. Can you honestly say that you never forgot Andrew? Be honest, Evie. You hardly remembered him.'

Now he'd gone too far. She made a move to free herself but his arms tightened. She gasped with outrage that he was daring to keep her prisoner.

'He didn't remember you either,' Justin continued remorselessly, 'because when a man loves a woman she's there with him, in his mind and his heart, every moment of the day.'

'Let me go—'

'Could you feel his body against you even when you were miles apart? Did the thought of him excite you? I don't think so.'

'How dare you—?'

She tried to struggle free again but it was useless. His face was close and she could feel his warm breath whispering past her cheeks, against her mouth. To her intense annoyance the sensation seemed to go right through her body, making her aware of him in a way that she would rather not have been at this moment.

'Did his kiss drive you wild, Evie, or don't you even remember that?'

She barely heard the last words, murmured as his mouth descended. She'd known what he meant to do but refused to believe it until his lips touched hers.

Even then she wouldn't face it. It wasn't possible that this awkward, arrogant, manipulative man should send shivers of excitement through her. It wasn't possible, *it wasn't possible!* She must hang on to that thought.

She tried to shut herself down and not be aware of her own feelings, but her body wouldn't let her off the hook. It insisted on responding to every sensation as his lips moved over hers again and again.

Her heart was a traitor too, pounding as it had never done before, almost as though it were in league with Justin. And while her mind seethed with indignation, her flesh ached for him to touch her more deeply, more intimately.

At last he loosened his grip enough for her to draw

back. She was breathing heavily with rage and something else.

'I'm warning you,' she gasped, 'if you don't let me go this minute, I'll do something that will make your ears ring for a week.'

Now he would lose his temper and she would have the satisfaction of a real knock down, drag 'em out fight. She was looking forward to it, every inch of her vibrating in anticipation, in a way that was new, violent and shocking.

But Justin disappointed her. There was no rage, no outburst. He just stood there looking dazed and confused.

'I'm sorry,' he said. 'I don't know what—I just wanted you to understand that this man—that you don't—'

'And I'm supposed to fall at your feet, am I?'

'No, that's—'

'You have the most unspeakable nerve. You think I have no feelings because that's what it suits you to believe. I've just lost the man I loved. I suppose the idea that I might be broken-hearted never occurred to you.'

'It might have done if you'd been a different woman,' he retorted.

'You have no idea what kind of woman I am.'

'I know you've got a lot of common sense—'

'Thanks a lot!' she snapped, insulted.

He threw up his hands. 'Now what have I said wrong?'

Since she couldn't have told him in a million years, she changed tack. But to be accused of common sense was a slur not to be forgiven.

'You seem to think you know everything about everybody, but this is my life. *I* decide how I feel—'

'You could if you were thinking straight,' he said. 'As it is, I'll spell it out for you. You're well rid of him. He was a waste of space.'

'You never even met him.'

'That's right, I haven't. And why? Because he isn't here when you need him. You were worried sick about losing your home, and what was he doing? Screwing around, that's what. He didn't do one single thing to help you.'

'It's not his problem—'

'Then it damned well ought to be.'

'Well, I confused him by sending out the wrong signals.'

'Give me patience!' Justin said in deep disgust. 'What happened to the independent woman I thought I knew?'

'She took the night off!'

'She's taken her whole life off if you're going to talk this way. Why must you blame yourself?'

'Have you never blamed yourself for anything?'

'Not if I could help it.'

'I can believe that.'

'Sometimes you have to admit you were wrong,' he admitted, 'but only a fool rushes into it.'

'Great! Now I'm a fool.'

'I won't answer that since everything I say seems to be wrong.'

'Hah! You noticed.'

She knew she was talking nonsense but her nerves were jangling.

'Look,' he said, with an air of exaggerated patience calculated to drive her to murder, 'I only kissed you. I was trying to make you feel better—'

'You conceited—'

'I mean by making you see things in a new light.

Maybe I did it clumsily—all right, yes, I was clumsy, but I—oh hell!'

He turned away, tearing his hair, but almost immediately swung back to face her.

'Fine, I did it the wrong way. But if you could just clear your head long enough to consider—'

'There you go again. Even your apologies are insults in disguise—and not that deep a disguise—'

'If you don't shut up I'll kiss you again.'

'Now there's a threat that'll keep me silent for years.'

He drew a sharp breath. His face was full of fury and for a moment she wondered if he would carry out his threat.

But he didn't. Instead, he snatched up a towel where he'd dropped it on a nearby chair and stormed out.

Evie ran upstairs. From her window she could watch Justin run across the sand to the sea. He'd removed his shirt, which was a pity because it brought back the sensation of being pressed against his bare chest.

She had never been so angry with him. Everything he had done was inexcusable: trying to dictate to her, daring to throw the light of common sense over her relationship with Andrew, kissing her, not kissing her.

She threw herself on to her bed, trying to quell the turbulence within. He was right. Of course he was right. Hadn't she always known that her relationship with Andrew was incomplete, because she'd always withheld part of herself? Hadn't she driven Andrew into another woman's arms, and secretly known what she was doing all the time?

She heard Mark moving in the next room and forced herself to be calm. By the time the boy came downstairs she was there ahead of him, smiling and preparing breakfast.

'Where's Dad?'

'He went for an early swim.'

'Can we go too?'

'Have some breakfast first.'

Justin came in a few minutes later, greeted them both, and said, 'I have to go away for a few hours today.'

Mark said nothing, but regarded his father with a face that was suddenly tense.

'Is that all right?' Justin asked, speaking to them both and neither in particular. If he was looking at anyone, it was Mark. But it was hard to be sure.

'That's fine,' Evie said. 'Mark and I will have a great day together, won't we, Mark?'

When he didn't answer she looked at him and found him staring fixedly at his father.

'Will you be away long, Dad?'

'Only until tomorrow.'

'Promise?'

'I promise,' he said, speaking gently. 'I'll be back tomorrow.'

'Where are you going?'

'That's a secret. But when I come back I'll have a surprise for you, and I think you'll like it.'

Mark nodded, seemingly satisfied. Justin ruffled his hair and went upstairs to change.

For a moment Evie was tempted to go after him, but she thought better of it. After a while he came downstairs, formally dressed, carrying a briefcase. This was a man intent on business, just as she had first known him.

Then she understood why Mark had asked if he were returning. He'd seen that, for his father, the holiday was over. In a few hours Justin would telephone, saying that he was staying in London and asking her to bring Mark home.

Fine! Evie thought with a touch of contempt. She wouldn't let his son down, even if he did.

They waved him off together and spent the day at the beach. Neither of them mentioned Justin. In the evening they played chess. Evie began by resolving to let Mark win a game or two, and ended up struggling to beat him even once. His twinkling eyes told her that he'd followed her thoughts.

She laughed with him, thinking how like Justin he looked. His mouth was different, gentler, with a touch of sweetness, but his nose was exactly the same, sharp and dominating his face, with a curiously flat bridge.

The phone rang. Mark ran to be the first to answer it.

'Hallo, Dad? When are you coming home? OK—I'll put you on to Evie—all right. I'll tell her.'

He replaced the receiver.

'Dad couldn't talk to you because he was in a hurry, but he says he'll be here first thing tomorrow.'

She answered vaguely. She was disturbed by a small knot of anxiety that was easing inside her, almost as though she were glad of his return. Even pleased, although pleased was perhaps going a bit far. She would admit to relief, but only for Mark's sake.

They tidied up and went to bed. Evie lay in the dark and tried to focus her attention on Andrew, wondering just how broken-hearted it was suitable for her to be. After a while she gave up. How could you grieve for a man whose face you couldn't remember?

In the early hours she awoke, hearing sounds from below. In a moment she was out of bed, pulling a light dressing gown on over her pyjamas and slipping quietly out on to the landing. The light was growing fast and she could see the man who had just arrived.

'Justin?' she called softly.

'Yes, come down. I have something to tell you.'

'Goodness, what's happened?' she asked, wondering at his businesslike tone.

She hurried down and saw him rummaging in his briefcase. He looked tired and unshaven.

'Have you been driving all night? You look done in.'

'Never mind that,' he said, sounding almost impatient. 'There's something I want you to see.'

'Is this the surprise you told Mark about? Shall I fetch him?'

'Later. I want you to see it first.'

'You're getting me worried.'

'No need. Here.' He'd found a large envelope in his briefcase and held it out to her. 'This is yours.'

'What is it?'

'Look at it,' he said curtly.

At first the words were a jumble, dancing before her eyes. Then she recognised the address of the cottage.

'It's sold,' she said at last. 'You mean the Nicholsons moved that fast?'

'Not them. Me. I bought this place yesterday.'

'You *what*?' Then her eyes fell on the price. *'How much?'*

The final price was fifty grand higher than the original asking price.

'You didn't really pay that?' she gasped.

'I had to. When the Nicholsons heard of my offer they raised theirs, which, I must admit I hadn't expected, considering that they tried to get it cheap. But, once they'd decided, they were determined not to let go. There was a bidding war, but I won because I kept going longer.'

'Yes, I can imagine that you did,' she said, dazed. 'But why—?'

'Look at the other paper. It'll tell you.'

The other paper was a deed of gift, making over the cottage to herself.

'I don't understand this,' she murmured.

'Surely it's clear enough? The cottage is yours. I bought it and now it's yours.'

She should have felt an uprush of gratitude, but there was only the old, uneasy feeling of a net closing about her. He hadn't done this for her sake, but for reasons of his own.

'But why are you giving it to me?' she asked.

His manner became even more impatient.

'What does it matter why? The point is, it's yours. You won't have to move out now. And since I paid over the odds you'll have plenty left when the debts are cleared. It's a very good deal for you.'

'Yes, it is, isn't it?' she said in a voice that was suddenly hard. 'And you really did pay over the odds, I can see.'

'Sometimes you have to, if it's the only way to get what you want.'

'I understand that,' she said slowly. 'It's really impressive, the way you never let anyone get the better of you. Not anybody. Ever.'

Something in her manner finally got through to him. He turned, regarding her with a puzzled frown.

'Evie, don't you understand? The cottage is yours. Yours to keep. For ever. It's what you wanted. Don't you have anything to say to me?'

She raised smouldering eyes to him.

'Yes,' she said fiercely, 'I do have something to say to you. *I shall never forgive you for this as long as I live.*'

CHAPTER SEVEN

JUSTIN stared at her. 'Did I hear that properly?'

'I think you did. What were you expecting? Gratitude? Well, maybe I'd be grateful if I didn't know the real reason behind this.'

His voice was hard. 'And you think the reason is what?'

'Control. Acquisition. I'm useful to you, because of Mark, and when something's useful you have to make sure it can't escape, right? So you buy it.'

He went pale. 'Is that what you think? That I'm trying to buy you?'

'What else? The perfect takeover bid, mounted under perfect conditions—the important one being secrecy so that the object of acquisition doesn't even know about it until it's too late.'

'Object of acquisition!' For pity's sake, listen to yourself! You're talking nonsense.'

'I don't think so. You've done a perfect job, behind my back, only I wasn't supposed to see the strings being pulled.'

'I tried to give you something,' he shouted. 'Something I thought you wanted. You've told me how much you love this place.'

'I was talking generally, not angling for a handout.'

'Yesterday you were crying about it.'

'Don't remind me about yesterday,' she said dangerously.

The way he'd kissed her as an assertion of power

rankled with her still, and drove her to lash him cruelly. She would think about it later. For now she only knew that the moment she had seen him her heart had felt a disturbance that was mysteriously linked to anger.

'The place is yours now,' he snapped. 'Do what you damned well like with it.'

'I can't. This isn't right. It mustn't happen.'

'You can't stop it. The sale's gone through.'

'I don't see how you can have done it in one day. All that money takes time.'

His shrug was a complete answer. What was a huge amount to her was a pittance to him. He'd probably handed over cash.

'I can't accept the cottage as a gift,' she said. 'Nor can I take the extra money. As soon as it's paid to the executor, and he's cleared the debts, I'll tell him to return you the balance.'

'That's ridiculous,' he shouted. 'Where's your common sense?'

'Obviously I don't have any. But I do have some self-respect, enough not to take charity from you.'

She heard his sharp intake of breath, and the look on his face was very ugly. She held out the papers and he snatched them.

'Go to hell,' he said with soft venom. 'Go there and stay there.'

Both tense with anger, neither noticed a figure looking down at them from the stairs, or heard the soft noise as he scuttled back to bed.

For a moment it seemed that Justin expected her to yield. When she didn't he simply walked out of the room, and a moment later she heard his car starting up. She sank down on the stairs, trembling violently.

She wondered what had come over her to have rejected his gift. To keep the cottage had been her heart's desire, and now it was hers, if she would only bend her pride a little.

But no power on earth could make her bend it for this man. His curt, businesslike tone as he'd outlined his methods, the way he'd crushed all opposition, the easy way he tossed money around, told her all she needed to know about his motives.

And it was all the worse because a corner of her heart had started to warm to him. If he'd done this in friendship she might have been tempted to accept. But Justin Dane didn't 'do' friendship.

She went back to her room and lay down, not expecting to sleep. But the fight had left her drained, and she dozed uneasily. When she awoke the sun was high, but Justin's car had not returned.

Looking out, she saw Mark sitting far out on the rocks. She dressed and hared out after him, ready with the words of reproach for slipping away alone. But they died on her lips when he raised his eyes and she saw the unhappiness in his face. Just like at the start, she remembered.

'Hallo,' she said, speaking cheerfully. 'You're out early. Anything interesting in the pool?'

'Some crabs. Nothing much. I just wanted to think a bit.'

'Well, it's a good place for it. Did you come up with anything?'

He shook his head. 'Thinking doesn't really help,' he said wistfully. 'It doesn't change anything.'

He was too young to believe that, she thought. Unable to find any words of wisdom she said, 'It's easier to think on a full stomach. Breakfast?'

He nodded. 'Then can we come back?'

'Yes, we'll spend the day here.'

She waited for him to ask if his father had returned, but he said nothing.

After breakfast they went back to the beach and explored the rock pools until Mark said, 'Here's Dad.'

Justin was coming across the sand towards them. He smiled at Mark, and then in Evie's general direction.

Mark greeted his father kindly but without eagerness. Nor did he ask about the surprise Justin had promised. She recalled his sadness of that morning and guessed that it was still there, suppressed beneath a polite smile.

It was like that for the rest of the day. On the surface all was calm. But beneath were tensions, only just held in check. In the evening Justin insisted on taking them out to a restaurant.

It was an expensive place and they all dressed up for it. She wondered why he'd done this until she realised that, in the fuss of waiters and choices to be made, the awkwardness between them was less noticeable.

He offered her wine, but refused it himself, explaining that he never touched alcohol.

Of course, she thought. Staying teetotal is a way of keeping control.

But then she castigated herself for dwelling so much on thoughts of him and his motives. There and then she made a resolution to put him out of her mind.

But that was hard when other people seemed so aware of him. At a nearby table sat two young women, both of whom seemed much taken with Justin. They regarded him with lustful appreciation, tried to catch his eye, smiled if his head turned briefly.

They were beauties that any man would be proud to have on his arm, and they were Justin's, if he wanted them, which he didn't seem to. She had to give him full marks for courtesy, for he gave her and Mark his whole attention.

She was forced to see him through their eyes as a vitally attractive man, with a presence and charisma that went beyond mere good looks, and she began to remember things she would rather forget: days on the beach with him stretched out beside her, half naked or fooling in the surf. From there it was a short step to being held against his bare chest as he kissed her fiercely, repeatedly.

It was useless to say that she hadn't wanted that kiss. Some part of her *had* wanted it, although she would go to the stake before letting him suspect.

Then came other thoughts—the way she'd awoken on the sofa to find him kneeling beside her, asking gently about her sadness. His unexpected kindness had touched her heart, making her vulnerable to him. But then he'd tried to turn it to his own advantage...

'Are you all right?' Mark asked her.

'I'm fine.'

'I thought you looked a little sad.'

'Not me,' she said untruthfully.

It was late when they reached home and Mark's eyelids were drooping. When Evie suggested that he go to bed he agreed without protest. Justin bade his son goodnight and immediately opened his computer.

'I think I'll go to bed, too,' she said.

'Fine,' he said. 'Goodnight.'

She regarded the back of his head with exasperation.

'Goodnight,' she said, and went upstairs.

She tucked Mark in and sat down on the bed. 'You didn't enjoy today, did you?' she asked.

He shook his head. 'It was like it used to be.'

'Used to be? When?'

'Just before Mum left. She and Dad—they were polite but it was horrible.'

Evie groaned. Why hadn't she thought?

'I'm sorry, Mark. We were just both in a bad mood. It didn't mean anything. Don't worry. Go to sleep, and everything will be all right in the morning.'

But when she'd gone to bed and switched out her light she wondered if she'd spoken truly. How could everything be all right after this?

She lay for a while, trying to get to sleep, but actually listening for the sound of Justin climbing the stairs. Instead she heard something from the next room that made her sit up in bed. There it was again—a wail from Mark's room.

She was out on the landing in a moment, pushing open his door to find the child sitting up, his eyes closed, tears pouring down his face.

'Mark,' she said urgently, taking him into her arms. 'What is it, darling?'

'Mum,' he wailed, 'Mum!'

She tightened her arms, feeling the frail body shaking with misery against her. He'd given up on words now and simply lay against her, crying uncontrollably. At last she felt his hands grasping her arms tightly.

'I'm sorry,' he hiccuped.

'There's nothing to be sorry about. But please, tell me what's the matter. Did you have a bad dream?'

'No, it was a lovely dream.'

'Was it about your mother?'

'Um!' He nodded against her shoulder.

'You miss her all the time, don't you?' she whispered.

'It's worse at night, because then I dream she's alive. She comes home to me and says it was all a mistake and she didn't mean to go without me. Then we run away together. Or sometimes she stays home with me. It was a mistake, you see. She didn't really leave me because she wouldn't do that.'

His voice rose on the last few words and he buried his face against her, shaking with sobs.

'No, darling, she wouldn't,' Evie murmured, racked for him.

Gradually he grew quieter. She continued to sit there, holding and soothing him, but actually alert, because her sharp ears had detected a faint sound from just outside the door.

'She would have come for me,' Mark said, 'if she hadn't died.'

'Of course she would. And I know she never stopped thinking of you, all the time.'

'Really?'

'Yes, really.'

'Then why didn't she come home? Do you think Dad stopped her?'

'No,' she said swiftly. 'I know he wouldn't do that.'

'You don't really know.'

'Yes, I do. He'd never do anything to hurt you. Mark, you must believe me.'

'But he wouldn't bring her home when she died.'

'That's different. When she was alive—'

She paused. She had no right to repeat to Mark what Justin had told her. After a moment she realised that she had no need to say any more. The child had fallen asleep against her shoulder.

Gently she laid him down on the bed and drew the covers up. Then she kissed his cheek before slipping quietly out of the room and closing the door.

It was dark in the corridor, but the sliver of moonlight from the window was just enough to show her Justin standing there, leaning against the wall, his head back, motionless.

'Waiting at the window every week,' he whispered.

'Justin—'

'Standing there for hours because today would be different—today she'd really come.'

Of course he'd heard his son's words, and his heart had understood. If only he could talk directly to Mark like this. She could see the tears on his cheeks. He didn't try to brush them away. Perhaps he didn't know about them.

She reached out and held him, enfolding him in the same gesture she had used to comfort his son, and at once she felt his arms go around her, clinging on to her as if he were seeking refuge.

'But she never came—' he murmured.

'Justin!' She took hold of him, giving him a little shake.

He looked at her despairingly. 'I was sure she'd come, but she never did.'

'You?' she echoed, wondering if she'd heard him clearly.

'She promised,' he said huskily. 'I knew she wouldn't break her promise—but I never saw her again.'

Only then did she understand that Justin wasn't empathising with his son's loss. He was talking about a loss of his own.

It was as though a pit had opened beneath her, and from its depths came an aching misery that left her shattered. It clawed at her, howling of endless despair, grief too great to endure. The man in her arms was shuddering with that grief and she held him more tightly, helplessly trying to comfort something she did not understand.

They mustn't stay here, she thought. Mark might hear

them and come out. Gently she urged him across the landing to her own room. He could barely walk.

Inside, she closed the door without switching on the light. He almost fell on to the bed, taking her with him, for his hands were holding on to her like grim death.

Once before he'd held her in an unbreakable grip, but this was different. Instead of arrogance, she felt only his need and desperation and everything in her went forward to meet it, embrace and console it.

'It's all right,' she murmured, just as she had done with the child. 'I'm here. Hold on to me.'

He kept his eyes fixed on her. He was still trembling like a man caught in a nightmare from which there was no escape.

'Justin, what's the matter? It's not just about Mark's mother, is it?'

'No,' he said hoarsely.

'Tell me about it.'

'I can't—so many things—there's no help for it now.'

'There's help for everything, if you've got someone who really wants to help you,' she said. 'But how can I, if I don't understand?'

'How can you understand, when I don't understand it myself?' he whispered. 'I want to ask why—I've always wanted that—but there's nobody to ask.'

She couldn't bear his agony. Without thinking about it, she leaned down and laid her lips tenderly over his.

'It's going to be all right,' she whispered. 'I'm going to make it all right.'

She had no idea what she meant, or what she could do to help him. But the details didn't matter. What mattered was easing his pain in any way she could. So she kissed him again and again until she felt him begin to relax in her arms.

It was unlike the other kiss in every way but one, and that was the slow burning inside her. But whereas that first excitement had been entwined with anger, this one was a part of pity and sorrow. She wanted him to find oblivion in her, lose himself in her completely, if that could give him a respite from suffering.

So she offered herself to him without reservation, waiting for the moment when his own desire rose and he reached out, taking over the kiss, turning her so that he was above her on the bed.

He checked himself for a moment, as though the earlier memory had come back to him. Seeing his doubt, she began to unbutton his shirt while her smile told him enough to ease the dread in his face. Then he was opening her pyjama top and laying his face against her warm skin.

He stayed like that for so long that she wondered if this was all he wanted, but then she felt his hands move on her with increasing urgency and she knew that they both wanted the same thing. And they wanted it now.

They made love quickly, as if trying to discover something they badly needed to know. And when they'd found the answer they made love again, but slowly this time, relishing the newly discovered treasure.

Afterwards there was peace, clinging to each other for safety in this new world, while the moonlight limned their nakedness.

She kissed him. 'Can you talk about it now?' she whispered.

'I'm not sure. I've never tried before.'

'Maybe that's the trouble. Talk to me, Justin, for both our sakes.'

'I don't know where to begin.'

'Start with your mother.'

'Which one?'

The answer startled her. She rose up on one elbow and looked down on him. After a moment he started to speak, hesitantly.

'For the first seven years of my life, I was like any other child. I had a home, two parents who loved me, or seemed to. Then the woman I thought of as my mother became pregnant.

'Almost overnight she lost interest in me. I found out why almost by chance. I overheard her talking to her sister, saying, 'It'll be wonderful to have a child of my own'. That was how I learned that she wasn't really my mother.'

'Dear God!' Evie said softly. 'Did you tell her what you'd heard?'

'No, I kept it to myself for months, pretending it wasn't true. But the pretence wore thin, especially when the baby was born, a boy.

'I was jealous. I started to have tantrums. So they called social services and said that I was "out of control" and I must go into care. After that I couldn't pretend any longer. I'd been adopted as second best, because they thought they couldn't have children. Now they didn't need me.'

She stared at him, too shocked to speak.

'I don't remember much about that day,' he said. 'I know I screamed at my parents not to send me away. I begged and pleaded but it was no use. They didn't want me.'

'Wait, stop,' she begged, covering her eyes as though, by this means, she could blot out the terrible story. 'I can't take this in. Surely they must have had some love for you?'

'You don't understand. I was a substitute. If they'd

never had one of their own I suppose they'd have made do with me, but now I was surplus to requirements. It took me years to see that, of course. All I knew at the time was that it was my own fault for being wicked.'

'How could anyone be so cruel as to put that burden on a child?' she burst out furiously. 'It's unspeakable. I suppose that's what *they* wanted to believe so that they didn't have to feel guilty about what they were really doing.'

'Yes, I worked that out in the end, too. But at the time I believed what I was told.'

'Where did they take you?'

'To what is laughingly known as a "home", which means an institution. At first I thought my mother would come and visit me. I used to stand at the window, watching the entrance. I *knew* she'd come. But weeks went by and there was no sign of them. Even then I didn't face it, not until one of the other boys jeered, "You're wasting yer time. Yer Mum dumped yer".

'Of course, then I knew, because in my heart I'd always known. The only way I could cope was to fight him. He was bigger than me, but I won because I hated him, not only because of what he'd said, but because his mother was taking him home the next day.

'The home wasn't a bad place. They meant well and they did their best. There was no affection because the staff turnover was so high, but I couldn't have dealt with that anyway. I'd learned enough not to want to get close to people, so I don't know what I'd have done if anyone had tried to get close to me. Something violent, probably.'

She shook her head in instinctive denial. At one time she might have mistaken him for a violent man, but now she sensed differently.

'I left when I was sixteen,' he resumed, 'and on the last day—'

He stopped, and a shudder went through him.

'What happened?' she asked softly.

He didn't answer at first. Then he said, 'Give me a minute.'

He rose and walked to the window. She stared at his broad back, wondering how she could ever have thought his size and strength alarming. All she could see now was that he was racked with misery. She went to stand beside him, turning him towards her, and had to fight back tears at what she saw.

He was actually shaking. Something was devastating him, and for a moment she thought he would be unable to speak of it.

At last he said, 'When I left they had to tell me the whole truth about myself. That was when I learned that my birth mother had given me away almost as soon as I was born.'

Evie stared at him, slowly shaking her head in speechless horror.

His laugh was harsh and bitter.

'You'll hardly believe this, but I was left on the orphanage doorstep like some Victorian foundling. If your mother does that, she can't be traced, you see. She's got rid of you completely.

'That was all they knew. I turned up one evening out of the blue. Apparently a doctor said I was about a week old. They did some research into the babies that had been born recently in that area, but none of them was me.'

'You mean your birth wasn't even registered?'

'Not by my mother. The orphanage registered me, of course.'

'It's awful,' she whispered. 'All this time, not knowing who you really are.'

'But I do know who I am,' he said with bitter irony. 'I'm the son two mothers didn't want. What could be clearer than that?'

'I used to wonder why you were so angry and suspicious all the time,' she said. 'Now I wonder how you've managed to keep your head together.'

'I'm not sure I have. For a long time I was crazy. I didn't behave well, either in the home or after I'd left it. I drank too much, brawled, got into trouble with the police, served some time in jail. That brought me back into contact with my adoptive parents.'

'They came to help you?' she asked, longing for some redeeming moment in this dreadful story.

'No, they sent a lawyer to say they'd get me a good defence on condition that I stopped using their name. They had an unusual name, Strassne, and since I still bore it people were beginning to associate this young low-life with them.'

'So that was when you became Justin Dane?' she asked. She would have liked to say something more violent, but was controlling herself with a huge effort.

'No, I became John Davis. My one-time "parents" insisted on doing it by deed poll, so that it was official and they'd never have to acknowledge me again. Then they paid for a very expensive defence, and John Davis was acquitted. They didn't even attend the trial.'

'So what happened to John Davis?'

'He didn't survive the day. I changed my name to Leo Holman. Not by deed poll. I just took off and gave my name as Leo wherever I went.'

'Don't you need some paperwork to get things like passports and bank accounts?'

'Yes, and if I'd needed those things it would have been a problem, but I wasn't living in a world of passports and bank accounts. I worked as a handyman, strictly for cash, got into trouble again, went inside—never long sentences, just a couple of months, but every time I came out I changed my name again. I lost track of how often. What did it matter to me? I no longer had a real identity, so it didn't matter how often I changed it.

'The last time I was in prison I met a man who put me straight. His name was Bill. He was a prison visitor, but he'd done time himself so he knew what he was talking about. He saw something in me that could be put back on track, and he set himself to do it.

'When I came out he was there waiting for me. He gave me a room in his own house, so that he could watch me like a hawk to see that I stayed on the straight and narrow. And he made me go to evening classes. I learned things and I found that I enjoyed having ambitions. Bit by bit I turned into a respectable citizen, the kind of man who needs paperwork.

'So I changed my name one last time. I was Andrew Lester at that time and I turned into Justin Dane. I did it officially, by deed poll, and I went to work in Bill's firm.'

'How did you choose the name?'

'Bill had a Great Dane I enjoyed fooling with. I forget where Justin came from. In the end he loaned me the money to start my own business. In three years I repaid him. In eight years I bought him out. Don't misunderstand that. He was delighted. I gave him a good price, enough to retire on. I wouldn't have done him down. I owed him, and I repaid him.

'After that I just made money. It was all I knew how to do. I didn't seem able to make relationships work.'

'What about your wife? You must have loved her?'

'I loved her a lot. I even told myself that she loved me, but we married because she was pregnant and I wanted a child badly. But it didn't work out. In the end she couldn't stand me. She said so. The only good thing to come out of it was Mark.

'I thought with him, at least, I could make a success, but I haven't. I don't know how. I'm driving him away as I seem to drive everyone away.'

'But what happened with your mothers—either of them—wasn't your fault,' she urged. 'It couldn't be.'

'Maybe not, but it started me on a track I don't know how to escape.' He gave a soft mirthless laugh. 'You'll hardly believe this, but when people tell me to get lost I feel almost relieved. At least it's familiar territory.'

He fell silent. Evie slipped her arms about him and leaned against his body as they stood there in the window. But she too said nothing, because in the face of such a terrible story there was nothing to say.

CHAPTER EIGHT

AFTER that they didn't speak of it again. He had said as much as he could bear to, and Evie's instincts told her to leave it. She must start getting to know this man again from the beginning.

Everything she had thought true about him was now reversed. Instead of the harsh bully, manipulating her for ulterior motives, there was a forlorn child desperately wondering what he'd done wrong to be so unloved. That child would remain a part of him all his life, making him so vulnerable to slights and rejections that he could only cope by being the first to attack.

She smiled to think how annoyed it would make him to be seen in this light. It was something she would have to keep to herself.

They didn't tell Mark why the atmosphere had suddenly become happier, and he never mentioned the nights he awoke to find Justin's bed empty, and went contentedly back to sleep. His air of strain fell away and he smiled more, but, like his father, he knew how to keep his own counsel.

One night, as they lay peacefully in bed, Justin said, 'So what was all that about Andrew?'

She gave a gasp of laughter.

'Don't remind me what a fool I was. I guess I wanted to believe I was in love with him, and the effort to convince myself was tying me in knots.'

'But why?'

'You once said that no man had ever offered me lifetime commitment—'

'I once said a lot of tomfool things. You shouldn't listen to me.'

'I try not to, but you're hard to shut out when you get going,' she said indignantly. 'And you really annoyed me that time, talking as though I'm some Victorian wallflower grasping at her last chance. I'd kick you if I had the energy.'

He grinned and kissed her. 'So what's the real story?'

'I've always been the one fleeing commitment. It sounded so boring. I love my life, the freedom, the variety—'

'The motorbike.'

'Yup. There was never a man who made me want to change it, but I thought, if I waited long enough, I'd meet one. And suddenly I was nearly thirty and Andrew was such a sweet guy that I—well—'

'You decided he'd "do".'

'You make it sound terrible, but yes, I suppose that's true. I was starting to feel lonely, so I decided on Andrew. But I was always forcing it, and of course he knew something was wrong.'

'When you'd stood him up often enough he got the message?' Justin said with the amiable derision of the conqueror for his defeated rival.

'Well, I'm glad he did, and found someone who suits him better.'

'You can't be sure he has.'

She gave a soft chuckle. 'Yes, I can. Anyone would suit him better than me, and that girl sounded as though he'd made her *very* happy.'

They lay in sleepy contentment for a while. She was wondering how to broach the subject on her mind. At last she murmured, 'Have you told Mark that you bought the cottage?'

'No. I wasn't sure what to say, when you were so mad at me.'

'Only because I misunderstood. I thought you were—never mind. I was wrong. I heard from the lawyer this morning. He's paid all Uncle Joe's debts and sent me a cheque for the balance.'

'So I suppose you're going to throw that back at me?' His tone was deceptively light, but now she could hear the dread beneath.

'Nope,' she said cheerfully, snuggling up to him. 'I'm going to put it in the bank and make whoopee!'

'I'm glad.'

'Seriously, I'll use it to do some repairs to the cottage—that is—if it's still mine.'

He'd seized her into his arms before she'd finished speaking, using his mouth to incite and tease her towards what they both now wanted. But through his desire she also sensed passionate relief that she had finally accepted his offering, taking the sting out of her earlier rejection.

It would be good to believe that the revelations had made everything right, or at least given her the key to helping him. With her he'd found a kind of happiness, but that alone could not slay the demons of dread and insecurity that were devouring him inside. The darkness was not so easily defeated.

He still flared up about small things. His temper always died quickly, and he would apologise in a way that revealed his fear that he'd drive her away. She forgave him readily, but she worried about him.

Even more troubling were the times that he controlled his inner turbulence and went away to suffer alone, returning with a bright smile and an air of strain.

Once, when Mark had gone to bed and a chilly spell had made them light the log fire and stretch out on the old sofa before it, she asked him, 'Justin, how long can you go on like this?'

He shrugged. At one time it would have seemed dismissive, but now she understood his confusion.

'As long as there is,' he said. 'What else can I do?'

'The first time I saw you I thought how angry you were. As I came to know you better I realised that you were angry all the time. No matter what happens it's always there below the surface, waiting for something to trigger it, never giving you any peace.'

'I'm sorry I lost it today—'

'That's all right. You said sorry at the time, and you bought Mark that computer game to make up for it.'

'Yes, and he put it on my computer and I couldn't get to it for hours,' he said with resignation. 'Be fair, I didn't lose my temper about that.'

'No, you showed the patience of a saint. You even let him teach you the game and beat you.'

He managed a faint grin. 'I didn't *let* him beat me. He beat me. And he enjoyed crowing at my expense. He's a great kid, Evie. I even think—'

'No,' she said urgently. 'You're not going to change the subject. It's you we're talking about. You're not happy—'

'Yes, I am,' he said, tightening his arms about her. 'A little more of Dr Evie's Magic Balm and I'll be sweetness and light all the time.'

'Not in a million years! Besides, I don't think I'd like you as sweetness and light. I wouldn't recognise you, for one thing.' He gave a muffled laugh against her hair. 'Besides, a magic balm only works on the outside. You need something to work on the inside.'

'Evie, I'm not ill.'

'You're being devoured alive, and that's a kind of sickness.'

'You do the psycho-babble very well,' he said lightly.

But she would not let him put her off. 'Stop that,' she said urgently. 'I know what you're trying to do.'

'You know everything, don't you?'

'I said stop it. You're trying to distract me because you don't want to confront it.'

'All right, I don't,' he growled. 'Why the hell should I want to?'

'Because you'll never resolve it otherwise.'

'What is there to resolve? It's the situation. It's my life. It can't *be* resolved.'

'Maybe it can.'

'Evie, listen. I know you mean well, but you have to play the hand you're dealt. You can play it well or badly, but you can't change the hand you start with.'

'But you can investigate it. And then, maybe, you'll discover you weren't dealt the hand you thought.'

'What do you mean by that?'

'I mean you should find out about your real mother, who she was, and why she couldn't keep you.'

He stared at her. 'Are you crazy?'

'No, but you might be if you try to carry this burden any longer. I think you're already starting to break under it.'

It was a risky thing to say. She waited. He gave her a black look, but he didn't deny it.

'Haven't you ever tried to find her?'

'Why would I want to find her?' he growled. 'So that I can say, "Hey, why did you toss me out with the junk? C'mon tell me, and that'll make it all right"?'

'But there might be things she could tell you that

would make you understand her better. Perhaps she had no choice. She was probably a young unmarried mother and it was very much harder for them in those days. At least try. It might make more difference than you think.'

'How could it? She gave me up. There's no way past that.'

'There is if she didn't *want* to give you up. She might have been pressured beyond endurance.'

'I'd like to see anyone try to pressure me to give up my son.'

'Don't be ridiculous!' she blazed. 'That is absolutely the stupidest thing I have ever heard anyone say. We're talking about a vulnerable girl. You're a grown man at the height of his powers. Nobody can bully you.'

'You're not doing badly.'

'I'm not bullying you, I'm just pointing out facts.'

'Right now I'm not sure there's a difference,' he said, eyeing her cautiously.

'Just because you can stand up to people it doesn't mean everyone else can. Honestly, Justin, that remark was plain idiotic.'

'All right,' he said harshly. 'I admit it. I was trying to get you off the subject. Do you think I want to let strangers poke and pry into my private life? Can you imagine how hard it was even to tell you? Suppose she wasn't a vulnerable girl. Suppose she was someone who just didn't want to bother.'

'All right, it's possible, but then I don't think she'd have given her baby away in secret. She'd simply have called social services. But neither of us really knows. That's why it's vital to find out.'

'You're forgetting that she never registered my birth. In a sense I never existed. All those agencies for reuniting people with their mothers can't help a man whose mother's name isn't on his birth certificate.'

'That's going to make it more difficult,' she conceded. 'But not impossible. I've got a friend that I'd like to give this to. He's a private detective, and he's brilliant.'

He was silent, racked by doubt. Evie could almost feel the violence of his feelings tearing him in opposite directions.

'I can see to everything,' she urged. 'You give me all the details and I'll talk to him. You won't even have to meet him if you don't want to.'

'All right,' he said softly. 'If I can leave everything in your hands, I'll do it.'

She held him close, praying that she'd done the right thing for him. If it turned out badly, she might have made his troubles a thousand times worse. But she knew that he couldn't go much longer.

It was time to leave the cottage and return to London. Evie took a last look around, thinking of how she'd arrived here meaning to pack up and say goodbye. And now there were to be no sad goodbyes. At least, not to the cottage. What the road ahead held for her and Justin she could not tell.

So that they could travel together he arranged for a driver to collect her van. As they drove home he said, 'It'll be very late when we reach London. Why don't you stay with us tonight, or maybe a few days?'

And she said that would be lovely, almost as though they hadn't planned it between them earlier. Mark grinned. He was a child who saw and understood a lot more than he was told.

Justin left for New York a couple of days later. Before going he showed Evie his office and all the files that concerned his birth. They were pitifully few, but they were a start.

When Justin had gone she contacted David Hallam, the private investigator who was a good friend.

'You're not giving me much,' he complained when he saw the material. 'Never mind. It'll be a challenge.'

On the night before Justin was due home David called her and said, 'You've really stirred things up.'

'You don't mean you've found something?'

He told her what he'd discovered, and she could barely contain her excitement. But she must be patient. She and Mark went to meet Justin at the airport, and she held back, letting the moment belong to father and son. Her time would come.

It came later that night when they were finally alone.

'I don't know how much it amounts to,' she said, 'but David has someone he wants you to meet.'

He tensed. 'Not—?'

'No, not her. A man. His name is Primo Rinucci, and his English stepmother had a son who was taken away from her at birth. For years he's been trying to find him for her. He's had feelers out with dozens of organisations and detective agencies, asking them to tell him if anyone with the right details contacted them. There's a chance that you're the man he's seeking.'

He turned pale. 'Dear God!'

'Justin, just think. If this works out, it means that *she's* been looking for *you*.'

'Don't!' he said in a harsh whisper. 'Don't encourage me to hope. *Evie!*'

'Yes, darling. Yes, *yes!*'

This might be the answer that would make him complete at last, and if they did not pursue it the doubt would torment them both. But she knew also that Justin was standing on a dangerous edge, and disappointed hope could destroy him. If that happened she would blame herself for ever.

'What else do you know about this man?' he asked.

'He comes from Naples and he's flying over here to meet you. I've provisionally set it up for the day after tomorrow.'

'I've got a meeting—'

'Change it.'

'Where do we go?'

'You want me to come with you?'

'I can't do it without you. Sometimes I don't think I can do anything without you. It's as though you're what links me to life. If that link were broken I'd just—' he fought for the words '—sink into a black hole and never come out again.'

It dawned on her that he was making what, in any other man, she would have called a declaration of love. But this man did nothing like the others.

He saw the understanding in her face and spoke in self-mockery.

'I'm making a pig's ear of it, aren't I?'

'Not really,' she said, smiling. 'I'm getting the message.'

'I'm glad, because there are some things—I can't do the "three little words" stuff.' He sounded desperate.

He might never say that he loved her, she realised. But her life had been full of men who could do the 'three little words stuff' easily, and she had wanted none of them. What she wanted was this clumsy bear of a man with his tortured, painfully expressed need.

'Do you remember the evening we collected Mark from the cemetery and you came home for supper?' he asked. 'The dogs were there, and their carry-on made you laugh.'

'Yes, I remember.'

'I'd never heard anyone laugh like that—such a sound—rich and warm—as though you'd found the secret of life. It seemed to—I had to follow—' he grimaced '—whether you wanted me or not.'

'A takeover bid,' she said, smiling fondly.

'Are you making fun of me?' He said it, not aggressively, but almost meekly, like someone who was trying to learn.

'Maybe just a bit,' she said, touching his face.

'You're being unfair. I do know that women are different from stocks and shares—'

'If only you could work out exactly how,' she teased.

He weaved his fingers through hers, drawing her hand to his lips, then resting it against his cheek.

'Laugh at me if you like,' he said, 'as long as you don't leave me.'

The meeting was set up in neutral territory. David hired a room in a London hotel and the four of them met for lunch, Evie carrying the file with all the paperwork.

Primo Rinucci turned out to be a tall man with slightly shaggy mid-brown hair, in his early thirties. Despite his name he spoke perfect English, with no trace of an accent.

Evie was prepared for anything, but in fact the truth was clear almost at once. When Primo first set eyes on Justin a stillness came over him and he drew a long breath. After that she knew.

She couldn't tell whether Justin had seen and understood. His manner was stiff and awkward and he scowled more than he smiled. David, with blessed tact, departed almost as soon as the introductions were made.

'Give me a call later,' he whispered to Evie.

When he'd gone the two men regarded each other warily.

'You are wondering what I can have to do with you,' Primo said. 'Let me tell you a little about myself. I was born in England and lived here for the first few years of my life. My father's name was Jack Cayman. He was English. My mother was Italian, and her maiden name was Rinucci.

'She died while I was a baby and my father married again, a young English girl called Hope Martin. She was a wonderful person, more a mother to me than a stepmother. Sadly, the marriage didn't last. When they divorced, my father insisted that I remain with him. Later he died. I went to Italy to live with my mother's parents, and took their name.

'But then Hope, my stepmother, learned where I was and came to see me. My family welcomed her, and my Uncle Toni fell in love with her. I was very happy when they married, especially as I was able to live with them. I felt I had regained my mother.

'It was years later, when I had grown up, that I learned that she'd had a child before her marriage to my father. She was only fifteen and her parents wanted her to give up her baby for adoption. They were furious when she refused.

'In the event she never even saw her child. They told her it had been born dead, which was a lie. It was a home birth and the midwife was her aunt. She took the boy away to another town, many miles away. Hope knew nothing about it.'

Justin said nothing, only stared hard at Primo. It was Evie who exclaimed in horror at what she'd just heard.

'Yes, it was wicked,' Primo said, looking at her warmly. 'Hope grieved for her "dead" child, but she grieved a thousand times more to think that he was alive and living apart from her, perhaps thinking she had abandoned him.'

Justin gave a small, convulsive jerk, but he didn't speak.

'How did she find out?' Evie asked.

'The aunt died. At the end she sent for Hope and tried to tell her what had happened, but she was too near the end to make much sense. Hope understood that her child had lived, had been stolen, and nothing else. She didn't even have the name of the town, because the aunt had gone to a place where she wasn't known. Apart from that, all she had was the date of his birth. This.'

He pushed a scrap of paper across the table. The date written on it was exactly two weeks before the date on Justin's official birth certificate.

'I began looking for him fifteen years ago,' Primo resumed. 'It took years to find the place where a baby boy had been abandoned soon after this date. At last my investigators narrowed it down to one possibility. Then I thought the search was over because this boy had been adopted by a couple called Strassne.'

There was silence in the room for a moment. Justin did not speak, but his grip on Evie's hand became painful.

'For several years he lived with them as Peter Strassne,' Primo said. 'But he assumed a new identity twenty years ago, and that was when the trail went cold. The deed poll said that Peter Strassne had become Frank Davis, but nobody ever heard of Frank Davis after that.'

Because he'd changed his name again, Evie thought sadly. *And then again and again. And every time the trail grew a little colder. By the time he became Justin Dane there was nothing left to link him with his earlier identities.*

'Once he'd seemingly vanished into thin air,' Primo resumed, 'my only hope was if he too was searching, and I might pick up his search. That is why I am here. I think I already know the answer, but will you tell me if your name was ever Peter Strassne?'

Slowly Justin nodded his head. Then he pushed the file of papers across the table. Primo examined it briefly, and nodded.

'I am satisfied,' he said.

'As easy as that?' Justin asked hoarsely. 'What can a few papers prove?'

'I told you I already knew the answer. I knew as soon as I saw you. Your resemblance to your mother is remarkable. There are tests that can establish your blood tie once and for all, but there is no doubt in my mind that you are Hope Rinucci's firstborn son.'

CHAPTER NINE

THE London to Naples flight left early, so the three of them spent the previous night in the airport hotel.

'Uncle Toni knows why I'm here,' Primo said as they sat over dinner the night before. 'But I didn't say anything to Mamma before I left, for fear of raising her hopes. But now I've called him and told him everything, and he's going to prepare her gently. She's dreamed of this for so long that the reality is going to come as a shock to her.'

'Will the whole family be there?' Evie wanted to know.

'Everyone, but for a while the others will stay out of sight.' He addressed Justin. 'The two of you will need to have your first meeting in private. Then we'll all gather.'

'Hope really has five other sons?' Evie asked.

'That's right, although not all of us were born to her. She and my father adopted Luke. Then there's Francesco. She fell in love with his father, Franco, while still married to Jack Cayman, which is really why my father divorced her. Carlo and Ruggiero are her sons by Toni.' He gave Justin an encouraging smile. 'So you have five brothers, one way or another.'

He didn't seem to notice that Justin's smile was faint and he'd spoken very little. He went on, 'Then Mamma will want to meet your son, Mark, her grandson. She'll be disappointed that he's not with you, but you were probably wise to leave him behind this time.'

'I'd like to get things sorted out first,' Justin said quietly.

'Of course. Signorina—' He turned to Evie and said in Italian, 'I'm delighted that you speak my language.'

'Only Italian,' she said in the same language. 'Not Neapolitan, except for a few words. But I want to learn more of your dialect.'

'I shall delight in teaching you.' He saw Justin frowning and said quickly in English, 'Forgive me. I'm being rude in using a language that you don't understand, but it's such a pleasure to discover a lady who speaks Italian so well. She will be a great help to you.'

He drained his glass.

'I think I'll have an early night.' Rising, he kissed Evie's hand, saying in Italian, *'Buona notte, moglie del mio fratello.'*

He departed.

Justin regarded her. After a moment he said edgily, 'Aren't you going to tell me what he said?'

'He just wished me goodnight,' she said hastily.

'No, he said more than that. Why should you conceal it?'

'Because it's a bit embarrassing. He called me his sister-in-law—wife of my brother. Forget it. I'm going to bed.'

He went up with her and they said goodnight at her door. But his knock came soon after.

'Are you all right?' she asked, letting him in. 'You've been very quiet all evening.'

He didn't reply at first, but walked about the room before saying abruptly, 'Evie, let's forget all this and go home.'

'You can't mean that, not after we've come this far.

You couldn't go away now, just when you're on the verge of discovering everything.'

'Am I? What is "everything"? Can you tell me that? At one time I might have agreed with you, but now I've met you I have another "everything". What connection can there be between her and me after all these years?'

'But you can't do that to her. She's expecting you now; it'll break her heart if you don't arrive. And in the years to come you'll regret not meeting her and finding out what you need to know. Justin, you're just making excuses—finding reasons. Why?'

He gave her a faint smile.

'You always see through me. Of course I'm making excuses. Because I'm afraid. I always thought of myself as strong. You have to make people see you like that because if they sense weakness they go in for the kill. But the truth is that I'm a coward and I've only just discovered it.'

'Don't be so hard on yourself. You're not a coward.'

'You know my weaknesses better than anyone, and you're the only person I could say that to, the only person I could trust that much. You're all I need. I want to spend my life with you. Nothing else matters.'

She smiled and touched his face tenderly.

'Darling, I love you, and it's wonderful that you say that, but—don't you see, we can't think about it now? What's going to happen tomorrow is so overwhelming that it's going to blot out everything else for a while. I'm here if you want me, but we can only go forward, not back.'

He nodded. 'Nothing could blot you out. I'll go forward if I have your hand in mine. Help me, Evie. With you I think I can manage anything. Without you—' His face clouded.

'But you don't have to be without me,' she said, taking him into her arms.

They made love tenderly, with her taking the initiative. She had never felt so strongly protective of him as at this moment.

Yet she could not ignore a small shadow at the back of her mind. He'd said he wanted to spend the rest of his life with her. It wasn't exactly a proposal, but she knew she could have turned it into one, had she wished.

Why hadn't she done so? Was it the old caution, that had held her back from marriage so often before? Or was it something more, something dangerous about this man, that warned her to beware, even while she felt the bands that linked her to him tighten around her heart?

The flight to Naples next morning went smoothly, and by early afternoon they were in the car sent to convey them to the Villa Rinucci.

Evie was so entranced to be back in Italy, and in a region that she'd always longed to explore, that she almost forgot everything else. It was the height of summer and the sun poured down over them as they took the coast road, then climbed up to the villa, with the Bay of Naples falling away below them.

Her first sight of the Villa Rinucci was pure magic. Seen from below, it was like a mini-palace made of honey-coloured stone. There were several wings and around the whole building was a covered terrace, the roof supported by high arches.

Looking out of the window, Evie thought she saw the figure of a tall, slender woman standing on the terrace, looking down at the car climbing the road. But the dazzling sun made her blink, and when she looked again the terrace was empty.

At last the car came to a halt in the courtyard on the other side of the house. A man was standing there.

'That is my Uncle Toni, and Mamma's husband,' Primo explained.

He was out of the car first, going forward to take his uncle's hand, then looking back to where Justin was getting out of the car, indicating him.

And there it was again, the slight start of astonishment as Toni Rinucci saw his wife's features in her son.

Primo introduced them quietly to each other, the men murmured something and Toni ushered them all towards the villa. As they approached, Evie could see faces at the windows and guessed these were some of the other sons, hovering nearby, but keeping a discreet distance.

When they were inside the villa, Toni Rinucci studied Justin more closely for a moment.

'Yes,' he said at last. 'Primo has assured us that you are the one, and now I see that he is right. If I did not believe that I would not let you near my wife. Since I told her she has been much disturbed, but she longs to see you. She is waiting for you in that room.'

Justin glanced at Evie, but she stepped back.

'This is just you and her,' she said. And he nodded.

Toni opened a door. Inside, a woman was sitting by a large window. The light was behind her, making her a silhouette. She rose as Justin entered, and Evie had a glimpse of the two of them moving slowly towards each other. A pause. Then Hope Rinucci's hands flew to her mouth in a gesture of joyful astonishment. And then they were in each other's arms.

Gently Toni closed the door.

'Signorina Evie,' he said, smiling, 'forgive me for not welcoming you properly before. Please believe that you are welcome in our home.'

He opened his arms in a huge Italian hug and she felt herself engulfed.

'My wife's maid will show you to your room,' he said when she finally came up, gasping for air. 'When you are ready, you will come down and meet some of the louts who hang around this house.'

There was muffled laughter from the gaggle of young men who had come downstairs but were still keeping a respectful distance, doubtless obeying orders.

Maria, the maid, showed her upstairs. Evie had an impression of a spacious building with warm red and brown flagstones, furnished in traditional style, with a great deal of polished wood. The effect was rustic, she noted, but the kind of elegant rustic that would take a great deal of money.

When she had freshened up Primo came to escort her downstairs, where Toni hugged her again.

'Primo has told us everything,' he said. 'How you helped and encouraged Justin in the search. My wife shall know of it. For now, you must have food and wine, and soon you will meet her.'

He led her out on to the terrace overlooking the bay and she stood gazing in wonder at the beauty until Toni offered her a glass of *prosecco*, the lightest possible sparkling white wine.

Now the other sons came forward to be introduced—Luke, the adopted one; Francesco, the love child; Carlo and Ruggiero, the twins, in their late twenties, full of zest and young, masculine attraction. Although not identical, they were sufficiently alike to show that they were brothers.

They plied her with questions about Justin, while contriving to make it clear that they admired her for their own sake. Ruggiero winked and gave her a soft wolf whistle, which prompted Carlo to say sharply, 'Mind your manners.'

He spoke in Italian and Evie immediately said in the same language, 'It's all right.'

That delighted them, and after that everyone spoke Italian. They were impressed by her and said so openly. Now the questions were about her, although only Ruggiero had the effrontery to look at her left hand and say, 'Then you aren't married to Justin? There's hope for the rest of us?'

'Behave yourself!' his father growled.

Ruggiero fell silent, but there was nothing meek in his demeanour and he gave Evie a conspiratorial wink.

A charmer and a ladies' man, she thought. He'll flirt with every girl in sight and it'll mean nothing. But he's harmless and likeable.

'Primo spoke as though you were already our sister-in-law,' Francesco explained.

'I've only known Justin a few weeks,' Evie said.

'But it was you who helped to set his feet on the road that led here,' Toni said. 'And it is you he chose to bring here with him. That means that in his heart you are his wife.' He raised his voice to add, 'And you will be treated as such by every man here.'

There were murmurs of, '*Si, Pappa.*' Toni turned back to her.

'If any of my sons offends you, please inform me at once, Signorina, and I will personally beat him black and blue.'

'I'm sure that won't be necessary,' she assured him, chuckling.

An hour passed, during which Evie made friends with them all. She was at ease and comfortable among these people. If only Justin could feel the same.

She thought of him, with Hope, the mother who had influenced his whole life by not being part of it. How was he coping?

At last there was a noise from outside. Someone hissed, 'They're coming,' and the next moment Hope Rinucci appeared, her hand tucked in Justin's arm. Together they came out on to the terrace.

Hope reached out to her husband, smiling through tears.

'He came back to me, Toni,' she said. 'He came back, as I always knew he would.'

'Of course he did, *carissima*,' he soothed her.

Justin kept his eyes fixed on his mother, as though what was happening had left him dazed. Evie tried to imagine what this moment meant to him, but it was beyond imagining.

She studied his face, seeking some sign of emotion, but she saw nothing. His expression was set and slightly fierce, much as it had been when he'd first told her his story.

She'd been partly expecting this. Justin would die before letting the world know how he felt. Even with her he found it hard. But surely she knew him well enough to read the signs?

Then, with a start of dismay, she realised that there were no signs. His face was the blank of a man who didn't even know what his feelings were.

At last he met her eyes and she saw his confusion. Years of dreading rejection had left him unable to react. She smiled back, trying to reassure him that it would happen later, when he wasn't under a spotlight.

But at this supreme moment, when there should be

joy and triumph, he was once more shut out and her heart ached for him.

Now that she saw Hope more clearly Evie understood why Justin had found instant acceptance. As Primo had said, the family resemblance was remarkable.

Carlo and Ruggiero studied their new brother with interest before shaking his hand. Then the others all offered their hands, signifying acceptance.

'Now,' Hope said, looking around at them, 'now I have all my sons beside me.'

Toni drew Evie forward to be introduced. Hope received her charmingly, but Evie didn't miss the shrewdness in the clear blue eyes, and knew she was being carefully inspected. She wondered what Justin had told his mother about her, and longed for a moment to talk to him.

It was a long time before such a moment came. Hope herself showed him to his room, clinging to his arm in a manner that Evie was glad to see. Nothing would do Justin more good than to have his mother claim him possessively like this. She dared to hope that soon his demons might be stilled.

She spent the rest of the afternoon with the twins, learning Neapolitan words. Then Toni showed her his library and she delighted him by studying his antique Italian books with real interest, and being able to translate them.

'You are an expert in my language,' he said, beaming.

'I hope so. It's how I earn my living, plus French, of course.'

'Pooh! French!' he said, dismissing a thousand years of French culture with a wave of an Italian hand. 'But

Italian—ah, wait until you see the people I can take you to meet. How I look forward to you being part of this family.'

'Please—' she said hastily.

'Of course,' he said, throwing up a hand. 'I understand that it's a delicate matter. I will say no more.'

The whole family joined up again for dinner that night. Justin sat beside Hope, who engaged him deep in conversation. Evie was glad to see that there was now less constraint in his manner. He could smile at his mother and speak naturally to her.

'When will I meet your son?' Hope asked him. 'My first grandchild. Indeed my only grandchild until another of my sons does his duty, which, I have to say, shows no sign of happening.'

There were grins and disclaimers around the table. Evidently this was an old bone of contention.

'Send for him,' Hope said. 'Bring him here tomorrow.'

It was charmingly said, with a radiant smile at Justin, but Evie noticed the hint of command. This was a woman used to announcing what she wanted and having her wishes fulfilled.

'Tomorrow's a little soon,' Justin said. 'I shall have to go and fetch him—'

'No, no, you were telling me about your housekeeper—Lily—she can bring him.'

'No, she's scared of flying,' Evie said. 'She told me so once. And Mark mustn't come alone. I'll go and collect him. I'll leave tomorrow and we'll be back the day after.'

The young men exclaimed over the idea of losing her,

but Hope thanked her in a way that allowed no further discussion. Justin threw her a look of gratitude.

When the meal was over Evie announced that she would retire at once, to make an early departure next morning. She would have liked to talk privately to Justin, but that could wait. This time belonged to Hope.

But later that night she had a surprise. As she was about to put out her light there came a knock on her door. It was Hope.

'I hope I don't come too late, but I had to have a brief word with you,' she said. 'We've had no chance to get to know each other, but I believe that nobody knows my son—' she lingered over the two words '—better than you.'

'I don't think that's really true,' Evie said hesitantly. 'I've known him only a few weeks.'

Hope gave an expressive shrug.

'Is time what really matters? Something tells me you know him better after a month than anyone else in a lifetime.'

'I don't believe he's let himself get close to anyone,' Evie agreed, 'except Mark.'

'Ah, yes, Mark. How I long to meet him. How generous of you to make it possible. I'll leave you now to get your sleep, and wish you a safe journey.'

She enfolded Evie in a scented embrace and departed imperiously.

Mark was waiting for her, eager to hear everything that had happened. Justin had given him part of the story and now Evie filled in with the rest.

On the flight back to Naples he kept looking at his watch.

'Counting the minutes?' she teased.

He nodded. 'Thirty minutes until we land, and thirty to get through Customs.'

'And then you'll meet your new family.'

'And you'll be there too? I mean, you're part of the family now, aren't you?'

'Well, not really.'

'But you and Dad—you know.'

'I'm not sure I do.'

'You *know*! He always used to cheer up when you wore your bikini.'

There it was again, the assumption that she and Justin were together for good. She tested the idea, wanting to know if the old alarm at commitment would start up. Instead she felt as if a smile was growing deep inside her.

As she'd expected, Justin and Hope were waiting at the airport. Hope kept her eyes on the boy as he neared her and Justin said, 'Mark, this is your grandmother.'

Mark and Evie had been practising this moment all the way on the plane and now he was ready. Gravely he offered his hand, saying, *'Buon giorno, signora.'*

Hope gave a cry of delight and was about to embrace him when she caught his eye, remembered how boys felt about being cuddled in public, and shook his hand instead, a piece of tact that won her Mark's goodwill.

While they sized each other up Justin drew Evie close, laying his cheek briefly against hers.

'Hope has been in agonies waiting for your return,' he said, adding softly, 'and so have I.'

In the car going home they were alert for Mark's needs, ready to smooth his path with this new and strange relative. But it was unnecessary. Hope and Mark were instantly on each other's wavelength and in a few minutes he was calling her Nonna, the Italian word for Grandma.

After that it was like a replay of their own arrival a few days earlier. Toni and the sons were there at the villa, this time offering a boisterous greeting that Mark seemed to enjoy. Evie could see that he was going to fit into the family even more easily than Justin.

Justin escorted her upstairs to her room and closed the door firmly behind them before taking her into his arms.

'I've missed you,' he murmured between kisses. 'Where have you been all this time?'

'All this time?' she teased him happily. 'One day?'

'You know I need you.'

'Don't tell me you've been thinking of me with all your new family to get used to. How are you getting on with your mother?'

'Well enough.'

'Well enough? Is that all you can say?'

'For the moment, yes. It's all a bit much—it'll hit me later, I dare say.'

'Yes, I suppose it's a lot to take in.'

'I know Hope is my mother. You've only got to look at us to see it. And yet—there's a part of me that doesn't believe it. I keep expecting to wake up and find that it was a dream.'

'But you won't,' she said tenderly. 'It's real. She's truly your mother, and the best part of all is that she didn't give you away. You weren't rejected. You were loved from the first moment. And you still are. That's what's so wonderful about it, that her love has been like an arc, stretching over the years from that moment to this, linking them.'

'Yes, of course,' he said. 'You put things so well. It takes me a little longer.'

'That doesn't matter. Things are coming together in their own good time. That's what counts. It's going to be all right, my darling. Everything's going to be all right.'

Later she was to wonder how she could have been so blind and stupid as not to see the pit opening at their feet. He had seen it but, in his inarticulate way, hadn't known how to tell her until it was too late.

CHAPTER TEN

THE Villa Rinucci was in turmoil. For days everything was dedicated to the great party at which Hope would introduce her new son to her friends. It would be organised along the same lines as her birthday festivities, but grander still. The whole world must know that she rejoiced in her son.

While she buried herself in menus and wine lists the two families worked at getting better acquainted. Justin spent time with Toni and Primo. His relationship with Primo was slightly edgy, but he worked hard at being cordial, conscious of what he owed him. They were both businessmen, and Primo had business interests in England, and on that level they could meet.

Francesco and Luke had left the villa to attend to their work, promising to return for the party. The twins still had a bedroom each at the villa, although both had apartments in Naples where, according to their mother, they 'got up to no good' and very much enjoyed doing so.

But for the moment their apartments were left empty as they devoted themselves to entertaining Evie and Mark. Mark gravitated instinctively to the boyish Carlo, adopting him as a favourite uncle. This was no surprise, according to his caustic twin, since Carlo had been blessed with the mind of a child.

Carlo responded in kind, and the cheerful insults flew back and forth, sometimes in English, in honour of the guests, but becoming more Italian as the atmosphere grew livelier. Mark, Evie was amused to notice, was making eager notes, desperate not to lose a single rude word, while she leaned close to Justin and translated for him.

The merry battle continued for most of the evening, engulfing the entire family, until Hope called them to order through her laughter. Mark went to bed blissfully happy and spent the next day practising Neapolitan insults until Carlo frantically covered his mouth, muttering, 'I'll tell you what that means when you're older.'

'Much older,' said Evie, who was also learning fast.

Her own preference was for Ruggiero, a dark horse. He was a quiet, thoughtful young man, with a kind of subdued fierceness about him that sometimes reminded her of Justin. But the great love of his life was his motorbike and, after the first startled recognition, he and Evie greeted each other as kindred spirits.

One day they vanished for several hours so that he could demonstrate his bike. There was a brief tense moment just before they departed, when Ruggiero explained formally to Justin that he was taking Evie away for the afternoon, 'with your consent.'

'Oi!' Evie said. 'With his consent or without it. I don't need his permission. Come on.'

She gave Justin's cheek a quick kiss and hurried out, eager to try the new toy.

They were out much longer than she'd intended, finally driving up the road to the villa, exhilarated and on the best of terms, to find the whole family watching their approach from the terrace.

'You're late for supper,' Carlo yelled down. 'We've eaten it all.'

'It was delicious,' Mark cried. 'The best ever.'

'But of course we saved you some,' Hope said, smiling. 'It will be ready when you've freshened up. There is no hurry.'

The meal was, as Mark had promised, delicious. She and Ruggiero dined together while Mark helped to serve them, chattering all the time. There was no sign of Justin.

She sought him out later.

'Aren't you going to tell me about your day?' she asked.

'I think I may be able to do some business with Primo. There's a lot to discuss, but I see it happening.'

'And you'll make a pot of money?'

'Hopefully.'

'Fine. Then you've had a good day.'

'I hope you enjoyed yours.'

'It was wonderful,' she said blissfully. 'As soon as we get back to England I'm going to sell my machine and buy one like his. The speed! I've never known anything like it.'

'I was worried about you,' Justin said quietly, with the smallest vibration of anger in his voice.

'There was no need. You knew I was with Ruggiero.'

'Driving on a strange bike over strange roads. And I don't even like to think what speed you were doing.'

'Then don't,' she said briskly. That 'with your consent' still rankled. 'I can control a bike at speed.'

'Control? You mean he let you ride that thing in front?'

'In the end, yes. No way was I going to be content riding pillion.'

'You're mad.'

'You've always known that. What's so different now?'

'I was worried,' he shouted. 'Can't you understand that?'

Instantly she was contrite. She had forgotten how he took things to heart.

'Yes, I can understand,' she said gently. 'Don't worry about me. I needed that ride, but I've got the madness out of my system, at least for a while.'

'Yes, promise me that you won't do it again.'

'I will not. I'll want another ride before I leave here.'

'But not in the front. Pillion is OK, but—'

'Justin, stop there. I decide what's OK for me, not you. Now let's leave this.'

His eyes were dark and angry.

'I'm not ready to leave it. I don't like you risking your life, and I don't like you gadding off for hours with another man—'

'Another man? You mean that boy who's two years younger than I am? Nonsense. I'm like an older sister to him.'

'Did he treat you like an older sister?'

'Of course he did,' she said, trying to banish the memory of Ruggiero's arms about her body when he had been riding pillion, and the gleam of admiration in his eyes that had had nothing to do with motorbikes.

He had flirted with her in a way that had danced to the edge of acceptability, and had then danced nimbly away again when she had fended him off with laughter. It hadn't troubled her. Flirting was one of the great pleasures of her life, but she always knew when to stop.

But Justin would never be able to believe that, she realised. Perhaps it was time to give up flirtations.

'He treated me like a fellow motorbike nutter. It's a club. We're all crazy about the same thing. Plus he was entertaining me to leave you free for your mother.'

'Hope has plenty to see to. You and I could have spent the afternoon together.'

'And miss doing business with Primo? Look, I'm sorry. Let's forget about it.'

'As long as you promise not to do it again.'

Part of her wanted to agree to whatever pleased him, but another part of her simply couldn't yield to possessiveness, even his.

'I said leave it,' she said quietly.

'I suppose that's my answer.'

'No, the answer is—stop trying to give me orders. Stop trying to control me.'

He took a sharp intake of breath and she looked up to find something in his eyes that might have been fear. They stared at each other, both equally shocked by the silly quarrel that had come out of nowhere and taken them both by surprise.

Then he pulled back quickly. 'Sorry,' he said. 'I'm sorry. I don't know what came over me.'

Softened, she reached out. 'Darling—'

'Just forget it, will you?' he said hastily. Then he turned and walked away from her without a backward glance.

Evie was left feeling saddened and angry with herself that she hadn't handled it better. A noise from above made her look up to see Hope at the top of the stairs. She wasn't looking at Evie and after a moment she walked away. It was impossible to tell how much she had heard.

Then Evie forgot everything in the rush of last-minute preparations. She spent a wonderful day among the fashion shops of Naples, returning with a black silk clinging creation that gave her a dazzling new persona, quite different from the boyish biker.

In this gown she was elegant and sophisticated. She would do Justin credit.

He knocked at her door just as she was trying to decide what jewellery to wear. She owned very little as most of her money went on the bike.

But Justin had the solution, holding up a diamond pendant and diamond earrings that were perfect with the dress.

'You bought these for me?' she asked in delight.

'No, they're from Hope. She asked me to give them to you.'

It passed across her mind briefly that he always referred to his mother as Hope, but then she was distracted by the beauty of the diamonds as she fixed the earrings into place.

'She bought these for me?' she asked in wonder.

'No, I think she already had them.'

'Put the pendant on for me,' she begged, turning her back.

He fastened the clasp, then let his hands rest on her bare shoulders. They were warm and strong, giving her a good feeling.

'I'm sorry,' he said. 'I shouldn't have got mad at you for going out the other day. I know you're not quite sane where motorbikes are concerned.'

'I'll let that insult pass,' she told him, smiling. 'Anyway, it was my fault too. I was cross with Ruggiero for asking your permission to take me out, and you got the backlash. I should have remembered that he's Italian and they have more formal ideas about families.'

He dropped a kiss on the nape of her neck and she shivered with pleasure.

'I don't think you should do that when we're going

to the party in a few minutes,' she said in a shaking voice.

'No.' He sighed. 'Perhaps it's not very wise. I just wanted you to know—well, anyway. Shall we go downstairs?'

'While we still can?'

'Yes,' he growled.

From the moment they appeared Evie knew that the evening was going to be a triumphant success. The food was laid out on long, groaning tables—Neapolitan grain pie, sautéed artichokes with baby potatoes, fruits, creams, the best wines served in fine crystal.

Hope had left nothing to chance, something which, Evie was beginning to feel, was typical of her. The young girl whose baby had been brutally stolen had grown into a woman of authority, armoured, imposing her will on life.

Times had changed. The child who once had to be hidden could now be announced to the world, and she was going to glory in it.

Justin and Mark stood by her side as a hundred guests arrived, and within an hour everyone in the room knew who he was. This might be Hope's night, but it was also his.

When everyone had something to eat and drink Evie looked for Hope.

'Thank you,' she said, touching the diamonds. 'They're beautiful. Justin said that they were your own.'

'Yes. They were given to me years ago by my husband. Toni knows I have given them to you, and he agrees. We hope that soon you will be one of us.'

She floated away without giving Evie a chance to confirm or deny it. That was her way. Hope Rinucci had made her wishes known. With amusement, Evie realised that she had been not so much welcomed into the family as ordered into it.

'You look lonely,' said a voice beside her in Italian. It was Primo.

'No, I'm not lonely. I've just been talking to Hope.'

'Has my mother told you what she's planned for you?' Primo asked with a grin.

'Something like that.'

'Don't be annoyed with her, Evie. She has a kind heart and she wants everyone to be as happy as she is.'

'I know that. I'm not annoyed.'

He held out his arms. 'The music's starting. Dance with me.'

As they waltzed he said, 'You're causing a sensation tonight. No man can take his eyes off you, and they all envy Justin.'

'Stop talking nonsense,' she told him demurely.

He laughed and they danced contentedly for a while. It was true, what he had said. All eyes were on her. Men clamoured for her hand, but she sat out the next dance, talking to Primo.

Then she saw Justin coming towards them and wondered if he would ask her to dance. But something stopped him when he was near, and he turned aside to sweep a beauty into his arms.

'Primo, you must stop doing that,' Evie said.

'What am I doing?' he asked innocently.

'Talking to me in Italian. That's what puts Justin off. It excludes him, you know that.'

His shrug was expressive. 'Excludes? Do you think he feels excluded now that he has been included in so much that he never had before? He's the hero of the hour.'

She stared. 'You dislike him, don't you?'

'Why are you surprised? He's not a man who's easy to like.'

'I suppose it's—all this talk about brothers.'

'But we're not brothers. There's no blood tie between us at all. He is my mother's son—and I am not.'

The touch of bitterness in his voice was like a blindfold being torn from her eyes.

'You're jealous,' she said incredulously.

'Of course I am. Why not? Because I'm a grown man and you think such feelings are only for children?'

'I suppose I meant something like that,' she said wryly. 'But it's nonsense, of course. There's always a small part of the child that never entirely grows up. It stays with the adult like a little ghost, haunting him and colouring all his thoughts and feelings.'

After a moment Primo nodded and said in a more sympathetic voice, 'I see. Him too.'

'Naturally. What do you think it was like for him, thinking himself unwanted by two mothers? You've nothing to feel jealous about.'

'I'm surprised at you, Evie. You of all people should understand Italians better, for I consider myself Italian despite my English father. We're not like the cold-blooded Anglo-Saxons. For us the family is still the centre of everything, and the mother is the centre of the family. That was true in the past, it is true now, and it always will be.

'Hope has been the only mother I ever knew. In my childhood we were exceptionally close. For years I regarded myself as her eldest son. Then I discovered that I wasn't. I began to wonder if our closeness had been an illusion. Was I no more than a stopgap for the son she'd lost?'

Evie made a sudden gesture. His words were so uncannily reminiscent of what Justin had said of his own adoptive parents.

'But it was you who found him,' Evie reminded Primo. 'You've searched for years.'

'For her sake. I wanted her to be happy. Now she is, and I am glad. But also—' he gave a sheepish smile '—I am jealous.'

'But you won't let it spoil things, will you?' she pleaded.

'Of course not. Despite what I said before, he is my brother. But who says that brothers have to agree all the time?'

She slipped away from him, brooding on his words and trying to ignore a little voice in her head that said something was wrong. On the surface all was well, with Justin, as Primo had said, 'the hero of the hour'.

And yet, she thought, troubled, and yet—

'Is it my turn now?'

She turned and saw Justin.

'I haven't been able to get near you all evening,' he said wryly.

'I could say the same about you,' she teased. 'I must be the only woman you haven't danced with.'

'And the only woman I want to dance with.'

He opened his arms and she went into them.

'I'm so happy for you,' she said. 'Who could ever have believed that it would all turn out as well as this? It's a dream come true.'

'More than that,' he said. 'How could I ever have imagined this?'

'Never,' she said happily. 'It just shows, you never know what's around the corner.'

He held her a little closer and she let her head fall on his shoulder, while the music played, soft and low. She thought back, just a few weeks, to before she had known this man. Now there was nowhere she wanted to be but in his arms.

She looked up, expecting to see him sharing her delight, but what she saw in his face startled her.

Instead of pleasure and satisfaction there was only confusion and a kind of bafflement. With a sense of alarm, she realised that she had never seen a man look so desperate.

'Must you go?' Hope pleaded the next day. 'Have I only recovered my son to lose him again so soon?'

'You won't lose me,' Justin said. 'I'll be back, but I must attend to my business.'

'Please, Dad,' Mark begged. 'Just a few more days? It's great here. Evie wants to stay too, don't you?'

Smiling, she shook her head. 'I have to get back to England too, but perhaps—' A thought had come to her, seductive in its promise of pleasure and joy.

She exchanged a silent look with Hope, who understood her at once and beamed.

'At least let Mark stay a little longer,' she said. 'Then I can be sure you will come back.'

Mark gave his father a beseeching look and Justin nodded.

'Of course,' he said. 'If that's what he'd like.'

Mark began a war dance of delight and his uncles Carlo and Ruggiero joined in. Justin relaxed and nodded.

'I'll come for him in September,' he said.

'And you will bring Evie with you?' Hope urged. 'And then we can discuss your marriage. Perhaps we can even have it here.'

'We can talk about that later, Mamma,' Justin said quickly.

'Of course, my son. I understand. I'm a steamroller, aren't I? I make plans for everyone and I don't let anyone else get a word in. It's just that I'm so anxious to welcome Evie into the family.'

Warmly she kissed Evie's cheek.

'My first daughter-in-law. How glad I will be to have you—'

'Mamma,' Primo murmured, 'you're doing it again.'

Everyone laughed heartily, except Justin, who gave only a faint smile. His mind seemed to be elsewhere. Evie was too preoccupied with thoughts of the coming blissful time, alone with him, to find this ominous.

Everyone came to see them off at the airport. Hope kissed her and whispered, 'Soon, my dear daughter.'

'I called Tom and told him to meet the flight,' Justin said when they were in the air. Tom was his driver.

'Will he take me to my apartment, or shall I call a taxi?'

'Don't be ridiculous,' he said, almost angrily. 'You're coming home with me. That is—' he became uneasy '—if you want to.'

She laughed. 'I just wanted to know what you had in mind.'

'I need to be alone with you. I haven't had that for days.'

She nodded vigorously.

It was late when they reached home. Lily opened the door, smiling to see Evie. Acting on instructions, she'd prepared a room for her and showed her up to it, followed by Justin.

'I've made a cold supper for you,' she said when Evie's bags were deposited in the bedroom, 'and it's on the table downstairs. Now, if it's all right, I'm going to bed.'

'Goodnight,' they both said.

The moment the door closed behind her they were in each other's arms, eager to make love and rediscover each other. He drew her down on to the bed, kissing her urgently as he removed her clothes and she removed his. And for a while it was as though the last week had never happened and everything was as it had been.

The sleep afterwards was deep and blissful. She awoke to the guilty thought that they hadn't eaten the supper after all and turned her head to share the joke with Justin.

He wasn't beside her on the bed, but by the window. He was naked, standing with his eyes fixed on her, so still that he might have been a statue. And the air was jagged.

'Justin, what is it?' she whispered. 'What's wrong?'

'I don't know. I woke up in a black cloud. It came over me while I was asleep, but it's as though I've been waiting for it. It was bound to happen.'

'So, you've got a touch of depression, but you're tired and you've had a lot of stuff to deal with. It'll pass.'

'I wish I believed that. But ever since I met my mother I've waited for the right feelings to come. At the party I looked around at them, my whole family, the features that so many of us share, and I kept saying to myself, *I've come home. This is it, the happy ending where I finally know who I am and where I belong.*

'And Evie, do you know what happened? Nothing. I repeated it again and again, waiting for the spring of joy that would make everything as it should be. But there's nothing there.'

'But my love, of course there isn't. It's much too soon. Only fairy tales give you an instant happy ending.

In life it takes longer. You haven't lived all these years in a vacuum. You've become a certain kind of person—'

'Harsh, suspicious, unfeeling—'

'Don't say that about yourself. You're not unfeeling, and I know that better than anyone. If anything you're hurt too easily, so you've tried to make yourself unfeeling, but it hasn't worked.'

'Don't you think I'd know more about that than you?' he asked quietly.

'No, I don't. You're the man I love and I'm going to go on loving. I know it won't be easy, but whatever demons you've got in your head I'll drive them away.'

'I wish I thought you could, that anyone could. I shouldn't have brought you home here with me, I shouldn't have made love to you. Forgive me for that. My only excuse is that I couldn't have borne not to. I had to be close to you again, and then to talk to you like this and tell you what's becoming clear to me, although God knows I don't want to face it.'

'What?' she asked, trying to quell the rising alarm in her. 'What is it that you don't want to face?'

'That we can't love each other and it's better if we say goodbye while there's still time.'

CHAPTER ELEVEN

THROUGH her shock Evie realised that this had always been coming. Underlying the joy at Naples, there had been something wrong. She'd sensed it without understanding, or perhaps not letting herself understand. Nor would she face it now. He was her life and she wouldn't give up without a fight.

'Who says we can't love each other?' she asked angrily. 'You?'

'What I *am* says it, and what I am can't be changed.' He gave a wry, mirthless smile. 'Oddly enough, you were the one who showed me that.'

'I did? How? When?'

'When you came back after that day with Ruggiero and I tried to stop you doing it again. You told me not to give you orders or try to control you. Do you remember?'

'Yes. And then you had such a strange look on your face—as though I'd said something terrible.'

'You had. You'd said exactly what Margaret used to say to me when we were married. I was possessive and controlling—'

'But that's only because you were afraid of losing her, because you'd lost everyone else. Surely you realise that?'

'Yes, of course. I did even then. But knowing why you're behaving intolerably doesn't mean you can stop yourself. I knew I was driving her further away from me every day. And I still couldn't stop.

'I saw her start to hate me and it made me worse. The more her love died the more I tried to force it back, and of course I failed because no woman can love a monster and tyrant for very long.'

'Don't say that about yourself,' she cried passionately.

'It's the truth. I know what I am and I can't be anything else.'

'You can,' she said stubbornly, 'because now you'll have me.'

He came forward in the faint light and stood beside her where she was sitting on the bed. She felt his warmth and breathed in the thrilling spicy scent of him as he put his hands on each side of her face, gazing down at her.

'I've told myself that,' he whispered, 'a thousand times when I've been trying to believe that I had every right to bind you to me. But I've always known that I have no right at all.

'Once I started thinking about Margaret I began remembering other things, how much I loved her at first, so much that it frightened me. But that didn't stop me turning into—what I became, what I still am. I destroyed Margaret and sent her off to her death. I won't risk doing that to you.'

She answered by reaching up, running her hands over his naked body and pulling him down beside her.

'Stop talking so much,' she said fiercely. 'It's all words. They don't matter. I know there are problems but we can beat them—like this—and this—'

She was kissing him as she spoke, speaking to him on the deeper level where they could find each other. But even as she did so she knew that this wasn't the way to convince him. She possessed his heart and his body, but his mind was fighting her. Without all three, he could never be truly hers.

As if reading her thoughts, he gave a convulsive jerk and pulled himself free.

'Evie, don't, please—'

'You can't destroy me,' she said passionately. 'I'm strong.'

'Yes. Strong enough to fight me, and fight me with the most devilish weapons, because you know the ones I find hardest to resist. But is that the love either of us wants? *She* fought me. In the end we did nothing else but fight, and I think—' his voice shook, as though the next words tore him apart '—I think, at last, I was actually trying to drive her away.'

'But why?'

'Because I learned to do that, long ago. Life's less painful if I'm the one who's doing the rejecting. I told you I was a coward at heart. Accept it.'

'I won't accept it because it isn't true. A coward could never have made the journey that you did to find out about your mother.'

'But it was your journey, that I took because you made me. Without you I'd have shut myself away in my steel trap. Let me tell you about that trap, because you need to know about it, and fear it. I was living there when we met. It's a small place, because that way I can guard every inch. It has two barred windows, but they're small too because it's easier to keep out the world that way.'

'Don't,' she cried in agony, putting her hands over her ears.

But he pulled them away and kept a firm grip on her wrists.

'You've got to know,' he said harshly. 'You've got to understand what I have to do.'

'I don't want to hear any more about that cage. We broke it open and we're taking it to pieces.'

'Once I thought so. If you only knew how I hoped for that, because you could break it open if anyone could. But you can't. Not even you.'

'I don't believe you're giving up on us that easily,' she cried.

'Because you don't know what I'm really like, the shadows inside me that I can't get rid of, not even now. That's why I have to make the decision for both of us, but don't ever call it easy.' He looked at her out of haggard eyes. 'Forgive me, Evie. Try to forgive me.'

'I won't forgive you,' she flashed. 'We've been given such a precious gift, and you're throwing it away.'

'Because the man I've grown into can't do anything else. Don't you see? That's the cage, and that's why it'll never be destroyed. I have to live in it, because for me there's no longer any choice. But I'm damned if I'll imprison you in there with me.'

'And what about Mark?'

'Mark's found what he needs with his new family. You did that for him, and I'll always be grateful.'

'And I'm supposed to just shrug my shoulders and go away, leaving you to shrivel?'

'You deserve better than to live in a cage.'

'Don't you?'

'It's a safe place. There's no feeling there.'

'Don't try to tell me you're unfeeling,' she raged helplessly. 'I know better.'

'You think you do.'

'Do you think a woman doesn't know if a man loves her when she's with him, when they lie together? I've seen your eyes and heard you whisper my name. You can't shut out those times or pretend they didn't happen. They were wonderful.'

'They were very enjoyable,' he said harshly. 'We're good in bed together. Nobody could deny that, but let's not get sentimental about it.'

His voice fell cruelly on her ears, leaving her too shocked to speak.

'You really fight dirty,' she whispered.

'Have you only just discovered that? Well, it's time you found out, and you're better off knowing the worst of me.'

'Stop trying to frighten me.'

'If you're not frightened, you ought to be. Go away from me, Evie. I just hurt everyone I touch. I can't help it. I wish we'd met years ago, but now it's too late for me. Can't you understand that?'

'No, and I won't believe it,' she flashed.

'What can't you believe? That I can plan to leave you at the same time as doing this?'

He pulled her hard against him, cradling her head for the most crushing kiss he'd ever given her. She returned it in full, driven as desperately as he. Like him she had something to prove, and she tried to prove it by more than meeting him halfway. Where he had been tender before, now he made love fiercely, but she contended with him in ferocity.

Only a few minutes ago she'd told herself that to unite with him physically but not mentally would be useless. Now she abandoned all thoughts of his mind. This might be her last chance, and she would win the game in any way she could.

And victory felt in her grasp with every fevered caress. He had said he couldn't do 'three little words', but he could love her with power and abandon, revealing the depths of his need with every movement. Her answering love was a promise from her soul. He must sense it and answer it. He *must*.

But in the last moments she felt her victory slipping away. It was over. He had loved her tonight as never before and, in that mood, he would sever himself from her for ever. She sensed that through her skin, her heartbeat.

When at last they lay in each other's arms she felt his face against her skin and knew that he was weeping.

Then she wept with him.

Evie told herself that she had been here before. A relationship that had looked promising came to an end and she was once more a free agent. There was sadness but there was also relief at her escape.

That was then. This was now.

In the past she had always been the one to call a halt, fearing for her liberty. This time it was like being tossed into a black pit.

She had loved Justin with an intensity of feeling that she'd never known before, giving herself to him, body, heart and soul, with a completeness that had surprised even herself. To love and be with him always had become more important than anything in life, even liberty.

Sometimes she could work herself up into hating him, reminding herself of his cruel words about getting sentimental, telling herself that he'd meant every one. If she worked hard, she could almost believe it.

At other times she was haunted by the conviction that he'd been forcing himself to say what would drive her away, not for his own sake, but for hers. That belief was the worst pain of all, because it meant that he'd chosen to withdraw into the bleak cage where no sun shone and where her love couldn't reach him. And he'd done it for her.

Before leaving his house she had returned to Justin the diamonds that Hope had given her.

'She meant these for her daughter-in-law,' she said. 'So I can't keep them.'

She was gone before Mark returned. The boy sent her emails, demanding to know when she was coming back, refusing to believe that everything was over. She could hardly believe it herself.

She wrote back, carefully explaining that she and Justin had decided that they had no future together, but that she would always like to hear from him.

He emailed her regularly. Sometimes he would add news about his father, who was apparently snowed under in work. There was never anything personal, except that he sometimes added, *Dad says hallo.*

She wrote to Hope, thanking her for her welcome, and the way she had underlined it with the diamonds.

I cannot keep them. But it will always make me happy to remember them.

Hope replied in a furious temper.

You've both taken leave of your senses. I don't want diamonds. I want the daughter-in-law that I love. I want a wedding and more grandchildren (not necessarily in that order. I'm not a prude.) I shall keep the jewels locked away until you both see reason.

Evie had to smile at that, recognising the loyalty and affection that lay beneath Hope's words, as well as the annoyance that the world was daring to disobey her.

The weather turned colder. Mark wrote to say that they were going to Naples for Christmas.

She could have spent her own Christmas with Debra and her family, but she made an excuse. The sight of Debra's husband and children was more than she could have borne just now.

She spent the festive season locked in her apartment working until she was exhausted, and remembering the words Debra had once uttered.

'One day I hope you'll fall hook, line and sinker for a man you can't have. It'll be a new experience for you.'

Her friend had been joking, but it wasn't funny any more.

When the doorbell rang on a freezing February day Evie didn't know who to expect.

'Mark!'

'Can I come in?'

'Of course.' She stood back and ushered him inside, glancing into the corridor outside. But Justin wasn't there and she forced back the brief surge of hope.

How quickly children grew! Mark had changed, even in six months. The young man he would soon be was starting to show in his face. He was also taller, as she realised when he hugged her.

She was longing to ask him a million questions—about himself, about his father and their life together. But she held off until he was sitting in her tiny kitchen, tucking into a hastily prepared snack.

'I'm glad to see your appetite is as healthy as ever,' she said. 'Another piece of apple crumble?'

He nodded, his mouth still full, and she loaded his plate again.

'How did you know my address?' she asked.

'You wrote it on the outside of the packet when you sent my memory stick back that time.'

'But that was ages ago. You made a note of it then?'

'We agreed to keep in touch.'

'Yes, we did. You really are your father's son, aren't you? He's ultra-methodical too.'

Merely talking about Justin was a pleasure. She forced herself to relinquish it. It was too dangerously sweet.

'So tell me,' she said, 'what's been happening. How was Christmas?'

'Great. Nonna's ever so nice, but I wish you'd been there. I wished it all the time. I kept thinking you might turn up as a surprise, but you didn't.'

'Mark, dear, it isn't possible. Your father and I aren't together any more.'

'But you could be,' he pleaded.

'No. It was never going to work out. I'm out of his life now, for good.'

'But I don't want you to be out of mine,' he said stubbornly. 'That's why I'm here. I want you to come to the funeral.'

'Whose funeral?'

'Mum's. He brought her home. He started talking to me one day, about Mum, and how I felt about her still being in Switzerland. I said I'd like to have her here, so he arranged for her to be flown back and reburied in that churchyard you saw.'

'That's wonderful,' she said. 'It's what you wanted, isn't it?'

He nodded, his eyes bright. 'I always wanted to have her home, but he didn't think it mattered, and I couldn't explain. But he's different now, Evie. He understands things he didn't understand before.'

She was silent, feeling a glow inside her that she had

thought never to know again. It was almost like happiness. For she knew, as surely as if Justin were standing there beside her, that she was responsible for this.

She had thought their love had turned into a barren thing, but if he'd learned the way to reach out to his son then some good had come from it.

He understands things he didn't understand before.

She could keep that and treasure it.

'The funeral's the day after tomorrow,' Mark said. 'Will you come?'

She gasped. 'Mark, I can't. I really can't.'

'But you must, because it's down to you, isn't it?'

'I may have said something to him once, but—no, it was his decision.'

'But you made him do it.'

She shook her head. 'Nobody makes him do anything.'

'You do. He did listen to you, although he pretended not to.'

She tried to deny it, but it was hard when he was saying what she longed to hear.

'Anyway,' she said, 'I expect your mother's family will be there. They might not like my being there.'

'She didn't have anyone. It'll just be Dad and me—and you.'

She was shocked by how badly she wanted to say yes. Just to see Justin again, speak to him, watch his face. All these things would be wonderful and terrible.

Then Mark stunned her again by remarking, 'He's still got your picture.'

'What picture?'

'One of the two I took of you that night you came to the house. Dad cropped it down to your head and printed it out small.'

'You saw him?'

His smile called her naïve. ''Course not. But he forgot to wipe it off my computer afterwards. So I checked his wallet, and it was there last week.'

'Mark, you shouldn't have looked in his wallet.'

'But I had to,' he said with an air of injured innocence. 'How can I find things out if I don't check the facts?'

'Don't you try to blind me with science, my lad,' she said, half laughing, half crying.

It was madness to feel suddenly full of joy. He'd kept her picture. Better still, he'd listened to her. In a way they were still part of each other's lives, even if they never met again.

'Mark, did you tell him you were coming here?'

The boy shook his head. Before she could speak, his mobile phone rang.

'Hallo, Dad. It's all right, I haven't disappeared. I came to see Evie. Dad? Are you there? I'm at Evie's apartment. I told her about Mum and asked her to come to the funeral, but she says she can't.'

'Let me talk to him,' she said, holding out her hand for the phone. 'Justin?'

'Yes,' came his voice after a moment, and even that one word, tinny and distorted as it was, had the power to move her.

'I just want you to know that Mark is quite safe. He'll be on his way home in a few minutes. Please don't worry.'

'I don't worry if he's with you, but I'm sorry he troubled you.'

'He's no trouble. And Justin—I'm glad—about his mother—'

'It was what he badly wanted. I should have seen that at the start. He says he's told you his idea.'

'For me to come to the funeral, yes, but it doesn't seem right.'

She stopped, hardly daring to let herself think further ahead.

Then he said, 'He wants it badly, but of course I'll understand if—I couldn't really expect you—'

'I'll come, of course I will. I didn't think you'd want to see me there.'

Silence. She wished she knew what she could read into it.

'Mark misses you,' he said at last. 'I think it would mean a lot to him.'

Say that you miss me, she thought wistfully.

Silence.

'Then I'll come.'

'I'll send my driver to collect him. Thank you for looking after him today. Goodnight.'

'Goodnight,' she said, trying to match his formal tone although it hurt her that they should have to be polite, like strangers.

'You're coming?' said Mark, who'd been listening. 'That's great.'

'Yes, I'll be there.'

'Did Dad sound angry?'

'No, he wasn't angry, he was just—he wasn't anything.' That was the only way, she realised, to describe the sense of blankness that had reached her down the phone.

But telephones made everything different. It would be all right when she saw him.

'While we wait,' she said cheerfully, 'why don't you tell me some more about Christmas? Did you find it a bit quiet, because Italians don't really celebrate Christmas. They wait until Epiphany on January 6th.'

'Yes, but Nonna said 'cos I was English I must have presents at Christmas, like always. And then, when it was Epiphany, she said I must have more presents because that's what everyone did. I tried to say I didn't expect two lots of presents, but Nonna told me I'd just have to put up with it.'

'I can just hear Hope saying that,' Evie mused, relishing the picture.

'And I learned lots of Neapolitan words. I remembered them for you.'

They chatted in this way until the bell rang, announcing Justin's driver. He said he would call for her again to take her to the funeral in two days' time, and bring her home afterwards.

When Mark had gone she plunged into her work and tried to think of nothing else. But pages passed before her eyes, making no impact. In the end she took the motorbike and rode at speed for hours until she no longer knew where she was. Which pretty much described her whole life, she thought.

For once the speed didn't bring the usual sense of release. She knew now that she was fleeing something that would always lie in wait, just ahead.

When the day came she chose an austere dark blue suit, and checked her appearance again and again. She was trying to stay calm, knowing that soon she would meet Justin again for the first time in months. And he would look different to her, because now she knew that he kept her picture with him all the time.

She wouldn't let herself think of what might happen then. That way lay madness. But, despite her good resolutions, the thought of seeing him after the long lonely months, studying his face, the way he smiled at her, all these made her heart beat faster.

Finally the cemetery came into view and at once her mind began to replay her last visit, in early summer when the leaves were green and the sun was high. Now it was the depth of winter—cold, wet, and miserable.

Mark came to meet her at the church door, taking her by the hand.

'Thank you,' he whispered. 'We're all ready.'

She was startled by the bleakness she found inside. As Mark had said, there was only himself and his father, with no family on his mother's side. Justin was standing in the front row with his back to her. He turned as she approached, and at first she didn't recognise him.

He was older and thinner, but that wasn't the worst of it. His face now had the hard, withered look that she'd feared to see.

'Hallo,' she greeted him softly.

He seemed to take a moment to respond, as though not quite sure where he was. Then he inclined his head a little towards her.

'Thank you for coming,' he said politely. 'It was important to Mark.'

'I'm glad he wanted me.'

The priest appeared, wanting to know if they were ready to begin. Justin nodded and glanced at Mark, who went to stand beside him, taking Evie's hand in his so that she was on his other side.

It was a short service. There was very little to be done. Justin kept his eyes fixed on the flower-covered coffin. Watching him, Evie remembered what he had told her about Margaret, how much he had loved her, and how it had all turned to hate.

What was he thinking now? Was Margaret there in

his heart again at this moment? Was there any room left for herself?

They moved outside to where the grave had been dug. Now she could see more clearly the flowers on the coffin—two bouquets of roses. One bore a card in Mark's childish hand.

To Mummy, with love always.

The card on the other was from Justin. It said simply, *Thank you.*

When the graveside rites were concluded Mark squeezed her hand, as if to say that everything was all right now. Evie looked at him, touched by the way he was reaching out to her, even at this moment.

Justin's face was like a rock, revealing nothing.

Everything was unreal. How could she be here with him, her heart alive to him as though the lonely separation had never been? As the service concluded, she saw him look at her. She went to stand in front of him, daring him not to face her.

'Are you really glad I came?' she asked. 'Not just for Mark's sake?'

He took a long time to answer and a chill crept through her.

'Yes, I'm really glad to see you,' he said at last. 'I've wondered how things were with you.'

'And I've wondered about you, whether you were well, how life was treating you.'

'It's treating me fine, as you can see.'

No, I can't see that. I can only see that your face is tense and weary, as it was when we first met.

'Do you see much of your family?'

'We have a standing invitation to Naples. Mark can go more often than I can, but Hope and I get on well.'

I thought I'd banished that defensive look from your eyes, but it's there again, and perhaps it always will be.

'I'm glad of that,' she said firmly.

'You did that for me, and I'll never forget it.'

No, in the end there was nothing I could do for you, my love.

'What about you? Have you been back to Italy?' he asked desperately.

'There hasn't been time. I've been swamped in work.'

'Well—I'm glad your career's going well.'

'Yes, very well, thank you.'

I'm grabbing all the work I can find. It fills the hours.

She'd been deluding herself with false hopes about this meeting. He hadn't wanted to see her, and now he was struggling for something to say.

'The driver will take you back as soon as you're ready,' he said. 'I hope we haven't taken up too much of your valuable time.'

There was an ache in her throat. Through the worst moments she'd clung to the hope that one day they would meet again.

But this was the meeting, and now she knew they were really at the end of the road.

When at last she could speak, she forced out words that were as formal and ugly as his own.

'Well, it's time I was going,' she said briskly. 'It's so nice to have seen you again. The best of luck.'

He drew a sharp breath and for a moment his face was constricted with pain.

'Evie,' he said harshly, 'are you all right?'

'No. You?'

He shook his head. But he would not yield.

'Goodbye,' he whispered.

She touched his cheek gently.

'Goodbye, my love,' she said. 'Goodbye.'

CHAPTER TWELVE

SHE began to lose track of time. Day seemed to follow day with little difference between them. Sometimes she felt as though she'd been translating the same book for ever and it was almost a surprise to receive three sets of galleys to check. At some time recently she must have worked on these books, but it felt like another life.

She sat at her screen for hours, crawling into bed at the last moment, getting up with the dawn, drinking black coffee before forcing herself awake with a cold shower.

Then it was back to work. Don't think. Don't listen to the phone that never rings. Don't wonder how you'll endure the rest of your life.

Mark still corresponded with her. She knew how often he went to Naples, and also how often Justin left him with his grandmother while he went away on business. She formed a vague idea that he was burying himself in work to avoid thinking and feeling, like herself.

She always worded her own emails carefully, in case Justin should see them. She couldn't bear to think of him knowing how she still pined for him when he had destroyed their love so decisively, although Mark ended every email with a hopeful, *Dad isn't dating anyone else.*

In spring she went down to the cottage. She'd been avoiding it, using the cold weather as an excuse. The truth was that she couldn't bear the thought of returning to the place where she had been with Justin, and had learned to love him.

But with the extra money he'd paid her from the sale she could do many necessary repairs, and at last the moment had to be faced. She bought a small car and drove down to Penzance.

The cottage was chilly and the emptiness felt more bleak even than she'd anticipated. There was the little kitchen where he'd cooked, and she'd begun to realise he had more facets than she'd imagined. There was the sofa where she'd awoken to find him kneeling beside her, regarding her with tender concern.

Her footsteps echoed on the flagstones, then up the stairs to the silent, empty bedrooms. She wondered how she could ever bear to be here again, but then she knew she couldn't bear to leave. This was the place where they had loved, and he would be with her here for ever.

She began to go swimming. The water was still chilly, but she found it bracing and would swim out a long way. The journey back would tire her, and that way she could get some sleep.

One morning she went out early and swam further than usual. At last she realised that it would be wise to turn back. She returned slowly, feeling the strength draining away from her while the shore seemed to recede instead of growing closer. Her arms and legs were heavy and she seemed to make no progress.

Her mind was growing fuzzy. It would be so easy to let herself fall asleep now.

Once before she'd come out this far and Justin had been alarmed, calling her back to safety, powering through the water to reach her. To tease him she had pushed on further, daring him to catch up.

That had been in the early days, before Andrew's defection, and everything had been a game, but when he'd been about to catch her she'd suddenly become very conscious of her near nakedness in the bikini, the way he was bound to seize her around the waist and draw her against him.

But he'd only grabbed her wrist and yelled something about showing a little common sense. She'd started to laugh, and he'd said, 'Hold on to me while we go back.'

She'd laughed harder, saying, 'Who needs to?' Then she had broken away from him and swam off, freshly invigorated by the sudden pounding of her blood.

She closed her eyes, reliving the moment, wondering why she hadn't seen the truth then. And would it have made any difference to the end?

'Eee—viee!'

The voice came from the sky, from the sea, from the air. It was all around her.

'Eee—viee!'

The sound narrowed down to a point on the shore. A tall, elegant woman stood there, calling and waving to her.

It was Hope.

Evie blinked, trying to realise that the impossible was happening. Somehow she brought her limbs back to life and began to make her way to shore.

As she reached shallow water and rose to her feet she stumbled, discovering just how exhausted she was. Without hesitation Hope began to wade in, oblivious to the damage to her couture clothes. Reaching Evie, she pulled her arm about her shoulders and supported her back to safety.

There, Evie could do no more than collapse on the

sand, looking up at Hope as she leaned over her, saying in a voice of total exasperation, 'Honestly, you're as bad as he is!'

Later, in the warmth of the cottage, when Evie had showered and dressed, Hope said firmly, 'Sit down and eat.'

Attired in Evie's towel dressing gown while her own clothes dried out, she had taken over the kitchen and concocted a delicious meal from whatever she'd found there. Eating it with relish, Evie recognised the hand of a genuine born home-maker.

This had always been inevitable, she realised. Part of her had known that Hope would never leave matters as they were.

'Are you angry that I came?' Hope asked, sitting at the table with her and pouring a cup of strong tea.

'Of course not. I'm glad to see you. But I thought you were in Italy, with Mark.'

'My grandson does not need me at the moment. He has the whole family to make a fuss of him. I came to England to see my son. He's the one who needs me now. You also.'

Evie gave a brief laugh. 'Oh, I'm managing.'

'Are you?' Hope asked, regarding her critically. 'It didn't seem that way out there.'

'I was just tired, getting my second wind before I swam back.'

'Perhaps, but something tells me that you were thinking dangerous thoughts.'

Before Hope's shrewd but kindly gaze Evie found that it was impossible to dissemble.

'Well, if I was, it was only for a moment,' she said. 'I'd have pulled myself together.'

'Of course. You are a woman. Somehow we always

pull ourselves together. But them—' She shrugged, dismissing and disrespecting the entire world of men.

She glanced around the cottage, taking in Evie's desk, the open books, the signs of relentless work. Watching her, Evie had the feeling that she understood everything.

'Do you ever sleep?' Hope asked at last.

'Only when I have to,' Evie admitted. 'For the rest of the time—' She shrugged.

'There is always work,' Hope agreed. 'It is as I thought. You cope better than he does.'

'You've seen him?' Evie asked eagerly. 'How is he?'

'I was with him yesterday. He's like you, working too hard, late into the night. His telephone rings constantly. He barks out his orders.' She gave a sigh. 'It is terrible.'

'We each cope in our own way,' Evie said.

'He isn't coping,' Hope said at once. 'He thinks he is, but actually he's dying. The outer shell is the same but inside he's crumbling to dust.'

'Don't,' she whispered. 'Please don't say any more.'

'But I have to. How else can I help my son? Evie, I've come to tell you that you must return to him. You *must*. Or he is finished.'

'But Hope, I didn't leave him. He sent me away. That was what he wanted.'

'Don't be ridiculous; of course that wasn't what he wanted. It's what he felt he had to do, for your sake. It was his idea of being strong, and of course he got it all wrong. He needs you. He can't survive without you.'

'He thinks he can.'

'Then you must show him his mistake. You must return to him, whether he agrees or not. If he protests, ignore him. Move in and refuse to budge. Evie, I beg you to listen to me. You're his last chance. I've never been able to do anything for my son before, but I must do this for him.'

Evie was silent, torn by temptation. The yearning for Justin was a cruel ache that pervaded her and reduced the rest of her life to rubble. And yet—

'I can't,' she said desperately. 'It isn't that I don't want to. I do. I want him so much, night and day, all the time, every minute, if you only knew—'

'You think I don't know that longing?' Hope asked wryly.

Evie had put her hands up to her head, almost tearing her hair, but at this she lowered them again.

'Yes, I suppose you do,' she said.

'When I was fifteen I fell in love with a boy a few years older. His name was Philip. He was wild and handsome and all the girls wanted him. My mother warned me against him. She said he was a bad lot. He came from a family of criminals and was just like them.

'But I didn't care. I was honoured that he chose me. I gave him whatever he wanted, sure that our love would last for ever. Of course, when I became pregnant, he didn't want to know. That was when I discovered how many other girls he had. Soon after that he was sent to prison.

'In those days unmarried mothers didn't have the help they have now. I longed to keep my baby, for I still loved Philip. I fantasised about going to see him in prison, taking our child with me. He would be so moved by the sight that he would love me again, and when he came out we would be together. Ah, the tales one tells oneself at fifteen!'

She sighed and fell silent. Evie put her hand over the older woman's and received a squeeze in return. They sat like that for a moment.

'Then my baby was born,' Hope resumed at last, 'but I never saw him. They said he'd been born dead and taken away at once. From that moment I grieved for him, and when I learned the truth it only made the grief greater, to think that he was alive somewhere and I might never see him.

'I did Jack Cayman a great disservice by marrying him without truly loving him. He had a son, Primo, and I think I tried to replace one son with another. Primo and I grew close, then Jack and I adopted another son, Luke. But you can't use one child to replace another.

'I tried to be a good mother to them, but then I met Franco and we fell in love. He was married. We couldn't be together, but Francesco was born from our love.'

'And Toni?' Evie asked shyly.

Hope gave a warm smile.

'Toni was the love of my maturity, and he still is. He always will be.'

But she did not say that Toni was the love of her life, Evie noted.

'When you both came to Naples last year,' Hope resumed, 'I was overjoyed. I looked forward to long talks with my son. I would tell him everything, and we would be united as mother and son. But—' She sighed and gave a helpless shrug.

'You didn't tell him anything?' Evie asked.

'Oh, yes, but only the bare facts. Of course, the child I'd dreamed of didn't exist. In his place was a man who'd turned himself to iron in order to endure what life had done to him. How could I share my thoughts and feelings? They would simply have embarrassed him.

'We spent long hours together talking about nothing of importance. At the end of it our hearts were still closed to each other, and I think now that his heart will remain closed, except to his son, and to you.

'He doesn't *feel* that I am his mother. He knows it with his head, but it's a meaningless word because he's never had a mother's love or care from me. That's why he always calls me Hope, never Mother.'

'Yes, I wondered about that.'

'Now I'm trying to do the only thing I can for him. He told me how he forced your parting, and why, and he's right in many ways. He *is* a dark man inside, and not every woman could cope with him. But I believe you can, and I'm here to beg you to go back and give him another chance.'

'But Hope—'

The older woman seized both her hands and spoke fiercely.

'I haven't been a good woman, Evie. I have been cruel and selfish and I've hurt many people along the way. I try to make up for it, but some things can never be put right. I've learned a great deal about men—perhaps too much.

'Some men are made to be husbands, and some to be lovers. I've known both kinds, and loved both kinds. A wise woman can sense the difference—' she gave a rueful smile '—but I was not always wise.'

'I think you're the wisest woman I know.'

'If so, I've bought that wisdom through hard and painful lessons. I told you I knew the yearning you are feeling—just for one man, because he's the only one who will do. I know when you should run from it because it will destroy you. And I know when you should listen to it. I tell you, this time you should listen. Because otherwise you will never be free.'

'How can I go back to him against his will? Maybe he secretly wanted a way out?'

'You wouldn't say that if you could see him now. If the two of you lose each other finally, you will survive, but I'm not sure that he will. He's strong in his way, but it's not the right way to help him now. You are connected to life in a way that he isn't.'

'If only I knew what was the right thing to do.'

'Listen to your heart. It will tell you all you need to know. It won't be easy for you. He's always going to be a troubled man, but he needs you desperately. And you'll have all his love, even if he finds it hard to tell you.'

Evie drew a sharp breath. 'I'll get dressed as fast as I can.'

Outside stood Justin's car and driver, both of which, Evie guessed, Hope had simply commandeered.

As they drove back to London Evie reflected, with wonder, on a lifetime spent avoiding commitment. Now she was plunging into a commitment so deep it was terrifying. But not as terrifying as a life spent without him.

When, hours later, they reached Justin's house, Hope let herself in with a key that perhaps she had also commandeered. Everywhere was very quiet, and at first Evie thought the place was empty. But then she saw him in the big garden, far away under the trees, in the fading light. She began to run.

When he looked up and saw her hurrying towards him, he grew very still. She half expected him to turn away, rejecting her, but at the last moment he opened his arms. When she went into them, they closed about her in a fierce grip.

But still he said, 'Go away, Evie. Don't do this,' while his arms held her tighter and tighter.

'Shut up,' she said. 'No more of your words. You won't get rid of me with words again. I'm staying, do you hear?'

He groaned. 'I'll break your heart. Don't you know that?'

'Yes, and I'll probably break yours. What of it? Hearts break and mend. But if we part again mine will break and never mend.'

She shut off his reply by kissing him. Her embrace held as much strength and determination as passion, and at last the message began to get through to him. The decision was no longer his. She had taken over, imposing her will on him, and all he needed to do was yield in peace and joy.

She drew back, taking his face between her hands. Months of anguish had left him thin and haggard.

'I'm here to stay, do you understand that?' she said. 'No more foolishness; we're going to be married.'

He nodded, smiling faintly.

'If you take me on, it's that lifetime commitment that you didn't want,' he warned her.

'Leave me to worry about that.'

'Evie, listen to me. Once this is done, I won't let you go, ever. I'll be jealous and demanding, possessive, selfish, unreasonable—'

'That's understood,' she said with a shaky laugh. 'I'll just kick your shins.'

'Be warned. Leave me before it's too late.'

'You fool, it was too late long ago. We just didn't realise it. It's all right.' She kissed him gently. 'It's all right—all right—'

Then he yielded, dropping his head on to her shoulder with a sound that was like a sob. She held him close, soothing him silently.

When he looked up, Hope was standing there in the gloom.

'Did you do this?' he asked.

She nodded.

'Thank you—Mother.' His voice lingered on the word.

Hope gave a little satisfied smile and moved away until she was lost among the trees. They could do without her now, and she had a wedding to plan.

The two in the garden didn't see her go. They had set their feet on a long, troubled road, where there would be bitterness as well as joy. But the joy would be there, all the sweeter for the struggle. And they would travel together, with no turning back.

HER ITALIAN BOSS'S AGENDA

PROLOGUE

'FEBRUARY!' Carlo sighed. 'Who needs it? Christmas is over and the best of the year hasn't started.'

'You mean there are no pretty tourists yet,' Ruggiero ribbed him. 'Don't you ever think of anything else?'

'No,' Carlo said simply. 'And you're just as bad, so don't deny it.'

'I wasn't going to.'

They were twins, not identical, but clearly brothers. Handsome, in the glory of their late twenties, they stood on the terrace of the Villa Rinucci, looking down at the Bay of Naples. It was late afternoon and darkness was falling fast. In the distance Mount Vesuvius loomed ominously, and below them the lights of the city winked.

Somewhere behind them their mother spoke.

'You would like my country, my sons. Every February, in England we celebrate the Feast of St Valentine, the patron saint of love. Flowers, cards, kisses—you two would be in your element.'

'Instead, it's Primo going to England,' Carlo observed gloomily. 'It'll be wasted on him. All he'll think of is business.'

'Your brother works hard,' Hope Rinucci reproved them, trying to sound severe. 'You should both try it.'

This was a slander, since these young men worked as hard as they played, which was very hard indeed. But they only grinned at their mother sheepishly.

'Why does Primo have to keep taking over firms, anyway?' Ruggiero asked. 'When will he stop?'

'Come inside and eat,' Hope ordered them. 'This is Primo's farewell dinner.'

'We give him a farewell dinner every time he goes away,' Carlo objected.

'And why not? It's a good chance to get the family together,' Hope said.

'Will Luke be here tonight?' Carlo asked.

'Of course he will,' Hope declared, a little too firmly. 'I know he and Primo have the occasional argument—'

'Occasional!' the twins groaned in unison.

'All right, most of the time. But they are still brothers.'

'Not really,' Ruggiero said. 'They're not related at all.'

'Primo is my stepson and Luke is my adopted son, and that makes them brothers,' Hope said firmly. 'Is that clear?'

'Yes, Mamma,' they both said in meek voices.

Inside the house there was warmth and the comfortable bustle of a family. But Hope looked around, dissatisfied.

'There are too many men here,' she declared.

Her husband and sons looked alarmed, as though wondering by what drastic means she intended to reduce the number.

'There should be more women,' she explained. 'Where are my daughters-in-law? I should have six by now, and I have none. I was so looking forward to seeing Justin marry Evie, but—' She gave an eloquent shrug and a sigh.

Justin was her eldest son, parted from her since his birth, but reunited the previous year. He'd come to Naples once with Evie, the woman he clearly loved. But then Evie had mysteriously vanished from his life, and when he'd returned at Christmas she hadn't been with him. Nor would he speak of her.

Gradually the big dining room filled up and, despite her disapproving words, she looked around her with satisfaction. Her sons had their own apartments in Naples, and it was a great day when she could gather them together in this house.

Her eyes lit up at the sight of Primo, her stepson by her first husband, an Englishman, although he now bore the Rinucci family name in honour of his Italian mother.

'It's been too long since I've seen you,' she said, hugging him. 'And tomorrow you're going away again.'

'Not for long, Mamma. I'll soon get this English firm into shape.'

'Why did you have to buy it at all? You were doing good business with it.'

'Curtis Electronics wasn't being run properly, so I decided to take it over. Enrico wasn't keen at first, but he finally saw it my way.'

'I'm sure he did,' Hope observed wryly.

Enrico Leonate had once been the sole owner of Leonate Europa, a firm for which Primo had gone to work fifteen years ago. He had learned quickly, made a great deal of money for his boss and for himself, and eventually had become a partner. Enrico was elderly and tired. Primo was young, thrusting and full of ideas. Enrico was glad enough to let him take the reins but, as he'd once ruefully remarked, it would have been all the same if he hadn't been. Sooner or later people tended to see things Primo's way.

Now he was telling Hope, 'I'll promote a few people, and tell them what I want.'

'That's if you can find anyone there who satisfies you. Since when did anyone live up to your expectations?'

'True,' he agreed. 'But Cedric Tandy, the present manager, recommends his deputy, Olympia Lincoln. I'll watch her closely.'

'And promote a woman?' Hope asked satirically. 'You—an equal opportunity employer?'

He looked surprised. 'I'll promote anyone who'll do as I say.'

'Ah! That kind of equal opportunity.' Hope laughed. 'My son, you make it sound so simple.'

'Most of life is simple if you know what you want and are determined to get it.'

She frowned, then forgot everything in the pleasure of seeing him here. As always, he had arrived at the perfect moment, not late but not too early, and elegantly dressed.

His appearance betrayed his dual heritage. From his long-dead Italian mother he had inherited dark eyes with a wealth of varied expressions, changing from one moment to the next. His English father had bequeathed him a stubborn chin and firm mouth, lacking the Italian mobility that characterised the other men.

'Luke isn't here yet,' she said in a low voice.

'He probably isn't coming,' Primo said cheerfully. 'I'm not his favourite person since I poached Tordini.'

Rico Tordini was a brilliant electronics inventor, claimed by both brothers, whose business interests were in the same line. Primo had secured him for his own firm.

'Luke says you stabbed him in the back,' Hope reminded Primo.

'Not a bit. It's true he spotted Tordini first, but I made him a better offer.'

'My dear, it's a bad business when brothers fall out.'

'Don't worry, Mamma. Luke will get his chance of revenge, and he'll take it.'

He spoke lightly. The running battle between himself and Luke had lasted years now, and provided spice to their lives. Without it they would both have felt something was missing.

Luke finally put in an appearance when the meal was almost over.

'*E, Inglese,*' Primo said, raising his glass in jeering fashion.

To call Luke an Englishman was Primo's favourite form of insult, a way of reminding him that he was the only son in this Italian family who was completely English.

'Better than being neither one thing nor the other,' Luke said with a grin, referring to Primo's dual ancestry and the fact that he was liable to 'switch sides' without warning.

'I'm glad you came,' Hope told him.

'Naturally.' Luke raised a glass sardonically in Primo's direction. 'I had to make sure we were really getting rid of him.'

Yet it was Luke who drove Primo to the airport the next day.

'I'm coming too,' Hope told them. 'Someone has to stop you two killing each other.'

'No fear of that,' Luke said lightly. 'It's more fun to plot a subtle revenge. That's the Italian way.'

'And what would an *Inglese* know of the Italian way?' Primo demanded.

'Only what he's learned from his mongrel brother.'

As Hope and Luke stood together watching the plane climb, she couldn't help giving a little sigh.

'Don't worry, Mamma,' Luke said, his arm about her shoulders. 'He'll be back in no time.'

'It's not that. People say how lucky I am that Primo never gives me cause for worry. But I do worry, because he's *too* reliable. He's so sensible, he never does anything stupid.'

'I promise you, if he's a Rinucci, he's stupid,' Luke said fervently.

'Indeed? And what does that make you, since you've always refused to take our name?'

He hugged her. 'I don't need it. I'm stupid enough anyway.'

CHAPTER ONE

IN THE London headquarters of Curtis Electronics tensions simmered. Employees hurried in, anxious not to be late, wondering who would be promoted and who pensioned off.

'They're not getting rid of me,' Olympia Lincoln said firmly. 'Not after all the work I've put into this firm, and the plans I've made.'

'It is rotten luck, this happening now,' Sara, her secretary, said sympathetically. 'Mr Tandy was bound to retire soon, and then you'd have had his job.'

'Grr!' Olympia said with feeling.

'The worst thing is not knowing when the new people will be here.' Sara sighed.

'Right. Even Mr Tandy doesn't know. "Some time soon" is all he can say. Maybe today, maybe next week.'

'Surely not today,' Sara objected. 'It's Friday. What sort of person makes his first day a Friday?'

'Someone who's trying to catch us out,' Olympia said at once. 'I'm blowed if I'm going to let anyone take me by surprise.'

'But today isn't just Friday,' Sara objected. '*It's Friday the thirteenth.*'

'Don't tell me you're superstitious.' Olympia chuckled. 'That's nonsense. People should make their own fate.'

'But Friday the thirteenth is bad luck.'

'It'll be bad luck for Primo Rinucci if he crosses me.

Now let's have some tea. I'll make it. You're looking queasy.'

'I'm fine really,' Sara said valiantly, if untruthfully. 'You shouldn't be making tea. You're the boss.'

'But you're the one who's pregnant,' Olympia said with a warm smile that transformed her face from its usual severe lines. She cultivated that severity, determined to make the world believe it. But her natural kindness had a habit of breaking through, although usually only Sara saw this and she was sworn to secrecy.

'That's better.' Sara sighed gratefully when she'd sipped the strong tea. 'Did you ever want children?'

'Once I did. When I married David I was madly in love and all I wanted was to be his wife and the mother of his children. Which probably makes me a disgrace to modern womanhood. But I was eighteen at the time, so maybe there was some excuse for me.'

'Did he appreciate this slavish devotion?'

'Did he, hell? He needed a working wife so that he could take courses and get diplomas that would help his career. When he moved onward and upward to the next promotion, plus the next wife, I was left with nothing. So I worked like the devil and made a career for myself.'

'You were unlucky, but not all men are like him.'

'Most of the ambitious ones are. They use us unless we use them first.'

'So that's what you do,' Sara agreed, regarding her boss sympathetically, and recalling various incidents in the last couple of years that now made more sense. 'Are you happy?'

'What's happy? I'm not *un*happy. I remember how I felt when David walked out, and that's never going to happen to me again. I'm going to get Tandy's job, you wait and see. I just have to work on—whoever turns up from Italy.'

'How's your Italian?'

'Not bad. I've been learning hard, but I suppose everyone else here has done the same.'

'None of the others will have prepared like you have, either in the head or the—' Sara made a gesture indicating Olympia's appearance, and Olympia laughed.

Both inside and out, her grooming was impeccable. Her mind was focused, steely. Her body was slender and elegant, clad in a blue linen dress.

She was tall for a woman, with long legs, a long neck and cleanly chiselled features. Her black hair was naturally luxuriant, but she wore it smoothed back against her head and twined into sleek braids behind.

In this she was illogical. The sensible thing would be to cut it off in a neat, boyish crop. But for once she couldn't make herself do the sensible thing. She wasn't sure why.

Her eyes were also dark, lustrous, with depths where humour still lurked occasionally, although she did her best to conceal it. She was a perfectly groomed creation, crafted to her own meticulous design.

In only one thing had she failed to achieve her own standards. At heart she knew that part of her was still the same girl she'd once been, the one she was trying to deny. That girl had been full of trust and eagerness, without a calculating bone in her body. She hadn't merely loved her husband, she'd worshipped him blindly. She'd also possessed a temper and an unruly tongue, which sometimes spoke before her mind was in gear.

All these things she'd striven to put right, and had mostly succeeded. Occasionally she was still betrayed by anger into rash speech, but she was working on that too.

Today was going to put all her skill to the test.

'Do you know who's going to turn up to look us over?' Sara asked.

'Probably Primo Rinucci. I've tried to research the firm on-line but there isn't much. There's two partners, Enrico Leonate and Primo Rinucci. I managed to find Leonate's picture on-line, but unfortunately there was no picture for Rinucci.'

'What does Signor Leonate look like?'

'Dull, middle-aged. Let's hope Primo Rinucci isn't the same.'

But even as she spoke Olympia was giving Sara a worried look.

'You're not well,' she said.

'I'll be fine in a minute.'

'Oh, no! You're going home. I don't want it on my conscience that anything went wrong with your baby.' She picked up the phone, dialled reception and ordered a taxi on the firm.

'Go home and call the doctor,' she said. 'And don't come back until you're a lot better.'

'But how will you manage without me?' Sara asked worriedly.

Olympia gave her a cheerful smile. 'I'll just have to stagger along somehow. Don't worry.'

She went down to reception, saw Sara into the waiting taxi and waved it off.

She was frowning as she returned to her office. She'd spoken reassuringly to Sara, but it was the worst possible time for this to happen.

She called Central Staff and explained that she urgently needed a temporary secretary, adding, 'the best you have. And quickly, please.'

'Someone will be there in five minutes.'

When she'd hung up Olympia took some deep breaths and closed her eyes.

'I will not let this get to me,' she said to herself. 'If things go wrong I will overcome them. I will. *I will*. I am strong. Nothing can defeat me.'

She repeated this mantra several times before opening her eyes and getting the shock of her life.

A young man was standing there, watching her with interest.

He was very tall with slightly shaggy brown hair, dark brown eyes and a wide, firm mouth. He seemed to be regarding Olympia with some amusement, but perhaps that was only her imagination. She hoped desperately that her lips hadn't been moving.

'Can I help you?' she asked coolly.

'I'm looking for Olympia Lincoln. They told me downstairs that I'd find her here.'

The Central Staff Office was downstairs. After the first surprise Olympia recovered. Male secretaries were quite common these days.

'I am Olympia Lincoln,' she said. 'I'm glad you got here quickly. They said they'd send me a replacement in five minutes, but—' She shrugged.

'Replacement?'

'Well, not permanent replacement, of course. Just temporary until my regular secretary is feeling better. Have you been here long—with the firm, I mean?'

'No, a very short time,' he said. He was watching her keenly and picking his words with caution.

'Never mind, you'll soon get the hang of it. We're in the middle of an upheaval at the moment. Curtis has been taken over by an Italian firm called Leonate Europa, and soon someone will arrive from Italy to make it official. We're all waiting in fear and trembling to learn our fate.'

He raised his eyebrows. 'Fear and trembling? You?'

She gave a half smile, pleased by the implication. 'Yes—well—I can do a good imitation of it if necessary.'

'Will it be necessary?'

'I'll tell you that when I've met His Majesty.'

'Who's he?'

'Primo Rinucci. The "great man" who's coming to whip us all into line. Damned cheek!'

'Isn't it a bit soon to blame him? He might be all right.'

Suddenly her carefully cultivated pose fractured under the burden of her anger.

'He's not all right. He's a predator who thinks he can snatch whatever he wants and to hell with everyone else. Ooh, I wish he was here so that I can give him a piece of my mind!'

'It's only a moment ago you were going to pretend to fear and tremble.'

'I'll do that first. *Then* I'll tell him what I think of him, coming here, disrupting my life, taking my promotion just when it's in my grasp, thinking his money can buy anything.'

'Money has a way of doing that,' he observed mildly. 'It's one of its virtues.'

'To hell with virtue, to hell with money and to hell with Primo Rinucci.'

The sight of her eyes, blazing with indignation, held him entranced. Men had lost their heads for eyes like that, he thought. As he was in danger of doing.

'I can see that this is going to be a meeting of Titans,' he murmured.

She returned to sanity, and sighed.

'Well, keep what you've just heard to yourself. I suppose I shouldn't have spoken so freely in front of you—'

'My lips are sealed,' he promised. 'I swear never to tell Primo Rinucci what you really think of him.'

'Thank you, but be careful. Since we don't know what he looks like, you might find yourself talking to him without knowing it's him. He's probably the sort of low life who'd keep his identity secret just to be mean.'

'Yes,' he said, with a touch of guilt. 'I suppose that's possible.'

'But then, his being Italian would be a giveaway.'

'Maybe not,' he couldn't resist saying. 'Not all Italians say *Mamma mia!* and wave their hands. In fact, I believe some of them are indistinguishable from normal human beings.'

Try as he might, he couldn't keep a note of irony out of his voice. Luckily she was too preoccupied to notice.

'But he'd have an accent,' she persisted. 'He wouldn't sound English like you and me.'

He cleared his throat, then seemed to go into a kind of trance. In truth he was struggling with a temptation more overwhelming than any he'd known in his life. A wise man would tell her the truth before it was too late.

But it was already too late, and never had he felt so reluctant to be wise.

'By the way, I should have asked your name,' Olympia said.

He played for time.

'What?' he asked vaguely.

'Your name.'

'My name.'

'That's right. What is it—your name?'

She spoke patiently, and her eyes showed that she thought she was dealing with a halfwit. Was that better than telling her that he was Primo Rinucci?

For one wild moment he teetered on the brink of the truth.

Tell her who you really are. Be honest. Play safe.

He took a deep breath. To blazes with honesty! As for safety—nuts to it!

'Jack Cayman,' he said.

It had been the name of his English father. It was many years now that he'd lived in Italy as a Rinucci. But his early years had left their mark, and he could still speak English without a trace of Italian accent. So it was easy for him, now, to look Olympia in the eye and claim to be Jack Cayman.

She extended her hand. 'Well, Mr Cayman—'

'You can call me Jack.'

'You can call me Miss Lincoln,' she said firmly, feeling that it was time she reclaimed the ground she'd lost in that burst of frankness.

'Yes, ma'am,' he said meekly.

'Now, the sooner we get down to work the better.'

'Would you just give me a few minutes first?' he asked hurriedly. 'I'll be straight back.'

'Of course. It's just down the corridor on the right.'

'Thanks,' he said, hurrying out of the door.

It was several moments before it dawned on him that she'd directed him to the gentlemen's convenience.

For the past week Cedric Tandy had been in his office half an hour early, so it was plain misfortune that when the crucial day came he was half an hour late.

'Oh no,' he moaned at the sight of the man waiting for him. 'Signor Rinucci—I assure you—'

'It's all right, Cedric,' Primo said pleasantly. 'I just thought I'd drop in for a chat.'

'Perhaps I can show you around and introduce you—'

'That can come later. I've been looking over the financial arrangements Enrico and I made for you, and it struck me that they were rather on the mean side. I'm sure you deserve something more generous.'

'Well—that's very good to hear but—Signor Leonate said that your firm couldn't pay any more—'

'You leave him to me. If he won't fund an increase I'll do it myself.'

Cedric gaped as Primo walked to the door and looked back.

'By the way,' he said, as if something had only just occurred to him, 'I'd rather nobody knew who I was, just at first. They think I'm Jack Cayman. It'll give me a chance to meet people in a more spontaneous manner. I know you'll back me up.'

Cedric might not be a genius at running a company but he'd learned shrewdness. He understood bribery. But he also understood about gift horses.

'Count on me,' he said.

Olympia looked up from the computer as he entered her office.

'You'd better come and study these files,' she said. 'They'll tell you a lot about how Curtis and Leonate have interacted since they started doing business a year ago.'

'I think it was actually more like fifteen months,' he said. 'It began when Curtis tendered to manufacture a new kind of computer plug.'

'Excellent,' she said. 'You've been doing your homework.' She rose and indicated for him to sit at the computer. 'Are you familiar with this system?'

'I think so,' he said, choosing his words with care. It was the same as the system in use at Leonate's head office in Naples and in all their other firms, and Curtis had adopted it recently at his own 'urgent recommendation.'

'I think it's a pain in the neck,' she said with a touch of annoyance. 'Our old system was much better, but Leonate insisted on this one so that we can network with their other companies.'

'Is it really a pain in the neck, or do you just hate your new bosses?' he asked with a faint grin.

'I can't afford to hate them.'

'But if you could, you would, huh?'

'I think I'd better not answer that. Let me explain how this all fits together.'

She proceeded to give him a run-down of the firm and its relations with Leonate. Her mind was clear and well-informed, and she had details at her fingertips. When his umpteenth attempt to trip her up failed he admitted to himself that he was impressed.

He had also to admit that he was finding it hard to concentrate through the distraction of her perfume. At first he hadn't been sure she was wearing any, so subtle and mysterious was it. But at close range the muted aroma just reached him, then faded, returned, faded again, teasing him with uncertainty.

The aroma, if there was one, was unlike anything he'd known before. He was used to women who dabbed on hot musk to entice him, but this had a cool, restrained quality that was almost like winter. Winter about to become spring, he thought: sweet-smelling fires in the snow, the smoke blown hither and thither, always on the verge of vanishing, always lingering.

The phone rang and she answered quickly.

'Sara? What's the news?'

'I'm in hospital,' came Sara's voice. 'It'll be months before I can work. I'm sorry, Olympia.'

'Don't worry about anything. If the baby's all right, that's what counts.'

'Bless you.'

Olympia replaced the receiver thoughtfully. Primo was watching her face.

'Your secretary's not coming back?' he asked.

'It seems not. In which case—'

She looked up as a shadow appeared in the doorway and a neat young woman hurried in.

'Miss Lincoln? I'm so sorry not to have got here earlier—'

'Was I expecting you?'

'Central Staff sent me. They said you needed a secretary.'

'But—' She gave a quick look at Primo, who let out his breath uneasily. 'But you—'

'It's a bit complicated,' he hedged.

'Will you wait outside, please?' she asked the newcomer pleasantly.

When the young woman had gone she faced him.

'I think you have some explaining to do. Just who are you?'

'I told you, my name is Jack Cayman.'

'But who is Jack Cayman? And why did he claim to be my secretary when he wasn't?'

'Ah, be fair. I never actually said that's who I was. You jumped to a conclusion.'

'Which you did nothing to correct.'

'You didn't give me a chance. You informed me why I was there, snapped your fingers, and I said, "Yes, ma'am, anything you say, ma'am." And let's face it, that's the kind of answer you prefer.'

He knew this was an exaggeration, but he was fighting with his back to the wall. Anything was better than the truth.

Or was it? This could be his last chance to make a fresh start. He took a deep breath, but before he could speak a voice from the doorway sealed his fate.

'Jack, my dear fellow, how good to see you!'

It was Cedric Tandy, advancing on him, smiling, playing his allotted part.

He made some reply. He had no idea what it was. Inwardly he was cursing.

'I see you've met Olympia,' Cedric burbled on, oblivious to the wreckage he was causing. 'That's good—excellent.'

'Oh, yes, we've met,' Olympia said with glassy-eyed courtesy. 'But we were still sorting out who's who.'

'I hadn't explained who I am and where I come from,' Primo said, giving Cedric a glance fierce enough to silence him. 'It's a bit difficult to—you might call me a sort of ambassador, an outrider, sent to prepare the land before the big guns arrive.'

'And was coming to my office a part of preparing the land?' Olympia asked with deadly brightness.

'Your name has been mentioned as one of the assets of the firm,' he said. 'Now we've talked I can see I'm going to rely on you for a lot of information. Perhaps the three of us can have lunch together, and exchange views.'

'Wonderful idea!' Cedric exclaimed.

'You're very kind,' Olympia said coolly, 'but I'm

afraid my lunch will be an apple at my desk. I've got a new secretary starting today, and I have to work with her.'

Cedric, aghast at this cavalier treatment of a man who came from the seat of power, began to mutter urgently, 'Olympia, I really think—'

'Naturally I respect your decision,' Primo interposed smoothly. 'Some other time. Cedric, why don't we go somewhere and talk?'

The two of them departed, leaving Olympia to reflect that she'd made a mess of everything, and it was all his fault.

She wanted to bang her head against the wall.

Or his.

Before leaving, Olympia looked in on Cedric, who informed her cheerfully that the newcomer had left an hour ago.

And he hadn't tried to talk to her again. Which meant that it wasn't just a mess. It was a complete and total mess. She ground her teeth.

In the firm's car park she headed for her new car, a prized possession whose gleaming lines usually brought her comfort. She surveyed them for a moment, trying to take the usual pleasure in this sign of success, but tonight something was out of kilter, as if a genie had threatened to rub a lamp the wrong way and snatch it all back.

Beneath her calm she was furious, more with herself than anyone else. Her plans had been laid so carefully. Primo Rinucci would arrive to find her one step ahead of him, which, of course, he would never suspect. She would play him like a fish on a line, as she had done before, although never when there was so much to win and lose.

And she'd blown it. Caught off-guard, she'd revealed her true feelings, something *you just didn't do!* Not if you wanted to reach the top as badly as she did.

Now he knew, and he would report back that she was not only stupid enough to mistake his identity, but hostile to her new employers. Great!

As she pulled out of the line and headed for the exit she became aware that another car had slipped in behind her. It followed her out on to the road and remained on her tail, keeping a safe distance, but definitely following. Glancing into her mirror she caught a glimpse of the driver and drew in a sharp breath. Him again!

Two impulses warred within her. One said this man came from the Leonate Head Office and she should be charming and recover lost ground.

The other said punch his lights out.

She compromised.

Half a mile later the road broadened out and she took the chance to draw into the kerb, get out and face him.

'Are you following me?' she demanded.

'Yes,' he admitted. 'I meant to catch up with you in the car park, but I just missed you. I thought we could talk.'

'You couldn't simply have suggested a meeting?'

'And get comprehensively snubbed? I don't think my fragile ego could stand it a second time in one day.'

'Fragile my foot!' she fumed. 'We "talked" this morning, and I'm still regretting it. You practised a wicked deception on me—'

'Not wicked,' he pleaded. 'Foolish, I grant you. I was stupid, it was a joke that went wrong, but when you just assumed that I was your secretary—well, can you blame me for playing along?'

'Yes,' she said firmly. 'It was unprofessional.'

'And not checking the facts was the height of professionalism, I suppose?' he said, stung. 'No, look, I'm sorry I said that. I don't want to turn this into a fight.'

'Then you're several hours too late. It became a fight the moment you thought I was there for your entertainment and tricked me into saying things that—' She shuddered as she recalled her incautious words.

'I didn't force you to say that stuff about "His Majesty" like "To hell with Primo Rinucci!" You were bursting to say it to someone.'

The stark truth of this didn't improve her temper.

'And I said it to you, thus finishing my prospects with my new employers.'

'I never said—'

'You didn't have to. If you don't tell them now you'll have to warn them later, otherwise they'll find out what you knew and your own prospects will be in danger.'

'Don't worry about my prospects,' he said coolly. 'I have the virtue of thinking before I speak. It's a great help. For an ambitious woman you have a remarkably careless tongue.'

'How was I to know that you—?' She bit back the last words.

'Wasn't an underling?' he finished. 'If I *had* been the worm beneath your feet that you clearly thought, it wouldn't have mattered, would it?'

'I'm not going to dignify that with an answer,' she seethed.

'Which is probably wise! No, look—forget I said that. I'm tired, jet lagged—'

'How can you be jet lagged from Naples?' she scoffed.

'The damned plane was delayed,' he yelled. 'It didn't get in until past midnight, and I got no sleep last night.

I'm not at my best, and I'm saying things I shouldn't. You're not the only one who can do that.

'So let's put an end to this now. I apologise—for everything. And I'd like to apologise properly over dinner.'

'No, thank you,' she said crisply. 'I have plans for this evening. I intend to spend it reading a book called *How To Spot A Phoney At Fifty Paces*. I thought I was good at that, but evidently I have much to learn.'

'I could give you some pointers.'

'No, you come under the heading of practical experience. After you I need further instruction. I'll probably take a crash course, with a diploma at the end of it.'

'I really screwed up, didn't I?' He sighed.

'Need you ask? Now, Mr Cayman, if you'll excuse me, I have to get home. I suggest you turn around and spend the evening writing a report for your employers. Be sure to include *everything*.'

'That's not how I plan to spend my evening.'

'If you follow me again I'll call the police.'

'What for? Surely you can deal with this situation without help. I'd back you against the police any day.'

'That was an entirely unnecessary observation.'

'I thought I was paying you a compliment.'

'Then we have different ideas about what constitutes a compliment. *Goodnight!*'

CHAPTER TWO

WITHOUT waiting for a reply, Olympia got back into her car and started up with a vigour that threatened to finish off the engine. Primo sighed, returned to his own car and pulled out.

What happened next was something he was never quite able to analyse, except to say that he was still mentally in Italy, where drivers used the other side of the road, and the steering was on the other side of the car. In daylight he might have coped better, but with lights glaring at him out of the darkness he briefly lost his sense of direction. The next thing he knew was an ugly scraping sound of metal on metal and a hefty clout on the head.

He swore, more at the indignity than the pain.

Olympia appeared, pulling open his door. 'Oh, great. All I need is a clown to ram my new car—hey, are you all right?'

'Sure, fine,' he lied, blinking and making a vain effort to clear his head.

'You don't look it. You look as if you were seeing stars. Did you hit your head?'

'Just a little bump. What about you? Are you hurt?'

'No, my car took all the damage. There's not a scratch on me.'

He got out, moving slowly because his head was swimming, and surveyed what he could see of the dent. There was no doubt who had hit whom, he thought, annoyed with himself for ceding a point to her.

'I'm sorry,' he groaned.

'Never mind that now. Let's get you to a hospital.'

'What for?'

'Your head needs looking at.'

'It's just a scratch. I don't want any hospital.'

'You've got to—' She checked herself. 'All right, but I'm not letting you out of my sight for a while. You can come home with me. No—' she added quickly as he turned back to the car. 'You're not driving in that state. I'll take you.'

'I don't want to abandon my car here.'

'We're not going to. If you hold a torch, I'll fix the tow.'

'Shouldn't it be me fixing the tow?'

'You've had a bump on the head. Do as I ask and don't speak.'

'Anything you say.'

He had to admit she knew what she was doing, attaching the two vehicles as efficiently as a mechanic. In no time at all they were on their way. Ten minutes drive brought them to a smart block of flats, where Olympia parked both cars efficiently.

'I'll call the hire firm first thing tomorrow,' he said, adding wryly, 'They'll be thrilled.'

'When did you hire it?'

'This morning.'

Her apartment was on the second floor. It was neat, elegant and expensively furnished with perfect taste, he noticed, but it seemed to him that there was something lacking. For the moment he couldn't define it.

'Sit down while I look at your forehead,' she said.

Unwilling though he was to admit it, his head was aching horribly, and a glance in the mirror showed him a nasty bruise and some scratches that were bleeding.

'It won't take a moment for me to clean that up,' she said. 'And I'll make you a strong coffee.'

He was glad to sit down and close his eyes. From somewhere in the distance he thought he heard her talking, but then he opened his eyes to find her standing there with coffee.

'Drink this,' she said.

'Thanks. Then I'll call a taxi to take me back to my hotel. I'm sorry about your car. I'll pay for all the repairs.'

'No need. The insurance will take care of it.'

'No, I'll do it,' he said hastily, with visions of form-filling and having to give his real name. 'We don't want to damage your no-claims bonus, and I'd rather the world didn't hear about this.'

'You think they might laugh?' she asked.

'Fit to bust,' he said gloomily.

The coffee was good. Almost up to Italian standard.

As he was finishing it there was a knock at the door. Olympia answered it and returned with a young man.

'This is Dr Kenton,' she said. 'I called him when we came in.'

He groaned. 'I told you I'm all right.'

'Why not let me decide that?' the doctor asked pleasantly.

He studied the bruise for a few moments, then took out an instrument which he used to look into his patient's eyes, before declaring, 'Mild concussion. It's not serious but you ought to go straight to bed and have a good sleep.'

'I'll go home right now,' he said, giving Olympia a reproachful look.

'Is there anyone there to look after you?' the doctor asked.

'Not really,' Olympia said. 'It's a hotel. That's why he's staying here.'

'Nonsense—' Primo protested.

'He's staying here,' Olympia repeated, as though he hadn't spoken.

'Ah, good.' Dr Kenton looked from one to the other. 'That's all right, is it? I mean, you two are—'

'The best of enemies,' Olympia said cheerfully. 'Never fear, I'll keep him in the land of the living. I haven't had such a promising fight on my hands for ages.'

Dr Kenton grinned and produced some pills from his bag.

'Put him to bed and give him a couple of these,' he said. 'I'll see myself out.'

When they were alone they looked at each other wryly for a moment until Primo said, 'If I'd thought about it for a month beforehand I could hardly have made a bigger foul-up, could I?'

'True,' she said, amused. 'But don't knock it. It's left me feeling so much in charity with you.'

He managed a faint laugh. 'Yes, there's nothing like having the other feller at a disadvantage to improve your mood.'

'There's a supermarket next door. I'll just go along and get some things for you, then I'll make up your bed when I get back. Don't even think of leaving while I'm gone.'

'Don't worry. I couldn't.'

In the supermarket she went swiftly round the shelves taking shaving things, socks and underwear. She had to guess the size but it wasn't hard. Tall, lean, broad-shouldered. Just the way she liked a man to be. Evidently her subconscious had been taking notes.

She looked for pyjamas too, but the supermarket's clothes range was limited to small items. Finally she stocked up on some extra groceries and hurried back, only half believing his promise to stay there.

But she found him stretched out on her sofa, his eyes closed, and got to work without disturbing him, putting clean sheets on her own bed, as there was no guest room.

'How did I get into this?' she asked herself. 'It's only an hour ago I was planning dire vengeance.'

When she returned to the main room he was awake and looking around vaguely.

'The bed's ready,' she told him.

'I'm afraid I don't have any night things.'

'That's all right. I got you some stuff in the supermarket. You'll find it in there.'

'Thanks. You've been very kind. I can manage now.'

His head was aching badly and he was glad to find the bedroom in semi-darkness, with only a small bedside lamp lit. When she was safely out of the room he removed his clothes and pulled on the boxer shorts she'd provided, meaning to don the vest as well. He would just lie down for a moment first.

It was bliss to put his head on the soft pillow and feel the ache slip gently away in sleep.

Olympia slept on the sofa. Waking in the early hours, she sat up, listening intently to the silence. There wasn't a sound, but a faint crack of light under her bedroom door told her that the lamp was still on.

Frowning, she went over to the door and hesitated only a moment before turning the handle quietly and looking inside. Then she stopped.

His clothes were on the floor, tossed everywhere, as though he'd only just torn them off before sleep overcame him. He'd put on the underpants, but not the vest, which was still loosely clasped in one hand as he lay on his back, his head turned slightly aside, his arms outstretched.

At first she viewed him with concern, in case he wasn't recovering properly. But then she realised that he was breathing easily, relaxed and contented. All was well.

It was lucky for him, she thought, that she wasn't the kind of woman to take advantage of a defenceless man; otherwise she would have let her eyes linger on his chest, smooth and muscular, and his long arms and legs. Propriety demanded that she withdraw, after she'd switched off the lamp.

Moving carefully, she eased herself along the side of the bed and reached for the switch. The sudden darkness seemed to disturb him for he muttered something and rolled over on the bed, flinging out an arm so that it brushed against her thigh.

She stood petrified, not wanting him to awaken and find her here, but realising that movement would be difficult. Between the large bed and the large wardrobe was a space too narrow for her to back away from his hand. Holding her breath, she took hold of his fingers, turning them enough for her to slip past.

But when she tried to let go she found that she couldn't. Suddenly his fingers tightened on hers. She twisted her hand, but it only made him clasp her more strongly.

Holding her breath, she dropped to her knees and put up her free hand, trying to release herself gently. A shaft of light from the window showed her his face, very near to hers, outlining the mouth that seemed different now. Earlier, she'd seen in it strength and a kind of jeering confidence, almost laughing at her even when he was trying to placate her.

But now, with its lines relaxed, it seemed softer, gentler, as though its smiles came naturally, and its laughter might be more real and spontaneous. Even delightful.

She drew a swift breath and rose to her feet, pulling her hand free and leaving the room without a backward glance.

Primo awoke suddenly. The pain in his head had completely gone and he was filled with a sense of well-being stronger than he had ever known before. It had something to do with the extraordinary woman who'd appeared in his life the day before and caused him to behave like a stranger to himself.

Lying there gazing into the darkness, not sure exactly where he was or how he'd got there, he wondered if he would ever recognise himself again. And decided that he wouldn't greatly mind if he didn't.

But then, he'd never quite recognised himself in all the years he'd had a dual identity.

He couldn't remember his mother, Elsa Rinucci, dead only a few weeks after his birth. In fact his earliest clear memory was of standing in the register office, aged four, while his father married a nineteen-year-old girl called Hope.

He'd adored her and had been on tenterhooks in case the wedding fell through. Only when it was over had he felt safe in his possession of a mother.

But no possession was eternally safe, he'd discovered. After two years, Hope and Jack had adopted Luke. He was a year younger than Primo, which everyone thought was charming.

'They'll be such companions for each other.'

And they had been, after a fashion. When they hadn't been squabbling and sabotaging each other's childish projects, they had formed an alliance against the world. But it had been an uneasy alliance, always ready to fracture.

His cruellest memory was of having his heart broken when he was nine years old. Jack and Hope's marriage ended in divorce, and she had departed, taking Luke but not himself. Only much later had he understood that she'd had no choice. He was Jack's son, but not hers. She could claim custody of Luke, but Primo had to be left with his father, feeling deserted by the only mother he had ever known.

There he had remained until Jack's death two years later, when his Rinucci relatives had taken him to live in Naples. To his joy, Hope had come to find him. That was how she'd met his Uncle Toni, and their marriage had soon followed.

Primo had taken the family name, and for a long time now had thought of himself as a Rinucci from Naples. But with the beautiful, maddening, fascinating woman whose bed he was occupying, that was the one person he couldn't be.

It was seven a.m., still dark at that time of the year, yet late enough for him to be thinking of rising. Pulling on his trousers, he went to the door and opened it a crack. It was still dark but a glow was beginning to come through a window, illuminating the young woman who stood there.

For a moment he didn't recognise her. This mysterious creature with the long black hair streaming down over her shoulders, over her breasts, halfway down her back, was quite different from the austere woman he'd met by day. The pale grey light limned her softly, bleaching colours away until she was all shadows.

She was looking out into the growing light as though the dawn itself was bringing her to life. She was growing brighter, more real, yet without losing her mystery.

Una strega, he thought, using the Italian word for a witch.

He was thinking not of an old crone stirring a cauldron, but of a temptress, endlessly enticing, teasing her prey to follow her to a place where anything could happen. Italian legends were full of such creatures, alarming even in their beauty, impossible to resist. With that long black hair she seemed to be one of them, plotting spells of darkness and light. A man who wanted the answer would have to follow her into the dancing shadows. And then it would be too late.

He shook his head, astonished at himself for such thoughts. He prided himself on his good sense and here he was, indulging in fantasies about witches.

But how could a man help it when faced with her fascinating contradictions? She showed an austere aspect to the world, scraping back her hair against her skull in a no-nonsense fashion and sleeping in pyjamas.

Nor were they seductive pyjamas. There was nothing frilly or baby-doll about them, no embroidery or lace. And she probably hadn't even realised that light from the right angle would shine through the thin material, revealing the outline of high, firm breasts, narrow waist and delicately flared hips. If she'd known that she would probably have worn flannel, he realised despondently.

He forced himself reluctantly back to earth and looked around the dimly lit room. When he saw the sofa with its pillows and blankets, it dawned on him that she'd slept there, while he occupied her bed.

He ought to move away. No gentleman would watch her while she was unaware, standing in a light that almost made her naked. So he limited himself to another two minutes before forcing himself to back off, closing the door silently.

He waited another few minutes, putting on his shirt and making plenty of noise to warn her. When he opened the door again he saw that the sofa had been stripped of sheets and blankets.

Olympia emerged from the kitchen, smiling. She was dressed in sweater and trousers and her hair was still long, although it had been drawn back and held by a coloured scarf.

'Good morning,' she said brightly. If he'd been thinking straight he might have thought the brightness rather forced, but he was long past thinking straight.

'How are you this morning?' she asked.

'A lot better for that sleep, thank you. In fact, thank you for everything, starting with making me come home with you. You were right about the hotel. It's a crowded place, but it would have been just like being alone.'

'Of course, you could always have asked them to send for a doctor,' she mused. 'But you wouldn't have done that. Too sensible. Men never do the sensible thing.'

'Actually, I usually do,' he said, making a face. 'That's my big problem, according to my mother. She keeps choosing wives for me but, according to her, I'm so sensible I drive them off. I tell her that when I'm ready to marry I'll find a woman as sensible as myself, and then neither of us will notice how boring the other one is.'

She laughed. From where she was standing no man had ever seemed less boring. A shaft of sunlight was falling on him, emphasising a masculine vigour that made him stand out vividly in her too-neat apartment. She found herself thinking of the countryside in summer, fierce heat, vibrant colours, everything deeper, more intense.

But the subtext of the story was that he had no wife at home. It alarmed her to find that she was glad to know that. It could make no possible difference to her. And yet she was glad.

She covered herself by turning it into a joke.

'You're in luck. I know several boring ladies who'd overlook a few deficiencies and make do with you.'

'Thank you, ma'am,' he said ironically. 'And while I'm thanking you I'll add the fact that you called the doctor last night, despite what I said. It was sneaky, but it was also the right thing to do.'

'Oh, I don't waste time arguing. When a man's totally wrong I just ignore him.'

'Now, that I believe.'

They laughed and she said, 'The bathroom's over there.'

He went in, taking the things she'd bought him, and had to admit that even her choice of shaving cream and aftershave were perfect. This was one very organised lady, who got every decision right.

But that was just one side of her, he realised. There was another side, with an unruly tongue that burst out despite all her efforts at control. That was the interesting side, the one he wanted to know more about, which was going to be hard, because it was the one she strove most fiercely to hide. But he wasn't going to give up now.

When he came out the room was empty and he could hear her moving in the kitchen. He looked around her apartment and again had the sense of something missing. Now he realised what it was. Like herself, the place was neat, focused, perfectly ordered. But what else was she?

What were her dreams and desires? There was nothing here to tell him.

He could find only one thing that suggested a personal life and that was a photograph of an elderly couple, their heads close together, smiling broadly. The woman bore a faint resemblance to Olympia. Grandparents, he thought. There were no other pictures.

Her books might give a clue. But here again there was nothing helpful. Self-improvement tomes lined the shelves, courses for this, reading for that. They had been placed there by the woman who wore mannish pyjamas and sleeked her hair back, not the witch whose black locks streamed down like water.

She emerged with hot tea. 'Drink this, you'll feel better. I hope you're hungry.'

'Starving.'

From the kitchen came the sound of a toaster throwing up slices at the same moment that there was a ring on the front doorbell.

'Answer it for me, would you?' she said, heading back to the kitchen.

At the door he found a young man in a uniform, clutching a large bouquet of red roses, a bottle of champagne and a sheaf of envelopes.

'This stuff has just arrived on the desk downstairs,' he said. 'There's a few others, mind you. The post's always heavy on St Valentine's Day, but the others are nothing to Miss Lincoln's. It's the same every year.'

'OK, I'll take them.'

The roses were of the very best, heavy with perfume, clearly flown in expensively from some warmer location. He managed to read the card.

To the one and only, the girl who transformed the world.

He returned to the main room just as she appeared from the kitchen.

'You seem to be very popular,' he said.

He was stunned by the look that came over her face as she saw the roses. Her smile was tender, brilliant, beautiful with love.

'Who are they from?' he couldn't resist asking.

'What's the name on the card?' she said with a laugh.

'There's no name,' he said, and could have kicked himself for revealing that he'd read it.

'Well, if he wants to keep his identity a secret,' she said carelessly, 'who am I to say otherwise?'

'There's a bottle of champagne and several cards.'

'Thank you.' She took them and laid them aside.

'You're not even going to read them?'

She shrugged. 'What's the need? None of them will be signed.'

'Then how will you know who sent them?'

'I shall just have to guess. Now, let's eat.'

Breakfast was grapefruit, cereal and coffee, which suited him exactly. While he was eating she relented enough to put the red roses in a vase, but seemed content to leave the cards unopened.

Could any woman be so truly indifferent? he wondered. Were her admirers really surplus to requirements?

Or was this another facet of her personality?

But she was a witch, he remembered, a *strega magica,* changing before his eyes to bemuse and mystify him. And he had no choice but to follow where she led.

CHAPTER THREE

OVER coffee he said, 'Considering the mess I made of your car last night, you'd have been quite justified to have abandoned me to my fate.'

'Yes, I would,' she said promptly. 'I can't think why I didn't.'

'Perhaps you're a warm-hearted, forgiving person?'

She considered this seriously before dismissing it.

'That doesn't sound like me at all. There must be some other reason.'

'Maybe you preferred to keep me around so that you could inflict dire retribution?'

'*That* sounds much more like me,' she said triumphantly. 'How did you come to have such a nasty accident?'

'I forgot that the English drive on the wrong side of the road.'

His droll manner made her laugh again, but then she said, 'You really do spend most of your time in Italy, then?'

'A good deal. I'm at home in many places.'

'And you're part of Leonate, and that's why you're over here?'

'Uh-huh!' he said vaguely.

'And then you have to report back?'

'I shall certainly describe what I find, but I think, for the sake of my dignity, I'd better leave yesterday's events out of it. I wasn't trying to trap you. I just acted on impulse. I have a peculiar sense of humour.'

'I have no sense of humour at all,' Olympia said at once.

'That would account for it,' he said. 'I'll make a note of that for my report.' He pretended to write, reciting the words slowly. 'No—sense—of—humour—at—all.' He seemed to think for a moment before adding, 'Problem—to—be—considered—at—later—date. Suggest—dinner. Then—duck.'

'Get outa here,' she said, laughing reluctantly.

'Do you mean that literally?'

'No, I guess you can finish your breakfast first.'

They shared a grin, and he wished Luke could have been here to see him now. Luke often accused him of having no sense of humour, and that was true enough—with any other woman.

But this one brought laughter welling up inside him, filling the world with light and warmth. It was strange that she could be a witch as well, but he would solve that mystery later. Or maybe he would never solve it. For the moment he just wanted to be here.

'So what do you say?' he asked.

'About what?'

'About dinner. Shall I duck, or make a reservation at the Atelli Hotel?'

She was impressed by the name of London's newest luxury hotel.

'That sounds delightful,' she said. 'But only if you're well enough to go out.'

'I'm fine now. We'll have to see about the cars this morning. Where do you take yours for repairs?'

'There's a good place about a mile away. Are you sure about paying?'

'Quite sure,' he said firmly. 'Enough of that. Aren't you going to open those Valentine cards?'

He had resolved not to ask, but his will, so often a source of pride to him, seemed suddenly to be pitifully weak.

'I guess I might,' she said casually.

The first one was an elaborate confection of red satin and lace which had clearly cost a fortune. The message inside read,

I'll never forget. Will you?

He glanced at her face, but beyond a faint smile it revealed nothing.

Slowly she opened the other two. Both were large with pictures of flowers. Neither bore a name or a message.

But her face changed as she looked at them, growing soft, tender, with a smile that was pure delight. When he spoke to her she didn't hear him at first.

'I'm sorry, what was that?' she asked, sounding as if she'd been awoken from a dream.

'I said, you obviously know the two guys who sent those cards.'

'I know who sent them, yes,' she agreed, hoping he wouldn't notice how she'd changed the words.

'And they must feel fairly sure that—I mean—'

'They're both people I'm very fond of, and they know that.'

'Yes, that's what I figured. But doesn't it get a bit complicated?'

'Why should it?'

'Well—do they know about each other?'

'Of *course* they do. What do you take me for?'

He was beginning to wonder.

'Which one of them sent the flowers?'

Olympia shrugged mischievously.

She made no further comment, but when she rose to go to the kitchen she lingered a moment to caress the velvety roses and inhale their scent with her eyes closed and a look of exhilaration on her face.

'I'll go and get ready,' he said abruptly.

When the bedroom door had closed behind him she slipped into the bathroom and took out her cellphone, which she'd made sure of taking with her. Before dialling she turned on the water so that there was just enough noise to muffle her words.

She heard the ringing tone, then a familiar male voice. 'Hallo!'

'Dad? They're beautiful.'

'Ah, they got there.' His voice faded as he turned away and she heard him say, 'They arrived OK,' followed by a woman's squeal of excitement.

'And the cards,' she said. 'They're both lovely, but you shouldn't be so extravagant.'

'We couldn't decide between them, so we sent both.'

'You're mad, the pair of you.' She chuckled. 'What other parents send their daughter Valentine cards?'

'Well, like we said, darling, you changed the world, being born like that, when we'd given up hope. Here, your Mum wants to talk.'

Her mother's cheerful voice came down the line. 'Do you really like them, darling?'

'It's lovely, Mum—as always. But what about you?'

'Oh, I got roses too.'

'So I should hope.'

'And next year—maybe there'll be a real young man.' Her mother's voice was hopeful. 'Oh, I know you said never again, but your father and I are keeping our fingers crossed.'

'Don't hope for too much, Mum. You married the only decent guy around. After Dad they broke the mould.' Then an imp of mischief made her add, 'Actually, there's one here now.'

'You mean a man who stayed the night?'

'Yes.'

'In your bed?' Her mother sounded thrilled.

'*Mum!* You're nearly seventy. You're supposed to be old-fashioned and puritanical and tell me to save it for marriage.'

'Your Dad and I didn't. Anyway, one must move with the times.'

'Yes, he was in my bed, but don't get too excited. There's only one bed in the apartment and he had a concussion so I looked after him, and that's all.'

'Is he good-looking?'

'That really has nothing to do with it.'

'Oh, nonsense dear! It has *everything* to do with it.'

'Well—all right, yes, he's good-looking.'

'As how?'

'He's in his late thirties, tall and—well, his eyes are—really quite something.'

'What did he think about your cards and flowers?'

'He was—interested.'

'You didn't tell him they were from your parents, did you?'

Olympia chuckled. 'Nope. You taught me that much savvy.'

'That's right. Keep him guessing. Oh, this is lovely. I must tell your father. He'll be so excited.'

'Mum, you've got a wicked mind.'

'Of course, dear. It makes life so much more interesting. Are you going to see him again?'

'We're having dinner tonight.'

'*Harold!*' her mother shrieked. '*Guess what!*'

There was an indistinct mumbling, followed by her father's bellow of, 'Best of luck, darling!'

She hung up feeling happier, as she always did when talking to her parents. She could never quite figure out how those two had come this far without discovering that love and marriage were snares for fools. She only prayed that they never did discover it.

For herself, it was too late to forget what she had learned. The finer feelings were not for her. There was ambition, and there was having a good time. Tonight she was going to enjoy them both. Jack Cayman was charming company, although it was true, as she'd told her mother, that his good looks were an irrelevance.

But what really mattered was that he came from the centre of power; he would know Primo Rinucci and could tell her how to aim for her goal. Tough times and hard work lay ahead, but a person could have some fun in the meantime, couldn't she?

She had a small twinge of conscience that perhaps she was being unfair to him, but only a small one. This was how the game was played.

She was really looking forward to dinner that evening.

As he gathered his things together, ready to leave, Primo was aware of an extra presence inside his head. He knew it was his conscience, hurling abuse at him, but as it grew more troublesome it was developing a personality uncannily like his brother's in his more disagreeable moods. It even looked like Luke. He began thinking of it as Lucas.

You ought to be ashamed of yourself, it informed him sharply.

'It's just a joke that got a little out of hand. I'll tell

her the truth when the moment's right—say, about the second glass of champagne. Now shut up!'

As he emerged he found Olympia looking worried.

'Are you sure you're all right to drive?' she asked. 'Why not call the hire company from here?'

'No need. I'll see you tonight, wearing my glad rags. Goodbye for now.'

To his relief the car's damage was no more than an ugly dent, and it still moved well enough for him to get back to the hotel.

Lucas howled at him all the way.

This isn't the way to behave. What would Mamma say?

She's always telling me I should do something stupid. Well, I'm doing it. And how!

He'd said 'glad rags' so Olympia chose a floor-length velvet dress in dark green with a tight waist, clinging hips and a dramatic neckline. Her necklace and earrings were gold, and dainty high-heeled sandals gleamed on her feet.

She'd bought the whole outfit in anticipation of some future celebration—promotion?—but tonight was the start of a new life, and it would do fine.

She spent a long time getting her hair right. She didn't want to be the stern Miss Lincoln tonight. In the end she drew it back more loosely than usual, then twined it into long braids that she wound around her head, giving a softened effect.

When he arrived his eyes flickered over her just enough to be subtle and flattering. He said nothing, but he smiled.

She allowed her own eyes to do the same. In his bow-tie and dinner jacket he was more handsome than he had any right to be.

Downstairs he handed her gracefully into a new car.

'The hire firm actually let you have another?' she asked in disbelief.

'I talked them round. What about your garage?'

'The damage isn't too bad. I told them to send the bill to me, as we agreed.'

'Fine. I'll transfer the money into your bank on Monday morning.'

'No need. Just give me a cheque.'

He murmured something non-committal and slid away from the subject. It was dawning on him that he wasn't cut out for a double life. There was so much to remember. He would get her bank details from the firm and deposit the amount in cash so that he wouldn't have to give a name. Tonight he could have taken her to dine at the hotel where he was staying, but they knew him as Primo Rinucci, so that was out. When the bill for dinner came he would pay it in cash and brave the puzzled stares.

And in future he would 'go straight'. It was less tiring.

They swept into the Atelli, arm in arm, and were ushered to their table. It was good to be treated like a queen, she thought. This man knew how to entertain a woman and make her feel valued.

It flitted briefly across her mind that if only he were Primo Rinucci, how perfect everything would be. But she shut off the thought. That way lay weakness. Tonight was 'time out' with a delightful acquaintance. No more than that.

When the wine had been poured and the caviare served he raised his glass to her and she raised hers back.

'To a great evening and no strings,' he said.

Such an unnerving echo of her own thoughts gave her a jolt.

'No strings,' she said slowly.

'We're going to enjoy ourselves, and to blazes with the rest of them.'

'Absolutely,' she said.

Solemnly they chinked glasses.

Over caviare, she asked, 'What part of the country do you come from?'

'North London. I'll probably go back there for a visit. My father's dead but some of his relatives still live there.'

'How come you live in Italy?'

'I go back and forth. I have some Italian family and I'm just as much at home in either country, although Italy's warmer, especially Naples.'

'Naples,' she said, relishing the word. 'I've always liked the sound of it. It conjures up such pictures.'

'Urchins and cobbled streets?' he teased. 'Don't tell me you've fallen for the romantic myth?'

'Certainly not,' she said quickly. 'Myths merely get in the way of reality.'

'Maybe one can have too much reality,' he suggested.

But she shook her head decidedly.

'No. Reality is what counts.'

Once he would have said the same, but now reality was seeming less important by the minute. What mattered were the spells being woven in the air about them. And what was reality, anyway?

'I expect you'll see Naples soon enough,' he said.

'I wish I could.' She sighed.

'If you want to get anywhere in the firm, you need to be familiar with everything. Perhaps you should start learning Italian.'

'What do you mean, start?' she demanded, offended.

'Beg pardon, ma'am. How advanced are you?'

She responded with a flood of Italian words, not all of which were accurate, but it was still a pretty good effort. He was impressed.

'How was I?' she asked.

'Not bad at all. You've been working hard.'

'You bet I have! Not just since I knew about the takeover, but before that, since the first deal. I knew your firm was going to be important to us, and I wanted it to be me that did the wheeling and dealing.'

He was amazed at the intensity in her voice and the flashing of her eyes. Here was no ordinary ambition. There was a driven quality to her.

'Leonate had better look out,' he said. 'Before they know it you'll have taken over. Perhaps I should warn them.'

'No need. I can make my point for myself.'

'I'll bet you can,' he said with a touch of admiration. 'The question is, would they be wise to take you on?'

She laughed, but then sighed.

'It's easy to talk, but I thought the prize was within my grasp this time, and look what happened.'

'Curtis?' He shrugged. 'A minor prize. But now there are others, bigger, more glittering.'

'Exactly,' she said, brightening again. 'It's just a question of making the right moves and convincing the right man.'

'And who is the right man?'

She took a deep breath. Her eyes were gleaming with the thrill of the chase.

'Primo Rinucci,' she said.

He stared, jolted out of the happy dream that had begun to swirl around him.

'Who?'

'Primo Rinucci. He's the power in Leonate Europa, even I know that.'

'Yes, but—you hate him.'

'How can I when I don't know him?'

'Well, you sure gave a good imitation of it yesterday. "To hell with Primo Rinucci" was the kindest thing you said.'

She made an impatient gesture as if to say this was an irrelevance.

'That was just talk. Now it's time for serious business.'

'And he comes under the heading of serious business, does he?'

'Winning him over does, although it's going to be harder than I thought, since he isn't here.'

'That would make it more difficult,' he agreed solemnly.

'I suppose he didn't bother to come to England himself because we're not big enough to take up his attention.'

'You're not doing very much for my ego,' he complained.

'I didn't mean—'

'Of course you did. Be brave. Admit it. You reckon Signor Rinucci hasn't got time to inspect his English acquisition, so he sends the small fry, like me.'

'Not at all,' she said quickly. 'He sent you because you're an Englishman and therefore better able to understand what you find here.'

'Thank you, ma'am. That was a very clever recovery. You don't mean a word of it, of course, because if you thought I mattered a bean you'd be trying to impress me instead of waiting for my boss.'

She laughed and didn't deny it.

'I wouldn't get far trying to impress you now, would I?' she teased. 'It's too late. You already know the worst of me. But he doesn't.' She looked at him in sudden anxiety. 'You won't tell him, will you?'

'What, that you abused him?'

'No, that I'm lying in wait for him. I don't want him to be one step ahead of me, always knowing what I'm doing, do I?'

'No, you don't want that,' he agreed awkwardly.

'So you won't tell him about me?'

'Not unless he asks me direct questions,' he said 'which I'm sure he won't.'

'Good. Then I'm going to lure the lion into my den.'

He grinned. 'I guess I don't qualify as a lion.'

'I see you more as a bear,' she agreed, giving the matter serious thought. 'Brown and grizzly, with a growl that you have to listen to very carefully to work out what it means today. Is he ferocious or is he in a mood to have his fur stroked? Better get it right, or who knows what could happen?'

It was subtle. It was clever. It was beautifully calculated to butter him up and soothe him down and, heaven help him, he knew he was going to fall for it even while he could see her pulling the strings.

'Congratulations!' he said admiringly. 'At least I've had my warning. You'll use me for practice, until the real prey turns up.'

She turned on him, eyes shining gleefully, head on one side.

'You don't mind, do you?'

'How kind of you to ask! Would it make any difference if I did?'

'You could always refuse.'

Sure, he could refuse! Like a drowning man could refuse to go down for the third time!

He met her eyes.

'I'm considering my options,' he said. 'But have you thought of the practical difficulties?'

'How do you mean?'

'Aren't you going to find it a little hard, running a lion and a bear in tandem?'

'Ah, but suppose the bear's on my side and he's helping me, discreetly of course?'

'Helping you—how?' he asked, with well-founded caution.

'Inside information. Practical advice. We could be a great team.'

'A team implies an equal bargain,' he protested. 'Advantage on both sides. What do I get out of it?'

'What do you want to get out of it?' she teased.

Suddenly his head swam. What did he want to get out of it?

When the wild dance of his senses had calmed a little he managed to speak.

'If that means what I think it does,' he said softly, 'you're a shameless hussy.'

'Not at all. You know the score.'

'Maybe I have my own method of scoring.'

'That will only make it more interesting,' she murmured, so softly that he had to strain to hear, and her breath whispered across his face.

Out of sight, he gripped the table.

'You're a wicked woman,' he said appreciatively. 'Scheming, manipulative, dishonest—'

'No.' She laid a finger over his lips. 'I'm not dishonest. I'm completely upfront about what I want and what

I'll do to get it. That's honest. It doesn't make me a very nice person, but it does make me honest.'

'Olympia, for heaven's sake! What a way to talk! Anyway, what do you mean by ''inside information''?'

'What's the best way to approach him? What kind of woman does he like?'

'The kind he's married to,' he replied, straight-faced.

Her eyes opened wide. '*He's married?*'

'Suffocatingly married for the last twelve years. He has five children and his wife's a dragon with gimlet eyes. She's a jealous fiend who inspects all his female employees with a machine-gun in her hand.'

'But Cedric says—' She checked herself, finally seeing the glint in his eyes. She leaned back in her chair, glaring at him.

'I ought to squirt something at you for scaring me like that.'

'It's all true, I swear it.'

'True, nothing! He's a bachelor. Cedric told me.'

'So you've been pumping poor Cedric?' he exclaimed in unholy delight. 'I can't wait to hear what you offered *him.*'

Suddenly she could no longer meet his eyes. 'The usual,' she murmured.

'And just—what—is the usual?' he asked, smothering his unease.

'Well—you know—'

'*Tell me.*'

'Whatever his heart desires. It has to be that, or there's no point.'

He drew a long, painful breath. If she didn't answer soon, so help him, he was on the point of violence.

'And what did Cedric's heart desire?' he asked with a deadly smile.

Olympia looked around in both directions before replying in a low voice. 'Cedric has a *particular interest*. He doesn't talk a lot about it because—well, people are so quick to make judgements—'

'But he knew you'd understand?' Primo said grimly.

'Oh, yes. He's shown me his whole collection, and I was able to complete it. He was really pleased.'

'Complete it?'

'Yes, he collects videos about dinosaurs, and there was one he'd never been able to get hold of. Luckily my father had it, so I copied it for him. Cedric eats out of my hand now.'

He stared at her. 'Dinosaurs,' he said, dazed.

'Yes.'

'You got him a video about dinosaurs?' he repeated slowly.

'That was what his heart desired.'

Her eyes were full of fun, telling him he'd been well and truly had. He tried to quell his laughter but it welled up inside him, finally bursting out loud enough to startle a passing waiter.

'You tricky, devious—' he choked.

'But whatever did you think I meant?' she asked, wide-eyed and innocent.

'I daren't tell you. You'd probably slap my face.'

Of course she'd followed his every thought, because she was a black-haired witch who could tease a man into her glittering snares, even when he knew he ought to run a mile. That was the sensible thing to do.

But he'd been sensible all his life, and suddenly it was impossible.

CHAPTER FOUR

IT TOOK him a while to stop choking with laughter and sit shaking his head as he regarded her in delight.

'You should be ashamed of yourself,' she said sternly.

'So should you,' he riposted at once. 'Now tell me, was Cedric's information worth the price?'

'No, I'm afraid Cedric's knowledge is limited. He couldn't even say what Signor Rinucci looked like, although he's met him. "Tallish", is the best he could do.'

'Yes, I don't think noticing details is poor Cedric's strong suit.'

'But you'll know. Is he good-looking? What sort of things does he enjoy? Come on. Tell.'

'Are you planning to seduce him?' he asked, avoiding her eyes.

'Certainly not. I'll be far more subtle than that. Seduction merely complicates things. Besides, when you say seduction, what exactly do you mean?'

'I'm disappointed in you, Olympia. I thought you were a strong woman, not one who backed away from facts. You know exactly what seduction means. The whole thing. Admit it. You haven't thought this through.'

'Not thought it through? If you knew just how many hours, waking and sleeping, I've spent working out this—'

'But you've never gone as far as the logical conclusion.'

'Look, there's seduction and there's seduction—'

'No, there isn't. There's only seduction, and you'd better know what you mean by it before you set out after this man. He'll want far more than a dinosaur video. Just how far are you prepared to go?'

'Not that far. What do you take me for?'

'A woman prepared to put her ambition before everything else. Before love, before happiness, before being a person.'

'That depends on what you mean by being a person. To me it means being a success. I want to impress him with my knowledge of business, my ability to speak his language, my willingness to commit myself to the job one hundred per cent.'

'And you're not going to use your womanly wiles at all? Is that it?'

She shrugged lightly. 'I may not be the kind of woman he likes.'

'Oh, he likes them all,' Primo said, throwing caution to the winds. 'He's dangerous.'

'Dangerous, how?' she asked eagerly.

He racked his brain, searching for ways to describe his 'other' self. He was beginning to find this exhilarating.

'He's a womaniser,' he said recklessly, 'a man without discrimination. If you've got any sense, you won't tangle with him.'

'Oh, but I love a challenge.'

'But he won't be a challenge. It's too easy to attract him on that level, but what happens afterwards?'

'Then I'll move on to Plan B.'

'You've got it all worked out,' he observed wryly.

'You have to work things out to get what you want.'

'And Primo Rinucci is what you want?'

'Not him personally. What I want is his power and influence.'

'And his money?'

'Not at all,' she said, shocked. 'Just his power. I can make my own money.'

'I just can't work you out.'

'Excellent. Then I'm on the right track. He mustn't be able to work me out either.'

'Can we forget Rinucci?' he said, a tad edgily. 'There are some holes in your reasoning that you'll have to consider later, but I'd prefer not to spend this evening on the subject.'

'What?' she said at once. 'What holes?'

He sighed and gave in. 'Well, for a start, there's the troop of lovers that you seem to keep dancing after you. Won't they get in the way rather?'

'What troop of lovers? I don't have any lovers. At least—' She seemed to consider. 'No,' she said at last. 'Not at the moment.'

'Admirers then. All those cards this morning, two without a message and one that said, *"I'll never forget"*. Who is he, and what won't he forget?'

'Ah, that was from Brendan,' she said with a smile. 'We had a flirtation a few years back and I get a card every year.'

'A flirtation, was it?' he couldn't resist saying.

'Brendan's a great one for pretty gestures at a safe distance. He always makes sure he's on the other side of the world in February. This came from Australia.'

'And the other two? And the red roses?'

Suddenly she burst out laughing, not a soft teasing sound but a chuckle of genuine mirth.

'You won't believe me when I tell you.'

'Try me.'

'They were from my parents.'

'*"To the one and only, the girl who transformed the world"*,' he quoted.

'They'd been married twenty years before I came along, and they'd given up hope. As long as I can remember they've sent me Valentine cards and flowers with messages about how I changed the world for them. They're such darlings.'

'Well, I'll be—is that for real?'

'Yes, I swear it's the truth. Didn't you see their picture on the bookcase?'

'Yes, but I thought they must be your grandparents.'

'That's because they're both nearly seventy.'

'But why didn't you tell me this morning?'

'Because I was enjoying myself. I don't mind being thought of as a woman with a host of admirers.'

'Miss Lincoln, you have the soul of a tease.'

'Sure I have. It's very useful. My husband got quite uptight about those cards at first. Right to the end I'm not sure he really believed my parents sent them.'

'The end? You're a widow?'

'Oh, no, he's still alive. He came close to meeting a sudden end a few times but I resisted that temptation.'

'Your better self asserted itself.'

'No, I don't have a better self,' she said cheerfully. 'He just wasn't worth the hassle. With my luck, I'd never have got away with it, so I let him live.'

She finished with a shrug, as though the whole thing was just too trivial for words, but he felt as though he'd had a glimpse through a keyhole. It was narrow, but the details he could see suggested a whole vista, waiting to be revealed.

The waiter appeared to clear away their plates.

'I gather he didn't deserve to live,' Primo said casually.

'That's what I thought, but I'm probably doing him an injustice. He wasn't really the monster I made him into. I told myself that love conquered all, and then blamed him when that turned out to be nonsense. And we married too young. I was eighteen, he was twenty-one. I suppose we changed into different people—or discovered the people we really were all the time.'

'I don't think this is who you really were all the time,' he said with sudden urgency. 'This is what he did to you.'

'He taught me a lot of things, including the value of total and utter selfishness. Boy, is that ever the way to get ahead! Tunnel vision. Wear blinkers and look straight down the line to what you want.'

He'd often said the same himself, but he couldn't bear hearing his own ruthlessness from her.

'Don't,' he said, reaching out swiftly and laying a finger over her lips. 'Don't talk like that.'

'You're right,' she said, moving her lips against his finger before he drew it away. 'It's too revealing, isn't it? I need a better act. How lucky that I have you to practise on.'

'Yes, isn't it?' he said wryly.

'I mean that I don't have to pretend with you. We can afford honesty. Why, what is it?' She'd seen his sudden unease.

'Nothing,' he said quickly. 'But the waiter wants to serve the next course.'

The mention of honesty had reminded him that he was sailing under false colours. But at the same time he had an exhilarating feeling of having found a new kind of honesty. His heart was open to her, his defences down as never before. Was this what Hope had been trying to tell him all the time?

'So your husband taught you all about selfishness?' he said.

'I guess I was a willing learner.'

It hurt him to hear her slander herself, but she seemed driven to do it, as though that way she could erect a defensive shield against the world.

'Did you ever want children?'

She hesitated a long time before saying, 'I wanted *his* children. I hadn't thought of myself as the maternal type at first. It was going to be a career for me, although I thought I'd probably want children later. Then I'd find a way to juggle them both.'

'So the career wasn't going to be everything to you?' he asked cautiously. 'Not like now.'

'No, not like now. But then I met David and it overturned all my ideas. I wanted to be his wife and have his babies so much that it hurt.

'Somehow it was never the right time for him. He said we were too young—which I suppose we were, and there were "things to do first". That's how he put it. I just said yes to whatever he wanted. It seemed a fair bargain as long as he loved me.'

She said the words with no deliberate attempt at pathos, but with a kind of incredulous wonder that anyone could believe such stuff.

'But he didn't,' Primo said gently.

She made no reply. She was barely conscious of him. Something had drawn her back into the person she used to be, naïve, giving and totally, blindly in love. The impression was so strong that she could almost feel David there again—confident, charming, with the ability to take her to the top of the world—then dash her down.

Never again.

'No, he didn't,' she said. 'I was useful to him, but only for a while. He used to wear expensive clothes because he had to make a good impression at work. I made do with the cheapest I could find because who cared what I looked like?'

'Didn't he?'

'You should have heard him on that subject. He was very good. "Darling, it doesn't matter whether your dress is costly or the cheapest thing in the market. To me, you're always beautiful." What is it?'

She asked the question because he had covered his eyes in anguish.

'I can't bear this,' he said. 'It's such a corny line. I thought it was dead and buried years ago.'

'Well, it rose from the grave,' she said tartly. 'And, to save you asking, yes, I fell for it. Hook, line and sinker.'

'I'll bet *he* wasn't wearing the cheapest thing on the market.'

'You're right. I bought him a shirt once—not expensive, but I thought it was nice. He sat me down, explained that he couldn't be seen in it, and asked if I had the receipt. He returned it to the shop, got the money back, then added some money of his own to buy what he called "a decent one". It was his way of letting me know what was good enough for him and what wasn't.'

'And you let him live?' Primo demanded, scandalised.

'I think I was kind of hypnotised by him. I wouldn't let myself believe what I was discovering. And he looked fantastic in the new shirt. If a man's incredibly handsome you somehow don't think he can be a jerk.'

She lapsed into silence and sat brooding into her glass,

trying to make a difficult decision. What came next was something she'd never been able to speak of before.

Yet here she was, on the verge of telling her most painful secret to a man she'd known only a day. But that day might have been a year, she seemed to know him so well. All her instincts reassured her that he was a friend and she could trust him with anything.

'Tell me,' he said gently. 'What happened then?'

She gave a faint smile.

'He had to work on a marketing project. By that time I had a job in the same firm. I was down at the bottom of the ladder but I understood the business and I helped him with the project. I'd done that before and, if I say it myself, the best ideas in that project were mine.

'In fact the layout and presentation were mine too. He used to say that my talent was knowing how to say things. I was flattered, until it dawned on me that what he really meant was that he was the one with talent, and all I could do was the superficial stuff.'

'But firms will pay big money for someone who can do "the superficial stuff". It's what marketing and presentation is about, and I'm surprised you don't know that.'

She gave him a shy smile that went to his heart.

'Well, I do know it now,' she said. 'But not then. I didn't understand a lot of things then. As far as I knew, David was the great talent in the family.'

'Because that's what he kept telling you?'

'Yes.'

'Meanwhile he stole your ideas and used them to climb the ladder?'

'He was promoted to be the boss's deputy. That's how he met the boss's daughter, who was also working there. One day I went up to the top floor to pay him a surprise visit. We'd had a row and I wanted to make up. Rosalie was there, leaning forward over his desk, with her head close to his.

'She scowled and demanded to know who I was, looking down her nose at me. I told her I was David's wife and she gasped. He hadn't told her he was married. Nobody in the firm knew. Our surname was Smith, which is so common that nobody made the connection.

'That night he came home late. I spent the time crying, like the wimp I was. When he got home we had a big fight. I said how dare he pretend I didn't exist, and he looked me up and down and said, "Why would I want to tell anyone about you?"'

'*Bastardo!*'

'I had nothing to say. She was so beautiful and perfectly groomed, and I was so dowdy. Soon after that we split up. There was a divorce and he married Rosalie. Since then he's gone right to the top.'

'Of course,' he said cynically. 'The boss's son-in-law always goes to the top.'

She nodded. 'His father-in-law is a rich man with a lot of power.' She gave a curt laugh. 'David has two children now. A friend of mine has seen them. She says they're beautiful.'

'And they should have been yours,' he said gently.

She was suddenly unable to speak. But then she recovered and said, 'No, of course not. That's just being sentimental. When the divorce came through I did a lot more crying, so much that I reckon I've used up all my tears for the rest of my life. That's what I promised myself, anyway. That was when I resumed my maiden name.

'It's silly to brood about the past. You can't rewrite

it. You can only make sure that the future is better. And that's what I'm determined to do.'

Primo didn't know what to say. She seemed to speak lightly but her manner was still charged with emotion. What unsettled him most was the way she'd revealed her pain with the sudden force of someone breaking boundaries for the first time. Now she seemed to be withdrawing back into herself, as if regretting the brief intimacy she'd permitted.

She confirmed it when she laughed and said, 'And that's the story of my life.'

'No, not your life, just one bad experience. But don't judge all men by your husband. Some of us have redeeming qualities.'

'Of course. I like men. I enjoy their company. But I'm always waiting for that moment when the true face shows through.'

'But suppose you saw the true face at the start,' he suggested, fencing, hoping to draw her out further.

'Does any man show his true face at the start?' she fenced back. 'Did you, for instance?'

'Yes, let's forget about that,' he said hastily. 'I prefer to talk some more about you.'

'Why? Is the truth about you so very terrible?'

He was wildly tempted to say that the truth about himself was something she wouldn't believe. But he recovered his sanity in time.

'Tell me about the new Olympia, the one who knows that love is nonsense.'

'At least she knows it's something you have to be realistic about.'

'I think you could lose a lot by being that sort of realist.'

'But don't you believe a person's head should rule their heart, and they should avoid stupid risks?'

'No, I don't,' he said, aghast. 'You could hardly say anything worse about any man.'

'Not at all. They're admirable qualities.'

'Yes, for a dummy in a shop window.'

'Have I offended you?'

'Yes,' he growled.

'But why? Most men like to be admired for their brains and common sense.'

He recovered his good humour.

'You've observed that, have you? Is it on your list of effective techniques for use against Rinucci? Item one, sub-section A. Make breathless comments about size of brain and staggering use thereof. Note: Try to sound convincing, however difficult. Sub-section B. Suggest that—'

'Stop it,' she said, laughing. 'Anyway, I don't know if it would work with him. Is he intelligent enough to make admiration of his brains convincing?'

'It doesn't matter. If he isn't, he'll never know the difference.'

'That's true,' she said, much struck.

'Personally I've always considered him rather a stupid man.'

'Stupid in what way?' she wanted to know.

'In every way.'

'Stupid in every way,' she repeated. 'That's a start.'

Primo grinned suddenly and hailed a passing waiter.

'Would you bring the lady a notebook and pencil, please?' he asked. 'She has urgent notes to make.' Turning back to Olympia, he said, 'Of course, if you were really applying yourself to the job, you'd have brought them with you.'

'I wasn't exactly prepared for the conversation to be so promising.'

'Always be prepared. You never know where any conversation might lead—*what are you writing?*'

'Always—be—prepared—' she said, her eyes fixed on the notebook which the waiter had just placed before her. Then she raised them and fixed them admiringly on his face. 'How clever you are! I'd never have thought of a difficult concept like that for myself.'

'Behave yourself,' he said in a voice that shook with laughter.

'But I was admiring your brilliant advice.'

'You were using me for target practice.'

'Well, some targets are more fun to practise on than others.'

The significant chuckle in her voice was almost his undoing. He longed to ask her to expand on the subject, but he felt she'd had it all her own way long enough.

'Enough,' he said severely. 'If you're going to do this, do it properly. Don't be obvious. Even a fool like Rinucci could see through that.'

'Really? Never mind, you can tell me what else to say. How old is he?'

'About my age.'

'That's young to be in his position.'

'He relies a lot on family influence,' Primo said, ruthlessly sacrificing his own reputation.

'It's going to take a lot of work filling this notebook. I'll need a section for his interests, clothes—'

'He's a fancy dresser. More money than sense. Ah, but I forgot. You're not interested in his money.'

'That's right. I just want to run him to earth, rope and brand him—'

'And generally get him in a state of total subjection.'

'You got it. And then—'

'Olympia, could we possibly drop the subject of Primo Rinucci?' he asked plaintively. 'He really isn't a very interesting man.'

'I'm sorry. Of course he isn't interesting to you.'

The waiter, proffering the sweet menu, saved him from having to answer, and after that he managed to divert her on to another subject.

At last she said, 'Maybe we should go. I should go to work tomorrow, to impress the boss.'

'But it is Sunday and he isn't here.'

'I meant you.'

'Yes, right—I'm getting confused. Let's go.'

On the way home they talked in a relaxed, disjointed way, then made the last part of the journey in silence. When he drew up and looked over to her he saw that she was asleep.

Her breathing was so soft that he could hardly hear it. She slept like a contented child, her face softened, all the tension smoothed out. There was even a faint smile on her lips, as though she'd found a rare moment of contentment.

He moved closer, charmed by the way her long black lashes lay against her cheek. If this had been any other woman, on any other night, he would have leaned down and laid his mouth against hers, teasing gently until she awoke and her lips parted under his. Then he would have taken her into his arms, letting her head rest against his shoulder and her hair spread out, flowing over his arm.

They would have held each other for a long moment before he finally murmured a question and she whispered her assent. Then, perhaps, they would have made their way together up to her apartment and closed the door behind them.

So many evenings had ended that way, in tenderness, pleasure and passion. But not with her.

With this woman passion was forbidden. Only tenderness was allowed, and so he watched her silently for several minutes, holding her hand but making no other move, until she opened her eyes and he said, in a shaking voice, 'I think you should go upstairs now. You won't mind if I don't escort you to your door, will you?'

He watched her walk into the building and kept his eyes on the windows he knew were hers until he saw the lights go on. Then he drove away quickly while he was still safe.

CHAPTER FIVE

As DAWN broke Olympia became half awake, seeming to exist in a limbo where there were no facts, only feelings and misty uncertainties, but they were very sweet. Perhaps more sweet for being undefined.

She seemed to be back in his car, dozing as they made the journey home. She couldn't see or hear him, but she was intensely aware of him. When he took her hand in his she was pervaded by a sense of deep contentment, as though she had come home to a place of safety, where lived the only person who understood.

She was smiling as she opened her eyes.

For once, the hours ahead of her were unknown, the decisions in the hand of someone else. After only two days he already seemed to fill her world. She was looking forward to the moment when she would meet him today and see in his eyes that he remembered last night, how they'd laughed and gazed into each other's minds and recognised what they found there.

When the phone rang she snatched it up eagerly.

'Olympia?'

'Jack? I knew it would be you.'

'Why? Did the ring sound impatient?'

She laughed, feeling excited. He was impatient to see her. He'd called to suggest a meeting today.

'Well, yes,' she said. 'It did sound a little impatient.'

'That's because I'm going through books and realising how much there is to do. If I spend the rest of the day working I'll just be ready to leave tomorrow. It ought to be today, of course, but since it's Sunday it'll have to wait.'

'Did you say you were leaving?' she asked, in shock, as much because of his businesslike tone as his words.

'I need to see the rest of the Curtis empire.'

'Empire? You mean the two other tiny factories?'

'That's right. I've studied them on-line and through correspondence. Now I want you to show them to me. Pack clothes for several days away, and I'll collect you first thing tomorrow. Bye for now.'

He hung up without further discussion, leaving her wondering if he was the same man as the night before.

The impression was reinforced when they met the next day. He was pleasant but impersonal. The evening they had spent together might never have happened.

Hadson's, the first factory, was in the south. As he drove they discussed business, how this small, out of the way place had come to be acquired, the computer peripherals that it made, how economic was it. Olympia spoke carefully, unwilling to be the one who revealed the awkward truth about Hadson's, which was that it was too small to survive. He would see it soon enough.

'You've gone very quiet,' he said at last.

'I've given you the facts and figures, but you need to form your own impression.'

To her relief he didn't press her further.

'Shall I call to say we're coming?'

'No, it's better to take them by surprise,' he replied coolly.

In another hour they reached the little village of Andelwick and went to the factory, where the surprise was very obvious. So was the alarm, almost fear. Introducing the forty staff, Olympia praised every one of them individually, trying to keep a pleading note out of her voice. Sounding desperate would not help them.

He was charming to everyone and invited the three senior staff to lunch. There he drew facts and figures out of them with skill and so much subtlety that they might not have guessed what lay behind it. But they did, Olympia realised with a sinking heart. They already knew the worst.

When they were alone he looked at her and said, 'Hmm!'

'Don't you dare say "Hmm!" to me,' she exploded. 'I know what you're thinking.'

'I'm thinking we're going to have to stay overnight. Is there a good hotel?'

'No hotels in this tiny place, but The Rising Sun does rooms. It's a nice pub, basic but clean, and the food's great. It's just down the road.'

'Fine. Will you go there now and do the bookings? Oh—and—' he was suddenly awkward '—I seem to have left my credit cards behind. Could you use yours?'

'Sure, no problem.'

He spent the afternoon studying the books, said 'Hmm!' again, and swept her off to The Rising Sun, an old, traditional building where she'd booked two tiny rooms with such low oak beams that it was hard to walk upright.

As she'd promised, the food was excellent and gave them vigour for the fight.

'You can't just dump this place,' she said fiercely.

'It's not viable, Olympia. You can see that for yourself. Forty employees!'

'Who all work their socks off for you.'

'They're now part of an international conglomerate—'

'So loyalty doesn't matter any more?'

'Will you let me get a word in edgeways? It might have been viable until two years ago, but now there's that other place, just down the road, Kellway's—who are operating in much the same line of work.'

'The council should never have allowed them to start up. They're just trying to squeeze us out of business.'

'Us?'

'Hadson's. It's just a unit of productivity to you, isn't it?'

'It's my job to see things in that way.'

'And to hell with the people! But Mr Jakes is a sweet old man and he's been the backbone of this place for years.'

'Perhaps he's ready to put his feet up?'

'No way, he loves that job and he wants to stick with it. And what about Jenny? It's her first job and she's so keen.'

'Yes, but—'

'And jobs are very hard to come by in this area. Did you know that? No, of course you didn't. All you care about is books of figures and money.'

'That's all I'm supposed to care about. And so are you.'

She missed the warning, yielding to the anger that was carrying her along.

'They're people, not just statistics.'

'This is business.'

'*To hell with business!*'

Silence.

He was regarding her wryly.

'If Primo Rinucci heard you say that, you'd be dead,' he observed.

Aghast, she saw the trap she'd created for herself.

'But he didn't hear me,' she said. 'Only you.'

'Only me,' he agreed with an odd inflection in his voice that she couldn't quite understand. 'I won't tell him, but sooner or later the truth will out.'

'What truth?' she asked in a hollow voice.

'That underneath that calculating, hard-as-nails exterior you've so carefully painted on there's a soft-hearted, empathetic, generous human being.'

'It's a lie,' she said fiercely.

He grinned and took a swig of the local beer before asking, 'Where did you get all that detailed knowledge of Hadson's?'

'I spent a week there once.'

'And got to know them all as people?'

'I did a detailed survey of the situation, as my job required,' she said stiffly.

'And made friends with them,' he persisted remorselessly. 'Liked them, felt for them.'

'I suppose one can be a human being without becoming an automaton.'

'Not really. Sooner or later the choice has to be made. My dear girl—'

'Don't call me that. I'm not a girl, I'm not yours and I'm not dear to you.'

'Isn't that for me to say?' he asked quietly.

She was silent a moment before saying, equally quietly, 'That's enough!'

He shrugged. 'Whatever pleases you. It's time I went to my room and spent some more time in the soulless pursuit of money. Goodnight.'

He left her there, wondering how she could ever have thought he was a nice guy. He was a monster who called her vile, unspeakable names.

Soft-hearted. Empathetic. *Generous* for Pete's sake!

She would never forgive him!

The following morning she rose to find that he had compounded his crimes. There was no sign of him at breakfast, only a note.

I'm tied up this morning, but I'll join you at Hadson's later. JC

Brusque to the point of discourtesy, she fumed. Perhaps he found writing difficult. He certainly seemed to have had a problem at the end of the note because there was an inky smudge just before his initials, as though he'd started to write something else, then scrubbed it out. Maybe he didn't know his own initials, she thought uncharitably.

Her morning at Hadson's wasn't happy. They all suspected the worst, and she could only confirm it.

'He says the place isn't viable,' she said with a sigh. 'It's just a matter of time now. I'm so sorry.'

'We know you did your best,' Mr Jakes told her and the others murmured agreement.

She was left feeling cast down. She had mishandled the whole business, failed to save their jobs and they were being nice to her. She could have wept.

He turned up in the middle of the afternoon and was received in near silence.

'Sorry to keep you waiting, everyone,' he said, apparently oblivious to the atmosphere. 'This morning's business took longer than I expected, owing to Mr Kellway's difficulty in making up his mind. But in the end he saw things the right way.'

'You've been to Kellway's?' Olympia asked, astounded.

'I've bought it. There's no room for both of you, so

there'll be a merger. Those who want to continue working are guaranteed a job at Kellway's. Those who don't can apply for voluntary redundancy.'

Forty faces turned accusingly towards Olympia.

'But she said you were going to close us down and chuck us out,' Mr Jakes said.

'Did you say that?' Jack Cayman asked.

'I—not in those exact words. But you said—'

'I said this place wasn't viable, and it isn't, on its own. A merger makes sense. I never mentioned chucking people out. That was your spin. You shouldn't jump to conclusions.'

'I—'

'Before we leave we'd better sort out who wants to stay and who doesn't. Mr Jakes, your position is protected. Kellway's is eager to get you.'

'You mean I don't get the redundancy?' Mr Jakes demanded.

'Of course, if you want it.'

'You bet I want it. I can go and see my daughter in Australia.'

Olympia stared. Was there anything she hadn't got wrong?

It took a couple of hours before they were ready to leave and then the cheers followed them. As they walked back to the pub he said, 'Do we have time to reach the other place tonight?'

'Just about.'

She took the wheel for the three hour drive. They said little on the journey, each saving energy for what was to come. This time the journey was to the Midlands and they managed to find a small hotel, just in time for the last serving of dinner.

Only when they were sitting over the soup did she say crossly, 'You made a complete fool of me.'

'I didn't mean to. You shouldn't have made that announcement without consulting me first.'

'I never thought you'd do anything like that. Anyway, suppose Signor Rinucci doesn't agree with you about this purchase?'

'He will.'

'Just like that?'

'Why not? It's the logical next step. You didn't see it because you haven't the right mindset, but you'll learn.'

'The right mindset for Leonate, you mean?'

'No, for any successful business. You're still thinking on a small scale and that's no use for an international conglomerate.'

'So how do I learn to think "international" if I can't get to meet the big boss?'

'Still fixated on him, huh?'

'You knew that.'

'Nothing's changed?'

'Nothing,' she said firmly.

'What about all that warmth and humanity you were showing signs of?'

'An aberration. I'll get over it. Besides, look what a mess I made. I got Mr Jakes all wrong. But you didn't,' she added as the realisation came to her. 'You understood him.'

'So maybe I'm not just figures and accounts?' he said with a slight inflection of teasing.

'Did I say that? I don't remember.'

'You're tired. That was a long drive and we have a lot to get through tomorrow. Let's finish the meal and get some rest.'

She was only too glad to agree. She felt as though

something had knocked her sideways, but she couldn't quite work out what it was.

Tired as she was, she found it hard to sleep. Lying awake for hours, she became aware of him on the other side of the thin wall. She could hear his bed creak, his footsteps on the floor, his window being pushed up as if he were drinking in the night air, then his bed again, sounding as though he were tossing and turning.

She wondered what he was thinking and why he should be as restless as herself.

The next day was more successful. As before, they arrived without warning and walked in as the manager was talking with a dissatisfied customer. It soon became clear that a trivial matter had been blown out of all proportion, chiefly because the customer had a quarrelsome nature.

He was inclined to take umbrage at the new arrivals, but within minutes Olympia had taken over, dazzled the man with her smile and calmed him down to the point where a sensible conversation became possible.

By the time she had finished, the order was not only rescued but increased and the customer was purring with content. Primo took them all to lunch and kept the manager locked in conversation while Olympia completed her demolition job on the customer.

They left town in time to get back to London quite early and laughed all the way.

'You did a great job,' he told her. 'I've never seen a fish reeled in so cleverly. How about we celebrate tonight?'

Her answer was a blissful sigh.

In mid-afternoon he dropped her at her apartment block.

'We'll go to The Diamond Parrot,' he said, naming

London's newest and plushest nightclub. 'Do you have a black dress?'

'I think so,' she said cautiously, knowing that she hadn't.

'Well, you'd better take the rest of the afternoon off to make sure,' he said, understanding perfectly.

He might have meant any kind of black dress, but the one she purchased was definitely slinky. It was made from silk and hugged her hips in a satisfactory way. When he saw it he gave a nod of satisfaction.

'That's just how I imagined you when I bought this,' he said, producing a black velvet box.

Inside was a delicate set of diamond earrings and matching pendant.

'A bonus for a job well done,' he said.

'From the firm?'

'Certainly from the firm. We cherish our valuable employees.'

He watched as she slipped the earrings into place, then turned so that he could drape the pendant around her neck. To his dismay he discovered that he was reluctant. Her long neck was white and perfect, an invitation that he must not accept. He tried to fasten the clasp without touching her, then backed off quickly, lest he yield to the temptation to drop a kiss on her nape.

'Fine, let's go,' he said in a voice that he hoped didn't shake.

She looked around with a little frown, as though in surprise. He turned away from that surprise, afraid of the insight it might create. She must never guess, not until he was ready to tell her, and they could laugh together, sharing the moment of discovery.

That time, when it came, would be sweet. But it couldn't be rushed without risking everything.

He hadn't yet defined what 'everything' might mean, but he knew that with each word, each step he had to be more careful. If this had been a conventional relationship he would have often taken her into his arms by now, kissing her long and fervently, letting passion take them wherever it might. But that was forbidden while she didn't know the truth. Even his thoughts were forbidden, although the struggle to rein them in grew harder every moment.

It was like conducting a clandestine relationship with a married woman, he thought in frustration. Except that he, himself, was the betrayed 'husband'.

Suddenly the evening ahead didn't seem like such a good idea. She would sit beside him, beautiful, glowing, and he must try to stay calm.

He groaned.

They found The Diamond Parrot in festive mode, having decided to make St Valentine's Day last a while longer.

'St Valentine's Week,' he murmured as they entered through dark red velvet curtains. 'It's original. I wish I could say the same about the roses and the glittering hearts.'

'They've really overdone it, haven't they?' Olympia chuckled.

A waiter showed them to a table on the edge of the dance floor. One or two couples were already smooching around to the music of a small band and a glittery chanteuse who crooned about moon and June.

For a while they talked little, but relaxed after the hard work of the last two days. Olympia felt good, knowing she had impressed him, and knowing also that she looked her best. From time to time she touched the delicate diamonds about her neck, puzzled again by the constraint she had sensed in his manner as he'd clasped it about her neck.

She had waited for the feel of his fingers gently caressing the sensitive nape, as any other man would have done. But there had been nothing but the most impersonal touch as he'd fixed the clasp. She hadn't even felt his breath against her skin, as though he were standing back to avoid her.

'You shouldn't be here,' she said. 'You should be making your report to Head Office.'

'After the roller coaster of the last few days I need to think about what I'm going to say. You make it difficult because you're never the same person from one moment to the next.'

'You don't have to tell them about me as a person, just as a businesswoman.'

'As a businesswoman you're impressive. What you did with that customer today—well—'

'That's just part of my repertoire,' she said with a chuckle. 'The trick is to get his attention first with the old-fashioned fluttering eye technique. Then, when he's got you down as a stupid bimbo, you bash him over the head with facts and figures. Leaves 'em reeling every time.'

'You're good at the fluttering eye bit, I take it.'

'Yes, but if you do it slowly it's more effective.

She gave a long sigh, lowering and raising her eyelids just once, very slowly. He drew a sharp breath. It was like seeing her eyes for the first time ever, unprepared for their impact. To make it worse, she gave a languorous smile, letting her lips fall apart very slightly.

'Is that what you plan to do with him?' he asked.

'Him?' she asked vaguely. 'Who?'

'Primo Rinucci.'

She was suddenly angry. Why did he have to drag Primo Rinucci into everything?

'You think that'll work, huh?' she asked in a slightly edgy voice.

'Sure to. Especially with all the practice you're getting on me. Teasing is always a good bet, especially when you manage to keep your distance at the same time. It'll stop him getting the wrong ideas. Either that or it'll incite him to more ideas. One of the two. You'll have to decide which you want. It wouldn't do to become confused.'

'It may not give him any ideas at all,' she couldn't resist saying. 'It seems to leave you cold.'

'It isn't supposed to give me ideas,' he pointed out. 'I'm just here to help you in your mission in life. When you've sharpened your claws on me, you'll bring your lion down.'

She chuckled suddenly.

'When I've done that, will you take pictures of me standing with one foot on his helpless form, like the old hunters used to do?'

'I'll even help you mount his head on the wall,' he promised. 'You can put it in the centre of all the other trophies.'

'What other trophies?'

'The others you've used for practice, with my head in the centre.'

'Uh-uh!' she said, shaking her head. 'You can stay cool about it. That's what makes you so valuable.'

It was a let-out and he should have seized it, but some demon urged him on to say, 'I should have thought it made me useless. If nothing works with me, how are you going to know what works with him?'

'Aha!' She seemed much struck by this point of view.

After considering for a moment she asked, 'Do you and he have the same tastes?'

'Pretty similar,' he said, crossing his fingers and wishing he'd never started this.

'Is he—or you—sophisticated or corny?'

'How do you mean, corny?'

'You remember those old Hollywood films where the heroine wore her hair tight back, then pulled it loose to signify that she was starting a new life? That kind of corny.'

'I don't think I ever saw those films,' he said, rashly tempting fate.

'Like this.'

With a swift movement, she tugged at her hair so that it came free, flooding over her bare shoulders like a black silky fountain. Some of it fell down the sides of her face, throwing her features into mysterious shadow.

Una strega. Una bellissima strega magica.

'That's how they do it,' she said, 'and the hero takes one look at her and goes gaga, because he's thinking, How can that grim-faced harpy have turned into this seductive creature? And she doesn't tell him the truth, which is that it took six hours and the entire make-up department, and if he's fool enough to marry her it's the grim harpy he'll find on the pillow in the morning. Oh, no, she lets him think it's the power of *ler-rrve*.'

The satirical inflection she put on the last word had him choking with laughter. At the same time, he wished she hadn't used the words 'pillow' and 'in the morning'. This was hard enough without her turning it into a testing ground for self-control.

'They tend to believe in *ler-rrve* in films,' he said. 'If they showed your point of view, nobody would go. No—leave it as it is.' She'd begun drawing her hair back again. 'Keep it like that while I do some thinking. It might give me some ideas to improve your technique.'

'I'm glad you have a sense of proportion about this,' she said. 'It's a great help. Unless—' She stopped as a horrible thought assailed her. 'Jack, you're not—? I mean, this isn't all pointless, is it? You'd have told me?'

'Told you what?'

'You know what I mean.'

'No, I don't.' In fact he did, but he'd be blowed if he'd let her off the hook that easily. Let her suffer for a change.

'You're not—are you?'

He gave her a twisted smile. 'Are you trying to ask me if I'm gay?'

'Well—are you?'

'On the principle that anyone who doesn't try to rush you into bed is pointing in the other direction? Hm! Well, it's a thought.'

'*Are you?*'

'Would it matter?'

'Of course it would matter. How could you advise me about him if you—?'

'Well, maybe he is too.'

'Is he?'

'How would I know? I've never propositioned him.'

She glared at him. 'Have I been wasting my time?'

'Doesn't your womanly intuition tell you one way or the other?' He was getting his own back now and it felt great. 'Am I not interested, or am I simply the perfect gentleman? Strange how hard it is to tell the difference these days.'

'You're enjoying this, aren't you?' she fumed.

'You bet I am. And why shouldn't I? The joke's been on me all this time, now it's your turn.'

'What do you mean? How has the joke been on you?'

With his feet at the very edge of the precipice, he pulled back sharply. He'd forgotten how little she knew.

'Nothing,' he said quickly.

'It must have meant something.'

'Then I'll just leave you to wonder. And in the meantime—Olympia—Olympia?'

The speed with which she'd switched her attention away from him would have been comic if it hadn't been dismaying. Now she was looking out into the semi-darkness on the dance floor.

'What is it?' he asked, taking her hand and squeezing it to get her attention.

'Nothing, I—I must have imagined it.'

'Whatever you imagined seems to have upset you. Can't you tell me?'

'I just thought I saw someone I knew—but in this light I'm probably mistaken.'

Unconsciously her hand had tightened on his until he winced from the pressure.

'Who is it?' he asked.

'My ex-husband.'

CHAPTER SIX

HE STARED at her. 'Your ex? Are you sure?'

'Yes, that's David—I think.'

'Does it matter?' he asked, shocked to realise that she was trembling. 'It's not as though you still love him—do you?'

'No, of course not. But it's the first time I've seen him since we split. Perhaps it isn't him,' she added, almost hopefully.

'But you can't be easy until you're sure?'

Suddenly her carefully honed confidence deserted her. 'What can I do? I can't walk over there and take a look.'

'You can if we're dancing.'

'But—'

'Olympia, you've got to do this. If you flunk it you'll never be able to look yourself in the mirror again.'

She knew it, but she was too nervous to think straight.

'Let's leave it,' she whispered. 'The past is the past.'

His hand tightened over hers. 'Nonsense. The past is never the past until you've faced it and told it to get the hell out of your way. What happened to the "can do" tycoon I've got to know?'

'She turned into a "can't do" wimp,' she said with a shaky laugh.

'No, she didn't. She just needs a friend to take her hand, like this.'

Giving her no chance to refuse, he drew her to her feet and on to the dance floor.

With a shock Olympia realised that he was finally

holding her. So many times he could have taken her into his arms, and so many times he'd refused. Now he'd done so under the guise of a dance. But that was what dancing was for—to embrace, to hold each other closely and feel the pressure of each other's body and the exchange of warm breath, without admitting that was what you were doing.

'Which way?' he murmured, his breath brushing her cheek.

'Near the orchestra.'

Closer and closer they went while her eyes searched the tables at the edge of the dance floor until she found what she was seeking.

Her first thought was to wonder how she'd ever recognised him. David was plumper, sleeker, beginning to lose his hair, and there was an expression of discontent on his face that mirrored that of the woman sitting near him.

Rosalie! It took Olympia a moment to identify this stodgy creature with the elegant nymph who had persisted in her memory, but this was Rosalie now.

'Is that him?' her partner asked.

'I think—yes, it is.'

'And the woman with him?'

'Rosalie, his wife.'

'He made a bad bargain when he traded you for her,' said her friend.

Now Olympia saw that there were six people at the table. David's father-in-law was there with his wife, David and Rosalie, and two men who Olympia guessed were business contacts being entertained. One of them asked Rosalie to dance. Smiling, she took the floor with him.

It seemed to Olympia that there was an element of

relief in that smile, as though anything was better than her husband's company. As she glided around the floor in her partner's arms, David watched them sourly.

Suddenly the movements of the dance brought Olympia close to the couple. Rosalie's eyes flickered vacantly over Olympia before moving on to the man holding her in his arms. She seemed suddenly interested, turning her head as she moved, trying to keep him in view. Only at the last minute did she really seem to notice Olympia and then there was a shocked look in her eyes, disbelief, almost outrage.

'She didn't know you at first,' Primo whispered, 'but she does now.'

'I guess I've changed a bit since those days.'

The dance ended and the other couple headed back to their table. But the next dance started at once and Olympia found herself whirled into it without a by-your-leave.

His hand was in the small of her back, holding her close against him as his legs moved against hers. The sight of David had been a shock, bringing back sharp memories that she'd spent years banishing, but, faced with the reality, they were fast fading. It was hard to be aware of anything but the man swinging her around and around, holding her so close that their bodies were as one.

The room was whirling about her, making her cling to him as the only fixed point in the world. He'd said he was her friend, and that was partly why she held him so eagerly. And partly it wasn't that at all. Everything seemed to vanish but his face. She must make him stop this, but she wanted him never to stop.

At last he slowed and the room came back into focus. Now, she could see David again, listening to Rosalie, who was talking to him with animation and pointing back on to the floor. He rose and they started to dance together.

'She's told him,' Primo murmured. 'Now he wants to see for himself if it's you. Look, they're working their way towards us.'

'Oh, no!' she said involuntarily.

'Why "oh, no!"? This is your moment of triumph.'

'Is it?'

'Isn't it? Look at them. Sad and middle-aged before their time because they've made too many compromises, betrayed too many people. Then look at you, young and beautiful as a mermaid, every man's head turned to you in admiration. They've had it, and now it tastes sour. You've got it all before you, and it's going to be great.'

'Yes,' she breathed excitedly. 'Oh, yes!'

'Let him find out what he threw away. Make him sorry he let you go. Then hold your head high and walk out of here with me.'

'You're right.'

Again there was that *frisson* of excitement at how totally he understood her, as though their minds were linked even more closely than their bodies.

Closer and closer they danced until she was a couple of feet away from the man who had once filled her world, then broken her heart when he'd declared her not up to standard.

As Jack had promised, there was satisfaction in seeing the shock in his face as he recognised her. Her partner kept her there, dancing on the spot so that David could be in no doubt who he was seeing. Olympia met David's eyes in a moment of blazing victory.

'Look up at me,' said a voice close to her ear.

She did so, and immediately felt his lips on hers. She gasped, almost stumbling, but his arms held her safe, keeping her in the dance so that her feet seemed to move of their own accord while her mouth relished his.

It meant nothing, she thought desperately. He was a friend, helping her to make a point to David, boosting her pride like the true friend he was. She must accept his kiss in the same spirit, keeping a cool head, ignoring the wild feelings that went through her.

'Is he watching?' she gasped against his mouth.

'His eyes are on stalks,' he murmured back. 'And so are hers. Let's give them a repeat run. Kiss me—as though you really meant it.'

'*Right!*'

Her arms slid up about his neck, one hand curving pleasurably against his head, drawing him down to her, ready for him, eager for him. She did as he'd said, giving it everything as though she meant it, and felt his answering response.

Now he'd released her hand and tightened both arms around her, holding her so that she would have been helpless to resist, if that was what she'd wanted. But she had no thought of resistance. Her body had been aching for this, longing to know how it would feel to be held by him, and all the time she had been denying her instincts the need had been building within her.

If only they were not in public so that she could yield to the need that was overwhelming her, the need to touch him again and again and offer herself to his touch.

But that was what she mustn't do, she thought wildly. Being alone with him would tempt her to reveal too much. Touch would follow touch, deeper and more intimate until touching wasn't enough.

However hard it was, she must try to keep her distance. But this felt like a very strange way of keeping her distance.

He released her just enough for her head to fall back so that she was looking into his face. He seemed to be frowning as though something had startled him, and she understood that reaction because she felt the same.

'What's happening?' she whispered.

'I'm not—quite—sure—'

And suddenly the world seemed to burst in a glitter of flashlights. People cheered, champagne bottles popped, red roses fell on them. Olympia saw that they were surrounded by waiters, all waving champagne and cheering.

'What on earth—?' she said.

A man in a glittering coat, who seemed to be the Master of Ceremonies, made his way towards them and bowed.

'Congratulations!' he cried. 'You are tonight's winners.'

'Winners at what?' she asked hazily.

'In our Lovers Competition. Every night this week, one lucky couple is declared our Premier Lovers—'

'But we're not lo—' she started to say, then gave up. She was being drowned out by cheering.

'Jack, what are we going to do?'

'Put up with it,' he said, close to her ear. 'We've no choice. It'll be over in a minute and we can slip away. In the meantime, try to look convincing. Smile. This is where the movie queen gives the hero the full power of her dazzling orbs and he goes weak at the knees.'

'Don't do that,' she begged. 'You're holding me up.'

He gave a crack of laughter, his eyes gleaming in appreciation of the joke.

The Master of Ceremonies was shouting, 'That was the most impressive kiss anyone's ever seen. How about another?'

Another cheer went up and the crowd began to chant, 'Kiss—kiss—'

'Jack—'

'We'll have to give them what they want, or they won't let us go,' he murmured.

'But we—'

'It can't be helped. Lie back and think of England.'

'You cheeky—'

'Hush,' he said, lowering his mouth to hers.

He was right. Who needed words when there were feelings like this? She gave herself up to what was happening, while all around them the crowd cheered and clapped.

When at last he released her she had a vision of David's face. It was a vacuous face, she realised, especially now, with his jaw dropping.

She had beaten him. The man who'd rejected her as dowdy and dull, who'd betrayed her love for money, had been made to regret it.

And she couldn't have cared less.

The Master of Ceremonies was dancing around them.

'It's wonderful what people will do to make sure they win,' he carolled.

'We didn't—' Olympia said breathlessly. 'We didn't know there was a contest.'

'You mean you normally act like that? Hey, folks, did you hear that? Boy, are these some lovers!'

More cheers, more applause.

'Can we sit down?' the Master of Ceremonies asked. 'Then we can sort out the details.'

She wanted to ask, what details? But she couldn't think clearly. Her legs were trembling, as though all the strength had drained away.

When they were seated at the table the Master of Ceremonies poured champagne and toasted them.

'And now for the big moment,' he said, 'when you get to choose your prize from among our glorious range. There's this—' He produced a catalogue showing some very fancy and high-priced entertainment equipment.

'Or there's this, a fortnight for two at a luxury health spa. Or two gift vouchers for the most expensive store in London. Or a vacation in any town in Europe, flights, hotel, the lot.'

He finished with an expansive gesture, like a man expecting applause. Primo indicated Olympia.

'It's her choice,' he said. 'Why don't you take the gift vouchers and blow the lot on clothes?'

'Oh, no,' she said. 'I've got a much better idea. I'll take the trip to Europe.'

'Wonderful!' the Master of Ceremonies exclaimed. 'And which city shall it be?'

Olympia smiled at Primo.

'Naples,' she said.

On the drive home he said, 'What do you want to happen about David? Shall I get Leonate to buy out his firm and fire him? Or employ him? Say the word.'

'No need,' she said contentedly. 'If I wanted revenge, I've had it. I'm so glad that happened. He really is in the past now. Thank you. You knew just what to do.'

'Good. Then can we talk about Naples?'

She gave a soft laugh. 'Your face was a picture!'

'I'll bet it was. You were winding me up, weren't you? Good joke.'

'That man said the Vallini Hotel was the best. Do you know it?'

'Yes, it's about halfway up the hill, overlooking the bay. It costs a fortune just to walk past it.'

'I like the sound of that,' she said with a sigh.

'But you weren't serious, were you?' he asked, sounding slightly alarmed.

Choosing not to answer this, she diplomatically closed her eyes and pretended to doze for the rest of the journey.

When they reached home he came upstairs with her, and it was only when they were in her apartment that she said, 'Actually, I wasn't joking back there. I'm going to Naples and I'm going to stay in that luxury hotel while I look around. I'm due for some time off. I haven't had any for ages, and you can authorise it. It's simple.'

'It's not a good idea.'

'It's a wonderful idea. It's fate. And after what happened tonight I'm even more certain that this happened because it had to.'

After what happened tonight. That stopped him in his tracks.

'Jack, I've been doing a lot of thinking—about the way things are going.'

'I know,' he said slowly.

'You know what I want and how determined I am to get it. It doesn't make me a nice person, but I can't change. I simply have to go for my goal.'

'Primo Rinucci. But he isn't here.'

'I know. And he's never going to be here, I see that now. So I must go to him.'

'*What?*'

'That's what I mean about fate. I can work on my Italian, learn some Neapolitan. It'll give me better chances than staying here.'

'But what about Curtis? It was your ambition to take over.'

'Well, maybe the world doesn't begin and end with Curtis. Maybe I'm broadening my horizons.'

'Which means—?' he asked suspiciously.

'Ambition alone is not enough,' she declared with the air of someone quoting eternal truth. 'Ambition plus flexibility yields results.'

He stared at her. 'Who said that?'

'I did.'

'I mean, who said it first?'

'I did. You just heard me.'

He passed a hand over his eyes, trying to get control of his thoughts.

'You sounded as though you were quoting an authority,' he explained.

'I was. Me.'

'Oh, well, in that case—!' he said wildly. 'Why not jot it down and put it in a book when you're running the Stock Exchange? *Notes On How I Did It.* You too can rule the world. Just roll over everyone like a steam-roller.'

'How dare you call me a steam-roller!'

'It's that or a three ton tractor. Take your pick.'

'Jack, where's your spirit of adventure?'

'It passed out under the table in the nightclub, and as far as I'm concerned it can stay there. Olympia, what's got into you? It's bad enough for you to be laying traps for this poor fool—'

'Don't call my benefactor a fool!'

'So now he's your benefactor?'

'He will be, when I've finished with him.'

'Then he *is* a fool,' he said recklessly. 'And so are you for hunting him down, because it'll frighten him off.'

'He won't even know. I'll just turn up in Naples, look around—'

'You're out of your mind.'

'You mean you won't help me?'

He took her shoulders, shaking her very slightly as though this would get him into her head.

'Olympia, you're living in a dream world. It's a delightful fantasy, but not if it means turning your back on what's happening between us.'

'We're having a pleasant flirtation. It's lovely, but it doesn't lead anywhere. We enjoy each other's company and then pass on. That's always been the deal.'

'I don't remember making any deal.'

'I was always honest with you. You knew my terms and you didn't refuse them.'

'Then I guess I just hoped you'd soon see things a bit more clearly. I don't think it's all on my side. Look me in the eye and tell me you don't feel anything for me.'

'After tonight, I can't. But I won't *let* it happen. I felt something like that once before, and I know where it leads.'

'I know where it would have led if you'd stayed with him. You saw him in the nightclub. You saw his wife, what marriage to him has turned her into. Be glad you escaped.'

'I am glad, but that's hindsight. All that kind of thing is over for me. You've always known that.'

'All right, I've known it, but I've tried not to believe it. And I won't believe it now. You keep trying to make me think badly of you—'

'I want you to see me as I am,' she flashed. 'I'm hard and cold—'

'You weren't hard and cold in my arms tonight.'

'That'll never happen again. I won't let it.'

'Stop it,' he said fiercely, seizing her in his arms and giving her a little shake. 'Don't talk like that. I forbid you.'

'Who are you to forbid me?'

His answer was to tighten his grip and pull her hard against him, kissing her with something close to ferocity.

For a moment she tensed against him, but then her refusal melted in the warmth and sweetness he could inspire in her with such treacherous ease.

'This is who I am,' he murmured against her lips. 'Don't you recognise me now?'

'Yes,' she whispered, kissing him back.

'You know me—you know me—'

She knew him. He was the one who haunted her dreams, resisting all attempts to banish him. She would escape him now while she still could—while there was time—but there was no time—

She kissed him again and again, each time promising that this would be the last.

'How can you leave when we have this?' he demanded hoarsely.

'Don't you see, it's because we *could* have this that I'm doing what must be done.'

'You mean you're running,' he said scornfully. 'Running like a coward who's afraid of life.'

The words were bitter, brutal, but he couldn't help it. The pain of her rejection was intense.

'Maybe I am,' she said. 'But I don't want to feel all that again, Jack, and you frighten me. You could take me to a place where I don't want to be—'

'If we were there together, like tonight—'

'It will never happen again. *I won't let it.*'

He drew apart from her, gasping.

'Wait here,' he said through gritted teeth, and walked out of the room without a backward glance.

He went all the way downstairs before he called Italy on his cellphone, taking no chance of being overheard. First he called Cedric Tandy.

'Cedric, I know it's late but I need a favour from you—'

It was a short call, very satisfactory, and ended with him saying, 'Cedric, you're a lifesaver. Go back to bed now.'

Next he spoke to Enrico, who wasn't best pleased at being hauled out of bed, but who also agreed to what Primo wanted, because people always did. After nearly half an hour he returned to Olympia. Secretly he was glad she'd forced the issue, driving him to a decision.

'It's settled,' he said when he rejoined her. 'I've been telling them about you and Leonate wants me to take you out there so that he can get to know you.'

'And what then?'

'You'll work in Naples for a while, then in a few months you'll know what you want to do. You may decide you want to return here and run Curtis. If so, you'll make a better job of it for having worked at the centre of things. Or you may decide that you like Naples and want to keep your job there.'

'What about you?'

'I'm flying out with you and staying for a while, to see you settled in, but I won't be living at the hotel. I have an apartment.'

'Wait, I can't get my head round this. Who'll run Curtis while you're away?'

'Cedric. His retirement package contains an option for another six months.'

'Does it? I saw it and I didn't see anything about another six months.'

'It's a recent development,' he said hurriedly, not choosing to tell her how recent. 'It gives me a breather while I make decisions about his replacement. He won't mind if I invoke that option. It keeps your options open too.

'And now that we've settled everything, I'll leave.' His voice became brisk. 'I want you in the office first thing tomorrow. There are arrangements to be made. Is your passport in order?'

'Of course.'

'Have you got the number that man in the disgusting jacket gave you to ring when you'd settled the date?'

'Of course.'

'Fine. Tell them we'll travel in two days. We'll sort out the final details tomorrow. Goodnight.'

He left without another word.

Olympia stood watching the closed door, feeling more confused than she'd been in her life. He threatened her peace, and she'd told herself that the time had come to escape him. But somehow he'd wrested control from her. The trip to Naples would be on his terms.

She'd outwitted him—and then she hadn't.

Suddenly the future was more exciting than it had ever been.

As he'd said it was all systems go in the office next morning.

'How can you leave so soon, when you've barely got here?' Olympia protested.

'But I'm only obeying orders,' he said innocently. 'Just a humble cog in the Leonate wheel, doing as I'm told, that's me.'

'Why don't I find that convincing?'

'Maybe you're just not a very good judge of character,' he said simply.

From then on packing and making arrangements about her apartment occupied all her time, and when she finally closed the door to start the journey to the airport she hadn't seen him for two days. She had to take a taxi. He didn't even bother to collect her.

She was glad of the time apart. It gave her a breathing space to get her ideas together and remind herself what really mattered. He was attractive, no doubt about it, but so what? She could enjoy a flirtation without compromising her mission, couldn't she?

But then these cool thoughts would be invaded by memories that were anything but cool: the way he'd held her in his arms, the fierce crushing kiss with a hint of some suppressed feeling that might have been desperation, the skilled movements of his lips, knowing so well how to incite her to respond.

He knew her too well. He could speak to her in a silent language they both understood. He was dangerous. She must escape him.

But she was glad with all her heart that he was coming with her.

He was waiting at the airport, greeting her with an air of tension that puzzled her.

'Are you all right?' she asked.

'Fine, fine. Just not too keen on flying.'

In fact he was an excellent traveller, but he'd just completed what he promised himself would be the last, the very last piece of trickery.

Realising that his ticket would be provided in the name of Cayman, he'd intercepted it when it had been delivered to the office the previous day, then booked himself another ticket in his true name and got to the airport early to collect it.

Now he was vowing that it would all soon be over. Safe in Naples, he would confess everything to Olympia over a glass of wine. They would share a laugh, and she would forgive him.

Eventually.

And he would never tell another lie as long as he lived. His nerves couldn't stand it.

CHAPTER SEVEN

'THERE it is,' he said as the volcano came into view in the distance. 'That's what you've been watching for, isn't it?'

'Vesuvius,' she said ecstatically. 'How fierce and magnificent it looks.'

The plane turned and now the lights of Naples were below them, like arms curving around the bay. Another few minutes and they were down.

Then they were in the taxi, climbing the hill to the Vallini, the grandest hotel that Naples had to offer. As soon as she stepped through the door she was enveloped in luxury. Uniformed staff murmured, '*Signorina*,' as they ushered her to her suite.

There she found a double bed of antique design but modern comfort, a marble bathroom and a sitting room with a balcony that looked out over the bay.

'I'll leave you for a while,' he said, 'while I check my apartment. I'll be back in a couple of hours.'

When he'd gone she had a long soak in scented water while the hotel laundry service pressed the creases from the black dress she'd worn to the nightclub. A hairdresser arrived and dressed her long black hair in elegant sweeps, some wound about her head, some falling.

It was a magical evening. He led her downstairs to his low slung sports car.

'Let me show you a little of my town,' he said.

They drove for an hour through narrow cobbled streets. Once she caught him stealing a smiling glance at her and knew it was a reminder of how he'd once teased her about 'urchins and cobbled streets'.

'But where are the urchins?' she asked at last and they both laughed.

They dined at a tiny *trattoria,* saying little. He forbade her to speak English and she struggled through the evening with her basic Italian.

'You're doing well,' he said. 'The more you practise it the better.'

'When do I start work?' she wanted to know.

'Let's enjoy a few days holiday first. Once I've introduced you to Enrico you'll be swallowed up.' After a moment he added delicately, 'And, of course, there's the other introduction you want.'

'Oh, yes,' she murmured. 'Him.'

For a moment she'd wondered who he meant.

'Yes, him,' he said, eyebrows slightly raised. 'Primo Rinucci. The man this is all about.'

'Well, there's no rush, is there? Let's not talk about him tonight. I don't want to think about work.'

'I'll swear it's years since you last said that.'

'Yes,' she said in surprise. 'It is.'

She wondered how anyone could think of work in this colourful place. Looking through the window by their table, she saw couples strolling through the narrow streets, lost in each other. It had been raining earlier and the blurred reflections of lights gleamed on the wet cobbles, giving a misty edge to the world. No, tonight she didn't want to think of work, or anything except the man with her.

She listened for the voice telling her to beware because he endangered her ambitions, but somehow it was muted. She would listen to it another time.

'What are you thinking?' he asked.

'You wouldn't believe me if I told you.'

'Then don't tell me. I'll work it out.'

'I wonder if you will.'

'I will, *strega*. I will.'

'*Strega?*'

'There are still gaps in your Italian. Look it up.'

'Tell me.'

'No.' He shook his head, his lips pressed firmly together. 'But I've thought of you as *strega* since the first day.'

'Is it a nice thing to be?'

'It changes. Mostly it leaves me not knowing what to think.'

'And that annoys you?'

'Only sometimes. At others—' He let the implication hang in the air.

'Tell me,' she begged again, but he only shook his head.

He drove slowly back to the hotel and saw her up to her suite.

'Go to bed and sleep well,' he said. 'I'll call early tomorrow.'

'Come for breakfast.'

'All right. And we'll plan the day. There's a lot I want to show you. Look—'

He led the way out on to the balcony where a brilliant full moon shone down over the bay. She stared out over the dark water, unable to believe such beauty.

His cellphone rang and he muttered something rude, turning back into the room to answer it. The next moment she heard his shocked exclamation.

Hurrying back into the room, she saw him standing with the phone to his ear, his eyes wide, his jaw gaping.

'What is it?' she asked urgently.

'OK, Cedric,' he said into the phone. 'Look, don't worry about it. It's not your fault. I'll take care of it. Don't blame yourself. I'm coming. Just hang in there.'

'You're going back to England?' she asked.

'Only for a couple of days. Do you remember a man called Norris Banyon?'

'Yes, he ran the accounts department, but he left suddenly a couple of weeks ago. I never liked him.'

'With reason, it seems. He was fiddling the books for years.'

'But how could he get away with it? Leonate had a firm of accountants swarming all over the books before you made your offer. They said everything was all right.'

'Yes, but Banyon had had time to cover his tracks, and he was there, day by day, thinking on his feet, always ready with an explanation for any question they raised. But as soon as the deal was concluded he left, taking a large sum with him. And, of course, the minute he was gone it began to unravel.'

'Is it disastrous?'

'No, it won't bring us down or anything. But Cedric blames himself.'

'That's not fair.'

'No, it isn't. I have to go back to calm him down. I'll get some more accountants in—a different firm this time—and they'll sort it out. Then I'll cheer poor old Cedric up. Since his wife died last year he's been alone. He has no children or close family, so there's nobody at home to help him cope.'

Olympia stared. She hadn't known Cedric's wife had died.

'That's really nice of you,' she said.

'Well, Cedric—er—did me a big favour recently.' He cleared his throat awkwardly.

'I'll come too.'

'Better not,' he said quickly.

'But I was his assistant. I can help with this.'

'He'd hate for you to know. I'll be back in a few days, when I've hired the new auditors. Until then, enjoy being a tourist and get to know my city.' He looked at his watch. 'There's a plane at dawn. I'd better go now.'

'You mean this minute?' she asked, horrified.

'I don't want to go but I think I must.'

'Of course. Give him my love.'

But she could have wept with disappointment. Something had started to happen, something that wasn't supposed to happen, and which she'd foolishly resisted. Now she was no longer resisting and she could see the road stretching out ahead, uncertain but inviting. Just not yet.

He hesitated over saying goodbye, holding her hand in his. At last he laid a gentle kiss on her mouth and hurried away. From the balcony she could see him leave the hotel, get into his car and drive away down the hill.

She looked back at her suite, the epitome of luxury, a symbol of the place she had wanted to be. But there was nobody there with her.

She thought of Cedric, too uptight to talk about his loneliness with the people he'd known for years. But Jack had known and responded with kindness.

He called her on the evening of the next day, telling her that things weren't as bad as they'd sounded, and he'd persuaded Cedric to stop beating his breast.

'I'll be with you soon,' he said. 'How are you occupying your time without me?'

'Reading dictionaries,' she said.

His voice reached her down the line, warm and amused, thrilling her from a distance of a thousand miles. 'So now you know what *strega* means. Do you like it?'

'Yes, I think I do. It could be interesting. But I won't know until you come back.'

'It'll be as soon as I can manage. And when I'm there we have a lot to talk about.'

'I know. Come back soon.'

When she'd hung up she sat looking at the phone, seeming to hear his voice in the air about her. For a moment the sensation was so strong that she nearly reached out, sure that she could touch him.

There was a suspicious wetness in her eyes and on her cheeks. She brushed it away, then went to bed and lay awake dreaming about him.

She whiled away the time by exploring Naples, but after the first day she was so footsore that she hired a car.

She went out into the countryside, stopped to eat at small inns and drove back as late as possible, trying to convince herself that she was having a good time. The land was beautiful, the bay was astonishing, but it was all wrong because *he* wasn't here.

She'd told herself that she must run from him, but running was useless. He could give her the kind of feelings she'd sworn never to know again, and to rejoice in them. That knowledge would be waiting around every corner.

And he knew. Of course he did. He'd played along with the joke, waiting for her to get over her fantasies and reach out to the real man. It had happened, and all could be well, except that it had happened in the wrong way, at the wrong time, when he wasn't even here.

Perhaps she'd needed him to go, so that the ache of

missing him told her what she wanted to know. But why, oh why, didn't he come back to her now?

Meanwhile she tried to occupy herself with being a tourist, but wherever she went she was thinking of him, planning how to tell him that she'd changed. How they would laugh together at the way she'd been overcome by her feelings! And then—

Every day she lunched at the *trattoria* where they'd eaten during his few brief hours here, at the same table if possible. Then she would search for something to fill the afternoon.

Despite all the historical sights, what attracted her most was the great building that was Leonate Europa. She longed to visit it, and even went so far as to turn into its underground car park. There she switched off the engine and sat behind the wheel, torn by temptation.

Surely it would do no harm to go in and introduce herself? After all, she'd signed a contract to work here. She could meet Enrico Leonate. She might even meet Primo Rinucci.

Then she smiled as she realised that she didn't care whether she met him or not. Only Jack counted now. Soon he would call to say he was returning. She would go to meet him at the airport and their time would come.

She started up the engine and began to edge her way out of the car park into the stream of traffic. It was late afternoon, the worst time of day to be driving. The traffic was at its most crowded and she was fast becoming confused by the car and everything around her. She remembered Jack attributing his accident to the fact that the English drove on the 'wrong' side of the road. Now she knew how he felt.

There was a blast on the horn from the driver behind

her. Startled, she turned the car swiftly to the side, realising too late that she'd chosen the wrong one.

'Damn!' she muttered, trying to brake, turn and see where she was going, all at once. '*Oh, no!*'

A shadow had appeared on her windscreen, a shadow that vanished with alarming suddenness.

'Oh, no!' she cried again, flinging herself out of the car. 'What have I done?'

'Covered me with bruises,' said a man's voice from the ground. Mercifully he sounded robust, even amused.

'I didn't actually hit you, did I?'

'No, I jumped out of the way when you swerved, and missed my footing.' He climbed to his feet, moving gingerly. 'Those kerbs are very sharp when you fall on them,' he complained, rubbing his elbow.

A bellow of sound from behind reminded her that other drivers were waiting to move.

'I've got to go,' she said, 'but I can't just leave you here. Can you get into my car?'

'Why don't I drive it for you?'

'That might be better,' she said with relief. 'The roads in Naples are—I don't know—'

When they were in the car and he was guiding them through the traffic he said, 'It's not just Naples. The roads in the rest of Italy are pretty hair-raising too. You're not Italian, are you?'

'You guessed! Neither are you by the sound of it. English?'

'Let's say I started out that way. Nowadays I'm not sure what I am. What's your name?'

'Olympia Lincoln.'

'Luke Cayman.'

'Cayman?' She looked at him quickly. 'Are you any relation to Jack Cayman?'

Before he could answer, a sleek sports car swept right in front of them, forcing Luke to brake sharply and utter a stream of Neapolitan curses. By the time things had sorted themselves out with lots of honking and bawling, Luke had had time to catch his breath and partly understand the situation.

Now, if ever, was the moment to watch every word. Brother Stuffed-Shirt Primo had certainly been up to something. But what? That was the million dollar question that he was going to enjoy exploring.

'Sorry,' he said at last. 'What was the name?'

'Jack Cayman. I met him in England. He works for Leonate. Surely you must be related? Two Englishmen with the same name, in Naples.'

As his thoughts settled he realised that he might have overreacted. Primo sometimes used his father's name for wheeling and dealing in England, thinking it would make him less conspicuous. It might mean nothing.

'It sounds like my brother,' he mused.

'Your brother?'

'That's right. We both come from England originally.'

'Are you part of the firm too?'

'Leonate? Not part of, but I'm in the same line of electronics and I've just sold them some goods, so I'd just dropped in to sign the papers. Jack and I don't see much of each other because he travels a lot. Look, I know a little *trattoria* just down here and I need some sustenance after the fright you gave me.'

She suppressed a childish desire to say, Oh, yeah? The mere idea of this man taking fright was incongruous. He was like a rock. A pleasant, attractive rock, but a rock just the same. It was there in the shape of his head and his jaw line.

When at last they were seated, eating pizza and drinking coffee, he said, 'I never take my car when I visit Leonate. The roads near it are so bad that it's quicker on foot. But how did you come to be driving out of that building?'

'I work there—well, sort of. I come from Curtis in England.'

'So you've been taken over?'

'I suppose I have. I'm here to learn the business and the language, and anything else I can.'

'Was that Jack's idea?'

'Mine mainly. I sort of forced his hand.'

'You—forced Pr—forced *his* hand?' Luke asked carefully. 'Not an easy man to force.'

She nodded. 'I wanted to come to Naples. A way presented itself and in the end he saw things my way.'

To Olympia's amazement Luke threw his head back and roared with laughter.

'You don't know how it sounds to hear you say that,' he said at last. 'That's how he talks—do it my way. And people always do, because he gives them no choice. I guess you've heard him.'

'No, I've never heard him say that,' she said. 'It doesn't sound like him at all.'

'Doesn't *sound*—? We can't be talking about the same man. Is something the matter?'

He'd noticed her looking over his shoulder and turned, half expecting to find Primo. Instead, it was his mother that he saw standing just inside the door, trying to attract his attention.

'Mamma!' He rose to embrace her and she hugged him back enthusiastically.

'I've been trying to call you, but you turned your phone off,' she reproved him. 'Now introduce me to your friend.'

'Mamma, this is Miss Olympia Lincoln. Miss Lincoln, this is my mother.'

Olympia regarded the newcomer with admiration. She looked between fifty and sixty, with an elegant figure and a face that was a tribute to the power of the massage parlour. She was fighting off encroaching age, and doing it very skilfully.

She shook hands with Olympia, giving her the welcoming but sharp-eyed look of a mother with too many unmarried sons. She evidently liked what she saw, for her smile broadened.

'Mamma, sit down and have coffee with us,' Luke said.

'I have no time. I must hurry back to the villa to finish preparations for tonight.' To Olympia she said, 'We're having a family party and you must come.'

'Oh, no—thank you, but—if it's a family party—'

'Of course you must come. I won't take no for an answer. Luke, you hear me now and bring this nice girl to us tonight.'

She paused to regard Olympia with admiration.

'We'll have some dancing and I just know you'll look wonderful in a long dress.'

'Mamma!' Luke covered his eyes.

'Well, she will. Crimson, I think.'

'Crimson?' Olympia exclaimed in surprise. 'I've never thought of it as my colour.'

'But it is. You must wear crimson, if not tonight then the next time I see you.'

She kissed Luke and hurried out before either of them could answer.

'You do realise that you've just been given your orders, don't you?' Luke said with a grin. 'Mamma's rather overwhelming, but she means it kindly.'

'I know she does, and she's made me feel so welcome.'

Luke suppressed the thought that this was because Hope was preparing to swallow Olympia alive in the name of 'acquiring daughters-in-law', and merely said, 'You will come, won't you? Just to keep her happy? She always gets cross if her sons turn up without girlfriends. She accuses us of only associating with the kind of girls a man can't take home to his mother.'

'Rightly?' Olympia asked, her eyes full of fun.

He cleared his throat. 'It's a long story. She thinks she's right and I just go along with it. We all do. But boy, does she ask a lot of questions! I swear it's like being interrogated by the Inquisition, but if you're there I'll be spared.'

'You won't, you know,' she chuckled. 'You'll just be asked a different kind of question, and probably twice as many.'

He groaned. 'How horribly true!'

'Questions are what mothers do,' she said sympathetically. 'One way or the other.'

'But you will come, won't you? It's the least you can do after knocking me down.'

'All right,' she said, laughing.

It would be better than spending the evening alone, wondering when Jack would return. She had tried to call him earlier but his cellphone had been switched off.

Luke drove her back to the Vallini and whistled at the sight of her destination. Once inside she went straight to the hire shop, seeking a suitable dress for that night. She was resolute in her determination to make her own choice, but somehow the gown that suited her best just happened to be deep crimson satin. She hired it and some gold jewellery, then bought gold sandals to go with it.

When the hairdresser had come to her suite and whipped up her hair into an elaborate confection, she was ready for the evening.

She tried to call Jack, but for the third time she couldn't get through. She frowned, puzzled by the odd silence and wishing with all her heart that he could be here and see her looking like this.

His brother was nice, but it was chiefly his relationship to Jack that made him so. She would see the house which had been their home and learn something about him.

If only he could be here, she thought sadly, regarding the vision in the mirror that he wouldn't see.

Luke's frank admiration was balm to her soul, although he couldn't resist saying, 'You'll give Mamma ideas, dressing like that.'

'It's not because of anything she said. This was the perfect dress. She was right about that.'

'I'll believe you. She won't.'

'Is it far?' she asked, diplomatically changing the subject.

'No distance. Just at the top of this hill. You'll see it as soon as we're on the road.'

Just as he'd said, the family home loomed up above them as they climbed the hill. All the lights were on and they seemed to blaze out a welcome over the whole of the surrounding city, the countryside, the bay, even as far as Vesuvius.

'When you're up there the volcano looks very near because there's nothing in between but clear air,' Luke told her. 'The least little murmur from Vesuvius, the tiniest puff of smoke, seems to be happening right on top of you.'

'You mean things happen even these days?'

'Nothing to worry about. The old man gives the odd grumble from deep in the earth, just to remind us not to take him for granted, but the last actual eruption was sixty years ago. Toni's father saw it happen and he used to warn us always to tell the truth, because Vesuvius was listening and would growl with displeasure if we offended. So every time there was the faintest murmur we all used to jump nervously.'

At last they swung into the great courtyard of the villa. As they left the car a door in the house opened and his mother emerged, throwing up her arms in joyful greeting.

'Mamma!' Luke called cheerfully, climbing the steps, Olympia's hand in his. 'You see, I've brought her.'

His mother gave him a perfunctory kiss before welcoming Olympia eagerly, her eyes flickering over the red dress.

'Perfect,' she said. 'It suits you, as I knew it would.'

'It's just an accident that she chose that dress, Mamma,' Luke said quickly. 'She told me so.'

'Of course she did. Olympia, my dear, you are very welcome. Now come and meet the rest of my family.'

As Olympia went into the house Hope drew Luke aside, murmuring, 'She'll make a beautiful bride.'

'Mamma, you don't know her.'

'I can tell these things. She *looks* like my daughter-in-law.'

'For which one of us?' he asked, amused.

'Whichever one she will deign to have,' Hope informed him caustically. 'She may take her pick.'

'Oh, no,' he said at once. 'She's all mine.'

'Congratulations, my son. Your taste is improving.'

As they entered the warm house Olympia turned towards her. 'Mrs Cayman—'

Luke's mother laughed. 'Oh, my dear, I'm sorry. We're all so casual about names. I'm not Mrs Cayman any more. That was years ago. I'm Signora Rinucci.'

'Rinucci? You mean—?'

'Toni's name is Rinucci, and this is the Villa Rinucci.'

'Then—you know Primo Rinucci?'

'My stepson. He should have been here tonight but he was called back to England very suddenly. But of course, if you work for Leonate you must know him.'

'No, I don't. Somehow we've always just missed each other.'

'Wait a moment,' said Hope, going to a cupboard and reaching inside.

She brought out a large photo album and laid it down on a small table, turning the heavy pages until she came to a picture and pointed to it.

'That's him,' she said triumphantly.

Smiling, Olympia gazed down at the face of Primo Rinucci. And her smile faded.

CHAPTER EIGHT

For a long moment Olympia felt absolutely nothing. What she was seeing was so impossible that there could be no reaction.

Her hostess was explaining, 'Primo was the son of my first husband, Jack Cayman. His mother was a Rinucci and he took the family name when he came to live here.'

Olympia barely heard the words. Her stomach was churning as the dreadful truth finally became real, sharp. This was Primo Rinucci. The man she had trusted, confided in, to whom she had revealed her whole ambitious strategy, had been keeping this secret all the time.

What a laugh she must have given him!

'So that's Primo,' she said at last, surprised to find that she could speak normally. 'No, I don't know him.'

She fought to remain calm. Nobody must suspect that she'd received a shattering blow. That would be to pile disaster on disaster. Instead she would smile and smile, concealing the turmoil in her heart.

'I never knew him,' she repeated quietly.

It was true. She'd thought she knew him so well, but all the time he'd been a stranger. The affectionate friend she'd trusted had never existed, because he'd been laughing at her, encouraging her to confide in him as she'd never done with anyone before, making a fool of her. When she thought of some of the things she'd said to him she went hot and cold.

Worst of all, she'd actually begun to believe that she

might fall in love with him. And all the time he'd been sitting back, enjoying the situation at her expense.

She must hurry away from here, get back to England, leave the firm and go where she need never meet him again.

'There you two are,' Luke said, appearing beside his mother. 'Mamma, everyone's looking for you. There's some sort of crisis in the kitchen.'

When she had hurried away he glanced at Olympia, concerned. 'Are you all right?'

'I'm fine, fine!' she said brightly.

'Come and have some champagne and I'll introduce you to everyone.'

She followed like an automaton, while behind the façade her mind seethed.

She had only herself to blame because she'd always known he was a deceiver. That first day he'd pretended to be her secretary. Just a little tease, easy to pass off as a joke. But he hadn't told her until someone else had exposed him. It had been a warning she should have heeded.

Instead, she'd blundered on blindly, convincing herself that it was only a game. But the bitter hurt that consumed her now was shocking, terrifying, and she almost staggered under its impact.

After the first concerned question Luke hadn't spoken again. But he'd glimpsed the photograph and seen her horror. Now things were coming together in his mind and he had a suspicion of the truth.

So brother Primo had kicked over the traces, he mused. And with a vengeance!

He took her to meet his family—Toni, his father, his brothers, Toni's elderly parents who were paying them a visit and were guests of honour. There were also some business acquaintances.

Now Olympia seemed pervaded by a glacial calm that Luke found disturbing. He'd lived long enough in Italy to be comfortable with shouting and smashed plates. But freezing control made him uneasy.

'Do you want to talk about it?' he asked gently.

'There's nothing to talk about.'

'Well, my family are crazy about you, especially Mamma.'

'I think she's wonderful. She's been so nice to me.'

Someone called Luke's name and he turned briefly away. Olympia's eyes sought out Hope and found her at the exact moment Primo walked through the door.

She drew a sharp breath and turned away, hoping she'd hidden her face in time. He wasn't supposed to be here. Why hadn't he let her know he was coming back?

Had he noticed her? Please, no! She needed a moment to get control of herself so that she could meet him calmly. At all costs she must be the one in charge of this situation. Just a few more minutes and she would be strong enough to outface him.

Hope was eagerly hugging Primo, exclaiming over his early return.

'You made it! I thought you were going to be trapped in England for ages.'

'No, I got through everything at the speed of light,' he said. 'I just wanted to hurry back here.'

This was true. The thought of what might be happening in his absence was making him nervous.

'You're here in time for the excitement,' she told him. 'Luke brought a really nice girl tonight. She'll make him an excellent wife.'

'You know that already, do you?' he asked, grinning.

'I knew the moment I set eyes on her.'

'So all you have to do is persuade her.'

'I'm halfway there already. I suggested—in the mildest possible way, of course—that she would look wonderful in a long crimson dress. And tonight she turned up wearing the very thing. She wants the same thing that I want and that's her way of telling me.'

'And what about what Luke wants?' Primo asked with a grin. 'Has anyone thought of asking him, or will he just take what's supplied as long as it's stamped Approved by Mamma?'

'Don't be cheeky. He knows she's right for him. If you could have heard the way he spoke of her tonight, the way he said, "She's all mine." Oh, it'll be wonderful to see him married. And then I must set to work on you.'

'Mamma, you set to work on me twenty years ago,' he said with a laugh.

'I want you to find a woman as perfect for you as this one is for Luke.'

'Well, that may have already happened.'

She gave a little shriek of joy. 'Is this the mystery woman, the one you've been dropping hints about and won't bring to meet your family?'

'How could I? We've been in England. But I'll bring her to meet you soon, I promise.'

'You've made up your mind?'

'Yes, definitely.'

She shrieked again and threw her arms around him.

'What's all the fuss?' Toni asked, appearing and clapping Primo on the shoulder.

'Primo's going to be married, and so's Luke,' Hope said ecstatically.

'I thought Luke only met her today,' Toni said. 'Isn't it a bit soon—?'

'What does time matter when two people are made for each other?' his wife reproved him. 'Perhaps we'll end up having a double wedding—Primo and his mystery woman, and Luke and his fiancée.'

'Mamma, will you calm down?' Primo begged. 'I can't even think of a wedding yet. There are—practical difficulties.'

'Well, if you're not careful, your brother will steal a march on you. Come and meet her.'

He followed her, happy to be home in the place he loved and wishing he could have brought Olympia with him. He had thought of her all the time he'd been away and every moment on the plane back. He'd even worked out how he would arrive without warning, take her by surprise and then tell her the truth.

But he'd reached her hotel to find that she'd gone out for the evening, nobody knew where. Resigned, he'd come to the party to please his mother, yet now he found his thoughts fixed on Olympia again. How he longed to bring her here openly to meet his family. He was smiling as he let his mother lead him across the room.

There was Luke in animated conversation with a young woman who stood with her back to Primo, her black hair elegantly dressed and streaming down her back in glossy waves.

That sight caused a nervous flinching inside him. Even from this angle there was something dreadfully familiar about her, but it couldn't be—it surely couldn't be—

Then she turned and the nightmare became real.

He was still some feet away from her and now that little distance seemed like a mile, going on for ever. He approached slowly, like a sleepwalker, transfixed, watching the ironic smile on her face until at last, after a long, long time, he stood before her.

'Olympia,' he murmured.

'*Signore!*' she murmured in return.

She was cool and composed, but her eyes warned him of trouble to come.

Hope embraced her.

'My dear, I want to introduce you to Primo, whom I was just telling you about. I can't believe you two haven't run across each other before.'

'Oh, no,' Olympia said silkily. 'I've never met Signor Rinucci before.'

She extended her hand and when he took it her fingers tightened in a grip that was painful, warning him to say nothing about the real situation. She needn't have worried. Nothing on earth would have persuaded him to tell anyone about this disaster.

'Never mind,' Hope exclaimed. 'The two of you have met now, and that's all that matters. *Yes, Toni, I'm coming!* I must see to my guests, but I'll be back.'

She hurried away, leaving the other two gazing steadily at each other.

'So you're Primo Rinucci,' Olympia mused, still smiling. 'I kept thinking I'd probably meet him before this, but somehow it never quite worked out. I'm not sure why.'

She gazed charmingly into his face, as though inviting him to speculate.

'Some things—are hard to explain,' he said vaguely.

'Oh, I don't think it's as hard as all that,' she said. 'Several reasons come to mind. I'm even a little surprised to meet him now, but it has all the charm of the unexpected, don't you think? Or perhaps charm is the wrong word.'

'Indeed,' he said vaguely.

He was trying to pull himself together, alarmed to

notice that she seemed perfectly in command of the situation while he was floundering.

'Is that the best you can manage?' she asked. 'You don't have a lot to say for yourself, do you? Strange, I remember you as such a clever talker.'

'Olympia,' he whispered, 'please don't jump to conclusions.'

'I didn't jump to this conclusion. It bounded out and socked me on the jaw. Inside I'm still reeling, but some things become clear even when you're in a state of shock. Don't you find that?' Her tone expressed merely interest.

'I'm in a state of shock right now,' he said wryly. 'But your powers of recovery seem remarkable.'

'Yes, but I knew first. Your mother showed me your photograph and gave me your name.'

And then he realised her sharp wits had told her all she needed to know. Now she had him at a hopeless disadvantage.

He pulled himself together and tried to match her amused tone, saying, 'Personally I enjoy dealing with the unexpected. You can get some pleasant surprises that way.'

'And some nasty shocks,' she said coolly. 'Not to mention severe disappointments.'

'Isn't it a bit soon to judge that?'

'I don't think so. Some judgements are best made immediately.'

'And some can be made too soon,' he murmured.

In the soft light it was hard to be sure but he thought she went a little pale.

'Yes, I discovered that years ago,' she said. 'I thought I was past having to learn it again, but I was wrong.'

The throb of hurt in her voice made him draw a sharp breath.

'Don't confuse me with David,' he whispered. 'I'm not like him.'

'You're right. David was a cheapskate but he was honest in his way. At least I knew his name.'

'I never meant to hurt you. Please believe that.'

'I do.' But the brief hope this gave him was dashed when she added, 'You never gave a second thought to whether you hurt me or not. Or even a first thought.'

'Come into the dining room, everyone,' Hope called. 'Supper is served.'

He looked a question at her, but without much hope, and Luke appeared at her side. As they walked away together Primo remembered his mother describing how Luke had spoken of Olympia—'She's all mine.'

He'd been away in England for only a few days, yet it seemed that they were almost engaged. He tried to ignore the faint chill this thought caused him and put on a smile for the other guests.

A malign fate caused him to be seated directly opposite Olympia, where he had a grandstand view of her and Luke, laughing and talking over the meal, sometimes with their heads together. The candles on the table were reflected in her eyes and their glow seemed to pervade her whole being. How could he blame Luke for seeming entranced by her? He was entranced himself. He had never seen her look so beautiful, but it was not for him.

After the meal came dancing and every man there competed to dance with her. To Primo's rage they generally raised an eyebrow in Luke's direction in silent acknowledgement that she was 'his' woman. Grinning, Luke would give his permission, then watch her with fond, possessive eyes. Primo fully understood that feeling of possessiveness. It was the same one that made him want to knock his brother to the floor, throw Olympia over his shoulder and run away to hide in a cave, where no man's eyes but his own would ever see her.

'Glorious, isn't she?' said a voice at his elbow.

It was Luke, having made his way around the edge of the floor to join his brother.

'How did I ever hit so lucky?' he mused.

'How long have you known her?' Primo asked, trying to keep his voice neutral.

'Only since today.'

'Today?' He was startled.

'She sent me flying with her car. I haven't picked myself up yet. Maybe I never will. That's fine. When the moment happens, it happens.'

'Are you telling me,' Primo said in a carefully controlled voice, 'that after less than a day—?'

'Why not? Some women are so special that you know almost at once. Look at her. Isn't that a lady who could slay you in the first moment?'

'Don't be melodramatic,' Primo said harshly. His head was throbbing.

'Sure. I forgot you're the one man in the world who couldn't understand love at first sight. Take my word, it's the best.'

'Yes,' Primo murmured inaudibly. 'It is.'

'You knew her in England, didn't you?' Luke added. 'What's the story?'

'There is no story,' Primo said repressively.

'Odd that. She won't talk about you either.'

'Then mind your own damned business,' Primo said with soft venom.

'Like that, is it? Why don't you ask her to dance? It's cool with me.'

This time the look his brother turned on him was murderous. But the music was ending and Primo marched swiftly over to Olympia and reached for her hand, saying, 'Let's dance.'

'I think not,' she said. 'I've promised this one.'

She slid easily into the arms of an elderly uncle whose name she had forgotten but who beamed at his luck. Primo watched them, planning dire retribution on his innocent relative. It didn't help when the uncle's wife stood beside him, sighing happily. 'Isn't she a nice girl to be so kind to the old fool? It's not often he has such fun.'

When the dance was over Primo took no chances.

'The next one is with me,' he said, taking firm hold of her hand.

'I'd rather not, if you don't mind,' she said, trying to break free and failing.

The music was beginning. Primo's arm was about her waist in an unbreakable hold and Olympia found that she had no choice but to dance with him.

Such forcefulness was new, coming from him, and it increased her anger. Yet that very anger also seemed part of the heady excitement that the drama of the situation was causing to stream through her.

'Who the hell are you to be high-handed?' she demanded furiously.

He gave her a wolfish grin.

'I'm Primo Rinucci, a man I've heard you describe as ruthless and power-mad. A man to be hunted down by a determined woman and used for anything she can get out of him.'

'I never said that.'

'You said plenty that meant exactly that. So why should you be surprised if I act up to your picture of me?'

'All right, enjoy yourself while you can. Tomorrow I'm on the first plane home.'

'I think not. You have a contract with Leonate.'

'I never signed any contract.'

'You signed one with Curtis that has a year to run. Leonate own Curtis, which means that I own you for the next year.'

'The hell you do.'

'The hell I don't! What happens to you now is up to me. Leave now and I'll freeze you out of the entire industry, for good. You'll be amazed at how far my tentacles stretch. How's that for ruthless and power-mad?'

'About what I'd have expected.'

'Good, then we both know where we stand.'

'Let me go right now.'

'Not until you see sense,' he said harshly. 'I admit I behaved badly but I didn't plan it. It was mostly accident—'

'Oh, please,' she scoffed.

'It got out of hand, and when you've calmed down I'll explain—'

'You will not explain because I don't want to hear.'

'Olympia, please—'

'I said let me go'

Luke was watching Olympia and his brother with mixed feelings. He'd only known her a few hours, but already she affected him strongly. He'd been looking forward to knowing her better, and then better still. Even his mother's wild hopes hadn't seemed totally fanciful.

And now this!

For he couldn't kid himself. Primo's arrival had

changed something drastically. If Olympia's face hadn't told him that, Primo's would have done. He'd seen emotions in his brother's face that he wouldn't have believed possible. He fixed brooding eyes on them and watched every detail.

When he saw Olympia wrench herself from Primo's grasp he went to her quickly.

'Why don't we slip away by ourselves?' he said. 'Mamma will forgive us.'

Hope's face confirmed it. When Luke signalled to her that he and Olympia were leaving she beamed and blew him a kiss, evidently convinced that the romance was proceeding perfectly.

'Olympia!' It was Primo, dark-faced with anger. 'You can't leave like this.'

'According to whom?' she demanded in outrage. 'Are you daring to give me orders? Just because you've had me dancing to your tune recently you think that's going to go on? Think again. It's over. Your cover's blown. Go on to the next victim and get out of my way.'

For a moment she thought he would refuse, he seemed so firmly set in her path. But then the tension seemed to go out of him and his eyes were suddenly bleak.

'Get out, then,' he said.

Taking Luke's arm, she hurried past him. She was suddenly afraid of Primo.

In half an hour they were seated in a small fish restaurant near the shore. Luke ordered spaghetti with clams and refused to let her speak until she had taken the first few mouthfuls.

She sighed with pleasure. 'Thank you. Now I feel so much better.'

'I had an ulterior motive,' he admitted. 'I expect to

be rewarded with the whole story. What did the *bastardo* do?'

It would have been superfluous to ask who the *bastardo* was.

When she didn't reply, he said gently, 'You did know him, didn't you?'

'Yes, we met in England.'

'But he didn't tell you he was Primo Rinucci?'

'No, he said he was Jack Cayman.'

Luke gave a soft whistle.

'The devil he did! Well, it was his father's name.'

'Yes, your mother told me. She says he's Italian on his mother's side.'

'We're never too sure how much of him is English and how much Italian, and I doubt if he knows either. He sometimes uses the name Cayman in business—'

'This wasn't business,' she said in a tense voice.

He didn't press her any further, but gradually she found it easier to talk. By the time they had finished the spaghetti and had passed on to the oven-baked mullet Luke had a hazy idea of what had happened. Not that she told him many details, but he was good at interpreting the silences.

He was astounded. Primo had done this? His brother, whose name was a byword for good sense, upright behaviour and totally boring probity, had not only lived a double life, but had managed to conduct a clandestine liaison with his own lover. For how else could it be described?

In fact Primo had behaved disgracefully.

Luke was proud of him!

'All I want to do now is go back to England and never see or hear his name again,' she said bitterly. 'But I've signed a contract and he says he'll hold me to it.'

'But of course you're not going home,' Luke said at once. 'You're going to stay here and make him sorry.'

She looked at him, suddenly alert.

'You're right,' she said. 'That's a much better way. Of course it is. I just couldn't bear the thought that he'd been having a big laugh at my expense.'

'But you had a laugh at his expense tonight. Did you see his face when he realised it was you? He looked as if he'd swallowed a hedgehog.'

'Yes, he did,' she mused as the moment came back to her, the details clearer now than they'd been at the time.

'There are going to be other moments like that, plenty of them, because you're going to get your revenge and I'm going to help you do it.'

She smiled at him.

'How?' she asked.

'I'll tell you.'

CHAPTER NINE

PRIMO stayed at the party as long as he could endure it, partly for his mother's sake and partly because he was afraid of what he might do if he followed Luke and Olympia. In the early hours he departed and drove around the city disconsolately until at last he turned the car to the place he had always intended to go.

As he drew up outside the Vallini he saw that the lights of her suite were still on. So she hadn't carried out her threat to leave. He let out a long breath of relief, discovering that his whole body was aching with tension.

The young man on the desk smiled, recognising him from a few days earlier. 'I'll just let her know.'

But Primo stopped him reaching for the phone. 'I want to surprise her.'

'I'm really supposed to call ahead, *signore*.'

A note changed hands.

'I guess you forgot,' Primo said with a conspiratorial smile.

'*Si, signore.*'

She took so long to answer the door that he wondered if she'd left after all. But at last she opened it. Her face set when she saw him but he was ready for this and put his foot in the door before she could slam it. With a swift movement he was inside, facing her fury.

'Get out of here!' she flashed.

'Not until we've had a talk.'

'We've had it. It's over.'

'You didn't let me say anything.'

'I let you say all that I was interested in hearing. Which was zilch. Just what do you imagine there is to say? I trusted you and all the time you were setting me up. I don't know what pleasure you got out of it, but whatever it was you should be ashamed.'

'I am. I never meant it to go so far. Please, Olympia, it was just a joke that got of hand.'

'You kept it going a lot longer than that.'

'Things happened unexpectedly. It all ran out of control.'

'I don't believe what I'm hearing. It ran out of your control? Primo Rinucci, the big boss, the man in charge, who snaps his fingers and people jump—'

'Cut that out,' he raged. 'You created a tailor's dummy and told yourself a load of stories about him, but he's not me. He never was.'

'Why didn't you stop me?'

'Because I was enjoying myself,' he said rashly.

'Ah, now we have it. You loved making a fool of me—'

'I didn't mean that. I meant—'

Somewhere there were the words that would tell her of the delight he'd known during those few days when he'd teased and incited her while falling under her spell. There must be words for the sweetness that had engulfed him, the sense of a miracle, so long awaited, that must be treated with care, lest it vanish. And more words for the fear that overcame him whenever he thought of telling the truth and risking everything.

Yes, there were words. If only he could find them.

'Well?' she demanded remorselessly.

'I didn't mean it to turn out the way it did,' was the best he could manage.

'No, you didn't mean to get caught out.'

'That wasn't what I—'

'Just how did you plan to tell me? Or didn't you?'

'Of course I was going to tell you, but it was hard. I knew you'd misunderstand.'

'Surely not?' she said caustically. 'How could anyone misunderstand a man who gives a false name and lures a woman into making a fool of herself just so that he can have a cheap laugh? Men do it every day, and women put up with it.'

'And what about what women do every day?' he demanded, stung to anger. 'You were planning a good laugh yourself, weren't you? When Rinucci turned up you were going to take him for a ride. You had it all worked out, down to the last detail, fluttering your eyelashes, plus the old hair trick culled from a hundred corny films.

'You even enlisted me to give you "inside information"—your own words—to weaken his defences, and never mind what a fool you'd be making of him when he turned up and I watched you bringing him down. I may have behaved badly, but that's nothing to the derision you piled on him—I mean me. Oh, hell!'

'You can't even sort out which of you is which,' she snapped.

'That's true,' he said wryly.

'What do you think it was like for me to find out the truth the way I did?'

'How could I have anticipated that? I didn't know you were going to be at my mother's.'

'I wouldn't have been if I'd known you were coming back. You kept very quiet about it.'

'I wanted to surprise you.'

'You sure as hell did that.'

'Olympia, please, I know I did wrong, but it wasn't for a laugh.'

'You'll never get me to believe that in a million years, so don't try.'

She turned and stormed away from him. She'd changed out of her glamorous red dress into serviceable trousers and sweater. Her face was free of make-up and her hair was dishevelled. It looked as if she'd torn down the elaborate arrangement then scragged it back any old how. A few wisps hung down over her face, softening the austere lines.

Despite her rage it was her misery that reached him most poignantly. Without the glitz she was pale and slightly wan, and even more beautiful in his eyes. He longed to reach out to her but he knew it wasn't the right time. She wasn't ready to hear what he had to say.

She was walking up and down the room now, brooding bitterly. 'All those things I said. I trusted you.'

The injustice of this made his temper rise again.

'Yes, you trusted me with a blow-by-blow account of the unscrupulous methods a woman adopts to bring a man to heel. A real eye-opener! I should write a book about it. Men beware! This is what they get up to. You turned me into a fellow conspirator with myself as the intended victim. I don't know who to feel sorrier for— me or me!'

'I warned you I wasn't a nice person,' she told him. 'Remember that day I said that I was up front about what I wanted and what I'd do to get it? You should have believed me.'

'I did believe you,' he shouted. 'How could I not when I was getting a demonstration every moment? You did a great job. Up front with *me,* not with him, although of course you couldn't have afforded to be. That's what you're really angry about, isn't it? You showed your weapons to the wrong man and now they're dead in your hands.'

'Don't worry, I'm not planning to use them on you.'

'But you *did* use them on me, and to hell with me and my feelings! Did you ever think of your victim? Suppose I'd fallen in love with you?'

'Be honest! You were in no danger of that.'

'Luckily for me I wasn't. I'm safe against your kind—'

'And just what is my "kind"?'

'Heartless, scheming, manipulative, calculating—take your pick. Yes, I'm safe, but you didn't know that. If I'd fallen in love with you that wouldn't have mattered, would it? Just a casualty of the war, only it wasn't my war, you heartless woman!'

In despair she stared at him. All the things that had seemed so simple before, when she had prided herself on being immune to feelings, now presented themselves in stark, livid colours, shocking in the light he turned on them.

When she spoke her voice shook. 'Then it's fortunate for both of us that you're so armoured—almost as armoured as I am.'

'Yes, I noticed that,' he said softly. 'When I held you, trembling in my arms, I thought how cold and indifferent you were.'

Her eyes glittered in a way he knew. 'I do it very well, don't I?' she said softly. 'I know all the right buttons to press, and I can press them in the right order.'

He paled. 'Are you telling me it was all an act?'

'Are you so sure it wasn't?'

Her words brought them to the edge of the precipice, showing him the disaster waiting below.

'Olympia, don't,' he said urgently. 'Don't do this, please don't, for both our sakes.'

'But what do you think I'm doing? Just being honest, that's all.'

'This isn't honesty. It's pride and revenge, and maybe you have the right, but don't do it. Don't ruin what we still might have.'

She gave a cruel laugh. 'You actually imagine that there might be something between us, after this?'

'I know it sounds crazy, but that's because we've been performing in masks, inventing other selves and thinking that's who we were. But if we could get clear of that and be ourselves—'

He left the implication hanging in the air and for a moment he thought he'd won. Her face softened and a weary look passed across it. But then she said, 'If we could do that we'd probably find we liked each other—and ourselves—even less. It's too late, Ja—' She broke off and a spasm of pain went over her face. 'Signor Rinucci.'

'Don't call me that,' he shouted.

'It's a useful reminder, in case I forget,' she cried back at him. 'Or in case you do.'

He closed his eyes. His world was disintegrating about him and whatever he did made it worse. He could only say her name in anguish.

'Olympia—Olympia—'

'*Don't*.'

They stood in silence, neither knowing what to say.

He looked around him and suddenly noticed things that he'd failed to notice before, and which now seemed ominous.

A half-packed suitcase stood open on the sofa and several clothes were draped over the back.

'Packing?' he breathed. 'Now?'

'Yes, now. I'm moving out of here tonight.'

'I told you, you can't go back to England.'

'I'm not. I've decided to stay and take up the job with Leonate. But I'm moving out of here tonight and going where you can't follow me.'

'There's nowhere I can't follow you, and I will.'

'You don't need to. I'm coming to work tomorrow. Or is that another of your fictions?'

'No, the job is there.'

'Then it's about time I met my colleagues, Signore Leonate and Signor Rinucci who, I understand, is the real power behind the throne. I'm longing to meet *him*—that is, if you can sort out which one he is.'

'Stop it,' he said violently. 'Are you going to beat me over the head with that for ever?'

'I can try.'

'So you reckon you're the injured innocent? I don't think so. I may have laid a small trap, but you made it bigger and jumped in with both feet. I'm sorry you feel foolish, but it's nothing to the kind of foolish that I'd have felt if things had worked out the way you meant.'

He came closer to her, seizing her arm so that she couldn't turn away from him.

'That was quite a plan you had, Olympia. Rinucci was going to turn up and you were going to use your wiles on him, and I was going to do what, exactly? Cheer you on from the sidelines? Suppose I'd warned him and brought your house of cards tumbling down? Did you think of that? Of course you didn't, because you never thought that far ahead.'

'How far ahead did you think?' she flung at him.

'Not far enough, which is why I don't blame you too much—'

'Big of you, considering that you started it.'

'That's arguable. You said a lot of things before you made the most cursory check who I was. The astute operator you want me to believe in wouldn't have done that. Perhaps I should question your skills a little more. Not your seductive skills, because we know about those—'

There was a crack as her hand connected with his face. Then something seemed to hold them both petrified. Her eyes were filled with anger, bitterness and insult. But there was also anguish and a kind of fear.

He saw it and his own anger died. Even at this moment he discovered that he couldn't bear to see her hurt. It made quarrelling very difficult.

'Let's say that makes us even,' he told her quietly. 'Now can we draw a line under it?'

'I don't know,' she said in a choking voice.

'But I do.' He turned her towards him and gently drew her close. 'That's it,' he said as he lowered his mouth to hers. 'No more fighting. It's finished.'

'You can't just—'

'Yes, I can,' he said, silencing her.

The last thought of which she was capable was, *How dare he?*

How dared he think that one kiss could make up for everything, and that she would simply do as he asked because his lips thrilled her? She would show him that he was wrong—she *must* show him that—just as soon as her strength came back.

But instead of returning it was draining away with every movement of his mouth against hers, as her body grew warmer, more eager to be his, and with less will of its own.

'The past is over,' he murmured against her mouth. 'It's the future that matters.'

'But how can we—?' she whispered back.

'I don't know. Who knows the future? We make it ourselves. Hold me.'

She did so, sliding her arms about his neck, part embracing him, part clinging to him for safety. There were no thoughts now, only the blind instinct to seek him, join with him, belong to him.

The past no longer mattered. She'd known she was falling in love with him. She'd faced it, accepted it, even welcomed it. Now she felt the warmth of his body communicating itself to hers and she knew that she needed that warmth, not only in her flesh but in her heart.

For too many years she'd been cold, hiding from love in her bleak cave. She knew now that only he could tempt her out. It was a risk, but every skilled movement of his mouth, his hands, urged her to take that risk and say, with him, that the past was over and they would make the future together.

In a haze of delight she was barely aware of him moving, drawing her after him in the direction of her bedroom. Not until she heard the door click did she get a sense of danger.

'Wait—' she said urgently.

He picked her up in his arms. 'Haven't we waited long enough?'

'But there's something I must—you don't understand—'

'I understand this,' he said, kissing her again. 'What else is there to understand?'

As he spoke he kicked the door open and walked into the grandiose bedroom, heading for the huge luxurious bed, so absorbed in his passion that he was close up to it before he realised that something was there that shouldn't have been.

A man was stretched out on the coverlet, his hands behind his head, grinning derisively.

'Hallo,' said Luke.

For a moment Primo could do no more than stare at his brother. Just as Olympia, earlier that evening, had told herself that what she saw was impossible, so now Primo closed, opened and closed his eyes, certain that the next time Luke would have disappeared.

But he stayed there, solid and, to his brother, thoroughly objectionable.

'You really should have warned me,' Primo said, speaking to Olympia but not looking at her. 'But if I'd been sharper I'd have expected it.'

'Will you please put me down?' she said edgily.

He meant to lower her with dignity but shock was causing the strength to drain away from his arms. They gave way abruptly and she ended up sprawling on the bed where Luke quickly took hold of her to stop her sliding off.

'No need to throw the lady about,' Luke observed. 'Not that I mind, you understand.'

Primo treated this remark with disdain. It was that or murder.

'What a picture!' he said softly. 'I should have known, shouldn't I?'

'How dare you?' Olympia flashed. 'Luke came here to help me to get out of this place.'

She scrambled to the floor, flushed and panting. Torn by conflicting feelings, bitterness and passion, she felt she would explode any minute. For a blinding moment she hated both of them.

'If you're thinking what I think you are—' she threw at Primo.

'He was waiting for you in your bedroom all the time,' he said with a thin smile. 'What do you expect me to think?'

'He's fully dressed, or haven't you noticed that? I told you, Luke came here to help me.'

'Hidden in your bedroom?' Primo demanded, almost savagely. The thought that Luke had been here all the time, listening, made him wild.

'That's where people usually do their packing,' Luke pointed out, indicating another open suitcase. 'I've just been fetching and carrying, acting like a maid.'

'Helping your mistress undress?' Primo asked coldly. 'Isn't that what a maid does?'

'Among other things.'

'Shut up both of you,' Olympia said fiercely. 'You—' she turned on Primo '—you do not own me, you do not give me orders, I am not answerable to you, except at work.'

'Where I expect you to be tomorrow morning,' he snapped. 'Be on time.'

'He's right, we'd better be going,' Luke said, scrambling off the bed. 'Olympia, I'll wait for you in the next room.'

'There's no need, I'm coming,' she said. 'Everything's packed.'

She began to close the suitcase, not looking at Primo. He watched her in silence for a moment.

At last he spoke in a harsh voice. 'Will you tell me where you're going to stay? Or needn't I ask?'

Now she looked at him and was startled by his face. She had seen him charming, and sometimes annoyed, but never coldly venomous, as now. Beneath the surface control he was in a bitter rage that threatened to engulf him, and for the second time that night she was actually afraid of him.

'You needn't ask,' she said. 'I'm staying in Luke's apartment.'

'Then get out of my sight and don't talk to me again,' he raged. '*Go on! Get out!*'

Since her car was still at the hotel, Luke took her to work the next morning and introduced her to Enrico Leonate. He was a plump elderly man with a genial manner and he welcomed her with open arms.

'Primo has told me so much about you,' he enthused.

'I hope he's explained that my Italian is very basic,' Olympia said.

'It will improve, and in the meantime we all speak English very well.'

'And besides, Miss Lincoln is a quick learner,' said a voice behind her.

'Ah, Primo,' Enrico cried. 'Come in. Miss Lincoln and I were just introducing ourselves.'

'Please call me Olympia,' she said to the old man.

'Then you must call me Enrico. Primo, here she is, and just as lovely as you said.'

'I don't think I said that exactly,' Primo replied coolly.

'But you—'

'Described her as businesslike, focused, intelligent, diligent and—as I said before, a very quick learner. She's particularly good at winning people over.'

'That's what we need,' Enrico roared happily.

'Don't accept everything Signor Rinucci says about me,' Olympia said lightly. 'He's prejudiced.'

'Of course he's prejudiced in your favour. He saw you at work in England.'

'That's very true,' Primo murmured.

'And you were impressed?'

'Oh, yes, it was an impressive sight. I believe I've said as much to you since, *signorina*.'

'You have indeed,' she riposted. 'But I was learning much from you, a true master in the art of manipulation.'

'That's his Italian side,' Enrico said triumphantly. 'It is our gift to see things from many angles at once. When you have been with us for a while, you too will have learned it. Primo will teach you.'

'You do the *signorina* an injustice,' Primo said. 'She has nothing to learn from me.'

Luke had been watching this exchange from where he'd been standing quietly by the window, his eyes alight with malicious pleasure. Now, as though feeling that he'd enjoyed the entertainment long enough, he roused himself to say, 'I'd better be going. Call me later, Olympia, and I'll collect you.'

'I don't want to be a nuisance,' she said. 'I could get my car from the Vallini and drive home.'

'You don't know the way yet. It was dark when we did the journey last night.' He gave her a warm smile. 'And how could you ever be a nuisance?'

'That's a very nice thing to say, but actually it's just a slur on my driving.'

'I was maintaining a diplomatic silence about your driving,' he said with a grin.

'Goodbye!' she told him firmly.

'Yes, goodbye,' Primo said without looking up.

Luke winked at Olympia and departed.

'Primo has told me how you took him around the Curtis factories,' Enrico said. 'Now I think he should return the favour and show you around the Leonate empire.'

'Actually, Enrico, that's a bit difficult,' Primo said. 'I've got a backlog of work to get through. I suggest that Signora Pattino undertakes this task.'

'As you say. Well, why don't you show Olympia to her office?'

'No, you do that. I have to get going. *Signorina*, I should like to welcome you to Leonate and hope that you will be happy with us.'

He said the last words like a robot and was gone instantly.

'Well, he really does have a lot to do,' Enrico said, sounding awkward. 'Let's go.'

That day was like the culmination of every ambitious dream she'd ever had. The office he showed her was modern, attractive and better than her old one. They discussed the firm and he was impressed with her knowledge.

'You've been learning about Leonate,' he said. 'Well done! You're everything Primo said you'd be.'

He swept her off to lunch, taking also Signora Pattino, his Personal Assistant, a comfortable, middle-aged woman who said she would enjoy being her guide in the coming days. Wherever she went she was welcomed as an asset by people who knew nothing about her except what Primo had told them.

But whatever he'd said was in the past. This morning he'd shown a cruel irony that reflected his true feelings now. Their conversation, superficially friendly, had been charged with hidden meaning that Enrico hadn't understood.

But Luke had understood every word.

CHAPTER TEN

PRIMO, descending into Leonate's underground car park prior to departure, saw his brother just drawing up and noticed sourly that he had a flashy new car. Which explained, he thought, why he hadn't recognised it outside the hotel the night before.

Luke got out of the car and hailed him cheerfully. 'Is she ready and waiting for me?'

'Since I haven't seen *Signorina* Lincoln all afternoon, I couldn't tell you,' Primo said frostily.

'Very formal suddenly. I expect that was her idea, and it's no more than you deserve. Did nobody ever explain to you that it's customary to introduce yourself to the lady at the start? With the right name, I mean. It does wonders for putting them in a good mood.'

'*She told you?*'

Luke shrugged. 'I hardly needed telling. At the party last night, it became very obvious what you'd done.'

'And I suppose you jumped at the chance to serve me an ill turn,' Primo raged. 'Something you've been waiting to do.'

'Don't blame me. I'm innocent in all this.'

'Am I supposed to believe it was an accident that she was at the villa?'

'Of course it was. Don't be a damned fool! It was bound to happen sooner or later. You shouldn't have left her alone.'

'I only meant to be away for a day,' Primo said

through gritted teeth. 'Things proved to be more complicated when I got there.'

'Things always do. What happened to the man who planned everything and took no chances?'

Primo glared at him with sombre resentment. He could have said that this man had died the moment he'd set eyes on Olympia, replaced by another who would take any wild risk to claim her. But hell would freeze over before he said this to his brother and enemy.

'You're really enjoying this, aren't you?' he snapped.

'The situation has its charm. Serves you right for playing such a tomfool trick! You're usually such a stick-in-the-mud. Not last night, though. If there's one man I'd never have expected to pick the lady up and carry her to bed, it's you. Pity I was there to spoil the fun.'

The last word was choked off as Luke found himself thrust back against the wall with his brother's hand at his throat.

'One more word and I won't be responsible for my actions,' Primo said murderously.

'Hey, calm down. All right, let's leave it.'

Primo released him, leaving Luke to rub his throat and take deep breaths.

'Another side of you I never suspected,' he said, slightly hoarsely. 'Well, well.'

'I'm warning you, Luke, she's not for you.'

'Isn't that for her to decide?'

'*Stay away from her.*'

'That would be hard since we're living together.'

'Don't fool yourself. She only went with you to revenge herself on me. She cares nothing for you.'

'You're sure of that, are you?' His eyes met Primo's in a direct challenge.

'Go to hell,' Primo said.

'If I can take her with me, I'll go anywhere. Ah, here she is.'

Luke went forward to greet Olympia with a kiss on the cheek, but Primo did not see this. He walked away to his own car, got in and drove away.

As Luke drove her home he asked, 'Did he give you a hard time today, demanding explanations and so forth?'

'Not at all. He barely spoke to me.'

'Good. Don't you go explaining anything. It's no business of his.'

'I know. It's just that it feels like deceiving him.'

'Not deceiving. Just leading him up the garden path. And let's face it, that's how you two communicate.'

She gave a wry laugh. 'That's true enough.'

Luke's home was on the southern boundary of Naples, in a recently built apartment block. Here everything was ultra-modern and shining. The computer was the latest, smoothest, most powerful of its kind. So was the internet connection, the printer, and 'all the other bells and whistles' as Luke cynically put it.

The same was true of everything in the kitchen, where the cooking arrangements were so complex that they could have propelled a spacecraft to the moon.

'But they also do a mean scrambled egg,' Luke had pointed out the previous night, then proceeded to demonstrate.

The apartment had two bedrooms, both with double beds and acres of wardrobe space. Her suitcases were still only half unpacked in the guest room, and now she hung up the rest of her things.

Luke knocked on the door. 'I've made you some tea.'

'Thank you,' she said fervently.

While they were drinking tea she said, 'I'd offer to

cook supper but I don't think I could cope with your kitchen.'

'Another time. You have a lot of reading to do, if that stuff you've brought home means anything.'

'Right, and I'm going to have to work hard because it's in Italian and I'm still learning.'

'Let me know if you need any help.'

She studied while he cooked, refusing to let her help. Nor would he allow her to help clear away after the excellent meal. After several hours devoted to files, with his assistance over awkward words, she felt she was beginning to get a grip on things.

How would it have felt if it had been Primo here, helping her out, caring for her with kindness? She closed her eyes. He no longer existed.

By the end of the evening she had a strange sense of contentment and safety. Luke even made her a mug of cocoa and said goodnight to her at her bedroom door.

She didn't see Primo for two days and then he dropped into her office without warning.

'Getting ready to go?' he asked, seeing her tidying papers on her desk.

'Yes, Signora Pattino and I are setting out tomorrow. I'm looking forward to it.'

She tried to speak normally, not letting him see how the sight of him affected her.

'Good. Enrico tells me that you're doing well.'

'He seems to have started with a good opinion of me. That must be down to you.'

'I told him what I thought, that your executive talents are considerable.'

'Even though you hate me?'

'I don't hate you, Olympia, and I hope you don't hate

me. You did what you had to do. I should have understood sooner. It would have saved us both a lot of pain.'

The pain was there in his face. She saw it when she looked up, and her heart went out to him.

But he didn't want her heart. He was still unyielding. Nothing in him was reaching out to her in return.

'Are you talking about Luke?' she asked.

'It hardly matters now.'

'Don't wave me aside like that. Of course it matters.'

'I just think you might have warned me that he was in your bedroom.'

'I told him to stay out of sight while I got rid of you. I meant to do that in ten seconds.'

'But you didn't—'

'I got angry with you and I forgot about him. He was only helping me pack—'

'And undress.'

'It was a hired dress. I had to leave it behind. I changed into something plain and useful, as you saw.' She folded her arms and gave him a challenging look. 'I promise you, they were not my seduction clothes.'

'True. I remember.'

'I've got to get going.' She turned away to her desk but he detained her with a hand on her arm.

'I just want you to know—I really didn't throw you down on to the bed. It was an accident.'

She gave a shaky laugh. 'I guess I knew that. You're not the caveman type—whichever one of you was there that night.' She saw him close his eyes suddenly. 'Hey, I was only joking. It's the past. Over and done with.'

'As you say, over and done with. But I wish you weren't living with Luke.'

'Maybe I'll find somewhere else later, when I know more about Naples.'

'I've got friends in the business. I could—'

'Primo, stop this. You can't organise me. Not everyone can be bought off with a hefty tip.'

'What do you mean?'

'I mean the hotel receptionist who didn't call ahead to warn me you were coming. He was apologetic when I went down. He didn't actually say you bribed him, but I guess you have your own methods of persuasion. Primo Rinucci always gets his own way, doesn't he?'

'Not always,' he said sadly. 'Sometimes even he knows when he has to admit defeat. Goodbye, *Signorina* Lincoln. I wish you well in your career.'

The soft touch of his lips on her cheek was unnerving. Then he was gone.

She and Signora Pattino were away for a week touring the Leonate factories in southern Italy. They got on well; Olympia drank in information about the firm and her companion was impressed.

Everything she had ever wanted would soon be hers, but now she wanted something more. And she had lost it.

But as they began the long drive back her courage revived. She was haunted by the memory of their last meeting, the sadness she had sensed in him despite his distant manner. He wasn't cold to her, whatever he might want her to believe. Sometimes she could still feel his kiss on her cheek.

They were working in the same building. She would have a hundred chances to take him aside, persuade him to talk. And out of that talk would come understanding and mutual forgiveness.

Surely it was the same with him. The time apart had allowed their tempers to cool and now they were ready to move on. The future could still be theirs. As she arrived back in Naples she was full of confidence and almost happiness.

Enrico welcomed her back jubilantly, and in Italian.

'Such glowing reports I've had of you! Everyone says you're wonderful.'

'Everyone's been very kind to me,' she said, also in Italian.

'Ah, Primo was right to praise you. If only he could be here to see your triumph. But I'll tell him next time I phone England.'

'England?'

'Yes, he had to go back. Cedric Tandy's confidence has been shaken by the Banyon episode, and he says he can't go on. So Primo's had to dash back and take over until a full-time replacement will be found. He'll be away for quite a while.'

Olympia often thought that Primo would have been surprised if he could have seen her at home with Luke, who acted like a kindly brother. Since he had an arrangement with a firm who cleaned the place and took care of his laundry she had nothing to do but think of her career.

Sometimes he would take her to the villa to have dinner with the family. Hope would overwhelm her with tender consideration, clearly trying to smooth their 'romance' along, which made Olympia feel slightly awkward but Luke seemed unperturbed.

Once, while she was there, the phone rang. Hope answered it, saying, '*Ciao, caro,*' and it soon became clear that she was talking to Primo. Olympia listened to the flood of Italian which was too rapid for her to follow in detail, but she could tell that there was no mention of him returning home soon.

Hope hung up with a sigh. 'I like to have them around me,' she said. 'I am unreasonable, since they are all grown men, but there! Mothers *are* unreasonable. And perhaps it's better for Primo and Luke to be apart just now.'

There was a slight buzzing in Olympia's ears. 'Why just now?' she asked, trying not to sound too curious.

'It's hard to say. All their lives they have been fighting. If it's not about this, it's about that. The last thing was a man they both wanted to employ, but Primo snatched him from under Luke's nose. ''Stole him'' according to Luke. But that's not important. There's something else, something that causes really bad blood between them.'

It gave Olympia a shock to realise that Hope still didn't know what had been between herself and Primo. She thought they had met for the first time at the party.

'Was that Primo?' Luke asked from the doorway.

'Yes, he is well and he sends his love to everyone.'

'Including me?' Luke asked in disbelief.

'Including you,' Hope said firmly.

'Perhaps I'd better test it for poison first.'

'Stop that,' Hope ordered him, suddenly stern. 'Whatever it is that has come between you, he is still your brother.'

'Sorry, Mamma,' Luke said sheepishly. He put his arms about her and kissed her. 'It's nothing,' he told her tenderly. 'You know that he and I have always been at odds about one thing or another.'

'But this time it's serious, I know it is. Why won't you tell me?'

'Because it's nothing. Come on, you know what we're like. If we're not scrapping we're not happy.'

After that he exerted himself to make her laugh and the matter was allowed to pass.

Primo wasn't mentioned again, but he stayed in Olympia's thoughts and perhaps Luke's too, because he suddenly began talking about him as they drove home that night.

'He's a contradictory man in many ways,' he mused. 'He can feel something with all his being, while doing things that go completely in the other direction.'

'Surely most people can do that?'

'Yes, but he takes it to extremes. Maybe it's the result of not really knowing whether he's Italian or English. You only have to look at how he behaved over our brother Justin.'

'Exactly who is Justin?' she asked curiously. 'I keep hearing odd bits of information but never very much. He's almost like a ghost.'

'For years he was a completely taboo subject. We all knew that Mamma had another son, but nobody knew what had happened to him. She was only fifteen when she became pregnant. She wasn't married, of course, and in those days it was a great stigma. What her parents did was unforgivable, but they must have been desperate.'

'What did they do?'

'Snatched her baby, handed it over for adoption and told her he'd been born dead.'

'Dear God!' Olympia exclaimed, shocked to the core.

'She never got over the loss of her baby. She married Jack Cayman and became Primo's stepmother. Primo couldn't remember his real mother and he adored Hope from the start. When they adopted me he wasn't best pleased. I was competition for her attention, you see. We've always fought and bickered.

'But I think the thing that really got to him, almost as

much as it did Hope, was when she discovered that her baby hadn't died after all. She went crazy trying to find him, but it was too late. He'd been adopted. She'd lost him.

'Her marriage didn't last. When it ended she took me with her, but Primo was Jack's son and she couldn't claim custody. But when Jack died Primo's Italian family brought him here and she contacted him again. Since she married Toni we've all been one big family.

'But Mamma never forgot her first son. She couldn't trace him, but when he turned eighteen she began hoping that he would try to trace her. No luck though.

'In the end it was Primo who found him. He contacted every private eye in England that he could find, putting down markers, saying he was to be notified if anyone likely turned up. And in the end it happened.

'But here's the strange thing. Primo was always jealous of Justin for displacing him as Mamma's eldest son. Yet he did it for her, because he knew what it meant to her. It took him fifteen years, and, when he got the first hint, he went over to England to meet him, check him out, then bring him back here.'

'What a wonderful thing for him to do,' Olympia said, touched.

'Yes, it was. My brother drives me nuts sometimes. He's pig-headed, too sure of himself, blinkered, obstinate—but then he'll do something that makes you stare, and wonder if you could be as generous as that. And I don't think most people could.'

His words brought back a memory—Primo talking on the phone to an agitated Cedric, calming him with kindness, promising to be there for him, no matter the inconvenience.

And that was the real Primo, the one who could empathise with someone else, even when it was against his own interests.

'Fifteen years,' she murmured. 'He would have been so young when he started.'

'True. Fifteen years of patient watching and waiting. That's very Primo. He knows how to take his time. Incredibly, he's still jealous. Mamma's thrilled about what he did for her. She calls him her hero. But he minds about Justin because he feels displaced.'

His words gave Olympia a strange feeling because they cast a new light on Primo's behaviour in England: watching and waiting, moving slowly towards his goal, keeping in the shadows while she tricked and teased another man—even though that man was himself.

She thought of the quiet, self-effacing generosity of someone who would spend years seeking a person he didn't really want to find, to please the mother he loved.

How she wished she could have known him under other circumstances! How different things might have been!

Life with Luke was contented. She found him easy to talk to and he soon knew all about her, including the story of her elderly parents. After an initial hesitation she told him about the Valentine cards and how she'd fooled Primo.

'So he was living with you?' Luke asked when he'd finished laughing.

'No, he just stayed one night.'

'Ah, I see.'

'No, you don't see,' she said, aiming a swipe at him. 'It was because he had a bump on the head.'

'Which you gave him?'

'In a manner of speaking. We had a little altercation on the way home and he crashed his car into mine.'

He eyed her askance. 'None of the men in my family are safe from you in a car, are they?'

'Anyway, Valentine's was next day and you should have seen his face when the cards arrived. And the red roses that my parents always send me.'

'Have they ever been to Naples?' he asked.

'Never. I took them to Paris once as a treat, but apart from that they've never been abroad.'

'I'm going to be away for a few days. Why not invite them to stay here?'

'You really mean that?'

'Why not? Give them a real vacation. They'll enjoy the *Maggio dei Monumenti*.'

'Whatever's that?'

'Literally it means May of the Monuments, although it starts in the last week in April. For a few weeks many museums and monuments open for free, and because they attract such crowds other things have started up at the same time—fairs, dance spectacles, that sort of thing.'

'Wait, I saw a puppet show in the street yesterday,' she remembered.

'That's right, it's just started, and now there'll be processions and concerts of Neapolitan songs. Spring is coming and it's a great way to celebrate. Call your parents and get them down for the fun.'

She did so, booked and paid for the tickets, and met them at the airport three days later. It was a joyous reunion, only slightly marred by her mother's immediate exclamation, 'Darling, you look so thin and tired. Are you working too hard?'

They behaved, as she afterwards told Luke, 'like a

couple of kids at the seaside for the first time.' She spent the weekend showing them around the city, now growing warmer as April passed into May. When she had to return to work they were sufficiently confident to make their own way around, and even to take a day trip to Pompeii to see the ruins.

The following evening Enrico took them all out to dinner, entertained them with outrageous stories and flirted like mad with Olympia's mother, while her father looked on in resignation.

'She's incorrigible,' he told his daughter. 'She always has been.' But he said it with a touch of pride.

They returned home to the disconcerting sight of Luke, asleep on the sofa.

'I got back early,' he said, getting up and rubbing his eyes. 'My business finished quickly, and I wanted to meet our guests.'

They were charmed by him, especially since he put himself out to achieve that very object. They all sat up late into the night eating pizzas, drinking wine and becoming the best of friends. By the time they'd finished he was calling them Harold and Angela.

There was an awkward moment when it became clear that Luke meant to spend the night on the sofa.

'Oh, but there's no need for that,' said Angela, anxious to be broad-minded. 'I mean—just because we're here there's no need for you to do anything different—'

'Let it go,' Harold begged, covering his eyes.

'But I only—'

'Darling, they know their own business best. Come to bed. Goodnight, you two.'

He said the last words hastily and almost carried his wife out of the room.

When they had gone Luke regarded her gleefully. 'I

think I've just been given your mother's permission to—'

'Yes, I know what she's given you permission *to*—' she said with heavy irony. 'Thank you for being nice to my parents. Now, I think I'll go to bed.'

'Are you sure you don't want me to come with you? Since it's all right with your mother—'

'Luke, I'm warning you—'

'All right. It was worth a try.' He gave a melancholy sigh. 'Back to the sofa.'

'Goodnight.' She was laughing.

He grinned. 'Goodnight.'

Next morning his mutual admiration society with Angela was increased when, owing to a failure in communication, she walked into the bathroom while he was in the shower. Retreating in haste, she confided to her daughter, 'He's got ever such nice legs, dear.'

'*Mum!* Does your husband know that you notice men's legs?'

'Only too well,' Harold moaned. 'I can't take her on the beach.'

She regarded them fondly. They had been married for fifty years and they were like a pair of crazy, loving children. This was how marriage should be, and how it so seldom was.

They've found a secret that I'll never find, she thought. *If I'd known, I might never have lost him.*

CHAPTER ELEVEN

OVER breakfast Luke called his mother, then announced that he was taking them all to the villa that night. Her parents exchanged looks and Olympia realised with dismay that this had given another twist to the screw of her supposed love affair with Luke.

But it was hard to deny it right now when she was still sore from Primo's behaviour. At least Luke was saving her face, which perhaps was his kindly intention. Living together was possible because his manner towards her was never loverlike.

Then she put the thought aside to concentrate on making her parents' visit memorable. They were guests of honour at the villa, treated like royalty, with the whole family lined up on the steps to greet them.

Toni kissed Angela's hand, followed by Francesco, then Carlo, then Ruggiero, then—

'Look who's here,' Hope said excitedly to Olympia. 'But I expect you already knew.'

'No, I didn't know Primo was back,' she said, trying to catch her breath.

She felt her hand taken into his, the shock of his warmth and strength. She was struggling to clear her head.

'I haven't contacted Enrico yet,' he said. 'But when I called home and Mamma said we had honoured guests, of course I had to be here.'

'Of course,' she murmured.

It was six weeks since she'd seen him, and he'd changed. His hair had lost its slightly shaggy look and was trimmed back neat and severe against his skull. It made him look older and slightly stern. Then she realised that the real change was in his face. He had lost weight and there were shadows under his eyes, which seemed darker, yet more brilliant.

Olympia suddenly remembered her mother's remarks about her own looks. So he too had lain awake through long, lonely nights, thinking of how different things might have been.

He greeted Angela and Harold with perfect courtesy, but with a slight reserve that afterwards made Angela whisper to her daughter, 'I don't like him as much as his brother.'

Hope swept the two elderly people away for a glass of wine. Primo surveyed Luke, standing just behind Olympia.

'Allow me to congratulate you,' he said, 'on your engagement.'

Olympia made a helpless gesture. 'Primo—look—'

She was about to say that there was no engagement, but Primo continued, 'And, while we're being formal, allow me to introduce *Signorina* Galina Mantini.'

Out of the corner of her eye Olympia had just noticed a young woman coming towards them. Now she registered that this was the most astoundingly lovely creature she had ever seen. She seemed to be about eighteen, with honey-blonde hair that reached almost to her waist, and a flawless, peachy skin. She laid a possessive hand on Primo's arm, gazed at him adoringly and giggled.

'Galina, this is my brother, Luke, and his fiancée, Olympia.'

The glorious Galina put out her hand and said, '*Buon giorno,*' in a soft, ravishing voice.

Olympia pulled herself together to return the greeting. Outwardly controlled, inwardly she was hurt and angry.

Her own sadness of the last few weeks suddenly seemed like a mockery. She'd thought his feelings were as deep as her own, when she'd merely been a passing fancy.

You should have known! How often had she said that about him? She hadn't been ready for this. But she ought to have been.

She was too preoccupied to notice Luke's eyes, flickering this way and that, bright with malicious interest. As they moved on into the house Luke gave his brother an understanding nod, which Primo met with a set, rigid face. But she didn't see that either.

Her parents seemed to be instinctively on everyone's wavelength, especially Grandpapa Rinucci, who seized on them with delight.

'What a fascinating man,' Angela said when she'd briefly escaped his clutches. 'Did you know he's actually seen Vesuvius erupt?'

'In 1944,' Luke said with a grin, 'soon after Italy was liberated. It lasted three days and he managed to grab a piece of lava as a souvenir. Ever since then he knows when the volcano is speaking to him personally. When anyone isn't telling the truth it sends a plume of smoke into the air.'

He said this like someone reciting words often recited before and Angela chuckled. 'You've heard it all before, haven't you?' she asked.

'Only about a thousand times,' Luke groaned.

'But we're really grateful to you,' said Toni, who was listening nearby. 'It's a long time since the old man had a brand new audience.'

Angela looked around her in delight, taking in the warmth of the whole family.

'You're so lucky,' she told Hope. 'So many sons and so good-looking.'

'But you too are lucky,' Hope said. 'The sadness of

my life is that I didn't have a daughter. I would have liked one as much like yours as possible.' Then she added conspiratorially, 'But perhaps soon you will share her with me?'

Angela nodded, also conspiratorial.

'Sons are a great trial,' Hope confided. 'I have six, and how many have brought girls to their mother's party tonight? Only two.'

Her accusing gaze fell on Carlo, who reddened.

'Mamma—I did explain—'

'I do not wish to discuss it,' she informed him loftily. 'Except to say that I have heard of that incident, and you should be ashamed of yourself.'

'I am, Mamma,' he said unconvincingly.

Ruggiero, his twin, chimed in beside him. 'He is. He's very ashamed of himself. And I'm ashamed for him.'

Under his mother's withering glance he fell silent. When Hope was sure she'd reduced her menfolk to abject submission she turned back to Angela.

'You should give thanks you never had boys,' she told her. 'They are nothing but trouble. But at least two of my sons are behaving properly tonight.'

Her smiling glance included Luke and Olympia, then Primo and Galina. She seemed to be waiting for someone to say something. But nobody did. At last Ruggiero said, with the air of a man desperate to break the silence, 'Francesco is bringing his girlfriend tonight.'

'Good. At least one of you knows his duty. And there he is.'

She went forward to greet Francesco who had appeared with a pretty, modest-looking young woman. Hope made much of her, to the knowing grins of the others.

Dinner was a riot. Harold was seated next to Grandpapa Rinucci, who spoke good English which, as he would tell anyone who would listen, he'd learned from the Allies in 1944. That was when Vesuvius—

And Harold won his eternal friendship by saying, 'Tell me about Vesuvius. It's fascinating.' Just as if he hadn't heard it once already.

To the amusement of the others, they plunged into an animated discussion. Letting her eyes drift past them, Olympia saw Primo and Galina, their heads together, absorbed in each other. Or maybe it was her plunging neckline that absorbed him, she thought bitterly. He hadn't waited long before replacing her. She'd been right not to trust him.

Having taken centre stage, Grandpapa Rinucci flowered. 'And when are you coming back for the wedding?' he demanded of Angela.

'Which wedding?' she asked eagerly.

'Any wedding. Primo's to Galina, Luke's to Olympia. We should have more weddings.'

'Count me out,' Olympia said firmly. 'I'm concentrating on my career. In fact, I don't even believe in love.'

'Oh, darling, don't say things like that,' Angela begged. 'She doesn't mean it.'

'Yes, she does,' Olympia declared, desperate to seize the chance to say this. 'Love is a snare for the unwary. My career is all I want.'

Before anyone could answer, there was a soft rumbling in the distance. At once a silence descended on the entire company and their heads turned towards the window.

The rumbling came again, and with one movement they all rose and went out on to the terrace. In the distance a soft plume of smoke rose into the night air and disappeared.

'Is it going to erupt?' Angela asked, thrilled.

'No, these little grumbles happen a lot,' Hope reassured her. 'It means nothing.'

'Oh, yes, it does,' Grandpapa insisted. 'It means that someone—' his eyes lingered on Olympia '—is telling white lies. Or maybe black lies.'

'Or maybe she meant every word,' Olympia said, managing to laugh it off.

Right on cue Vesuvius growled deep in the ground and sent up another plume. Everyone laughed and there were knowing cries of 'Aha!'

The meal was almost over and nobody returned to the table. Seeing that her parents were happy, Olympia relaxed slightly. Now she could afford to think of herself and what had just happened. It was only a joke, not worth a moment's thought. She wasn't superstitious.

Suddenly Primo was beside her. 'May I refill that for you?' he asked, indicating her glass.

'No, I've had enough, thank you.'

He took the glass from her and set it down. 'You're looking very well,' he said politely.

'So are you. Are you back for good now?'

'No, just for a few days, then I'm going back to finish putting the new arrangements in place.'

'How is poor Cedric?'

'Enjoying his retirement. On his last evening we went out and got a little "drunk and disorderly" together.'

'You? Drunk and disorderly? Surely not?'

'I used to in my younger days.'

'That's hard to imagine, but I expect you planned it all beforehand, so much of this to drink, so much of that, always stay in charge of the situation.'

Primo gave a curt, mirthless laugh.

'You've just described my brother, not me. Luke's the cold, hard-headed one, planning everything to suit himself.'

'I haven't seen that in him.'

'No, he's different with you, I'll give him that. But if you make the mistake of marrying him you'll find out in the end.'

'Then the two of you are much the same,' she flung at him. 'Maybe that's why you're always at odds. It's a toss-up which of you is more determined to arrange life to suit himself.'

That got to him, she was glad to see. He flinched.

'I'm not as bad as you think.'

'Aren't you? Then tell me this. I've been thinking back and remembering that Cedric had met you before. He knew it was you all the time, didn't he?'

'Yes,' he admitted reluctantly.

'How did you persuade him to keep quiet? His pension didn't suddenly double, did it?'

'Not quite double.'

'So you bribed him, just like you bribed the hotel receptionist. You only have two ways of dealing with people, haven't you? Delude them, and bribe them. Did you ever try approaching anyone straightforwardly? Or don't you know how?'

'Olympia, please—'

'All right, I've finished. We don't need to talk any more.'

'So when is the announcement?'

'What announcement?'

'Of your engagement to my brother. Isn't that why your parents are here?'

'No, it's pure chance. They're just staying with us for a few days.'

'With us?'

'Staying at Luke's apartment.'

'I see.'

'No, you don't see. He said I could invite them while he was away but then he came back early.'

'Like a good prospective son-in-law. They love him. Your mother was telling me how wonderful he is, and your father longs for the day when he'll give you away.'

'And you heard what I said.'

'Yes, I did.' He gave a wry grin. 'So did Vesuvius, and you know what he thought of it.'

'Don't tell me you're superstitious.'

'You can't live here without being superstitious. The old man over the bay can tell when you're lying.'

'That's it. That's enough,' she said furiously. 'I spent weeks talking nonsense with you—'

'You should know. You did most of the talking.'

She breathed hard. 'I'm going back to join the others now,' she said, and walked away.

She shouldn't have talked to him. It had been a mistake, one that she wouldn't make again.

The party split into small groups to drink coffee. Hope was talking about her first son, Justin, snatched from her at birth.

'It will be the holidays soon and then perhaps Justin will return with my grandson,' she said, smiling at Olympia. 'And then you will meet him.'

'I'll really look forward to it,' Olympia said. 'I think it's wonderful how you found each other at last.'

'That's what Primo did for me,' Hope said, regarding him fondly. 'He gave me back my eldest son.'

'No, Mamma,' he said, looking uncomfortable. 'You can't give one person to another. If they find you it's because they want to. Justin was seeking you and in the end he would have found you himself.'

Olympia thought Hope was preparing to say more, but then she checked herself, as though she'd realised Primo wanted to end the subject.

'Is there any hope that we'll see Evie again?' Luke asked.

'I fear not,' Hope said sadly. To Olympia she explained, 'Evie is the woman who came here with him the first time. She'd done so much for him, and anyone could see that they loved each other, but now they seem to have broken up.'

'Then perhaps they did not love each other,' Toni pointed out.

'Why do you say that?' Olympia asked impulsively. 'Sometimes people love each other and still break up. It doesn't mean the love wasn't there, just that they couldn't find the path that led to each other.'

Hope made a sudden movement of interest. Several of the others turned to look at Olympia, but she couldn't see if Primo was one of them as her head was turned away from him. Even so, she sensed him grow still.

'I think you are right,' Hope said, nodding to her. 'I know that Justin is a difficult man. He says so himself. He wouldn't be an easy husband for any woman, but I think Evie could have been the right wife for him, if only—' She sighed.

'If only someone would help them,' Olympia said impulsively.

'You think so?' Hope asked. 'But how?'

'Talk to them, make them talk to each other. Knock their heads together.'

'If only—' Hope murmured. 'But then my family would say I was an interfering busybody.'

'Let them,' Olympia said robustly. 'People sometimes call me an interfering busybody, but I've never let it stop me yet.'

This caused a general laugh and Hope patted her hand.

'I knew there was a reason I like you so much,' she said triumphantly.

As the evening drew to a close Olympia sought refuge in the cool night air, from a position where she could glare at Vesuvius across the bay.

'You're a real pain in the butt,' she informed him. 'In future, shut up.'

He loomed in tactful silence. He'd had his fun.

It was a relief to be away from the chattering crowd. Her head was starting to ache from the confused impressions she had received tonight.

Primo's face was in her mind, pale and strained as she'd seen him in the first moment, then cool and smiling as he'd introduced his glamorous companion.

'Oh, it's nice to be out in the fresh air!'

It was Hope, further down the terrace, echoing Olympia's thoughts.

She was about to speak up when she heard Primo's voice, saying, 'Yes, come and sit down for a moment, Mamma. You're looking tired.'

'I am, but it's been a wonderful evening. Galina and Olympia are both so beautiful. I wonder when—'

'When we'll see Justin again,' he interrupted her quickly.

'Yes, that too. Every family party feels as though something is missing.' Hope sighed.

'But you used to say that before we found him,' he reminded her. 'Then he was truly missing. Now you know where he is, and that he will come here again soon.'

There was a silence, then Primo said, 'Are you thinking of what Olympia said?'

'Of course I am. It's so tempting to think that she was right, because then I'd have an excuse to act.'

'And you always like an excuse to act.'

The words were not said in criticism. Olympia could hear the fond humour in his voice.

'True, but I suppose my wise son would counsel caution?'

'You do me an injustice, Mamma. I think Olympia is right.'

'You, agreeing with Olympia? I thought you didn't like her, chiefly because she and Luke are in love.'

'You're wrong—' Primo sounded as though he'd been about to blurt something out, then checked himself. 'You're wrong, Mamma. I do not dislike her, and I think she'll make an admirable wife for Luke. But she's also a wise woman who's learned some hard lessons about love.'

'You sound as if you know her well.'

'I do know her, better than you think. Tonight she spoke to you out of her wisdom and her pain. You should listen to her. If Evie and Justin belong together then we should do everything possible to help them overcome whatever troubles them.'

'*You* say this?'

'That surprises you?'

'A little, because although it was you who found Justin, I don't think you feel like a brother to him.'

'That doesn't matter. I know now that to find the ideal person and then lose them because—'

Olympia heard him take a sharp breath and then go on with difficulty.

'Because of what?' Hope asked curiously.

'Because of their own foolishness, and because there was nobody to help them find the way that they had lost—it can happen too easily, and then the worst thing is to know that it was your own fault. I wouldn't wish it on any man. Not Justin. Not Luke.'

'Not yourself?' Hope asked gently.

Primo gave a curt laugh. 'I can take care of myself.'

'Can you, my son? I thought so once. Now I've begun to wonder. Once you seemed so strong—'

'I'm much stronger now, Mamma. A man is always better for making discoveries—especially about himself. From what you say, Justin has discovered many things, but they have left him confused. Olympia has spoken the truth. You must help him through that confusion.'

'And you? Are you confused?'

Primo spoke quietly. 'No, Mamma. My confusion is over. Now, come inside. It's getting chilly.'

Olympia didn't move but sat there silently until she knew that they had gone. She discovered that her face was wet, but she couldn't remember when she had started to weep.

As part of the *Maggio dei Monumenti* celebrations Enrico was laying on a ball for all the 'notables' as he called them. His guests included most of the Council of Naples, who organised the festival, the older Neapolitan families and many of his employees. This year the number of employees was greater and included many from England, to mark the successful merger.

He had persuaded Angela and Harold to extend their visit for a few days and join him. On the night they set off, with Luke and Olympia, for one of the local *palazzos,* now owned by the city, where he had hired the ballroom.

It was a grand occasion. The Rinuccis were there in force—Francesco with the girlfriend on whom Hope was pinning expectations, Primo escorting Galina, who looked like a model in a white satin dress that plunged down at the front, down at the back and up at the side. She had exactly the perfect figure to get away with it and Olympia reckoned that if Primo was making a point then he was doing it in style.

She herself was elegant in deep blue silk, but she was glad she hadn't worn white. She could never have competed with the luscious Galina.

Enrico was ebullient. The occasion had gone to his head and he was set on marking it symbolically. He gathered Primo and Olympia to him to receive directions.

'It will be a wonderful evening,' he enthused, 'and the culmination will be the moment when the two of you take the floor together for the waltz.'

'Surely that's not really necessary,' Olympia said.

'Of course it's necessary. We are celebrating the merger of our two firms, ushering in a time of peaceful co-existence, of happy union—'

'It's two firms not two kingdoms,' Olympia pointed out. 'Can we keep a sense of proportion?'

'I agree,' Primo said through gritted teeth. 'I think you should forget this idea.'

'I will not forget it,' Enrico spluttered, enraged. 'It is essential to tell the world of our blissful—'

'Well, I don't feel blissful,' Olympia said firmly. 'Why can't *you* dance with someone?'

'If I do, my wife kill me,' he said mournfully. 'No, it must be you.'

'No,' they both said together.

'What nonsense is this? I demand that you dance together.'

They yielded to placate him, and took the floor for the first dance.

'I'm sorry about this,' Primo growled.

'Don't worry. I'm getting to know Enrico's little ways by now. He's harmless. We only have to smile and be polite, then go our separate ways.'

'Our separate ways. Do you know how melancholy that sounds?'

'New roads always lead to something,' she reminded him.

'But suppose it isn't the place we want to go?'

'You have Galina waiting on your road. She'll probably take you somewhere interesting.'

'Shut up,' he said softly. 'Don't talk like that, do you hear me?'

'Why not? What difference can it make now?'

'You speak as if I'd betrayed you. But if you can say Galina, I can say Luke. Tell me that you're not in love with him. Let me hear you say it.'

'Didn't I once tell you that I never fall in love with unsuitable men?'

'Yes, and I asked what kind of man did you fall in love with. You said you couldn't remember. But that was then. This is now.'

'And life grows more complicated as time passes.'

'Witch,' he said bitterly. '*Strega.*'

'Yes, you should beware of me.'

His mouth was so close to hers that she could feel the whisper of his breath across her lips. The sense of sweet pleasure was so intense that she felt faint. She longed for him to kiss her, longed for it so intensely that nothing else mattered. She was swept by a desire to forget all her careful, self-protective plans and kiss him first.

At any moment she would do so and the world could think what it pleased—any moment—

The music slowed. It was over. People were applauding the dance that symbolised the creation of the new firm. In the midst of the applause Primo led her to Luke, inclined his head in a little bow and walked away, back to Galina.

The next morning they went their separate ways.

CHAPTER TWELVE

OLYMPIA saw her parents off at the airport.

'We've had such a lovely time, darling,' Angela said, 'and it'll be so lovely coming out for your wedding. Luke's a delightful young man, but don't you let the other one put a stop to it.'

'The other one—put a stop to it—?'

'Primo, the one who stands about scowling at you and Luke. Watch out for him, because he'll block it if he can.'

'I'll be careful,' Olympia promised. 'But don't count on my marrying Luke. Things aren't always what they seem.'

'Don't be silly, dear. I've seen the way he looks at you. Goodbye, now.'

Three days later there was news from England.

'Mamma's done it!' Luke announced triumphantly as he came off the phone. 'Don't ask me how, but she's made Justin and Evie see sense and the wedding's going to take place here, next month.'

Olympia spent an evening with Hope, who was happily deep in wedding plans. She had a natural gift for organising that was almost as great as Olympia's own, and soon the entire family had been turned into lieutenants, scurrying hither and thither at her command.

Justin, Evie and Justin's son, Mark, were to stay at the villa and arrived two days early.

'I know it's not usual for the bride and groom to start from the same house,' Hope said to Olympia, 'but neither of them has a home here, and this way I can keep an eye on them.'

'You're afraid they're going to escape you again,' Olympia teased. Hope laughed and didn't deny it.

Toni and Primo, newly returned from England, went with her to the airport to greet them, and that evening everyone congregated at the villa. Olympia was immediately taken by Evie's wit and her ready laugh, which obviously covered a sharp intelligence. Justin was an interesting man, apparently harsh, yet seeming to cling to Evie. If she left his side his eyes followed her around the room.

Mark was already a favourite with the family and now he won Olympia's heart with his cheeky antics and his happiness at being there. After Hope, he was the person most anxious for the marriage to take place without delay.

'He's a bit like Primo, when I married his father, Jack Cayman,' Hope confided. 'He wanted a mother so badly. I'll never forget the way he smiled when he finally felt certain of me.'

But that certainty had proved an illusion, Olympia thought. His 'mother' had been taken from him and, although she had been restored later, he'd never felt completely safe again.

Hope's use of the name Jack Cayman brought a host of other memories back. Now she saw how Primo's early experiences had shaped him. Beneath the apparently solid self-confidence was something rootless, constantly mobile, as though he were seeking something that could never be found.

It didn't take much insight to deduce that much the same was true of Justin, whose life had been built on even greater confusion. Snatched from his mother at birth, he had later been rejected by his adoptive parents and abandoned in an institution. He'd reached manhood angry and bitter, caring for nobody, ready to do anything.

Against all the odds he'd made something of his life and was now a wealthy man and the head of a huge firm. But the scars remained and they had made him reject Evie, who loved him, for her sake. Now, thanks to Hope's intervention, things had come right for them, and the whole family had joined to wish them well.

Since Primo had been the one to find him first, Justin had asked him to be his best man. Toni was to give the bride away as Evie had no family. And the day before the wedding Olympia's parents arrived, at Hope's invitation, the clearest signal that she was still plotting.

On the morning of the wedding the entire Rinucci family gathered at the villa, which made an impressive sight. Some were staying there, some had travelled up early in the morning, until at last everyone was there.

Galina, as always, was a knockout in a light blue chiffon dress that contrived to be fairly restrained, for church, while leaving no doubt about her glorious figure. Olympia's honey-coloured linen, which had seemed so elegant in the mirror, now looked dull. In fact, she told herself that she looked almost middle-aged beside Galina's vibrant youth.

Primo noticed her and drew Galina across for a greeting. The morning sun flashed off something around the girl's neck, which closer inspection proved to be a gold chain with heavy, elaborate links.

'Isn't it beautiful?' Galina squealed when Olympia admired it.

'Did Primo give you that?' Luke asked.

Galina just giggled. Olympia stared out of blank eyes. A gift so valuable was a declaration of intent.

'It's time the groom was leaving for the church,' Hope said, bustling over. 'And those of you who are going with him, the car's ready outside.'

Justin appeared, dreadfully pale, and was taken in charge by Primo. A few minutes later the two of them departed together, with Galina.

More cars were lined up before the house; people started checking themselves in the mirror, taking care of last minute details.

Then everyone was silenced by the arrival of the bride. Evie had chosen a simple ivory-coloured dress with a short veil held in place by flowers. She looked beautiful, but she also looked honest, calm and strong. In fact she was exactly what the man she loved most needed.

And Hope knew it, because she gave her new daughter a special mother's embrace before taking her hand and putting it in Toni's.

'You will give her away,' she said, smiling, 'and then she will be ours.'

No bride could have asked for a better welcome, Olympia thought as she and Luke headed out to the cars. But she knew now that it could never be hers. There could be no marriage between herself and Luke, whatever other people thought, and it was time for her to leave.

His brotherly kindness had lulled her into a sense of security and she had lingered too long. But now it was time to depart and set a distance between herself and the Rinucci family. That way she need no longer see Primo with Galina.

But then she thought of working with him, seeing him

day after day, and knew that moving home wasn't enough. She must go away entirely, back to England, to another job. It would mean starting again.

But I can do that, she thought. I've done it before.

The wedding ceremony was an impressive ritual, but the most impressive part was when two people claimed each other with quiet fervour. Then the organ pealed out and they started back down the aisle into the sunlight, where the photographer was waiting.

So many photographs to be taken, so many family combinations. Nobody must be left out, and Olympia found herself kindly dragooned into many pictures where she felt she had no right to be. But Hope was determined and nobody could stand up to her.

'Not if they want to live,' Luke commented wryly.

Then the formal reception, the speeches, Justin almost inarticulate, having to be rescued by his son, saying cheekily, 'Dad hasn't got much Italian yet, so I'll do it.'

At last the tables were cleared for dancing. Olympia watched the bride and groom, standing well back against the wall, a glass of champagne in her hand.

'Making plans?' Primo's voice asked ironically.

'Oh, shut up,' she said, abandoning tact.

'But how much longer can you keep us all on tenterhooks while you delay the announcement? Soon you will be my sister-in-law—or you would be, if I acknowledge that *Inglese* as a brother.'

'Primo, will you please stop talking nonsense? Of course I'm not going to marry Luke.' She faced him, suddenly angry and too full of regret to care much what she said. 'How could you ever have believed it for one minute?'

'Because you went to live with him.'

'Only because I was angry with you. You should have

known that. You *did* know it. Where have your wits been all this time?'

He stared at her. 'This is my fault?'

She thought of Galina and sadness overcame her.

'No, mine too, I suppose. I wasn't very clever from the start, or I'd have seen through you.' She gave a wry smile. 'Let's face it, you didn't really do it very well. You didn't fool me. I fooled myself. I wanted to believe in my own cleverness. I've nobody to blame but me, so I think we should part friends and forget it ever happened.'

'Friends?' he murmured, and then, '*Part?*'

'Yes, I'm leaving. It's time this was over. I'm going back to England.'

He stared at her, seemingly unable to think of a reply. When it came it wasn't the one he would have chosen.

'You can't. You've got a contract.'

'Sue me.'

She turned and began to walk away, moving out on to the terrace. But he came after her and pulled her round to face him.

'People will see,' she said frantically.

'Let them. It's time we had this out. You've been playing me for a sucker for far too long.'

'*I've* been—?'

'Everything you've done recently has been done to punish me. Living with that *Inglese,* making my whole family see you as a couple. You were teaching me a lesson, weren't you? I thought better of you.'

'Oh, don't give me that,' she said angrily. 'We both behaved badly. We both thought better of the other, and we were both disappointed.'

'Which seems to leave us about even,' he said, giving her a curious look.

'Yes.' She sighed. 'And that's a good place to finish.'

'Are you sure about that?' he asked, looking at her strangely. 'Some people might say it was a good place to start.'

'What?'

'Don't you realise that what you've been saying for the past few minutes gives us the best chance we've ever had? Olympia, for the first time we can be honest with each other. That's a great start.'

There was a gleam far back in his eyes that obscurely disturbed her, but she refused to take any notice. She had made her decision and this time she would stick to it.

'I can't believe you're saying this. After what we did to each other—'

'That was bad, and we needed some time apart to get over it, but we've had that and now we're ready—'

'Will you stop telling me what to do?'

'Somebody needs to, because you're lost and confused. Almost as lost and confused as I am, but this is where it stops. Tell me that you love me.'

She gasped in outrage. *'Is that an order?'*

'Yes, it is! And look sharp about it, I'm tired of waiting.'

'The devil I will!' she said, trying to turn away again.

'The devil you won't,' he said, pulling her back. 'Now listen to me. I stood there in that church, watching Justin and Evie and wondering how I'd ever let things go this wrong.'

'But so did I—'

'Then tell me that you love me.'

'Now, look here—'

'Say it—'

Before she knew it his lips were against hers and his arms about her.

'Say it,' he muttered.

'I'm blowed if I—'

'*Say it!*'

But in the same instant he made it impossible for her to say anything, kissing her until she was breathless and incapable of thought. She had deadened herself to emotions, not once but twice—first for David and then, recently, trying to kill her love for Primo. But now the sweet, uncontrollable feelings rose up and refused to die down.

She loved him. She might deny it from now until kingdom come, but it would still be true.

'Say it,' he murmured again. 'Or I'll kiss you forever until you do.'

'In that case, my lips are sealed.'

He was laughing, his body shaking, sending tremors through her too.

'I love you, I love you,' she said. 'But don't stop.'

All tension and sadness seemed to melt away in kiss after kiss. She was only distantly aware of a door opening and closing behind her, but then she felt Primo draw back a little in dismay.

'Well, well,' said Luke's voice.

Shocked, she whirled and saw him standing there, leaning against the wall, regarding them both with apparent amusement.

'So you reached the finishing line at last,' he said. 'I thought you would if I was patient.'

'You—?' she said uncertainly. 'You mean you—all this time—?'

'I think I've been rather clever,' Luke said with a grin that might have been aimed against himself. 'That first night, when you got mad and wanted to leave, I had to find a way to keep you in Naples—'

'Why?' Primo asked at once.

Luke gave a crack of derisive laughter.

'Because I knew she was the one woman who could bring you down, of course. And I wasn't going to miss the fun. And has it ever been fun! The sight of you not knowing whether you were coming or going has been the best laugh I've ever had. I've seen jealousy on your face that you could barely control. I've seen you driving yourself crazy because you wanted something you couldn't arrange to have, and you couldn't even admit it to yourself. Did I enjoy that? You bet I did!'

Primo began to swear softly under his breath. Olympia couldn't follow the names he called his brother, but they must have been outrageous because Luke relished every one of them.

'Don't!' Olympia got diplomatically between them. 'Don't let anything spoil it now. Primo, whatever his reasons, your brother did us a favour.'

'Don't call him my brother—'

'Of course he's your brother,' she insisted. 'Only a brother would do you a huge favour and insult you afterwards, and then laugh at you and with you—'

'You're going to be a good influence on him,' Luke observed. 'You could even knock some of the nonsense out of him.'

'Luke, you were never in love with me, were you?' she asked hopefully.

He shrugged. 'Maybe just a bit. But not enough to worry about. I've been a perfect gentleman so that you could stay here without worry, and it all worked out right.' He grinned suddenly. 'Mind you, there might be a problem. Your mother likes me better.'

'I'll bet she does,' Primo murmured. He still eyed Luke askance, but he was calming down.

Olympia kissed Luke's cheek and was enfolded in a brotherly hug. As he turned to go, Primo called, '*Hey, Inglese!*'

He waited until Luke looked back before saying quietly, 'Thank you.'

'Hah! You think you've won, but she'll lead you a merry dance, and I'll be there, laughing all the way. Starting with the altar. I want to be your best man.'

'I wouldn't have anyone else.'

Luke walked away.

'Yes, I think I've won,' Primo said. 'I *know* I've won. I've won everything I want in the world.'

He seized her in his arms again. Neither of them saw Luke turning at the last minute. He watched them for a moment, then touched his cheek where Olympia had kissed it and murmured, 'Maybe just a bit.'

Olympia's conscience was troubling her.

'What about Galina? You weren't trying to make me jealous, surely?'

'No, because I didn't think I could. I wanted to save my face, so that when you and Luke announced your engagement I wouldn't be standing there alone like a lemon.'

'But if she's in love with you—'

That made him roar with laughter.

'My darling, as far as Galina's concerned I'm an old man. She's eighteen. I only know her because her parents are friends of mine. When she found out what was happening—and it's hard to keep anything from that girl—she said, "What you need is window-dressing, Uncle Primo, and I'm the person to help you." So I turned up with her on my arm, just to save my dignity.

She came to my rescue again after that, but she'll be glad it's over so that she can go back to boys of her own age.'

'She doesn't really call you uncle?'

'I swear she does. She kept coming out with it all that evening, and I had to keep frantically reminding her not to. Let's find her so that I can tell her that she's off duty from now on.'

They found Galina a few moments later, dancing smoochily with Ruggiero, so absorbed in him that it was with great difficulty that Primo attracted her attention. Then he pointed to Olympia, giving a thumbs up sign. Galina smiled, waved and touched the heavy gold chain about her neck. Then she hooked an arm around Ruggiero's neck and forgot all about Uncle Primo.

As they walked away, Primo said, 'What did you think of the chain—my thank you gift?'

'Very pretty.'

'Wait until you see the one I will buy you.'

In another room Luke found solitude and a bottle of good whisky.

There Hope discovered him a few minutes later.

'I saw what happened,' she said fondly. 'It's what you were planning all the time, isn't it? You always knew it would be Olympia and Primo in the end.'

'I guess I did. But Mamma, sometimes you have to ask yourself, if a man acts like such a clown when he's wooing his woman, isn't another man entitled to step in and—?' He finished with a shrug.

'So why didn't you?' she asked, holding out a glass for Luke to pour her a whisky.

'I nearly did. There were nights when I stood outside

her bedroom door while my worse and better selves fought it out. My worse self put up a brave fight—'

'But your better self always won?'

'Unfortunately, yes,' he said savagely, and she laughed.

Then he sighed. 'It wouldn't have been any use. Primo's the one for her, I could see that.'

'So you played Cupid. I always knew that you were really a good brother.'

'Don't say that,' he said hurriedly. 'Think of my reputation.'

Hope laughed. 'All right, I'll keep quiet about it. But we both know the truth, which is that you have a kind heart, a *brother's* heart.'

He grimaced. 'Yes, it's just a shame that it asserted itself now, and about *her*.'

'Somewhere there is a woman for you. You'll get over Olympia.'

'Sure I will—say, in about a hundred years. In the meantime, perhaps I'd better go away for a while.'

'Far?' Hope asked in alarm.

'No, only as far as Rome. A man there owed me quite a lot of money. He couldn't pay so he signed over some property he owned. It's likely to prove more of a curse than a blessing, as I gather it's in a bad way. There have been no improvements to speak of for a long time, and there's a lawyer giving him grief. He describes her as the devil incarnate, which means she'll give me grief as well.'

'She?'

'*Signora* Minerva Pepino. I've already had a letter from her that practically took the skin off my back.'

'Good. She'll keep your mind occupied.' She kissed

him. 'Go to Rome, my son, and come back for Primo's wedding. Perhaps you will bring a bride home of your own.'

'I doubt it. Be content with two daughters-in-law, Mamma.'

'Nonsense. I want six. Now, come back and join the party.'

She departed, humming. After a moment Luke followed her and stood, unnoticed, watching the revelry. Justin was dancing with his bride, his harsh face softened by happiness. Primo circled the floor with Olympia, both enclosed in their own cocoon of joy.

Luke watched her and knew that she had forgotten him.

'I had to go and be a "good brother", didn't I?' he groaned. 'It was bound to happen one day, but in heaven's name, why now?'

He stood for a moment watching Primo and Olympia—soon to be his sister—held close in each other's arms, absorbed and happy.

'Why now?' he murmured.

The wedding was over. The house was sleeping, except for the two in the gardens. It was dark out there, except for the moon, and the only sound was of two lovers whispering.

'I never meant to lie to you,' he vowed, 'but the moment we met I knew you had to be mine. I'd lived such a safe, sensible life, but none of that meant anything after I saw you. I wanted to be wild and even stupid.'

'Well, you were certainly that,' she told him fondly.

'Are you going to be a nagging wife?'

'One of me is. The others haven't decided.'

'Ah yes,' he said, understanding her at once. 'We'll

always have that now. An infinite variety—very handy for playing away—'

'Planning to be unfaithful, huh?'

'Only with you, *amor mio*. Only with you.'

Her deep, delighted chuckle brought the world to life. In the moonlight he saw her pulling at her hair, becoming a witch before his eyes.

'You know this one, don't you?' she teased. 'It's the corny film where the heroine lets her hair fall loose and the hero goes weak at the knees, and swears to love her for ever.'

'Yes,' he said, taking her joyfully into his arms. 'That's exactly what happens…'

THE WEDDING ARRANGEMENT

CHAPTER ONE

I'M CRAZY to leave.

The words pounded in Luke Cayman's head as he packed his bags on the day after his brother Primo's engagement.

I should stay and fight for her.

Yet he got into his brand new state-of-the-art sports car and headed out of Naples 'like a bat out of hell', as he put it.

It was a relief to get on to the *autostrada*, where he could let it rip, driving the two hundred miles to Rome at the top of the legal limit and making it in two and a half hours.

Once there, he checked into a five-star hotel in Parioli, the wealthiest and most elegant part of the city, and indulged himself with the best of Roman cuisine and wine, which he drank in brooding silence.

I should have stayed.

But there was Olympia's face in his mind, as he'd last seen it, her eyes fixed blissfully on Primo, her fiancé, soon to be her husband. Who was he trying to kid? He'd never stood a chance.

He was just thinking of an early night when a hand clapped him on the shoulder and a hearty voice said, 'You should have told me you were coming.'

Bernardo was the hotel manager, a plump, hearty man in his mid-forties. Luke had stayed here before on business trips to Rome, and they had always been on good terms.

'It was a last-minute decision,' Luke said, trying to sound cheerful. 'I find myself the owner of a building in Rome and it needs my attention.'

'Property? I thought you were in manufacturing.'

'I am. This place was given to me in repayment of a debt.'

'Round here?'

'No, Trastevere.'

Bernardo raised his eyebrows. If Parioli was Rome's most elegant area, Trastevere was its most colourful.

'I gather it's in a poor state of repair,' Luke said. 'When I've put it right, I'll sell it.'

'Why not just sell it now? Let someone else bother with the repairs.'

'Signora Pepino would never let me get away with that,' Luke said with a grin. 'She's a lawyer who lives and works there, and has already bombarded me with letters saying what she expects me to do.'

'And you'll do what this woman tells you?'

'She isn't a woman, she's a dragon. That's why I didn't tell her I was coming. I can get a look at the place before she starts breathing fire at me.'

'Is that the only reason?' Bernardo asked, regarding him shrewdly.

Luke shrugged.

'Ah, a lovely lady broke your heart and now—'

'No woman has ever broken my heart,' Luke said sharply. 'I don't allow that to happen.'

'Very wise.'

'I let myself get a little too close to a woman, although

I knew she was in love with another man. It was a mistake, but mistakes can be put right. A wise man sees the danger and takes action.'

'And you managed that with your customary efficiency?'

'My what?'

'You're known as a man who believes in good order, keeps things in proportion, and stays invulnerable. I envy you. It must make life simple. But now you need to get blissfully roaring drunk, with good companions who will put you safely to bed afterwards.'

'For pity's sake, Bernardo, how often have you seen me like that?'

'Not often enough. It's unnatural.'

Luke gave a reluctant laugh. 'Maybe, but it helps a man stay in charge of his life, and that's what matters. Goodnight.'

He went to his room quickly, suddenly uneasy in Bernardo's company. For a moment he'd seen himself through his friend's eyes, a man who prized good order and self-control above all else: a cold, hard man, who gave little and counted it out carefully first.

It wasn't so far from the truth, he thought. But it had never troubled him before.

He checked the messages on his cellphone and the words, *Call your mother,* appeared on the screen. Grinning, he called Hope Rinucci, his adoptive mother, and the only one he had known.

'Hi, Mamma. Yes, I got here safely. Everything's fine.'

'Have you met Signora Pepino yet?'

'I've barely arrived. I've had a meal, that's all. Let me settle in before I confront her. I need all my courage.'

His mother's exasperated voice reached him down the line. 'Don't pretend you're afraid of her.'

'I am. I'm shaking in my shoes, I swear it.'

'You'll go to hell for telling lies, and serve you right.'

He chuckled. She always made him feel better.

In his mind he could see her in the Villa Rinucci, high up on the hill. She liked to take phone calls on the terrace, looking out over the Bay of Naples, the most glorious view in the world, according to her. It would be dark now, with only the twinkling lights breaking through the black velvet, but the beauty was still there.

'Are you exhausted after all the festivities?' he asked.

'I've no time for that. I'm planning the party for Primo and Olympia's engagement.'

'I thought we had that last night.'

'No, that was just the tail end of Justin's wedding,' she said, naming her first son. 'One wedding begets another, and naturally we toasted Primo and Olympia, but they'll want a proper engagement celebration of their own.'

'And if they don't they're going to get it anyway,' he said with wry fondness.

'Well, you can't expect me to pass up the chance of a party,' she said reasonably.

'It would never occur to me that you'd pass up the chance of a party,' he said truthfully. 'And after that, there's the wedding, unless Olympia's mother has some mad idea of organising it herself.'

'Oh, no, we discussed that last night, and she quite agrees with me.'

'You mean she can't stand up to you any more than the rest of us,' he said with a laugh.

'I don't know what you mean,' Hope said, affronted. And she really didn't.

'I look forward to it. I won't miss the chance to gloat over brother Primo's downfall.'

'You'll meet the right one for you,' Hope said, like all mothers.

'Maybe not. I might just settle for being a curmudgeonly old bachelor.'

Hope crowed with laughter. 'A handsome boy like you?'

'Boy? I'm thirty-eight.'

'You'll always be a boy to me. Your wife is next on my list, and don't you forget it. Now, go and have a good time.'

'Mamma, it's eleven o'clock.'

'So? The perfect time for—anything you want.'

Luke grinned. His mother had never been a prude—one reason why her sons adored her. Toni, her husband, was far more strait-laced.

'I need to be clear-headed to deal with Signora Pepino.'

'Nonsense! Just turn your charm on her, and that'll do the trick.'

Hope Rinucci was convinced that all her sons had the charm of the devil and no woman could resist them. With the younger ones it was possibly true, but Luke knew that charm wasn't his strong suit. He was a tall, muscular, well-made man with features that were regular enough to pass for good looks. But his face fell naturally into stern lines and he smiled little.

It had been different with Olympia. In the few weeks he'd shared his apartment with her he'd forced himself to behave like a gentleman, knowing that her heart was already given to his brother, Primo. It hadn't been easy keeping his infatuation under control, and the strain had almost propelled it into outright love.

He knew that under Olympia's influence his nature had thawed, almost to the point of charm. But he was on his guard against it happening for a second time. Authority, no-nonsense, stubbornness: these he did well. Not charm.

But since there was no arguing with a mother's partiality he didn't try. They finished the conversation affectionately and he hung up, feeling strangely uneasy again. Something was wrong. He didn't know what, but he had an uncomfortable sense that the trouble lay with himself.

As always, when something disturbed him, he took refuge in work, pulling out the folder that contained the details of his newly acquired, if unwanted, property.

It was called the Residenza Gallini, a grandiose name that presumably promised more than it delivered, and, from the plan, seemed to be a five-storey building, built around four sides of a courtyard. The heart of the folder was the correspondence with Signora Minerva Pepino, a severe and ferocious lady whose very name was beginning to worry him.

It was easy fighting a man. You could go in with fists flailing. With a woman subtlety was needed, and Luke, who didn't 'do' subtlety any more than he 'did' charm, felt at a disadvantage.

She had opened hostilities with a reasonably restrained letter enquiring when he intended to come to Rome and set in motion the vast amount of work that was necessary to bring the property up to the standard essential to her clients, who lived there in conditions that were a disgrace.

He had replied assuring her that he would arrive 'as soon as was convenient' and venturing, in the mildest possible way, to suggest that she exaggerated the conditions.

She had treated his mildness with the contempt it deserved, blasting him with a list of necessary repairs and including the probable prices, whose total made him gulp.

But now he felt he was getting her measure. The tradesmen who'd given these estimates were probably friends or relatives, and she was on commission. He began to be offended at the way she clearly thought she could bully him, and repeated his assurance that he would come to Rome when it was convenient.

And so it had gone on, each growing more quellingly polite as their annoyance rose. Luke imagined her as a woman carved out of granite, probably in her fifties, ruling her world with grim efficiency, crushing all disagreement. Even her name was alarming. Minerva was the goddess of wisdom, known for her brilliant intellect but also for being born wearing armour and wielding a spear.

He would visit Rome and act like a responsible landlord. What he would not do was let himself be ordered around.

He put the folder away. Suddenly his room felt too quiet, its very luxury pressing in on him like a stifling blanket. Coming to a sudden decision, he took the cash out of his wallet and put it in his pocket along with the plastic card that was the key to his room. Then he locked the wallet in the wall safe, and headed downstairs.

It was a balmy night and he was warm enough in his

shirtsleeves as he walked away from the hotel and hailed a taxi to take him the length of the Via del Corso, with its late-night cafés and glittering shops. At the bottom they swung right, heading for the Garibaldi Bridge over the River Tiber.

'Here will do,' he called to the driver when they had crossed the river.

He knew now that he must have reached the part of Rome known as Trastevere, a name which literally meant 'on the other side of the Tiber'. It was the oldest part of the city, and still the most colourful. The light streamed on to the streets, accompanied by song, laughter and appetising smells of cooking.

He plunged into the nearest bar and was soon enveloped in conviviality. From there he drifted to another bar, relaxed by some of the best local wine he had ever tasted. Three bars later he was beginning to think that this was the way to live.

He wandered out into the cobbled street and stood there, gazing up at the full moon. Then he studied the street, realising that he had no idea where he was.

'Looking for something?'

Turning, he saw a young man sitting at one of the outside tables. He was little more than a boy, with a charming, mobile face and dark, vivid eyes. When he grinned his teeth flashed with almost startling brilliance.

'Ciao!' he said, raising his glass in tipsy fellowship.

'Ciao!' Luke answered, coming to sit at the table beside him. 'I was just realising that I'm lost.'

'New here?'

'Just arrived today.'

'Well, now you're here, you should stay. Nice place. Nice people.'

Luke signalled to a waiter, who brought two fresh glasses and a full bottle, accepted Luke's money and departed.

'*Very* nice people,' the boy repeated.

'I probably shouldn't have done that,' Luke said, suddenly conscience-stricken. 'I think you've already had enough.'

'If the wine is good, there's no such thing as enough.' He filled both glasses. 'Soon I shall have had too much, and it still won't be enough.' A thought struck him. 'I'm a very wise man. At least, I sound like one.'

'Well, I guess it makes a kind of sense,' Luke agreed, tasting the wine and finding it good. 'I'm Luke, by the way.'

The young man frowned. 'Luke? Lucio?'

'Sure, Lucio if you want.'

'I'm Charlie.'

It was Luke's turn to frown. An Italian called Charlie? 'You mean Carlo?' he asked at last.

'No, Charlie. It's short for Charlemagne.' The boy added confidentially, 'I don't tell many people that, only my very best friends.'

'Thank you,' Luke said, accepting the honour with a grin. 'So tell your friend why you were named after the Emperor Charlemagne.'

'Because I'm descended from him, of course.'

'But he lived twelve hundred years ago. How can you be sure?'

Charlie looked surprised. 'My mother told me.'

'And you believe everything your mother tells you?'

'What Mamma says, you'd better believe, or you'll be sorry.'

'Yes, mine's that way too,' Luke said, grinning.

They clinked glasses, and Charlie drained his, then quickly refilled it.

'I drink to forget,' he announced gleefully.

'Forget what?'

'Something or other. Who cares? Why do you drink?'

'I'm trying to nerve myself to confront a dragon. Otherwise she might eat me.'

'Ah, a female dragon. They're the worst. But you'll slay her.'

'I don't think this lady is easily intimidated.'

'You just tell her you're not standing for any nonsense,' Charlie advised. 'That's the way to deal with women.'

So now he had two pieces of advice for dealing with the situation—use his non-existent charm, or try to impose what this naïve boy fondly imagined to be 'masculine authority'.

They passed on to the next bar, and then the next, until it began to feel like time to go home.

Suddenly they heard a shout from the next street, then the sound of a child crying and an animal squealing and suddenly a crowd of young men came stumbling out of the shadows. The one in front was carrying a puppy that was squirming to escape. With them was a boy of about twelve, who continually tried to rescue his pet, but was thwarted as the lout tossed the puppy to one of the others.

'Bastardi!' Charlie exclaimed violently.

'I couldn't agree more,' Luke said.

They moved forward together.

The sight of them made the louts pause just long enough for Charlie to seize the puppy. Two of them tried to snatch it back, but Luke occupied them long enough for Charlie to give the animal to the child, who grabbed it and vanished, leaving him free to concentrate on the fight.

Two against four might seem an unequal conquest, but Charlie was furious and Luke was powerful and they managed to stop them chasing the fleeing child until there were further sounds from the narrow alleys, shouts, sirens, and all six were surrounded and carted off to the nearest police station.

The knock on the door could only be Mamma Netta Pepino. Nobody else knocked in exactly that pattern and Minnie was smiling as she went to answer it.

'It isn't too late?' Netta asked at once.

'No, I hadn't gone to bed.'

'Every night you stay up late, working too hard. So I brought you some shopping because I know you don't have time to do your own.'

This was a fiction that they had shared for years. Minnie had an expensive law practice on the Via Veneto, and a secretary who could have done her shopping. But the habit of relying on Netta had started years ago, when she had been eighteen, the bride of Gianni Pepino, and this warm, laughing woman had embraced her.

It had been that way through the years when Minnie studied law, and had continued as her practice built up to its present success. Gianni had been dead for four years now, but Minnie had neither moved to a more luxurious home, nor weakened her links to Netta, whom she loved as a mother.

'Proscuitto, Parmesan, pasta—your favourite kind,' Netta intoned, dumping bags on the table. 'You check.'

'No need, you always get it right,' Minnie said with a smile. 'Sit down and have a drink. Coffee? Whisky?'

'Whisky,' Netta said with a chuckle, heaving her huge person into a chair.

'I'll have some tea.'

'You're still English,' Netta said. 'Fourteen years you live in Italy and you still drink English tea.'

Minnie began putting the shopping away, pausing as she came to a small bunch of flowers.

'I thought you'd like them,' Netta said, elaborately casual.

'I love them,' Minnie said, dropping a kiss on her cheek. 'Let's put them with Gianni.'

Filling a small vase with water, she added the flowers and set it beside a photograph of Gianni that stood on a shelf. It had been taken a week before his death and showed a young man with a wide, humorous mouth and brilliant eyes that seemed to have a gleam deep in their depths. His naturally curly hair was too long, falling over his forehead and down his neck, and increasing the charm that glowed from the picture.

Next to him stood another picture, of a young girl. Once she had been the eighteen-year-old Minnie, her face soft, slightly unfinished, still full of hope. She hadn't known grief and despair. That came later.

Her face was finer now, elegant, more withdrawn, but still open to humour. Her fair hair, worn long in the first picture, now just brushed her shoulders, a length chosen for efficient management.

She changed the position of the flowers twice before she was satisfied.

'He will like that,' Netta said. 'Always he loves flowers. Remember how often he brought them to you? Flowers for your wedding, flowers for your birthday, your anniversary—'

'Yes, he never forgot.'

Neither woman thought it strange to speak of him both in the present and the past, changing from sentence to sentence. It came so naturally that they barely noticed.

'How's Poppa?' Minnie asked.

'Always he complains.'

'No change there, then.' They laughed together.

'And Charlie?'

Netta groaned at the mention of her younger son. 'He's a bad boy. He thinks he's a big man because he stays out late and drinks too much and sees too many girls.'

'So he's a normal eighteen-year-old,' Minnie said gently.

In fact she, too, had been growing a little uneasy at her young brother-in-law's exuberant habits, but she played it down for Netta's sake.

'It was better when he was in love with you,' Netta mourned.

'Mamma, he wasn't in love with me. He's eighteen, I'm thirty-two. He had a boyish crush, which I defused. At least, I hope I did. Charlie's of no interest to me.'

'No man interests you. It's not natural. You're a beautiful woman.'

'I'm a widow.'

'For too long. Now it's time.'

'This is my mother-in-law talking?' Minnie asked of nobody in particular.

'This is a woman talking to a woman. Four years you are a widow, yet no man. *Scandoloso!*'

'It's not quite true to say there have been no men in my life,' Minnie said cautiously. 'And, since you live right opposite me, you know that.'

'Sure. I see them come and I see them go. But I don't see them stay.'

'I don't invite them to stay,' Minnie said quietly.

Netta's answer to this was to give her a crushing hug.

'No man ever had a better wife than my Gianni,' she said. 'Now it's time you think of yourself. You need a man in your life, in your bed.'

'Netta, please—'

'When I was your age I had—'

'A husband and five children,' Minnie reminded her.

'That's true, but—ah, well, it was a long time ago.'

Netta had a generous nature. In all things.

'I'm quite happy without a man,' Minnie insisted.

'Nonsense. No woman is happy without a man.'

'And, even if I wanted one, it wouldn't be Charlie. I'm not a cradle-robber.'

'Of course not. But you could make him listen. Where is he tonight? I don't know. But I'm sure he's with bad people.'

'And I'm sure that when you get home you'll find him there looking sheepish,' Minnie assured her.

'Then I go home now. And I tell him he should be ashamed for worrying his mother.'

'I'll tell him, too. Come on, I'll walk home with you.'

Minnie's home was on the third floor, overlooking the courtyard. Some of the other homes were also occupied by Pepinos, since the family had always liked to live within hailing distance of each other. As they went out on to the iron staircase that ran around the inside of the courtyard, they could see lights in the other windows and shadows passing across them.

Then, up the stairs to the fourth floor on the other side, to the front door of the home Netta shared with her husband, her brother and her youngest son, when he was at home. There was still no sign of Charlie.

'He'll be home soon,' Minnie said soothingly. 'He's just trying his wings.'

She kissed her mother-in-law and wandered back to her own little apartment. As always, it felt very quiet when she let herself in. It had been that way since the day her young husband had died in her arms.

She was suddenly very tired. Netta's conversation had steered her close to things she normally tried not to think of.

From his place on the shelf Gianni seemed to follow her around the apartment with his eyes. She smiled at him, trying to find reassurance in his presence as she had so often before. But this time she couldn't sense him smiling back.

The kitchen table was scattered with papers. Reluctantly she sat down to finish her work, but her mind couldn't concentrate. It was a relief when her cell-phone rang.

'Charlie! Mamma's been worrying about you. Where have you got to? You're *where*?'

CHAPTER TWO

THE young policeman looked up with admiration as Signora Minerva strode into the station.

'*Buona notte*,' he said. 'It's always a pleasure to see you here, *signora*.'

'Be careful, Rico,' she warned him. 'That remark could be construed as harassment. You're reminding me that my relatives are always in some sort of trouble.'

'No, I was saying how pretty you always look,' he replied, hurt.

Minnie laughed. She liked Rico, a naïve country boy, overwhelmed by his assignment to Rome, and wide-eyed about everything, including herself.

'Always?' she teased.

'Every time your relatives are in trouble,' he said irrepressibly. 'How an important lawyer like yourself comes to be related to so many criminals—'

'That's enough!' she told him sternly. 'I grant you, they can be a little wayward, but there's never anything violent.'

'Signor Charlie has been in something violent tonight. His shirt is torn, he's bleeding. Huge big fight. The fellow with him is even worse. He's a big, bad man with a nasty face.' Rico took a deep breath as he came to the real crime. 'And he doesn't have any papers.'

'What, nothing?'

'No identity card. No passport.'

'Well, we don't all carry our passports around with us.'

'But this man speaks Italian with an accent. He is a foreigner.' He added in a low, horrified voice, 'I think he's English.'

'So was my mother,' Minnie said sharply. 'It's not a hanging crime.'

'But he has no papers,' Rico said, returning to the heart of the matter. 'And he won't say where he's living, so he's probably sleeping in the streets. Very drunk.'

'And he was fighting Charlie?'

'No, they were on the same side—I think. It's hard to be sure because Charlie's drunk too.'

'Where is he?'

'In a cell, with this other fellow. I think he's afraid of him. He won't say a word against him.'

'Does "this fellow" have a name?'

'He won't give his name, but Charlie calls him Lucio. I'll take you to him.'

She knew the way to the cells by now, having come here so often to help her relatives, who were as light-fingered as they were light-hearted. Even so, she was aghast at the sight of her young brother-in-law, seated lolling against the wall, scruffy, bruised and definitely the worse for wear.

Rico vanished to find the key, which he'd forgotten to bring. Minnie stood watching Charlie, wishing he didn't look so much like a down-and-out. But his companion was even worse, she realised, as though he'd fought ten men.

Tall, muscular, unshaven, he looked strong enough to deal with any number of opponents. Like Charlie he wore a badly torn shirt and his face was bruised, with a cut over one eye. But, unlike Charlie, he didn't look as if it were all too much for him. In fact, he didn't look as though anything would be too much for him.

So this was Lucio, a thoroughly ugly customer, brutal, with huge fists to power his way through the world—a man used to getting his own way by the use of force. She gave a shudder of distaste.

Then Charlie seemed to half wake up, rub his eyes, lean forward with his hands between his knees and his head bent in an attitude of dejection. 'Lucio' came to sit beside him and put a hand on his shoulder, shaking him slightly in a rallying manner.

Charlie said something that she couldn't catch and Lucio replied. He, too, was inaudible, but she sensed that he spoke gently. Then he grinned, and the sight surprised her. It was ribald and full of derision, yet with a hint of kindness, and it seemed to hearten the boy.

Rico returned. 'I'll let him out and you can talk with him in an interview room,' he said, 'well away from that one.'

The sound of the key turning made both men look up. Rico opened the door and addressed Charlie in a portentous tone.

'Signor Pepino, your sister is here. Also your lawyer.' Trying to be witty, he added, 'They came together.'

Out of the corner of her eye Minnie saw Lucio stiffen and throw a sharp look at Charlie, then at her. He stared as though thunderstruck. His eyes contained both a frown and a question as they looked her up and down in a considering way that was almost insulting.

In this she did him an injustice. Luke was beyond thinking anything except that this couldn't possibly be happening.

Pepino? A lawyer?

She was Signora Pepino? This dainty fair-haired creature was the dragon? And he, who'd laid such plans for gaining the upper hand, found himself in a police cell—

dishevelled, disorderly, hung-over and, worst of all, dependent on her.

Great!

Charlie tried to fling his arms about her, hailing her emotionally as his saviour.

'Get off, you ruffian!' she told him firmly. 'You look as if you've been rolling in the gutter and you smell like a brewery. I suppose you're relying on me to get you out of here?'

'And my friend,' Charlie said, indicating Luke.

'Your friend will wish to make his own arrangements.'

'No, I've told him you'll look after him too. He saved my life, Minnie. You wouldn't abandon him to his fate when he's poor and alone and has nobody to help him?' Charlie was in an ecstasy of tipsy emotion.

Minnie groaned. 'If you don't shut up I'll abandon *you*,' she told him in exasperation.

'I'll take you to an interview room,' Rico said.

'No, thank you, I'll stay here and talk to both of them.'

'Stay here?' Rico asked, aghast. 'With that one?' He pointed to Luke.

'I'm not afraid of him,' she said crossly. 'Perhaps *he* should be afraid of *me*. How dare you do this to my brother?'

Luke leaned against the wall, regarding her ironically through half-closed eyes.

'Look,' he said, sounding bored, 'bail your brother out or do what you have to. Then go. I can manage for myself.'

'Lucio, no!' Charlie exclaimed. 'Minnie, you must look after him. He's my friend.'

'He's a lot older than you and should know better,' she said firmly.

'That's right, it's all my fault,' Luke said. 'Just leave.'

He promised himself that when they next met he would be washed, shaved and well-pressed. With any luck she might not even recognise him.

'What did you mean about saving your life?' she asked.

Charlie launched into an explanation which was more or less accurate considering the state he was in. The word 'puppy' occurred several times and by the end Minnie had a rough idea that the stranger had come between Charlie and superior odds, although perhaps not as melodramatically as he described it.

'Is that what happened?' she asked Luke in a gentler tone.

'Something like that. Neither Charlie nor I like seeing a child bullied. Or a puppy,' he added after a moment.

'What happened to the child?'

'Grabbed the puppy and ran. Then there was a bit more fighting, and someone must have called the police.'

'Well, I'm glad you were there with Charlie, Signor—'

'Lucio will do,' he said hastily.

'But I can't represent you if I don't know your name.'

'I haven't asked you to represent me.' Inspiration made him add, 'I can't afford a lawyer.'

'It'll be my gift, to show my gratitude.'

Luke groaned, mentally imploring heaven to save him from a woman who had an answer to everything!

'As Charlie says, I can't just abandon you,' Minnie went on. 'But you must be quite frank with me. Where are you living?'

'Nowhere,' he said hastily, imagining her mirth if he gave the name of the hotel.

'Sleeping in the streets?'

'That's right.'

'But it makes my job harder. So does your lack of identity. How come you don't have an ID card?'

'I do.'

'Where?'

'I left it in the hotel,' he said before he could stop himself.

'But you just said you were sleeping in the streets.'

'I'm not at my best,' he said, inwardly cursing her alertness. 'I don't know what I'm saying.'

'Signor—whatever your name is, I don't think you're as drunk as all that, and I don't like clients who mess me around. Please tell me the name of your hotel.'

'The Contini.'

Silence.

She looked him up and down, taking in every scruffy, dishevelled detail.

'All right, you're a comedian,' she said. 'Very funny. Now, will you please tell me where you're staying?'

'I just did. I can't help it if you don't believe me.'

'The most expensive hotel in Rome? Would *you* believe you, looking the way you do?'

'I didn't come out looking like this. I left everything behind in case of pickpockets.' He looked down at his disreputable self. 'Now I don't suppose any pickpocket would bother with me.'

'*If* you are telling the truth, and I'm not sure I believe it, I still need your name.'

He sighed. There was no help for it.

'Luke Cayman.'

For a moment Minnie didn't move. She was frowning as though trying to understand something.

'What did you say?' she asked at last.

'Luke Cayman.'

She drummed her fingers. 'Is that a joke?'

'Why would you think so?' he fenced.

'I thought maybe I'd heard the name before, but perhaps I was mistaken.'

'No, I don't think you were,' he said deliberately.

They regarded each other, each with roughly the same mixture of exasperation and incredulity. Charlie looked blank, understanding nothing.

Suddenly his expression changed and he took a deep breath. In a flash Minnie was at the door, calling for Rico, who came running.

'You'd better get him out quickly,' she said.

Rico did so, guiding Charlie down the corridor to where he could be ill in peace.

'Let's get this settled,' Minnie said. 'I do not believe that you're Luke Cayman.'

'Why? Because I don't fit your preconceived notion? You don't fit mine, but I'm willing to be tolerant.'

'You think this is very funny—'

'Well, no, this isn't how I'd have chosen to meet you. With a bit of conniving I dare say you could get me locked up for years. Look me in the eye and say you aren't tempted.'

'Well, I'm not,' she snapped. 'It's the last thing I want.'

'Very virtuous of you.'

'Virtuous, nothing!' she said, goaded into candour. 'With you locked up, the Residenza would be in limbo, with no hope of getting anything done. You may be sure I'll do my best to make you a free man.'

'I see. If anyone's going to give me grief, you'd prefer it to be you.'

'Exactly.'

Charlie returned, looking pale but slightly better, and

glanced back and forth between them, sensing strain in the air.

'We were discussing strategy,' Minnie said.

'I've decided not to hire you,' Luke told her. 'I'd feel safer if you just leave me to my fate.'

'No,' Charlie burst out. 'Minnie's a good lawyer; she'll get you out of trouble.'

'Only because she's got far more trouble planned for me,' Luke said with a derisive grin.

'Please, let's not be melodramatic,' Minnie said coolly. 'I shall treat you exactly as I would any other client.'

'You see?' Charlie urged. 'Honestly, Lucio, she's the best. They call her the "giant slayer" because she'll take on anyone and win. You should see the battle she's preparing for the monster who owns our building.'

'I can imagine,' Luke murmured. 'A monster, eh?'

'Yes, but she's says he's going to die a horrible death,' Charlie said with relish.

'Literally, or only legally?' Luke asked with interest.

'Whichever seems necessary,' Minnie said, meeting his eyes.

'I gather you'll make that decision at a later date.'

'I like to keep my options open.'

'When she's finished he'll wish he'd never been born,' Charlie added.

'Does this monster have a name?' Luke asked with interest.

'No, Minnie just calls him the "devil incarnate".'

'Stop talking nonsense, both of you,' she said severely. 'I've got to work out what we're going to do. You'll be in court in a few hours and you can't go looking like that. Charlie, I'll send someone down with clean clothes for you. Signor Cayman, you'll need fresh clothes, too, and your ID card. How do I get them?'

'I could call the hotel and ask them to arrange it,' he said reluctantly. 'But I don't want them to know I'm here.'

'You're right. Can I get into your room?'

'Yes, I brought the card with me.' From his back pocket he drew the sliver of plastic that acted like a key at the Contini and handed it to her, giving her the code. 'It's on the third floor.'

'I don't believe I'm doing this,' she said, half to him, half to herself.

'Try to forget that I'm the devil incarnate,' he said. 'That should make it easier.'

Charlie looked from one to the other, baffled.

'You can explain it when I'm gone,' she told Luke.

Rico opened the door for her. At the last moment she turned to look back at Luke and said, 'By the way, I didn't call you the devil incarnate.'

'Thank you.'

'I called you "the creature from the black lagoon". I'll see you later.'

Heading north, she swung her car on to the Ponte Sisto, the bridge that would take her over the Tiber in the direction of the Contini Hotel. As she drove, she seethed.

She had been furiously angry for years. The man who'd owned the Residenza had been a reprobate who had resisted her attempts to make him spend money on the property. When she'd moved the law against him he'd always found a way to wriggle out.

And then, just when she'd thought she had him cornered, he'd pulled a final rabbit out of the hat, signing over the building to Luke Cayman, so that she had to start again. It was a moot point whether she were angrier with him or Luke Cayman.

And now, to find herself defending the enemy, was enough to make her explode.

A cool head would dictate placating him, saving him from the gallows—figuratively speaking—then turning on the charm. But she was too incensed to consider it.

By now dawn was breaking, covering the sleeping city with a soft white mist. In the distance she could see the Contini, a huge, luxurious building created from an ancient palazzo. She could hardly believe that the ruffian she had left in the cells was actually staying here.

Luckily the night receptionist was dozing and it was easy to slip past. On the third floor she found Luke's room without trouble. It was large and lavishly appointed, with a balcony.

She went out and stood regarding the view as the light grew brighter. To her right lay the lush green lawns of the Borghese Gardens. To her left she could see the Vatican, the early sun just touching the dome of St Peter's. Between them glided the River Tiber.

It was a marvellous scene, full of peace and beauty.

A rich man's scene, she thought crossly. For only a rich man could afford to stand in this exact spot and see such wonders spread before him. And one particular rich man had thought it amusing to leave his wealth briefly behind and go out slumming it for fun.

He'd got more than he'd bargained for, but in the end he had only to send someone to his expensive hotel, to go through his expensive clothes and put everything expensively right for him. And all the while his tenants lived in a building that was falling apart.

For a moment she was so livid that she almost stormed out, leaving everything behind. Let him take his chances! See how funny he found that!

But her professionalism took over. She would do her job.

She surveyed the suits in his wardrobe until she found one of a dark charcoal colour. To go with it she chose a white shirt and a dark blue silk tie. Then she rummaged in the drawers for clean socks and underpants. As she had more than half expected, he wore boxer shorts.

Well, it wouldn't be a satin thong, she mused with a faint smile. *Not him.*

She packed everything into a bag she found in the wardrobe, then opened the wall safe using the plastic card that had opened the door. Inside she found his wallet and checked it for the ID card. It was there, and so was something else—a photograph of one of the loveliest young women Minnie had ever seen.

She was wearing trousers and standing, leaning against a wall, her thumbs hooked into her belt, one foot up against the wall in a pose that emphasised her height and slender grace.

Like many beautiful women Minnie was fascinated by beauty of a different kind in others. Where she herself was fair, this was a brunette with marvellous dark hair streaming down to her waist, giving her an exotic, mysterious look.

She was also wonderfully tall. As a child Minnie had dreamed of growing to five foot ten and becoming a model. In the end she'd had to settle for five foot four, or 'nothing very much' as she'd crossly put it.

But this was how she'd always longed to be, with legs that went up to her ears and a neck that came from a swan.

'Grr!' she said to the picture. 'Who are you? His wife? His fiancée? Girlfriend? Whoever you are, you've got no right to look like that.'

She replaced the picture carefully in the wallet, which she then put in her own bag, to take to him.

From a distance she heard the bell of St Peter's, chiming seven o'clock, and realised that the light was growing fast, the city was waking and she still had much to do.

She should call Netta, but a quick rummage in her bag revealed that she'd left her cellphone behind. Using the bedside phone might be indiscreet. That left Luke Cayman's own cellphone. After a brief hesitation, she took it and dialled. When Netta answered she kept her tone light.

'Netta? That silly boy has been up to his tricks. He drank too much last night, got into a brawl and he's at the police station.'

She heard Netta give a little shriek and hastened to add, 'Don't worry, I'll sort it. It's not the first time.'

'Oh, Minnie, you will get him out, promise me.'

'Don't I always? But I need you to get down there with some clean clothes so that he can look good in court. It'll just be a fine and when you get him home you can make him sorry he was born.'

After a few more reassurances she hung up. Before putting the phone away, she studied it a little, tempted by its state-of-the-art appearance, and making a mental note to replace her own with one exactly like this beauty.

Nothing but the best for him, she mused.

She was about to switch it off when it rang and, before she could stop herself, she answered it.

'Pronto!'

The action was completely automatic, and only when the word was out did she realise what she'd done.

The caller was a woman, sounding a little surprised at hearing Minnie.

'*Scusi?*' she said. 'Is this Luke Cayman's phone or do I have a wrong number?'

'No, this is his phone. If I could explain—'

The other voice became warm and charming. 'My dear, there's no need for you to explain. I understand perfectly. I should apologise for calling so early, but I overlooked the time. Please ask Luke to call his mother when he can spare a moment.'

'Yes—yes, I'll do that,' Minnie stammered, for once not in control. 'Er—it won't be in the next few minutes, I'm afraid—'

'That's all right. I was once young myself. I'm sure you're extremely beautiful.'

'But—'

'*Ciao!*' The line went dead.

Well, that was that, she thought crossly.

Luke's mother thought she was his girlfriend, rising from the sheets after a night of passion, and about to dive back in for another riotous round of pleasure.

She could have screamed with vexation.

For precisely one minute she sat there, taking deep breaths. Then she finished packing, taking care to switch off the phone before it could ring again, and hurried out of the room, just managing not to slam the door behind her.

At the police station she showed Luke's ID card at the desk before going to the cell.

'There's just the "drunk and disorderly" to deal with, and I assume you have no previous convictions?'

'None,' he assured her.

'You'll go before a Justice of the Peace in a couple of hours. He'll fine you and that'll be the end of it.'

He was looking in the bag she'd brought. 'You've

done a great job. These will make me look like a pillar of the community.'

'Hmm!'

'I won't ask what that means. I'm sure you're longing to tell me.'

'But you're not going to give me the satisfaction. Very wise.'

He declined to answer this, but his harsh face softened and there was briefly a devil in his eyes. Suddenly Minnie remembered his mother's mistaken assumption, and she had a horrid feeling that she might be about to blush.

'I'll see you in court,' she said, and departed with dignity.

Netta returned home with Minnie to cook her some breakfast while she showered, ready for court later that morning.

'Bless you,' she said, emerging in a towelling dressing gown to sit down before muesli and fruit juice. 'Don't worry. Charlie's going to be all right.'

'I know. You'll take care of him like you've done before. And also of that nice young man.'

'Nice—you mean that brute with him? You know nothing about him.'

'Rico let me into the cell to see Charlie, and we all had a talk. I'm glad you are helping him, too.'

'Don't be fooled, Netta. I can see that he's been to work on you, but you needn't feel sorry for him.'

'But of course I must be concerned for the man who saved Charlie's life,' Netta said, scandalised.

'Saved his life, my left foot!' Minnie said with frank derision. 'I don't believe he did any such thing.'

'But Charlie says so,' Netta persisted.

'After what Charlie's taken on board I wouldn't rely on him for the time of day. And I wouldn't rely on this other character for anything. He's our new landlord. The enemy.'

'But he's not our enemy, *cara*. He explained to me how it happened, how he did not want the Residenza—'

'That isn't going to make him a better landlord,' Minnie pointed out.

'He told me that he thought he had offended you, and how he feels most desolate—'

'Did he, indeed?' Minnie said with grim appreciation of these tactics.

'And I said I was eternally grateful to him for saving my Charlie, and he was welcome in our home at any time.'

'You might well say that, since he happens to own it.'

'Then everything is all right.' Netta beamed. 'We are all friends, and he will make the repairs—'

'And double the rent.'

'You will talk to him, be nice, make *him* nice.'

'Netta, listen, this is one very clever man. He's been to work on you, and achieved exactly what he wanted. You're putty in his hands.'

'Twenty years ago, I would have been,' Netta said with a sigh.

Minnie refused to allow her lips to twitch. 'Don't think like that,' she said with an attempt at severity. 'It's just giving in to him.'

'OK, *you* give in to him. Such a man was made for a woman to give in to. Or many women.'

'Then they'd be very foolish. He knows what to say and do, but it's all meaningless. I'd love to know what really happened in this fight.'

'He was defending Charlie and the little puppy—'

'I think he was probably just fighting the puppy,'

Minnie said cynically. 'I expect it bit him. Good for the puppy!'

'Why are you so unkind to the poor man?'

It would have taken too long to explain, so Minnie just said, 'I'll get dressed and we'll go.'

CHAPTER THREE

Two hours later she presented herself before the Justice of the Peace, Alfredo Fentoni, clad in the voluminous black robe of the advocate. Fentoni, who knew her, smiled benignly, addressed her as *Avvocato*, and they began.

Minnie had to admit that Luke was much improved. The suit spoke of sober respectability, and a shave had transformed him into something resembling an ordinary man.

But only resembling. Now that she saw him at his best, she realised how far from ordinary he was. In the cell she'd been aware of brute force. Now she was even more intensely aware of the skill with which he disguised power. That made him a cunning man as well as a forceful one, and all the more dangerous for that.

It seemed odd to be regarding him as dangerous when his fate was in her hands, but he was no longer the down-and-out she'd met that morning. In fact, that had been an illusion. The reality was this other man who strode into the court as though he owned it, and took up position in the dock with an air of impatience, as though he were doing them all a favour.

She was his advocate, and obliged to do her best for him, but the temptation to bring him down a peg was almost irresistible.

The trial began. What happened then, Minnie could only ascribe to a malignant fate, making her life as difficult as possible. By dubious means Luke had contrived to wrap himself in a halo, at least as far as Netta was concerned. Now events conspired to give that halo a new brilliance.

The four oafs from the night before were also in the dock, grinning and scowling by turns. They had their own lawyer, ready to challenge Minnie on every point, and it soon became clear that they were trying to establish themselves as innocent victims.

They were all small and wiry compared to Luke's impressive size, and at one point their lawyer flung out a hand in his direction, inviting comparison. A sensible man would have let his shoulders sag, or at least done something, no matter how useless, to shrink himself.

Luke, to Minnie's total exasperation, stood up straight and folded his arms in an attitude that contrived to be aggressive. She could have torn her hair.

She redoubled her efforts, concentrated all her forces, managed to trip the oafs up, made them contradict themselves and showed them up for what they were.

Everyone relished the moment when the ringleader stumbled into silence while Minnie simply spread her hands as if to say, You see! The massed ranks of Pepinos began to applaud, and were firmly shushed by Netta.

More than a lawyer, Luke thought, unwillingly impressed. A consummate artist, a force of nature.

And he was going to be her next challenge. He was beginning to enjoy the prospect.

At last Fentoni declared that he was fed up with the lot of them, and imposed hefty fines all round.

One of the oafs, incensed at this 'injustice', made a lunging movement at Charlie, but found himself facing Luke, who stepped in quickly and took hold of his ear. While he twisted and yowled with pain Luke raised an eyebrow in the direction of the police, as though asking what he should do with this object. An officer hastily intervened. Fentoni promptly doubled the oaf's fine, and the session was over.

Netta beamed at Luke, then beamed some more when he insisted on paying Charlie's fine as well as his own. Charlie's brothers crowded round, slapping Luke on the back. Minnie groaned.

'Netta, he is not a hero,' she tried saying firmly. 'Charlie would probably never have been in trouble if he hadn't met him.'

'You've quite decided that I'm to blame,' Luke said, appearing beside her. 'Aren't you at least supposed to believe in your client?'

'You are not to blame,' Netta told him firmly. 'Tonight we have a big party at our home, and you will be the guest of honour.'

'You're too kind, *signora*,' Luke said impressively.

'You'll have no trouble finding the Residenza Gallini,' Minnie said darkly. 'You'll know it by all the bits falling off the building.'

'And if I don't notice them, I'm sure you'll point them out to me,' he said smoothly.

He was about to turn away when Minnie remembered something and stopped him. 'You need to call your mother,' she said in a low voice. 'She called you this morning while I was in your hotel room. I took a message.'

As she turned he stopped her with a hand on her arm. 'You will be there tonight, won't you?'

'Of course I will, if only to stop you deluding my poor family any more.'

His grin jeered at her. 'You haven't had much luck so far.'

'I'll improve with practice. Don't forget your mother,' she said in a voice that put an end to the conversation.

He took out his cellphone, which she had returned to him earlier, switched it on and dialled. Hope answered at once.

'Darling, I'm so sorry,' she said. 'I didn't mean to be indiscreet, but I forgot it was so early.'

'What do you mean?'

'This morning, when I called and the phone was picked up by that young lady. She sounded charming, but of course I got off the line at once.'

It dawned on him what she was talking about.

'No, Mamma, it's not like that.'

'Nonsense. When a young lady answers a man's phone at seven in the morning it's always "like that".'

He looked around and found Minnie's eyes on him. Of course she could guess every word his mother was saying. In outrage he turned his back on her.

'Mamma, listen to me—'

'Yes, my son,' she said and obligingly fell silent.

That stumped him. It had been the bane of his life that he had a mother who listened. Unlike other mothers, she didn't brush his explanations aside, thus giving him a permanent excuse—'But Mamma, I *tried* to tell you—' She simply sat there waiting, while he tied himself in knots.

Comparing notes with his brothers, he had found them all similarly afflicted. It had made growing up very hard. Now she was doing it again.

'You've got the wrong idea,' he growled.

'I hope not. I thought she sounded very nice. There was something in her voice, a soft vibration that's always there when a woman has a passionate nature.'

'*Mamma.*'

But then she surprised him with a great burst of laughter that rang down the line.

'Don't be silly, Luke, I'm only joking. She was probably the chamber maid bringing you an early breakfast. I expect you were in the shower.'

'Yes,' he said, filled with relief.

'It was wrong of me to tease you, but I would be pleased to think you were forgetting Olympia so soon.'

'Olympia?' he asked blankly. 'Oh, yes—Olympia.'

When he hung up a few minutes later he saw Minnie regarding him with a look he chose to interpret as cynical amusement.

'Do you mind telling me what you said to my mother?' he demanded.

'Very little. It was mostly of the "um—er" variety, and she needed no encouragement to think what you think she was thinking. She plainly believes that women clamour for a scrap of your attention and swoon with desolation if you don't look their way.'

He had been going to tell her that it was Hope's idea of a joke, but before he could do so she added, 'This was your first night in Rome and she reckoned you'd pulled already? Who are you? Casanova?'

'In my mother's estimation, yes.'

'Or did she think there was a simpler explanation, and that money came into it somewhere?'

'No, she knows I don't have to use money. At least, not in the sense you mean.'

'Is there another sense?' she demanded, aghast.

'I have been known to buy a lady dinner and the best champagne before a night of mutual pleasure. But nothing as crude as you're suggesting.'

Of course he wouldn't, Minnie thought before she could stop herself. This man would never have to pay a woman to get into his bed. The thought didn't improve her opinion of him. If anything, it added to his sins.

'I'm sure my mother never suggested any such thing,' he added.

'No she was very kind and assured me that she "quite understood perfectly". I suppressed the impulse to tell her that hell would freeze over first.'

'First?' he asked innocently. 'First before what?'

She regarded him icily. 'Before you wrap me round your little finger the way you've done with the others. Netta, *cara*.' She turned to embrace Netta who'd appeared beside her. 'I must be going to my office now.'

'Then you can give Signor Cayman a lift to the Contini,' Netta suggested quickly.

'I don't think—' Minnie began.

'But of course you can. It's just a little way past the Via Veneto.'

'The Via Veneto?' Luke queried.

'That's where my office is,' Minnie said. 'I'll give you a lift if you wish. Goodbye, Netta. I'll see you tonight.'

Luke didn't speak until they were on the road.

'I thought your office was in the Residenza. That was the address on your letters.'

'You might say I have two practices,' Minnie said. 'There's my official one in the Via Veneto, and my unofficial one here in Trastevere.'

'And the unofficial one is for friends, relatives—any of the locals likely to end up in a police cell?' he hazarded.

'I also act for my neighbours when they need help with a tyrannical, money-grubbing—'

'Meaning me?'

'No, meaning Renzo Tanzini. I fought him for ages

and then he—' She checked herself suddenly. 'This isn't the time.'

'No, this is where I thank you for helping me out. Send me your bill, and Charlie's, and I'll settle them promptly.'

'There's no need for that.'

'It's a good chance for me to get into Netta's good graces.'

'Surely you've managed that already?'

'And that makes you madder than anything, doesn't it? In your ideal world she'd hate me as much as you do.'

'I don't hate you, Signor Cayman, I merely require fair dealings for your tenants.'

'And you don't think you'll get them from me?'

'The tone of your letters didn't inspire hope.'

'The tone of *your* letters made me think of an elderly harpy with hobnailed boots.'

She gave a wicked chuckle that he found oddly pleasing. 'And I'll crush you, wait and see.'

He barely heard the words. Something in her voice had alerted him and, against his will, he found himself remembering Hope's words. '*...a soft vibration that's always there when a woman has a passionate nature...*'

Nonsense. Hope had invented it to tease him, and the power of auto-suggestion made him hear it now. Nevertheless, he found himself trying to provoke her into a response.

'I'm sure you'll try.'

'Oh, I'll do it,' she promised, 'but not just yet.'

Did he imagine it, or was there a special vibration in her tone as she said the last words?

They had reached the Via Veneto and were gliding along its length.

'Which office is yours?' he asked.

'Up there on the left.'

He studied it as they went past, and was impressed. He made the rest of the journey in thoughtful silence, breaking it only briefly when she dropped him at the hotel. She barely acknowledged his goodbye, speeding away in a dashing style that he couldn't help admiring.

His phone rang. It was Olympia, the girl he'd 'lost' a couple of days ago. It felt like a couple of years, so much had happened.

'Luke, are you all right?'

He stretched out on the bed. 'Of course I am. Don't worry about me.'

'It's just that you left so suddenly, and I didn't have a chance to say goodbye—and thank you.'

Her voice was sweet and husky, and now he remembered how it could entrance him. That, too, seemed to have slipped into the past a little.

'How's Primo?' he asked.

'As grateful to you as I am for bringing us together.'

'Don't start painting me as a noble loser,' he begged.

'A noble, generous loser.'

'Olympia, *please*!'

She laughed and it was charming, but his heart was safe. He hung up, feeling relaxed.

He stripped and went into the shower to scrub the police cell off. Now his thoughts were all of the coming battle, and how he should confront Signora Minerva. She had surprised him by being younger, prettier than his mental picture. Yet instinct told him that she was also more formidable and totally unpredictable.

Now he recalled something from early that morning. When Minnie had swept out of the cell on her way to his hotel, he and Charlie had been left to talk things over, and Charlie had said, 'Minnie and my brother Gianni adored each other. She hasn't been the same since he died.'

'She's a widow?' he'd said, surprised, for there was something about her air of glowing life that hadn't made him think of a widow.

'Has been for four years. And it's not for lack of offers. All the men are after her.' He'd sighed. 'Including me.'

'You're just a kid.'

'That's what she says. Not that it would make much difference if I weren't. I'm not Gianni. Gianni was everything. When he died, she died.'

It had meant little at the time, but now he tried to connect that picture with the vibrant, lovely woman he'd encountered since, and it was no use. It didn't fit. The surface denied the reality. Or maybe the other way around. How did a man tell?

Mentally he set that down on his plan of campaign. It could be very useful.

Even if he hadn't known where the Residenza was Luke would have spotted the party from a great distance. The courtyard was glowing, lights were on all over the building and more light poured out into the street.

He was reminded of the Villa Rinucci in Naples, his home for many years now, ever since Hope, his adoptive mother, had married Toni Rinucci. It stood high on a hill, and at night its lamps could be seen for miles inland and out to sea.

He had always loved the place. Even after he'd moved out to his own apartment in Naples, he'd looked up the hill at night before going to bed, and the sight had warmed his heart.

There was a wide gulf between the luxurious villa and

this down-at-heel tenement, and it was disconcerting to have the same feeling here as he found at home.

It was the lights, he told himself reasonably. Light always created the illusion of warmth and friendliness, and he wasn't going to start being sentimental about it.

But there was also the laughter and the sound of welcoming voices, and these, too, spoke of home, so that when he entered the Residenza he was smiling.

Behind him came the taxi driver, puffing under the weight of Luke's contribution to the party. When Netta called down to him from an upstairs window he indicated the cases of beer and wine. Cheers broke out above and the stairs shook under the pounding of feet. Several young men burst out into the courtyard, scooped up the cases and Luke with them. In moments he was upstairs, being embraced by Netta, who screamed joyfully in his ear, making him wince.

He'd met all the family briefly that morning, but now he met them again. Alessandro, Benito, Gasparo—all Charlie's brothers—plus Netta's brother Matteo, his wife Angelina and their five children. Netta's husband Tomaso slapped him on the back, hailing him as a saviour, and various other uncles and aunts clamoured for his attention, until he thought the little apartment would burst at the seams.

He couldn't see Minnie but in the crowded room it was hard to be sure, so he looked again, and then again. But there was no sign of her. He found himself curious to know how she would dress for this party.

Charlie bounded up to him, offering a drink.

'Thanks, but I'm sticking to orange juice,' he said. 'I'm not taking any risks tonight.'

'Go on, have a beer.'

'Don't press him, Charlie,' said a female voice. 'He doesn't want to end up burdened with you again.'

It was her. How long had she been standing there? When had she come in?

She was dressed with a flamboyance that surprised him. He'd never pictured her in trousers, but there they were, dark purple, fitting snugly over her hips, topped off with a silk blouse of extravagant pink. The effect was stunning.

Her fair hair was drawn back off her face, emphasising her delicate bone structure and fair skin, and she might have been a different person from the austere advocate of the morning.

'Thanks for coming to save me,' he said.

She laughed directly into his face. At five foot four inches she had to look up to him, but she still gave an impression of looking him in the eye, he realised.

'I reckon two doses of Charlie in one day is more than the strongest man should be asked to bear,' she said. 'Let me get you an orange juice.'

She fetched it, then had to turn to look after another guest. He watched her, unwillingly impressed by her neat, shapely figure. It was hard to reconcile this flaming creature with the woman Charlie had described, who'd died with her husband. There was something there he couldn't work out, something mysterious and intriguing.

The room was filling up as more guests arrived. Some of them gave him curious looks, and he guessed the news of his identity had gone around. He became lost in a maze of introductions. Every girl there wanted to flirt with him, and when someone put on some music there was dancing.

In such a small place it seemed impossible that anyone could dance, but they managed it. Luke plunged in with every sign of enjoyment, although he was actually growing tired after so long without sleep. But not for the world would he pass up the chance to win over his tenants, thus making them easier to deal with and, incidentally, giving himself the great pleasure of making Signora Minerva nervous.

At last he had a free moment just as Minnie was passing.

'You can't just go like that,' he said, grasping her hand. 'You and I have to dance with each other.'

'Have to?'

'Of course. When two countries are at war it's customary to mark a truce by having the two heads of state dance together.'

'I believe that only happens when the war's actually over.'

'Then we'll set a precedent,' he said, putting an arm about her waist.

Minnie might have demurred longer, but someone collided with her, pushing her closer to him.

'Very well,' she said. 'Just for the look of the thing.'

'You're all graciousness.'

Glancing up, she found him regarding her with a look that was half irony and half an invitation to share the joke. Drat him, she thought, for having a kind of fierce attractiveness that could get under her guard, even if just for a moment.

'How are you feeling now?' she asked.

'More human. A lot poorer.'

'You wait until you see my bill. That really will make you feel poor.'

'And Charlie's,' he reminded her.

'You don't think I'd charge Charlie, do you? He's my brother-in-law.'

He shook his head in despair for her.

'Why did you tell me that? You should have charged me over the odds for him and put the money into a fund for repairs.'

'Yes, I don't make much of a schemer, do I?' she agreed ruefully.

'You prefer to confront the foe full-on, rather than plot behind his back. Brave but foolhardy.'

'Plotting isn't my style. Besides, I've slain a good few foes in my time.'

'Is that a threat or a challenge?'

'Work it out.'

Minnie wished the room were a little less crowded so that she wasn't crushed so hard against his body. She'd seen that every woman in the place admired him, and there was something in that consciousness that infiltrated her own, so that she could understand their feelings, while assuring herself that she was safe from sharing them.

But she would have felt safer still if she could have danced a few inches away. The room was hotter than she'd realised, and it was getting harder to breathe.

As soon as she could she excused herself. 'I must go and help Netta. Enjoy the party.'

He nodded and let her go. He was beginning to be very conscious that he'd spent the previous night in a police cell, wide awake.

He'd meant to catch up on his sleep at the hotel that afternoon, but he'd become involved in business phone calls and in the end there had only been time for a cold shower. Now he knew it hadn't been enough. His eyes insisted on closing, no matter how hard he fought to keep them open.

At last, taking advantage of the crowd, he slipped out of the door and found himself by the railing that overlooked the courtyard. Too public. Where could he find a little privacy?

He discovered a small corridor that went through the building, connecting the staircase to the outer apartments that overlooked the road. It was deserted and he sank down to the ground, thankful for a place where a man could rest his head in peace.

He'd return to the party soon, but, just for a few minutes, he would close his eyes...a few minutes...a few...

CHAPTER FOUR

AFTER handing round more drinks, Minnie went into the kitchen to help Netta make coffee.

'You looked good together,' her mother-in-law observed.

'Just doing my duty,' Minnie said. 'It was purely formal.'

'How can you be formal with him? He is a *man*.'

'So are a lot of other people here,' Minnie observed, trying not to understand Netta's meaning.

'No, they are not men, like he is,' Netta insisted. 'Boys, feeble creatures who look like men but don't measure up. He is a *man*. He can bring you back to life. Why were you so careless as to let him leave?'

'Has he left?'

'Can you see him anywhere? He's slipped out with a woman, and they've found a quiet place to do things that—'

'Yes, I can imagine what they're doing.' Minnie stopped her hastily. 'I suppose he has every right to please himself.'

'He should be pleasing himself with you,' Netta said stubbornly. 'And you should be pleasing yourself with him.'

'Netta, I only met him today.'

'Huh! I only knew Tomaso one day before I had his clothes off. Oh, it was glorious! Of course he was useless at everything else but I got pregnant and we had to marry.'

'That sounds like an argument for staying a virgin.'

'Who wants to be dried up and withered?' Netta demanded.

Soon afterwards Minnie took the chance to slip away. Her nerves were jangling in an unfamiliar rhythm and she badly needed to calm them.

Taking up a bottle of mineral water, she went out of the front door, rejoicing in the cool night air. She took a long gulp of the water and felt better, then she began to drift down the stairs.

Perhaps Netta's right, she thought, *and I am dried up and withered. But I wasn't always...*

There had been a time when she and Gianni had seemed to exist for passion alone, a time when every night had been a scorching delight, every dawn a revelation, when life's chief good had been the shape of Gianni's body, the hot spicy scent of him.

But that time had ended. She'd told herself that his death had brought all desire to an end, and she was content to have it so. She was used to Netta's attempts to talk her into a different mood, and she'd always laughed them off. Suddenly, mysteriously, she couldn't do it any more.

Then she heard a noise from nearby. It came from one of the corridors that ran through the building, linking the inner staircase with the apartments that faced outwards.

Signor Cayman, she thought wryly, *taking his pleasures.*

But this didn't sound like a man in the throes of physical delight. More like snoring.

She crept inside the corridor. There was Luke, sitting on the floor, leaning against the wall, dead to the world. She dropped to her knees and, with the aid of one weak lamp in the ceiling, made out his face, slightly to one side, relaxed for the first time.

She'd seen his mouth tensed in the hard line of a man determined to have his own way, or twisted in derision, but now it was softened into a more attractive shape, one that it was just possible to associate with pleasure. Pleasure for himself, pleasure for the woman who kissed him...

She stopped, annoyed with herself for letting her thoughts wander in this direction. A woman who'd lived almost like a nun for four years should have herself under better control by now, except that somehow control grew harder as time passed.

It's Netta's fault, she thought, *talking about him and me like that.*

She was about to walk out and leave him, but her conscience stopped her. She couldn't let other people find him here. She gave him a gentle shake on the shoulder. It took several shakes before he opened his eyes.

'You've been sleeping like a baby,' she said, her eyes gleaming at him in the darkness.

'Oh, Lord, did anyone notice I was gone?' he groaned.

'Does it matter?'

'That place is full of young lads who can carouse all night and then start again without any sleep. At one time I could have done it, too, and I'm damned if I'll let them suspect I can't do it still.'

Minnie smiled and produced the bottle of mineral water, unscrewing it for him.

'Thanks.' He drank deeply and felt better. 'Whatever happened to my misspent youth?'

'You spent it,' she said sympathetically.

'Yes, I guess I did.'

'I wonder how. I'll bet you'd never seen the inside of a cell before last night.'

'There's no need to insult me,' he said drowsily. 'When I was younger I had my moments—I should be heading back to the hotel soon. I'll say goodbye to Netta and then—'

He tried to get up and sank back. His brief doze, far from refreshing him, had started dragging him down to the depths of sleep, and there would be no escape until he'd gone all the way to the bottom and surfaced gradually.

'You'll never make it,' she said. 'I've got a better idea. Stay here a moment.'

He fell asleep again as soon as she left, and awoke to the feel of her shaking him by the shoulder.

'Come on,' she said in a tone of command.

He had a vague awareness of going down a flight of stairs and along a corridor until they stopped outside a door. She took out the key that she had been to fetch, and opened the door of an empty apartment.

'This is between tenants at the moment,' she said. 'Of course you'll find it a bit of a comedown after the Contini—'

'If it's got a bed, it's fine,' he murmured.

'It's got a bed, but it's not made up.'

She reached into a cupboard to find a pillow that she tossed onto the bed, followed by some blankets.

'Hey, steady there,' she said, catching him swaying. 'Now lie down.'

'Thanks,' he mumbled, collapsing thankfully, and doing it so fast that she went down onto the bed with him.

'OK, let me go,' she said.

'Hmm?'

'Let me go.'

But the grip of his arms was unrelenting. He was too far out of it to heed her protests, but he was holding her against his chest in a grip she couldn't break.

She told herself that there was nothing lover-like about his clasp, and she must be as unaware of him as he presumably was of her. But the warmth of his great body was reaching her, enveloping her, taking control in a way that was alarming.

For a moment she was almost tempted. It was so long since she'd known the first moments of thrilling sensation with their implicit promise of what was to come, and it was hard to turn away now.

Yet she forced herself. Weakness was something she couldn't afford. That was the code she lived by, and she wasn't going to forget it now. Putting out all her strength, she managed to prop herself up a few inches, just far enough to deliver a well-aimed sock on his jaw.

Like magic he went limp, and she managed to get free.

'Sorry about that,' she said, untruthfully.

'Mmm?'

She tucked a blanket around him, and slipped quietly away.

At dawn Luke awoke and lay with his eyes still closed, trying to sort out his impressions. They were very confused.

A soft, warm, female body lying against his own—his head spinning—

He opened his eyes.

He was in a place he didn't recognise. The narrow bed beneath him stood in the corner of a small room which had a chest of drawers, a chair and a lamp. Nothing else.

He rose and pushed open the door leading to a living room with a small kitchen leading off. Like the bedroom it was sparsely furnished, containing only a sofa, two chairs and a table. The only other room was a small bathroom.

If only he could remember, but he'd been barely awake and had received only impressions. He'd held a woman close to his body and she'd been moving urgently—in the motions of love? Or trying to get away?

And who? Not the gazelle-like Olympia, who had sometimes filled his dreams, but someone shorter, more strongly built, with a powerful right hook he thought, as he recalled the reason his jaw was tender.

The sound of the front door made him turn. It was Signora Pepino, sauntering in and standing there, surveying him with a cheeky grin.

He barely recognised her. He'd seen her as 'Portia' in an elegant black gown, giving a commanding performance in the courtroom. Last night at the party she'd been glamorous in silk and velvet. Both of those women had been 'Signora Pepino'.

But this was 'Minnie', an urchin in old jeans and blue T-shirt. He wished she would stay the same woman for more than a few hours.

'So you're up at last,' she said with an air of teasing. 'This is the third time I've been back. You were dead to the world. Do you feel better?'

'Ye-es,' he said cautiously, making the word half a question, and feeling his jaw tenderly.

To his relief, she burst out laughing.

'I'm sorry about that.'

'It was you?'

She surveyed him with hilarity. 'Another woman would feel insulted by that question. Do women thump you so often that you can't remember them?'

'You're the first—I think.'

'Are we back to your misspent youth again? I'm not sure I want to know the details.'

'Fine, because I can't recall them.' He felt his jaw again. 'But I won't forget you in a hurry.' He looked around. 'Where did I see a bathroom?'

'No use. Everything's turned off. Come up to my place and I'll make you some breakfast.'

Now he could see the courtyard in broad daylight, and appreciate how cleverly the tenants had made the best of it. It might have been a dreary place with its dark bricks, plain construction and the staircase that ran around the inner wall looking like a fire escape. Indeed, it probably doubled as a fire escape, but it was also the way to get from one home to another.

But the dwellers here had fought back with flowers. There were several different kinds, but mostly geraniums, for Italians had a passion for geraniums, with their ability to spread colour and cheerfulness over the grimmest scene.

They were everywhere—white, red, purple, rioting over railings, trailing from pots, smothering ugliness. Just the sight of them lifted his spirits.

Minnie's apartment turned out to be opposite the one they'd left, but one floor higher. Whereas his had been a shoe box, barely big enough for one person, hers could manage two, three at a pinch, and had a cosy, friendly air.

She produced some towels and directed him to the bathroom.

'Breakfast will be ready when you've showered,' she said.

She hadn't quite finished cooking when he came out, and it gave him a chance to look around and see her home. Anything he could learn about her would be useful in the coming battle.

It was cosy and unpretentious, slightly shabby but delightful. He suddenly noticed a photograph standing on a shelf, with a small vase of flowers beside it. The man resembled Charlie, although he was older, and Luke realised this must be Gianni.

'That was my husband,' Minnie said, coming to stand beside him.

Gianni had a wide, laughing mouth, gleefully wicked eyes and the same air of irresponsible charm as Charlie.

'You can see that he's a Pepino,' Luke observed.

'Yes, they're a tribe of madmen,' she said with a slightly wistful smile. 'I love them all. He used to say that I'd have married any one of his brothers, just to be part of the family, but he knew he was special to me as no other man could be. Put it away, please.'

When he hesitated she took the picture from his hand and replaced it on the shelf.

'I'm sorry; I didn't mean to pry,' he said.

'You weren't. It's just that I find him hard to talk about.'

'After four years?'

'Yes, after four years. Sit down and have your breakfast.'

She was still smiling, still pleasant, but unmistakeably a door had been shut.

She served him eggs done to perfection and coffee that was hot, black and sweet. He was in heaven.

'I've seen people collapse at the end of a party before,' she said, sitting opposite him, 'but never from orange juice.'

'That's right, rub it in. At one time I could have seen that crowd under the table.'

'I doubt if you could ever have competed with Charlie,' she advised him.

'Was he really named after the Emperor Charlemagne?'

'Yes.'

'But why?'

'Because of Charlemagne's father. He was a king called Pepino.'

'And since the family name is Pepino—?' he hazarded.

'It stands to reason that they're descended from royalty.'

'But that was twelve hundred years ago.'

'So?' She shrugged. 'What's twelve hundred years to an ancient and royal family?'

'Do they really believe it?'

'Absolutely.'

'But surely it can't really be true?'

'Who cares as long as it makes them happy?'

'Isn't a lawyer supposed to care about the truth?'

'No, a lawyer cares about the facts. It's quite different. Anyway, that's for the courtroom. In real life a nice, satisfying fantasy is better.'

'You're like no lawyer I've ever known. You've got that office in the Via Veneto, which is the most expensive part of town, and yet you live here which is far from expensive. Perhaps I should double your rent.'

Her head jerked up. 'You *dare*—?'

'Calm down; I was only teasing. It seemed right to play up to your idea of me as Scrooge—sorry, Scrooge was an English villain—'

'You don't have to explain that to me. I'm half English.'

'You are?'

'My father was Italian, my mother was English. I was

born here, and lived here until I was eight. Then my father died, my mother returned to England and I was raised there.'

Luke stared at her. 'That's incredible.'

'Unusual, maybe, but hardly incredible.'

'I mean that it's a sort of mirror image of my own experience. I'm completely English by birth. When my parents died I was adopted. But my adoptive parents divorced after a few years and my mother married an Italian called Toni Rinucci, from Naples. I've lived in Naples ever since.'

'So that's why you have an English name?'

'Yes. The Rinuccis are a family of English-Italian hybrids. Primo, my nearest adoptive brother, had an Italian mother, so he calls me *Inglese*, as an insult.'

She gave a gasp of delighted recognition. 'When Gianni and I were teasing each other he used to say, "Of course you're half English so you wouldn't understand," and I used to throw things at him.'

'Didn't you like being half English?'

She shook her head vigorously. 'I always wanted to think of myself as Italian. I got back here as soon as I could, and I knew at once that I'd come home, my real home. I met Gianni soon after, and we were married quickly. We had ten years. Then he died.'

She delivered the last few words briefly, and got up to make some more coffee. Luke said nothing, wondering at the sudden change that had come over her.

After a moment she returned, apparently cheerful again.

'So now you know why I live here. I love the whole family. Netta's a mother to me. Gianni's brothers became my brothers. I shall never leave.'

'But don't you ever feel the need to move on? I don't

just mean to another address, but emotionally, to the next stage in life?'

She frowned a little, as though wondering what the words meant.

'No,' she said at last. 'I was happy with Gianni. He was a wonderful man and we loved each other totally. Why would I want to move on from that? After total happiness, what is the "next stage"?'

'But it's over,' he said gently. 'It was over four years ago.'

She shook her head. 'No, it's not over just because he died. When two people have been so close, and loved each other so much, death doesn't end it. Gianni will be with me as long as I live. I can't see him, but he's still with me, here in this apartment. That's my "next stage".'

'But you're too young to settle for permanent widowhood,' he burst out.

'Who are you to say?' she demanded with a touch of anger. 'It's my decision. Gianni was faithful to me. What's wrong with me being faithful to him?'

'He's dead, that's what's wrong with it. Can't there be more than one man in the world?'

'Of course,' she said simply, 'but only if I want there to be.'

There was no more to say. She had closed the subject quietly but firmly. For a moment he glimpsed an iron will beneath the charming exterior. She would not be easily moved from a decision once taken.

'Thank you for breakfast,' he said. 'I'll be going now.'

'Let's fix an appointment so that we can go over this building and I can show you what needs to be done.'

'You've already given me a comprehensive list.'

'Yes, but the reality is worse. Shall we say tomorrow? I have a free afternoon.'

'I'm afraid I don't,' he said untruthfully. 'I'd like to arrange my own timetable. I'll call and speak to your secretary.'

Her wry look told him that she wasn't fooled. He met her eyes, letting her know that he wasn't going to be a pushover.

Before leaving he said, 'Can I have the key to the place where I slept last night? I'd like to look at it again. Thank you.'

The next few days were packed with work. The day she'd lost had to be made up and she had several new clients, so there was little time to reflect on the fact that Luke didn't contact her.

She took to going home late to avoid the curious looks of her fellow tenants. She knew they were excited at the prospect that she could really help them now, and they would be disappointed to know that matters had stalled. If Signor Cayman, as she persisted in thinking of him, did not call her, they would expect her to call him, and she didn't know how to explain that pigs would roost in trees first.

Nor could she have told them that one part of her was glad not to meet him again. When she thought of what she'd told him about Gianni and their lasting love, she was aghast at herself. She never discussed her husband with strangers, yet she'd found herself saying things to this man that she'd barely confided to Gianni's family. For some reason she cared that he should understand, but it made no sense, and it obscurely alarmed her.

Then a client suffered a crisis, forcing her to travel to Milan and stay for a week. During that time there was no call from him, according to her secretary. On the night before her return to Rome she decided that enough was enough, and called the Contini.

'I'm sorry, *signora*,' the receptionist said, 'but Signor Cayman checked out this morning.'

She flew back to Rome calling herself every name she could think of. He'd returned to Naples and her best chance was gone.

It was late but as she entered the courtyard Netta, followed by her menfolk, came hurrying to meet her, arms open.

'Darling, you're so clever,' Netta cried, enfolding her in a gigantic hug.

'No, I'm not. Netta, I've been stupid—'

'Don't be silly! You're a genius! Charlie, Benito, take her bags. Can't you see she's tired?'

Minnie found herself swept in and up the stairs.

'We've been longing for you to come home so that we could tell you how proud of you we are,' Netta said gleefully. 'It was a master stroke. You're simply a genius. Everyone says so.'

'Netta, will somebody please tell me what I've done that's so clever?'

'Oh, listen to her!' Netta chortled.

'But what—?'

Minnie fell silent as they reached the second floor. The door to the vacant apartment opened and a man emerged, regarding her satirically.

'What—are you doing here?' she asked slowly.

'I live here,' Luke informed her. 'I've just taken this apartment, although I have to say it's in shocking condition. First thing tomorrow I shall complain to the landlord.'

* * *

Meetings of the Residenza Tenants' Association always took place in Netta's home. This time the atmosphere was buzzing.

Netta dispensed coffee and cakes, besieged on all sides by neighbours who assumed that she was in the know. But what she could tell them was disappointingly thin.

'I've hardly seen her since she came home. She's been in her office early and late. There's been no chance to discuss anything.'

'But she must be talking to him privately,' was the consensus. 'Look at what he did today. She must have made him do it.'

But Netta said no more, unwilling to confide her suspicion that Minnie knew nothing about Signor Cayman's interesting activities that day.

At last the door opened and Minnie swept in, a mass of files under her arm, the picture of efficiency. To their disappointment, she was alone.

'All right, everyone,' she said crisply. 'We have a lot to talk about tonight. Things have changed, but we can turn this to our advantage—'

She stopped as the door opened, and her face showed her dismay.

'Sorry I'm late,' Luke said.

'What are you doing here?' The words were out before Minnie could stop them.

Luke's face assumed a look of diffidence. 'I thought this was the meeting of the Tenants' Association,' he said meekly. 'Did I come to the wrong place?'

He was drowned out by a chorus of welcome. Arms reached out to him. At first he seemed inclined to hold back, as if unsure, but then he let himself be drawn in.

And it was all an act, Minnie thought indignantly. If you believed this man was shy, you'd believe anything.

'Yes, this is the tenants' meeting,' she said, 'but I hardly think it's appropriate for you to be here.'

'But I'm a tenant,' he said, hurt. 'Haven't I the same rights as anyone else?'

She drew a long, careful breath. 'You are also the landlord—'

'Then I should be here, and you can tell me what you think of me,' he said with a winning smile.

'Signor Cayman, if you've been reading my letters you know very well what your tenants think of you.'

'But you were writing to me as landlord,' he pointed out. 'I'm here as a tenant, and I have several suggestions for dealing with the shady character who owns this building. I know his weaknesses, you see.' He added confidingly, 'There's nothing like inside information.'

This produced a ripple of laughter. Minnie had to respect these clever tactics, although she couldn't help feeling excluded. She was their friend and defender, yet he was taking over, make her superfluous. Suddenly she was shivering inside. It was a feeling she hadn't known since she'd returned to Italy, fourteen years earlier.

She knew what he was up to, pretending friendship only to turn on them later. But she wouldn't let him get away with it.

'You're quite right,' she said, giving him a cool smile to let him know that battle had commenced. 'But the really valuable inside information is held by me—information about this building and what it needs, what your tenants need. Without that, you know nothing. And if you really want to be well informed, *signore*, I suggest we start to inspect the building right now.'

That should show him that she had regained the initiative.

Then Enrico Talli spoke up.

'But Signor Cayman is already doing that. He inspected my place this morning, and Guiseppe's home this afternoon. He was most interested in what he saw, and has promised to take care of things.'

Minnie drew a long, slow breath.

'That is excellent news,' she said, hoping that her confusion and dismay weren't obvious.

'But what about me?' an elderly woman piped up, incensed that Enrico had received favoured treatment. 'When do you look at my place?'

'This is Signora Teresa Danto,' Minnie explained.

Luke smiled at the old lady. 'And what is wrong with your apartment, *signora*?'

'It's in the wrong place,' she said. 'I want you to move it.'

'That might be a little beyond my powers,' he admitted.

'It's on the top floor,' Minnie explained. 'And it's too large for her. Teresa needs something smaller and lower, so that she doesn't have to climb so many stairs.'

'Then perhaps I should take a look now,' Luke said, rising and offering Teresa his arm.

This brought a cheer from the assembled company, who all seemed to consider themselves invited. In a procession they left the room and followed Luke up the stairs to the top floor.

CHAPTER FIVE

TERESA'S flat was in reasonable condition, but too large for one person. As soon as they entered Luke's eyes were drawn to a low table on which stood a photograph of an elderly man.

'My husband, Antonio,' Teresa said with pride. 'This is where we lived together. Now he is gone, and this place is too big for Tiberius and me.'

Tiberius turned out to be an imposing black cat, sitting on a window sill, washing his face and observing proceedings with the indifference of one who knew that he would be all right, whoever else wasn't.

'Please move us on to a lower floor,' Teresa pleaded. 'I'm too old for those stairs, and Tiberius doesn't like heights.'

'In that case,' Luke said at once, 'you must take my flat, and I'll move into yours.'

There was a cheer of approval from the residents, and they all trooped downstairs to Luke's flat.

'We can start on the exchange tomorrow,' he said. 'It'll need redecorating—'

'Oh, no,' Teresa said quickly. 'It's lovely as it is.'

'It's not,' he said, surprised. 'It's a dump.'

'But redecorating will be expensive,' she said anxiously.

'Only to me, not to you. And, since it's so small, the rent will be lower than you're paying now.'

Teresa was ecstatic. 'Lower rent? Then Tiberius can have fish every day.'

'I guess he can,' Luke said, amused.

The old lady was as excited as a child who'd been promised a treat. She insisted that everyone must return to her home to celebrate and, since the tenants of the Residenza were always ready for a party, it was only a moment before the procession was making its way upstairs again.

Luke was the hero of the hour. Minnie, watching him cynically, could only wonder at the ease with which he was winning everyone over. His clever stunt with Teresa did nothing for the rest of them, but they didn't seem to notice that.

He made his way across the room to her. 'Aren't you pleased that I'm doing the right thing?'

'Never mind me. It's them I want you to please.'

'The truth is that hell will freeze over before you concede that I might have one good point.'

'Well—' she floundered.

Then she saw him looking at her with one eyebrow cocked and something on his face that might have been real humour.

'Maybe just one,' she conceded.

He grinned. 'That really had to be dragged out of you with pincers, didn't it?'

'Of course it did. I'm a dragon, remember?' She held out her hand. 'Goodnight.'

'You're not going?' he asked, scandalised.

'I ought to do some work—'

'Work won't do your headache any good,' he said shrewdly.

She stared. 'How do you know I have a headache?'

'Something in the way you keep closing your eyes. It's true, isn't it?'

'Yes, but it's just a little one.'

'It'll grow into a big one if you don't take care of it. No work. Come with me.'

'Why?'

'We're going to have a civilised coffee and a civilised talk, and celebrate our truce.'

'Haven't we already done that?'

As she spoke he was curving his arm around her, not touching her but shepherding her in the direction he wanted to go. She smiled and went with him, content to get out of the noise and glare.

Having urged her towards the stairs, he got in front of her.

'Just in case you fall,' he said. 'It's a long drop.'

'Hey, I won't fall apart because of a little headache,' she protested. 'I'm as tough as old boots.'

'Sure, I can see that by looking at you.'

As they went down, the noise faded behind them and she felt as though she were being engulfed by peace and quiet. It was a strange sensation to enjoy with Luke, but pleasant.

Coming out of the arch into the street, she took deep lungfuls of air, turning her face up to the sky with an expression of ecstasy.

'I suppose I look crazy,' she said when she opened her eyes to find him watching her.

'No, you look like someone who should do that more often. Feel better now?'

'Yes, it's a bit stuffy in that courtyard.'

They began to stroll through streets where *trattorias* were still open, their lights gleaming on the cobblestones. Luke saw an all-night pharmacy on the corner and slipped in for a moment.

'Just something for your head,' he told her, emerging, 'in case you find you're not as tough as you think.'

'Sometimes I'm not,' she agreed. 'Sometimes I just want to lie down and go to sleep.'

'You missed a trick there,' he said. 'Never admit a weakness to the other side. I shall pounce on it and use it to undermine you.'

She gave a rueful laugh. 'Will you?'

'Well, maybe not this time.'

'Besides, I already know your weakness.'

'I don't have one,' he said at once.

'You're a man who suffers badly if he doesn't get enough sleep. Look at the way you were after Netta's party. One night without sleep and you collapsed into a crumpled heap. You'll never take over the world like that.'

'I guess I won't. Dammit! What a pity you noticed.'

'Never mind. I won't tell anyone. I'll just "pounce on it and use it to undermine you".'

With every step Minnie felt she was walking deeper into calm content. The battle was far away. She would fight him tomorrow.

He steered her into a café where they could sit at a table on the pavement. The owner evidently recognised Minnie, for he held up a tall glass, raising his eyebrows in a question.

'What's that?' Luke asked.

'They do a delicious dish of strawberries, cream and ice cream. I used to eat it a lot before I moved to the Via Veneto and became pompous.'

He ordered coffee for them both and a sundae for her.

'Take this for your head,' he said, offering her what he'd bought in the pharmacy.

'Thanks. I'll leave it for a moment. It may not get bad enough for me.'

He watched with pleasure as she tucked into her sundae, thinking that it was like watching a child let out of school.

'They all lean on you, don't they?' he said suddenly.

'What?'

'The night we met, you came out to defend Charlie, and he's not the only one, is he? Rico let out a few interesting things while we were in the police station. You're in and out of that place, hauling them out of the consequences of their own mistakes. Shoplifting, low level smuggling, selling hot goods in the market—'

'It's all minor stuff. They're family.'

'They not *your* family. They've just latched on to you and loaded you with all their problems.'

'Why shouldn't they? I'm the strong one. I like it.'

'OK, you like it, but even the strong one needs a rest some times. Does anyone ever think of you?'

'Yes, Netta. She's been better than my own mother.'

But, even as she said it, she knew what he meant. On the surface Netta was the matriarch of the family, but in fact it was herself, and it was a lonely position.

She tried to remember the last time she'd walked through the streets of Trastevere like this, and she couldn't. It passed across her mind that under other circumstances Luke would have made an ideal friend.

Suddenly she realised that they were being watched. A young boy was standing on the edge of the circle of light, trying to attract their attention.

Luke noticed him and smiled. 'Hey there!'

As the boy came forward Minnie saw that he was holding a puppy.

'Is that—?'

'That's my friend,' Luke said. 'And *his* friend. So they're OK. Good.'

'I'm glad to see you well, *signore*,' the boy said with

formal politeness. 'I wanted to thank you for helping us the other night.'

'That's all right,' Luke assured him. 'It all ended happily.'

'But you were arrested—I know they must have fined you—and I have some pocket money—'

'There's no need for that,' Luke said. 'It's all sorted, and nothing for you to worry about.'

'You are sure?'

'Completely sure,' he said gently. 'But perhaps you shouldn't stay out so late another time.'

Right on cue a window opened somewhere above them and a woman's voice screeched, 'Giacomo, come home at once.'

'Yes, Mamma,' he called back in a resigned voice. He thrust the puppy towards Luke. 'He, too, would like to thank you.'

Luke rubbed the animal's head. There was another screech, and Giacomo hurried away.

'Why are you looking at me like that?' Luke asked.

'I guess I really did misjudge you. If there's one man in the world I wouldn't have thought—'

She was confused, less by discovering that there really had been a puppy, but by the kind way he'd spoken to the boy.

'It comes from having younger brothers,' he said, picking up her thought.

'Are you a mind-reader?' she asked in wonder.

'Well, it's easy with you, since I know where you're coming from. I'm the devil and all his works, and anything that doesn't fit that pattern takes you by surprise.'

She began to laugh and choked slightly, waving a hand before her face as if to fend him off while she got over it. He took hold of her hand and held it until she'd finished coughing.

'I suppose there'll come a day when we're not on opposing sides,' he mused. 'When that happens, there are things I'd like to discuss with you.'

It was hard to know how to answer him since his eyes were on her hand, not her face. But he didn't seem to expect an answer and, after holding her fingers between his for a moment, laid his cheek briefly against them and let them go. When she looked up he'd gone inside to pay the bill.

They walked on slowly. The moon was rising, making lovers draw back into the shadows, as she and Gianni had once done, she remembered. But there was no ache tonight, only a sense of peace that was almost happiness.

Even a group of lads kicking a football about down a side street couldn't disturb her. When the ball accidentally came flying in her direction she kicked it back with a neat movement that made Luke look at her with new respect.

'I can do more than stand up in a courtroom, you know,' she said, and they laughed together.

At last they came full circle to the Residenza and he saw her to her door.

'Have those pills before you go to bed,' he said.

But she shook her head.

'I don't need them now. I haven't had a headache for—I don't know. It slipped away without my noticing.'

'I'll say goodnight then.' He held her hand for a moment before turning away.

Back in his own home, he called Hope at the villa. When they'd discussed inconsequential things for a few minutes he said, 'I expect you see a lot of Olympia?'

'She and Primo were here tonight.'

'Next time, give her a message for me, would you?'

'*Caro*, is that wise? She and Primo love each other so much—'

'And I'm really glad they do. I wouldn't spoil it for the world. Mamma you told me once that everyone you love changes you in some way. So tell Olympia—just tell her I said thank you.'

Over the next few days the exchange took place. Luke had Teresa's furniture moved down for her, then he set about moving some furniture into his own place. This caused much hilarity among his tenants, as various items were hauled up five floors of stairs too narrow for them. The men turned out to help, and enjoy a laugh and a beer. The rest of the tenants came out to line the stairs, cheering and applauding as each item reached another level without doing anyone an injury.

After that it was Luke's turn to give a house-warming party. It was colourful and noisy and it competed with other Residenza parties as one of the best there had ever been. Minnie was working late, but she slipped in at the last minute to share a glass of wine and see how happy Teresa was.

'But I know you'll miss this place,' Minnie said, 'because it was the home you shared with Antonio.'

The old woman shook her head wisely. 'My home with Antonio is in here,' she said, pointing to her heart. 'And it will always be there. Bricks and mortar are nothing. You must be ready for what life offers you next.'

A stillness came over Minnie, and she had a strange sensation of hearing distant sounds from mysterious places, inaudible to anyone else but conveying a message to her. She turned away and saw Luke standing nearby.

It disturbed her that he might have witnessed that eerie moment.

'I'm sorry you couldn't arrive sooner,' he said.

'I tried, but I brought you a house-warming present. Here.'

It was a book about Trastevere, full of history and local colour. When he tried to thank her, she gave him a brief smile and slipped hurriedly away, running down the stairs to her own home, desperate to be alone. She locked the front door behind her, and stood for a moment with her back against it, as though barring the world. Teresa's words had got to her, and she could hear the distant music again.

She poured herself a glass of wine, took the photograph of Gianni from the shelf and curled up on the sofa, watching his face, waiting for the moment when he would become real.

She had done this many times before, and had devised a technique for making it happen. It was important to be patient. Trying to rush things would make it harder, so she let herself relax, holding the picture loosely in her lap, looking down on it with eyes that were vague and almost unfocused. Gradually the outlines of the room blurred, faded, retreated, leaving only him behind. And then he was there.

'I don't know what's the matter with me.' She sighed. 'Everything's in a muddle and I don't understand.'

He spoke in her mind. *Is it him?*

'Partly. He's playing a sort of game, but it's not a game to them.'

But if they benefit from it—?

'Will they? There's something going on here that I don't understand.'

Maybe it's really very simple, and Netta's right.

'No,' she said quickly.

Carissima, why are you angry?

'Because he's taking them away from me.' She sighed, facing the truth at last. 'My family, my friends, the people who looked to me—now they look to him. Since I lost you, they're all I have, and they're all I want.'

But suddenly there was silence. She waited for a long time, hoping for something more. But it was over.

Carissima, why are you angry? How often in their squabbles had he said that to her, gently teasing? She was the one with the temper, he the relaxed, good-natured one who waited until the storm had blown itself out.

Suddenly she felt very tired and lonely. She drew the picture up to her chest, folding her arms across it, hanging her head and thinking of Teresa, who could take Antonio with her wherever she went.

All about her the building was growing silent, lights going out. A couple remained on the outside staircase, but after a while even they moved away, unseen by anyone except Luke, who was looking out of his window, watching for the moment the staircase would be empty.

At last he slipped out of his front door and silently went down to Minnie's home. Watching her face, just before she'd left the party, he'd seen real hurt there, and it troubled him. He knew he was being unwise. Her power to make him feel protective was something he should fight, but he wasn't sure how.

One window of her living room looked out directly on to the staircase. The curtains were half open and he stopped to look in. The lights were low inside, but he could see her curled up on the sofa beside a small lamp. Then he realised that her lips were moving and her eyes were directed at Gianni's photograph, resting in her lap.

He drew in his breath and stood quite still, unwilling

to believe what he saw. But he had to believe it when she drew the picture up against her chest, her arms crossed over it as though clinging on for safety.

No, he thought despondently. Not clinging. Embracing. Because there was nobody else in the world that she wanted to embrace. She had found comfort, but not from himself.

He crept away. This was no place for him.

As part of furnishing his new home, Luke bought a couple of self-assembly bookshelves, which he set about putting together, soon realising that he had no gift for this. Trying to use a screwdriver, he slashed the back of his fingers, leaving him bleeding.

With no sticking plaster in the place, he was forced to wrap his hand in a handkerchief and go out to the pharmacy at the end of the street. As he emerged on to the staircase he saw a woman on the level below him, going down the last flight to the ground, then under the archway that led into the street. She was severely dressed in dark clothing and for a moment he was sure it was Minnie. He called down, but the woman didn't seem to hear him, and in another moment she had vanished.

He ran down the stairs and out into the street, but it was crowded and although thought he glimpsed her, he couldn't be sure. As he made his way down the street there was no sign of her.

In the pharmacy he bought a large packet of sticking plaster. On leaving he turned left down a small alley which would lead him to the Residenza by a back street. The little alley meandered for a while before emerging near the rear of a church. From here he could see the graveyard. It was a pleasant place, small and grassy, crowded with headstones that were warmed by the afternoon sun. While he stood watching, Minnie emerged from the church.

She was no longer alone. The other members of the family were with her, having probably come on ahead and met her in the church. They were walking in a little procession, led by Netta, with Minnie beside her and the Pepino brothers following. Luke stayed quite still, almost hidden among the trees.

They were all here together, dressed as mourners, which meant that this was a special day, Gianni's birthday or the anniversary of his death. He wondered what it meant to her after four years. Did she grieve for that charmer as a memory, or as a husband? Was he still alive for her?

Unwillingly he remembered the picture in her apartment, the way she'd embraced it as though it was the only comfort on earth. How often did she renew those flowers she kept beside it? How often could you renew love before it wore out?

They were drawing nearer, towards a grave that lay a little apart from the others. Netta was weeping as she approached it, and so were some of Gianni's brothers, but Luke was barely aware of their grief. His eyes were fixed on Minnie.

Alone among the family she was quiet. Her face was pale but composed as she knelt by her husband's grave. Then she rose and turned her attention to comforting Netta.

They were gathering around the grave now, loading it with flowers and talking to Gianni as though he were still one of them. From their smiles some of them seemed to be cracking jokes with him.

Luke knew he should move on, but something impelled him to stay a little longer and see this through to the finish. They were rising to their feet, moving slowly away.

Then, at the last minute, Minnie paused and turned for a last look, and Luke drew a sharp breath as he saw everything he would have liked to deny.

Her face was no longer composed but ravaged, desolate, anguished. All her life's joy was buried there, and Luke covered his eyes, suddenly unable to endure it.

When he raised his head again Minnie was looking directly at him with an expression of indignation and anger. He groaned. She would think he had been deliberately spying on her.

She turned away, contemptuously it seemed to Luke. He stood watching as the family disappeared into the church, then he hurried away, seeking to get back to the Residenza as fast as possible.

He needed time alone to think. Before his eyes she had changed into someone else. He'd known her, or thought he had, as sharp, funny, cool, in control. The other night he'd watched as she'd talked to Gianni's picture, but she'd done so with a gentle melancholy. The grieving, devastated woman of today was different, terrible.

Inside the flat he waited, listening, until night fell and the building was quiet. At last he descended the stairs to her apartment. The lights were on, but the curtains were closed. What was happening behind them? Had she taken shelter in her private world with Gianni, the world that excluded everyone else, especially him?

After a long time the curtains parted, revealing her face, but at once she let them fall.

'Minnie,' he cried, knocking on the door. 'Minnie, please open up. I must see you.'

There was no sound or movement, and he thought she

was going to ignore him. But then the door opened a few inches.

'Go away,' she said.

'I'll go when we've talked. Please let me in.'

Reluctantly she stepped back from the door. When he'd closed it behind him Luke stood looking at her. Their brief friendly intimacy of the other night might never have been. Now she was really his enemy, and for reasons that had nothing to do with the Residenza.

'I came to say I'm sorry,' he said.

'You were spying on me, and you think "sorry" covers it?' She spoke with her back to him.

'I wasn't spying. I'd been to a shop and happened to walk back that way. It was pure chance; please believe me.'

When she turned he was shocked by her face, which was pale and dreadful, as though she were living on the edge of endurance. 'All right, I believe you,' she said tiredly. 'But it's none of your business, and I don't want to talk about it.'

'Do you ever talk about it, with anyone?'

She shrugged. 'Netta sometimes—no, not really.'

'Don't you think you should?' he asked gently.

'Why?' she asked wildly. 'Why can't I have some privacy? Gianni and I—this is mine. It's *mine*. Can't you understand that? It's between Gianni and me.'

'Except that there is no Gianni,' he said, suddenly harsh. 'He's just a memory now. Or maybe no more than a fantasy.'

'What does that matter? He made me happy then and he makes me happy now. Not many people ever have that kind of happiness. I want to keep it.'

'But you can't keep it. It's gone, but you'll turn your back on life rather than admit it.'

'Who cares about life if I've got something better?'

'There *is* nothing better.'

'People who say that don't know. They don't know what it's like to be so close to someone that it's as though you were one person. Once you've had it, you always have it. You *can't* let it go. Why should you try to make me?'

He'd been asking himself that, and the answer scared him.

'Can't you see that you're too young to live with a ghost?' he said, almost imploring.

'The only thing I can see is that you have no right to interfere in my life. What I do or don't do has nothing to do with you.'

'You can't prevent me wanting to stop you throwing your life away.'

'It's mine, to do with as I please,' she said, angry and frustrated that he wouldn't understand. She paused, took a deep breath and spoke with an effort. 'Look, I'm sure you're a nice man—'

'Be honest. That's not what you really think of me.'

'All right, No! I think you're a smug, patronising, interfering, arrogant so-and-so, who's playing games with my mind for the fun of it. I don't like you. You're too damned sure of yourself. Is that honest enough for you?'

'It'll do for starters.'

'Then please go and leave me alone.'

'Why? So that you can have another chat with a man who isn't there?' he demanded harshly. 'Which of you dislikes me most? Him or you?'

'Both of us.'

'Do you do everything he tells you?' he shouted.

'Get out!'

He hadn't meant to say his last words but her stubbornness was causing something cruel and dangerous to rise in him, and it made him leave, fast, shutting the door sharply behind him. Outside, he stood on the staircase for a moment before going slowly down to the ground and out of the courtyard, to spend the rest of the night wandering the streets of Trastevere in a black mood.

CHAPTER SIX

THE next day he received a call from her secretary, making a formal appointment in her office. He wore a respectable suit in dark grey, with a snowy white shirt and a dark red tie, and was glad of it when he saw her office, a large, impressive room, the walls lined with legal books.

Almost as if inspired by the same thought, Minnie too wore a grey suit with a white blouse. He briefly considered making a mild joke about their similarity, but a glance at her face changed his mind. She was pale, with very little make-up. Her hair was drawn back against her skull in a way that seemed designed to deny life—or, perhaps, to send him a message.

'There was no need for that, you know,' he said gently.

'I'm not sure of your meaning.'

'Aren't you? I thought you might understand. Oh, well, never mind.'

'Signor Cayman, if we keep to the matter in hand I think we'll make more progress.'

Her voice was cool, self-possessed, the voice of a woman in control of the situation. But he heard in it something else, a tension that made him look at her more closely, and realise that her eyes were dark and haunted.

'I'm sorry,' he said suddenly.

He hadn't meant to speak the words, but they burst out.

'There's no need for apologies,' she replied coolly, 'if we can just stick to business.'

'I didn't mean that. I meant I'm sorry for the things I said the other night. I had no right—it was none of my business—'

'Excuse me,' she said swiftly, and left the room before he could realise what she meant to do.

He frowned, hardly able to believe that she'd fled him, unable to cope with what he was saying. How deep a nerve had he touched with his rash words?

The secretary brought him coffee. He drank it, then passed the next few minutes standing at the huge window, looking out over Rome. From here the view was breathtaking, with its distant view of the dome of St Peter's, glowing under the sun. If he hadn't known it before he would have known now that Signora Pepino was a supremely successful lawyer who could afford everything of the best. It gave a new poignancy to her refusal to leave her shabby old home.

Minnie appeared ten minutes later, her composure restored.

'I apologise for that,' she said. 'I remembered a phone call I had to make.'

She seated herself, indicating for him to take the chair facing her desk. 'I gather you've now been over the building extensively and seen for yourself what needs to be done.'

'I have,' he said, sitting down and opening his briefcase, 'although we may not have the same ideas as to what needs to be done.'

'You've seen the state the place is in?'

'Yes, and I don't think repairs are any more than sticking plaster. What that building needs is to be renovated from top to bottom. It's not just a case of flaking plaster, but rotten woodwork needing to be ripped out and replaced.'

'Your tenants will be very glad.'

'Minnie—'

'I think *signora* would be more appropriate,' she interrupted, looking not at him but at the computer screen.

His temper began to rise. If she wanted to play tough, OK. Fine!

'Very well, *signora*, let me make my position plain. My tenants are paying about half the going rate for property in that area, which is perhaps why my predecessor got into financial difficulties.'

'Trastevere isn't the wealthy part of Rome—'

'It's coming up in the world. I've researched the area, and I know that Trastevere has been growing more popular over the last few years. People who couldn't afford the high prices in the rest of Rome started moving in and doing the place up. So then Trastevere prices started to rise. It's actually becoming fashionable to live there.'

'I see where this is leading. You've had an offer from a developer and you're planning to sell us out. Forget it. Your predecessor tried that, but I stopped him by proving that the tenants are protected. They can't be got out for at least ten years. That scares the developers off, except that some try bullying tactics. But even they can be made to wish they hadn't started anything, as you'll find out if you tangle with me.'

'Can I get a word in edgeways?' Luke snapped. 'Whatever needs to be done at the Residenza I want to do it myself, and I want the rest of you to help me. As for bullying tactics—if that's what you think of me, I don't know why we're even bothering to talk. To hell with you for thinking such things!'

He threw down his papers and strode across to the window, staring at the view without seeing it. All he could see was the turmoil in his own mind, where she had the power to cause such havoc. Her opinion of him shouldn't matter, yet her contempt seemed to shrivel him.

'I apologise,' she said, behind him. 'I shouldn't have spoken so strongly. I don't like being taken by surprise, and you surprise me all the time. So I—I go on to the attack.'

'I really am sorry about the other day,' he risked saying. 'I didn't mean to spy. It was an accident.'

'I know. It's just that there are times when I don't like to be looked at.'

'I think that's most of the time,' he suggested gently.

'Well—never mind that.'

'But I—damn!'

The telephone had rung. She snatched it up and spoke to her secretary, finishing with, 'All right, put him through.'

She made a placating signal to Luke and spoke into the phone for ten minutes.

When she'd finished he asked, 'Could you block your calls until we've finished?'

'Not really. I have some important stuff coming through this morning—'

'And it gives you a convenient escape from me, right?'

Before she could answer, the phone rang again. Moving fast, Luke lifted the receiver and slammed it back down. Then he grasped Minnie's hand and began to walk out of the room, forcing her to go with him.

'What do you think you're doing?' she seethed, trying to pull free.

'Taking you to where there's no escape,' he said, not loosening his grip.

On the way through the outer office they passed the secretary, whose curious gaze forced Minnie to look cheerful.

'Just take messages until I'm back,' she called.

'But when will that be?'

'I have no idea,' she managed to say before the door closed behind her.

'What kind of man are you?' she demanded as they went down in the lift.

'A man with a short fuse, a man who doesn't like being messed about, a man who believes in direct action.'

'So your answer is to take me prisoner? Where are you going to put me? In a dungeon?'

'Wait and see.'

But he grinned as he said it and there was something in the sight that sent a sudden *frisson* through her. It was confusing not to know what he had in mind, but also strangely intriguing. His unpredictability should be maddening—it *was* maddening, she hastily corrected herself. But right now she was intensely curious.

After all, it might actually turn out to be a dungeon.

The ride to the 'dungeon' was by one of the horse-drawn carriages that travelled the streets of Rome.

'Borghese Gardens, the lake,' Luke called to the driver as they got in and seated themselves.

'You're going to throw me in?' she asked.

'Don't tempt me,' he growled.

She decided to wait and see before taking any hasty action. Not that there was much action she could have taken with her hand firmly clasped in his.

New York had Central Park, London had Hyde Park, Rome had the glorious Borghese Gardens, known as the 'green lung' of the city, a hundred and fifty acres of trees, lawns, shaded wandering paths and cool water.

At the top of the Via Veneto the driver turned his horse into the gardens, and soon they were trotting beneath trees through which the sun slanted, until the lake burst on them, its water glistening, the artificial temple on the other side white and gleaming in the glow of summer.

Leaving the carriage, Luke led her to the place where boats could be hired, but suddenly a tremor shook her and she tried to pull away from him.

'Not here, Luke.'

'Yes, here,' he said firmly, keeping tight hold on her hand. 'We're going to take a boat and relax and talk and forget everything except that it's a beautiful day.'

'But—'

'Hush,' he said, raising the hand that was holding hers so that she could see the tight clasp as well as feel it. 'I told you there was no escape and I meant it. Today, *Signora Avvocato*, you're going to do as you're told—for once.'

Not releasing her, he took a small rowing boat, and indicated with his head for her to get in. She did so, and he silently congratulated himself. Evidently the odd display of 'male authority' could be risked, even in this day and age.

She settled in the stern, watching him as he took the oars and headed out into the middle of the lake.

'You were right,' she mused. 'There's no escape.'

He had a mysterious feeling that she meant something else, but she fell silent.

'Do you mind?' he asked cautiously. 'I'm sorry I got pushy.'

So much for male authority, he thought.

'It doesn't matter,' she said, and again he had the sensation that she wasn't really talking to him. 'It had to happen. I suppose I was being silly.'

'I seem to see a new you all the time,' he observed. 'In party mood, mother hen, the stern lawyer today—'

'You've seen me as a lawyer before,' she reminded him. 'Think of our first meeting.'

'That was different. That court was your stage. You commanded it. But I haven't seen you before like you are today, holding yourself in and fighting the world. Or is it only me?'

'No,' she said after a moment. 'As you say—the world.'

'You do a lot of fighting inside yourself, that nobody knows about, don't you?'

She nodded.

'Or perhaps Gianni knows?'

He knew it was a risk but, instead of trying to jump out of the boat, she shook her head.

'Did he ever know?'

'When he was alive there was nothing to fight,' she said simply.

He pulled on the oars, drawing them nearer the centre of the lake, sensing that the further they went the more she relaxed, as though a spring inside her was visibly uncoiling.

'*Signora*—' he began.

'Minnie.'

'Then could you please take your hair down? It's scaring me.'

She laughed and pulled her hair free, letting it fall around her face, as close to dishevelled as he had ever seen it.

'Is that better?' she asked.

'Much better,' he agreed. 'Now you look like the real Minnie.'

'You know nothing about Minnie,' she assured him.

'True, because she keeps changing and confusing me.'

'I could say the same about you. You've had a few

different guises yourself—convict, party animal, ruthless tycoon. I merely adapt to keep up with you.'

'And what am I now?'

'Caveman! Hauling me off like that to a place where there's no escape.'

'Well, there *is* no escape, unless you want to jump into the water. I don't know if it's deep but it's certainly dirty.'

For answer she gave the most delightful chuckle he'd ever heard from her. It subsided into a sweet, wistful smile.

'What is it?' he asked.

'How strange that you should have said that to me. It's exactly what he said.'

'He?' Luke asked, but he had an uneasy feeling that he already knew the answer.

'Gianni. This is where he proposed to me. He hired a boat just like this one, rowed me out into the middle of the lake, and said, "Marry me!"'

She fell silent, looking into the water, reliving the moment.

Luke stared, shocked as the implications dawned on him. Then he groaned and clutched his head with one hand, so agitated that he forgot the oar, which swung away from him in the rowlock. Minnie leaned forward to take hold of it.

'Don't panic,' she said, sliding it back to him.

He didn't seem to see it. He was staring at her, aghast. 'That was why you didn't want to come on the lake?'

'Yes.'

'This place is special, and I forced you... Oh, Lord, I'm sorry. I shouldn't have done that. What a mess!'

'Stop being so hard on yourself.'

'Have I ruined it for you?'

'Of course not,' she said gently. 'Nothing could ruin it for me. It doesn't depend on other people. I'm even glad that you made me come here. I've never been back since he died, and it's been like a wall rearing up in front of me. Now you've helped me get over it.'

Her air of strain had fallen away, leaving her calm and content. She had said, 'It doesn't depend on other people', and he saw that it was true. She had her own world where she lived with Gianni, and nobody could touch it.

Luke cursed the ill luck that had made him bring her here. He'd meant to draw her away from Gianni's ghost, but it was himself from whom she'd withdrawn, back into her private place, leaving him outside.

He took the oar from her, feeling the brief touch of her hand. Slight as it was, it unnerved him.

He said no more for a while, but rowed in silence while the sun rose high in the sky and he grew uncomfortably hot in his sedate jacket.

'You're not dressed for rowing,' she said kindly. 'Why not take your jacket off?'

He removed it gratefully and she took it from him, folding it neatly and laying it beside her.

'And the tie,' she said. 'Take that off and open your shirt. Right now you need to be comfortable rather than dignified.'

'Thanks,' he said, stripping off the tie and handing it to her.

It was bliss to open the top buttons and feel the air on him, but after a few minutes he discovered a downside to this. Perspiration cascaded from him as he rowed, soaking his shirt, making it cling to him, outlining the muscular shape of his torso.

For some reason he felt awkward. With any other beautiful woman he would have enjoyed the chance to impress her as part of the normal process of flirtation. But for her that wasn't good enough, and he felt uncomfortable, even ashamed.

He glanced at her and was relieved to find that she apparently hadn't noticed. She was leaning back, her head tilted up to the sky. Her eyes were closed against the sun, and there was a half smile on her lips. He watched her, entranced, knowing that he could have stayed like this for ever.

He pulled on the oars with renewed vigour, relishing the mass of physical sensations that were rushing in on him at once. Exertion had made his blood pound and his heart beat more strongly, and now his memory seized on the night of the party, when he'd fallen asleep, she'd led him to bed and had to struggle to free herself.

He couldn't actually recall her thumping him, but the feel of her body writhing against his was there with him now. And suddenly he knew why. The touch of her hand, a few minutes ago, had revived that other moment when they had been as close as lovers, in flesh if not in spirit.

Now his body felt alive, vibrant, and the knowledge that it wasn't the same with her, that there was no way he could reach her, had the effect of intensifying every feeling almost to the point of desperation.

In an urgent attempt to distract his own thoughts, he said, 'Did you accept Gianni at once?'

'I didn't say anything,' she remembered dreamily. 'I was too dumbfounded to speak. I was madly in love, but I'd thought it would take me ages to wring a proposal out of him. Suddenly there it was, and all I could do was open and close my mouth like a goldfish.'

'What did he say?' Luke pressed her.

He despised himself for weakening and asking the question, but if she didn't tell him soon he'd go crazy.

'He said, "Either you say yes or I tip you in the water." So I said yes. Afterwards he told me he wished he hadn't done it that way, as he'd never know whether I'd married him out of love or to save myself from getting wet.' She laughed. 'I told him to work it out.'

'Did he ever manage that?'

'Let's just say we were very happy,' she said softly.

He was silent. There was nothing to say.

After a moment she asked, 'Why are you looking at me like that?'

'I was wondering how often this happens. Do you see Gianni everywhere?'

She considered this seriously. 'I don't "see" him. He's just there, part of me.'

'But I meant places.'

'Yes, he's in all the places. Anywhere we were together, he's still there. We often used to come on this lake and remember what happened.'

He was longing to ask if Gianni was there with them now, but he bit the words back. Why torment himself?

'I should return to the office,' she said with a little sigh.

'Let's not go back. Let's stay on the water, then go and have some lunch and to blazes with them all.'

'I can't,' she said reluctantly. 'I have clients coming in this afternoon.'

'Put them off.'

'Luke, I can't. I mustn't. I can't just abandon people who need my help.'

'But we haven't talked about anything.'

'Serves you right for being a caveman.'

And with that he knew he would have to be satisfied. Turning the boat he pulled back to shore and helped her out. A horse-drawn carriage was passing and took them back to the Via Veneto.

At the door of the building she paused. 'We'll talk business another day,' she said.

Luke didn't want to talk business with her. He wanted to kiss her. But he bade her a polite farewell and left.

A few minutes walking in the sun were enough to dry his shirt. He called the bank and made himself an appointment for later that day. He passed the time with an excellent lunch at which he drank only mineral water to keep his head clear. By now he was functioning as a businessman, so he sat at the table for another hour, jotting down figures.

The meeting at the bank was very satisfactory, and he emerged with the feeling of having matters under his control, something which always made him feel better.

But he was restless, and to ease it he walked all the way back to the Residenza while the light of the city faded and the yellow lamps came on. It was almost dark when he arrived.

Some of his neighbours were sitting on the stairs of the courtyard and he lingered with them, exchanging pleasantries. But he didn't stay long. It had been a hot day and a humid evening, and he was longing for a shower. As he climbed the final stairs he allowed himself to glance down at Minnie's windows, something he hadn't allowed himself to do under the curious eyes of his neighbours. There were lights on. She was in.

Briefly he considered crossing over to see her, but he sensed that she would prefer to be left in peace. After watching the lights in her flat for a while he closed his door and went into the bathroom. There he stripped off, got under the shower and reached out to the boiler.

It exploded.

* * *

After that his impressions piled in on each other. The hideous noise, the crack on his head as he was hurled back against the wall, flames, the terrible helplessness of lying on the floor, half in and half out of consciousness, unable to move and save himself.

From a distance he heard fists pounding on his front door until it flew open and people burst in. Some dragged him out of the bathroom, others fought the flames. The pain was terrible, yet he didn't lose consciousness, only turned his head from side to side, trying to understand what was happening.

They wanted to carry him outside where he would be safer, and he thought vaguely that they shouldn't do that because he was naked. He tried to say something, but when he looked up he found Minnie's face above him. Somehow she was cradling him in her arms. Tears poured down her face and she was sobbing, 'Oh, God, not again—*not again*!'

Then he blacked out and knew no more until he awoke to find himself in hospital. There was a searing pain down his right side, starting with his face, which felt red-hot, and going down his arm, where it was almost unbearable. He made a sound which was half gasp, half groan, and a woman's face appeared in his consciousness.

'You're awake. Good. The pain-killers should start to take effect soon.'

Luke gave a grunt of thankfulness.

'What happened?' he whispered.

'Your boiler blew when you were right in front of it and you caught the full blast. You're lucky you aren't dead.'

'I feel pretty near it.'

'Your right side is most affected. You have mild burns

all down the right of your body, and more severe ones on your arm. But they'll heal. You're in no danger.'

He remembered now. He'd just stripped off, prior to having a shower when the world had exploded about him. With horror he realised that the woman talking to him was a nun.

'Oh, Lord!' he groaned. 'I'm sorry, sister—'

'Doctor,' she said firmly.

'Doctor, I hope I didn't outrage the sensibilities of the sisters.'

'Don't you worry, young man,' she said cheerfully. 'We're not easily scared. Besides, you were decently covered by the time you came in. Your neighbours took care of that.'

'Good,' he said thankfully.

But then more memories assailed him. Minnie—she'd been there when they'd dragged him free. He'd lain naked in her arms, and she'd cradled him, weeping, 'Oh, God, not again!'

He tried to think. Had it really happened or was it just his feverish imagination? But the pain-killers were taking effect and suddenly he lost consciousness.

CHAPTER SEVEN

HE SURFACED again, having lost track of time, but seeing that it was still dark outside. Turning his head painfully, he saw Minnie standing at the window with her back to him. He tried to speak but the sound that came out was weak, and she didn't turn towards him. He wished he could see her reflection in the dark glass, but her head was bent.

Minnie, standing at the window, knew that he had stirred, but needed a pause before she could look at him. She kept her head lowered, lest he see her face, and her tears should reveal too much.

She could still hear the explosion. It happened again and again in her head until she thought she would go crazy from the endless repetition. Then everything slowed and she seemed to be wading through glue as she ran to him, her heart pounding at the sight of the smoke and flames.

It was playing back again, the moment she'd rushed in to find them dragging him out of the bathroom and laying him out on the floor, dropping to her knees beside him, cradling him in her arms—like that other time—watching life ebbing away—*Please, not again!*

She'd held him against her, willing him to live, begging, praying, imploring some unseen power, because she couldn't bear to go through it a second time.

They had taken him from her arms to get him down the stairs. She'd followed and insisted on going in the ambulance with him.

Now he was safe, his injuries treated, his outlook good. She ought to be glad and relax, but inwardly she was screaming while the tears poured down her face.

'Minnie.' His voice was barely a croak, but her ears seemed specially sensitive to him, and now she couldn't hide any longer. She dried her eyes and forced herself under control. When she turned to him she even managed a smile.

Through a haze Luke watched her come towards him and lean close.

'You're all smudgy,' he whispered.

She rubbed her face. 'It's the smoke.'

'Sorry about that. Were you injured?'

'Not at all. Never mind me,' she said with soft urgency. 'I'll go soon and let you rest, but first, how do I contact your family?'

'There's no need for that. I'd rather not worry my mother. She'll think it's worse than it is.'

'You were lucky it wasn't.'

'I was lucky in my neighbours, who came to my rescue so fast. Still,' he added wryly, 'I suppose, having won me over, they wanted to keep me alive until the repairs were done.'

'Stop fishing for compliments. You're a popular man.'

'But you can't think why.'

At one time she would have enjoyed bantering with him, but now there seemed to be a lump in her throat and she was afraid of weeping again.

'I haven't given the matter any thought,' she said, trying to speak steadily. 'Now, can we please be serious for a moment? I ought to let someone know about this. What about your girlfriend?'

'What girlfriend?'

'The one whose picture you keep in your wallet. I

found it the first night when I was collecting your things. She has lovely long black hair.'

'Oh, her!'

'Oh, her? Is that any way to talk about the lady in your life?'

'Hardly that.'

She was silent for a moment before she spoke, choosing her words carefully. 'Does she know she's been relegated to "Oh, her!"?'

'Olympia wouldn't care. To her I was never any more than "Oh, him!"'

'Yet you kept her picture.'

'I'd forgotten it was there. Better tear it up now she's engaged to my brother Primo. In fact—I don't know—what was I going to say?' His mind seemed to be filled with clouds.

'Never mind now,' she said. 'Get some rest. I'll come in tomorrow.'

'Thank you for—what you did—it was you holding me, wasn't it? Or did I imagine that?'

'Go to sleep,' she said.

'Mmm!'

She waited and, when she was sure that he was asleep she kissed his forehead. He stirred, but did not awaken, and she slipped out silently.

The next day he felt better, although still woozy. Netta came to see him, bearing a huge gift of fruit, and chattered non-stop.

'Everyone asked after you. Benito and Gasparo and Matteo, and they sent you some beer, but the hospital wouldn't let us give it to you.'

'They're funny about that,' Luke said with a weak grin.

'Such a mess you were, we thought you would die. So

we called the ambulance and when they carried you off we followed. All except Minnie. She came with you.'

Did she cradle me, naked, in her arms? he thought.

'I'm glad I've got such nice neighbours,' he said.

Netta continued bawling kindly confidences at him until a sister came to his rescue and ushered her out.

'Thanks,' Luke said when the sister returned. 'She's a dear, but—' He gave an expressive shrug, then wished he hadn't because it hurt his arm.

'No more visitors today,' she said.

'Ah—well, if Signora Minerva Pepino should come, I want to see her. She's my lawyer and we're planning legal action against my landlord.'

He slept again and when he awoke it was dark outside and Minnie was sitting beside him. Her dishevelled, grimy look was gone and she was her impeccably neat self again.

'Are you feeling better?' she asked.

He was still talking in a husky whisper, but he managed to say, 'Yes, I guess I'm well enough for you to say, "I told you so."'

She smiled faintly. 'I was going to save that for later.'

'Go on, get it over with. Aren't you glad that I ended up my own victim? Doesn't it serve me right? Minnie, what's the matter?' She'd covered her eyes suddenly and when she spoke her voice shook.

'Don't say things like that, just—don't.'

'You're not crying, are you?' he asked in disbelief.

'No, of course I'm not,' she said hastily, brushing her eyes. 'But you could have died in that blast.'

'Teresa *would* have died in it,' he said huskily. 'She's old and the shock alone would probably have finished her off. I'd have had that on my conscience.'

'Then she's very lucky that you took over,' Minnie

said gently. 'We all are. Thank God you're still alive and it's no worse than a burned arm and face.'

He gave a derisive grunt. 'That's no loss. Women never pursued me for my beauty. I might do better as "scarred and interesting".'

'You're not going to be scarred. Here.'

She took out a small mirror and gave it to him. He surveyed himself critically and grunted again.

'My face looks like a boiled lobster.'

'Only down one side,' she reassured him.

He gave a bark of laughter and immediately winced.

'Just a little redness,' she said. 'It'll go and your looks will be unimpaired.'

He looked at her askance. 'My face was always shaped for scowling rather than smiling. Now it feels too tender to smile much, anyway. Tell me about the apartment.'

'Blackened with smoke. The fire was put out almost at once, but it's not habitable.'

'I want you to do something for me—I mean, please. Get the right people in, not just to my place but everywhere. I want every boiler in the building replaced, and that's just for starters. When I'm back home there's a lot more to be done. I want to oversee it personally.'

'You need to be better before you can think about anything.'

'Will you come and see me again?'

'Of course.'

The nun he'd spoken to earlier appeared by his bed, and smiled at the sight of Minnie.

'*Signora*, I am glad to see you. Signor Cayman tells me that you are both planning to take very stern action against the landlord.'

Minnie's lips twitched. 'He said that?'

'Oh, yes, and it's good. Such landlords are beneath

contempt. If I had yours here I would put arsenic in his coffee.'

'So would I,' Luke said, darting a wicked glance at Minnie.

'You're looking tired,' she said. 'It's time I was going.'

She gave his hand a brief squeeze and departed, leaving him to the tender mercies of the sister.

In three days he was feeling better. He still lacked energy but the only sign of injury was his heavily bandaged arm and hand.

The Pepino family visited every day. Netta would call in briefly to ask if she could get him anything, and the men lingered to play cards.

'Netta, I want to get out of here,' he said one evening. 'Is my place really so bad?'

'You can't live there,' she said at once. 'Not for ages.'

'What about a hotel? Do you know one nearby?'

'You can't live in a hotel. You come to us.'

'I couldn't impose on you. There would be so much work—'

Netta began to weep noisily. In the outpouring that followed several things were stressed—her lonely life since so many of her sons had moved out, how happy it made her to have someone to look after, but, of course, at her age she couldn't expect to know the joy of being needed, and if he preferred to go among strangers then she would try not to complain, but it was very hard on a poor woman who only wished him well, et cetera, et cetera.

Her sons listened to this with groans that showed they'd heard it all before, and her husband leaned over to Luke, remarking cynically, 'You may as well give in now.'

Luke agreed and yielded, grinning. Netta's tears dried as if by magic, and she graciously accepted the financial terms he offered. It was agreed that he would be collected the next day.

Minnie arrived soon after, to be greeted by the news. She expressed herself pleased, but there was a slight reserve in her manner that Luke thought he understood.

Even so, he might have been surprised to hear them talking in Netta's kitchen that night.

'What are you playing at?' Minnie demanded furiously. 'And don't give me that innocent look because you're as devious as an eel.'

'Bad girl. You should respect your mother-in-law.'

'I'll respect her when she stops trying to marry me off.'

'Marry? Who says marry? I'm looking after an invalid, that's all.'

'That's all, my left foot! This is part of a devious plan.'

'So? I'm your Mamma, you've said so often. And a Mamma is supposed to be devious to help her daughter.'

'I do not need help,' Minnie declared, trying to sound firm.

But she knew, from experience, that it was easier to be firm with the wind than with Netta in full cry.

'Of course you need help,' Netta said. 'Four years you are a faithful widow. Now you find a happy life for yourself.'

Minnie eyed her with wry affection. 'So this is all about my happiness, is it?' she challenged.

Netta shrugged expressively. 'He's rich. You marry him, we won't have to pay rent ever again.'

'Netta, you don't know what you're playing with. This

isn't a game where you can move people around the board like pawns. I—I don't want him here. I think he should stay in hospital a little longer.'

'If he's here he's in your power and that's what you want.'

'Really? So now you're an expert in what I want?'

'Sure. You want a man.'

'Not this man,' Minnie said stubbornly.

'Yes, this man. He's the one. I, *your Mamma*, tell you so.'

'Will you keep your voice down?' Minnie asked frantically.

'Then be a good girl and do as you're told. You want him here where you can work on him, like any clever woman.'

'Well, maybe I'm not a clever woman.'

'That's true. You're a very clever lawyer, *cara*, but a stupid woman.'

'Thanks,' Minnie said crossly.

'Don't sulk,' Netta advised her. 'Mamma knows best.'

'She's right,' Tomaso said, looking into the kitchen. 'You listen to Netta. She's got it all worked out.'

'You should be ashamed of yourselves, the lot of you,' Minnie said, but she spoke without anger.

Their affection warmed her even while she told herself that they were scoundrels conniving for their own benefit. That was true, but it wasn't the whole truth. Their schemes were survival ploys, and their love for her was genuine. So, as often before, she allowed herself to be seduced by the comfort of their embrace. The fact that she disapproved of them did not make that embrace one whit less comforting.

She was in court the following day and so missed seeing Luke's triumphant return to the Residenza. Coming home late, she saw Netta's lights on, and Charlie keeping watch on the stairs to waylay her.

'She's here,' she heard him call inside.

They swarmed out to engulf her and sweep her inside, where Luke rose to greet her. He was smiling and composed but she sensed an air of strain. When Netta ordered her to sit down and eat, Luke insisted on bringing some of her supper from the kitchen and helping to serve her.

'You look as if you should be in bed,' she told him quietly as he poured her coffee.

'I'm a bit tired, but Netta's looking after me wonderfully, and they're making me feel like one of the family.'

'That's what I'm afraid of,' she said softly. 'They're lovely people, but—'

'But exhausting. I know. Don't worry. Netta says she's going to be like a mother to me. Tomorrow I have strict orders to stay in bed until the nurse comes to change my dressing. Then I'll get up and go up to look at what's left of my home.'

'Don't overdo it. You need all your energy for getting well. Is your room comfortable?'

'Yes, I've got Charlie's room. He's kindly moved into a tiny place that looks like a box cupboard.'

'It would have been better if you'd had that one.'

'Thanks,' he said, surprised.

'No, I mean it's down the end of the corridor and fairly quiet. Charlie's room is in the centre, and always noisy.'

'Well, it's still kind of them, and I won't be here for long.'

Before she left, Minnie took Netta aside.

'He looks very tired,' she said.

Netta sighed and nodded. 'Perhaps this wasn't a good idea. With so many of the family around and the others dropping in, he can't rest properly.' Suddenly she brightened and seemed to think of something. 'I know, why don't you put him in your spare room?'

Minnie groaned. 'This is what you've been planning all the time, isn't it? Netta, you are unspeakable, you are shameless, you are—ooh, I wish I could think of something bad enough.'

'I know,' Netta said penitently. 'I'm very bad. But you will take him, won't you?'

'I will not. I refuse to be a party to your schemes, do you hear? I don't know how you have the nerve to—of all the—*Goodnight!*'

She grabbed her bag and got out of the apartment while she could still control herself, leaving Netta to explain to Luke that there had been an urgent call from a client.

Minnie meant to stay away for the next few days, but the memory of Luke's strained face haunted her.

Part of her wanted to take him in, care for him and enjoy doing so. But part of her shied away. Being honest, she didn't hide from the reason. It was connected to the minutes when he'd lain in her arms, burned, bleeding, helpless.

His nakedness had left no doubt of what she'd often suspected, that he was magnificently built with broad shoulders and strong thighs, designed for power. Suddenly the power had gone, leaving him vulnerable, his eyes closed, his head slumped against her. The desire to protect him at all costs had been overpowering, and that was what she feared now—to be overpowered, not by him, but by the strength of her own feelings.

She'd stroked back his hair, caressed his face and shoulders, held him against her heart, weeping frantically. And for a few blinding minutes she'd cared for nothing and nobody else on earth.

Now, despite her resolve to stay away from danger, she knew he wasn't well, and she had an uneasy feeling that she'd abandoned him when he needed her. So she called the following evening, meaning to stay just a few minutes.

She found the place in uproar and Netta weeping.

'I meant everything to be all right,' she wailed, 'and now everything is all wrong, and I don't know what to do.'

'But what's happened?'

'My sister Euphrania and her husband Alberto are on their way here to visit us. They will arrive tomorrow and expect to stay here but we have no room. Oh, what am I going to do?'

Suppressing a desire to murmur, 'Stop overacting,' Minnie drew Netta firmly aside.

'This is another of your schemes,' she said, 'but it isn't going to work. He's not coming to my place.'

Netta gave her a pathetic look. 'What will become of him?'

'You'll have to pass on to Plan C, won't you?'

'Pardon?'

'Yesterday was Plan A and it didn't work, this is Plan B, and it's not working either.'

Netta's eyes gleamed. 'The day isn't over, *cara*.'

'Your day will be over for good if you don't stop this,' Minnie threatened. 'I won't have him at any price.'

Netta giggled. The sound infuriated Minnie.

'I will not invite him, Netta. Understand me once and for all, the answer is *no*!' She added, more in hope than conviction, 'And that is final!'

She stormed away so fast that she collided with Luke coming along the corridor, and he winced before he could stop himself. In the brief harsh close-up view of his face, she saw that he was at the end of his tether.

'I'm sorry,' she said. 'I didn't mean to hurt you.'

'I'm fine,' he lied. 'Minnie, is there a good hotel near here?'

She hesitated, seeing a malign fate draw closer, ready to suck her in, and there was no way to avoid it without kicking him when he was down.

'Not a hotel,' she said. 'Not among strangers.'

'I'm a grown man. I can take care of myself. Netta, there you are. I was just wondering about a hotel.'

'I don't think that's a good idea,' Minnie said reluctantly.

'But of course it is,' Netta cried, to her astonishment. She named a hotel. 'It's a lovely place. You'll be very comfortable there.'

'He will not,' Minnie said hotly. 'It's a dump run by swindlers.'

Netta became an avenging angel. 'The night porter is my cousin's uncle's brother.'

'I rest my case. Swindlers who fleece the guests and provide bad food. Luke could die in his room and not be discovered for days. No way. He'll stay with me.'

'I wouldn't dream of troubling you,' Luke said at once.

'It's no trouble,' she snapped.

'Then why did you say earlier that you wouldn't take him at any price?' Netta demanded.

In the icy silence that followed, Luke looked from one to the other.

'Did you say that?' he asked, sounding only mildly interested.

'I—may have said something like it, but I've changed my mind. I don't want your fate on my conscience, so you're coming to stay with me.'

'Don't I get a say?'

'No. And that's final.'

'You say "final" very often,' Netta mused. 'Only then things turn out not to be final at all.'

'Netta, I'm warning you—' She checked herself and drew a long, slow breath. 'Please be kind enough to collect Luke's things.'

'Suppose I say no,' Luke said. 'Perhaps I don't want to.'

She turned on him, breathing fire. 'Did I ask what you want? You are coming to stay with me, and that's the end of it. No more argument.'

'You'd better do what she says,' Netta told him. 'When she's made up her mind, she never changes it. Never, *never* does she change her mind—'

Then, perceiving that she had pushed her beloved daughter-in-law as far as was safe, she fell silent.

'Then I guess I'll just have to agree,' Luke said with an air of meekness that did nothing to improve Minnie's temper.

She glanced at the other woman, expecting to see her relish her triumph. But Netta had left the field of battle while she was winning.

The whole family helped him move the short distance to Minnie's flat, where Netta got to work on his bed.

'Come and see if it's all right,' she commanded Luke, guiding him, not to the spare room, but the large bedroom with the double bed.

'I'm taking the spare room,' Minnie told him. 'Netta says you toss and turn a lot, so you'll be more comfortable with the extra space.'

'I can't take your room.'

'It's all arranged,' she said. 'So quit arguing.'

He didn't want to argue. He didn't want to do anything

except collapse on the double bed, which looked wonderfully inviting. Minnie, reading his face, shooed everyone out so that he could have some peace. The last one to leave was Netta, and Minnie went with her to the door.

'You're disgraceful,' Minnie told her amiably. 'There was no need to hurry it tonight.'

'Best if neither of you had time to change your mind.'

'It won't work, Netta. Luke and I just aren't on that wavelength.'

'Hmph! Much you know! Goodnight, *cara*.'

Minnie laughed and kissed her. 'Goodnight.'

She closed the door and went back to the bedroom where she had left Luke. But he was already sprawled across the bed, fast asleep.

CHAPTER EIGHT

LUKE settled into a peaceful routine in which he slept a lot, had his dressings changed by the visiting nurse, and entertained visitors.

Teresa came every day with Tiberius. If Luke had been her hero before, he was doubly so now that he had received injuries that would otherwise have descended on herself and possibly the cat.

'The dear old girl has somehow persuaded herself that it was all a plot against Tiberius's life,' he told Minnie one evening, 'and that I charged in at the last moment, seized him up and put myself between him and the blast.'

'What was Tiberius doing taking a shower?'

'He's a cat of many talents, according to Teresa.'

'And nobody will ever make her understand the truth,' Minnie said ruefully. 'That, but for pure chance, you'd have been the villain and I'd have been suing you, on Teresa's behalf, for every penny you have.'

He grinned. 'Better luck next time.'

They had fallen easily into this way of talking, still opponents, but teasing each other almost like brother and sister. In the mornings she would rise first and bring him coffee. When she'd left he'd embark on the awkward business of washing himself with only his left hand, and the nurse would help him finish dressing.

After that there would be a procession of Pepinos and various other neighbours, bearing food and entertainment. The afternoons became a card school, with Luke insisting on small stakes and being careful to lose.

Minnie would return when the evening was half over, looking tired and with a briefcase full of files. Once he tried to prepare a meal for her and made such a clumsy mess of it that she asked pointedly if he were trying to destroy her home as well as his own.

It was Netta who did the real cooking, sweeping in every evening with an elaborate meal that she swore she'd 'just thrown together', then sweeping out and not returning until the next morning, which surprised him. Such restraint was unlike Netta.

After supper Minnie would settle down to work while he watched television. He'd offered to turn it off but she assured him this wasn't necessary, as her concentration was deep enough to blot out distractions. And it was true, he realised, regarding her bright head bent over the papers. Her private world was always there, the door open invitingly.

He only wished he knew who was waiting for her in there. It hadn't escaped his attention that she'd removed Gianni's picture from his sight.

One evening Minnie put her books away, then yawned and stretched. From behind the half-open bedroom door she could hear Luke talking into his phone, and heard him say, 'Mamma.'

As he hung up she pushed the door right open. 'Cocoa?'

'Lovely.'

He came out and settled on the sofa until she returned with two mugs.

'Have you told your mother what happened to you?' she asked.

'Not yet. I'll tell her when I'm human again.'

'Tell me some more about your family. How many are there?'

'Eight, including our parents.'

'Six brothers and sisters?'

'Just brothers. Hope, my adoptive mother, had a son when she was fifteen and obviously unmarried. Her parents gave him up for adoption and told her he was dead.'

'Swine,' Minnie said succinctly.

'I agree. None of us knew anything about him for years. Hope married Jack Cayman, a widower with a son called Primo, because his mother had been Italian. And they adopted me. I don't think it was ever a very happy marriage, and it collapsed when Franco, Primo's uncle, came visiting from Italy, and he and my mother fell in love and had a son.

'After the divorce she got custody of me, and Primo stayed with his father, but Jack died a couple of years later and the Rinuccis took Primo to Italy. Hope went to look for him, and that was how she met Toni, Franco's brother, and married him.'

'What about Franco? If she had his baby, didn't she go to him after the divorce?'

'No, he already was married with two children, and he felt he couldn't leave his wife.'

'Doesn't that make family reunions a little tense?'

'They don't happen often. Franco lives in Milan, which is a safe distance.'

Minnie was counting on her fingers. 'So how do you get six sons?'

'Toni and Hope had twins, Carlo and Ruggiero. And then last year the first son, Justin, turned up, and there was a big reunion. He came to Naples to be married—'

Luke's voice trailed off as he realised something that astonished him.

'What is it?' Minnie asked, looking at him more closely.

'He married barely six weeks ago,' he said, sounding dazed.

'Is that odd?'

'I left the next day, so it means that I've only been here for six weeks.'

So much had happened that he seemed to have known her for ever, yet it was all crowded into that short space of time. He knew it was true, and yet he couldn't believe it.

'Just six weeks,' he murmured, looking at her.

She met his eyes and he knew that she had understood. Suddenly the truth was there between them, undeniable, even for her. He reached forward to touch her face with gentle fingers.

'Minnie—' It was no more than a whisper.

'Luke—please—please—go on telling me about your family.'

The moment was over, so fleeting that it had barely happened, and even he, the least subtle of men, knew that to try to prolong it would be to court disaster.

'Yes,' he said. 'Well—we're an odd family, some related, some sort of related, some not related at all.'

'But the only one not at all related is you,' she said shrewdly. 'You're a Cayman in the middle of a family of Rinuccis. Don't you feel left out?'

He considered this.

'I'm not sure. Justin isn't a Rinucci either. He's Justin Dane.'

'And Primo, presumably, is a Cayman too.'

'No, he took the family name years ago. I could have done the same. Dear old Toni said he considered me as much his son as his own boys, and I was welcome to be a Rinucci if I wanted.'

'But you didn't want to?' she asked, sounding puzzled.

'Do you think that's strange?'

'I can't understand anyone choosing not to be part of a family if they had the chance. It's so—so cold outside.'

'I'm not exactly outside, or only to the extent that I choose to be. I guess there's just something pigheaded in me, something that makes me stay outside the tent, or at least to be free to leave when I want. Does it matter?'

'I suppose it might matter to the people who tried to welcome you, and maybe were left feeling rejected.'

'I think they understood.'

'Of course they understood, if they loved you, but that doesn't mean they weren't hurt.'

He frowned, but before she could speak she checked herself.

'I shouldn't have said that, please forget it. It's your business. I love being part of a large family, and I forget that some people feel suffocated by it.'

'No, not suffocated,' he said quickly. 'It's just that— you're right. I'm the only one that isn't related by blood to any of them. I'd never really thought of that before, yet I suppose, in a way, it's always been at the back of my mind that they all belong together in a way that I don't.'

'But that's meaningless,' she said earnestly. 'I'm not related by blood to the Pepinos, but I'm still one of them, because they want it and I want it.'

They said no more, but her words stayed with him, keeping him awake long into the night. There was, in her, an open-hearted acceptance of life, and a need to seek and embrace warmth, that he knew to be lacking in himself. And he had never been so conscious of it as now.

The work he'd ordered was getting under way. Engineers had surveyed the building, identified several other boilers that they considered dangerous, but passed most of them as safe.

'It doesn't matter,' Luke told Minnie as he folded up the papers one night. 'I want them all replaced. Every one. And stop giving me that cynical look.'

'I'm *feeling* cynical. You're playing the hero again, the grand gesture—'

'Give me patience!' he roared. 'Woman, will you stop thinking the worst of me at every excuse?'

'I don't need an excuse, and don't call me woman.'

'What would you prefer? The creature from the black lagoon?' he asked, reminding her of their first meeting in the cell.

'No, that's my line,' she said, laughing, for these days their battles had lost the hostile edge and were more like humorous fencing.

'Anyway, it's nothing to do with playing the hero. It's Netta. Her boiler doesn't need replacing, but if you think I'm going to face her with *that* when Signora Fellini next door is having a new one, you can think again.'

'Coward!' she said amiably.

'Sure I'm a coward. Netta scares me—not as much as you do, but enough.'

'Oh, yes, you're very scared of me! Who do you think you're fooling?'

She'd been cooking and was now sitting beside him on the sofa, her face flushed from the heat of the kitchen, and prettier than he had ever seen it. Suddenly all his good resolutions deserted him, and he reached out, cupping his left hand behind her head and drawing her face close to his.

'If I weren't terrified of you, you harpy, I'd kiss you right now.'

'But you are terrified of me,' she reminded him in a voice that wasn't quite steady.

You could take that two ways, he thought: as a rejection, or a dare. He was always up for a dare.

Moving clumsily, he managed to get his bad right arm around her as well.

At this distance Minnie couldn't miss the disturbing smile on his lips, and an even more disturbing look in his eyes.

'I'm getting braver by the moment,' he said. 'Still nervous of your right hook, though.'

'No need for that,' she murmured. 'I wouldn't fight an injured man. It wouldn't be—correct.'

'That's right,' he said, lowering his lips. 'I might sue.'

In the four years of her widowhood she'd had light flirtations, short-lived relationships that had died almost before they lived. A kiss and it was over, dying in disappointment and despair.

But Luke's kiss was different, shocking in its intensity. Briefly Minnie put up a hand to protest, but then let it fall away. Sensations that she'd banished from her life were threatening to take control of her. They were purely physical, unmixed with tenderness, but thrilling, driving caution out.

It was crazy, reckless to kiss him back, but she found herself doing it, using both arms to clasp him, one hand seizing his head in a mirror image of his own movement, so that she could press her mouth more closely to his.

Now there was no going back, even if she'd wanted to, but there was nothing she wanted less. All the sensuality she'd suppressed was rising up to torment her, crying out that there was life still to be lived. The skills she'd thought she'd never need again clamoured for use, reminding her of how sweet it was to be held in a man's arms, especially a man like this, who knew how to use his lips to tease a woman until she melted.

She opened her mouth a little, teasing him back, inviting, while her hands explored him, relishing the shape of his head, his shoulders. Every movement was a violation of the rules she lived by but she didn't care. There would be time later for regrets—but there would be no regrets—regrets—

Suddenly the word shrieked at her out of the darkness. She lived with a secret that caused her such bitter regret that there was almost no room in her life for anything else. She'd survived on caution, and she was throwing it recklessly away.

She must escape the trap her own madness had created for her, and there was one way, one weapon calculated to drive him off.

Fighting the pounding of her heart until she could control herself, Minnie pressed her hands against Luke's chest, just enough to let him know that she meant it. He drew back a little, regarding her with eyes that held a question, and a hope.

'This is a bad idea,' she said.

'Minnie—' His voice was urgent.

'You really are a very brave man,' she said, hoping she didn't sound breathless and trying for a light humorous tone.

He regarded her, still with the same disturbing gleam that made it so hard for her to laugh.

'Why, are you going to thump me after all?' he murmured, giving her a quizzical look that almost sent her back into his arms.

'Much worse than that,' she said. She drew right away from him, leaning back on the sofa and regarding him humorously. 'Luke, you're such a clever man, I'm amazed that you didn't see through it.'

'See through what?'

'Netta's cunning little plan. Do you think it was an accident that her relatives suddenly announced a visit when you were there?'

'It seemed a bit odd, especially as there's been no sign of them.'

'Of course not. That visit was conveniently cancelled as soon as Netta achieved her object, which was to get you down here, with me. Luke, wise up! Don't you see what she's trying to do?'

'You mean—you and me?'

'She's trying to marry us off.'

'She's what?'

'Netta is setting up a match between us. If she can bully us up the aisle, all the Residenza problems are solved—she *thinks*. I've tried to make her understand that she's got it all wrong, that there's no way you and I would ever think of getting married. But as fast as I fended off one plan she came up with another.'

'She's trying to—?'

'She's an arch conspirator. Don't worry, I have no designs on you. I only brought you here because you looked so wretchedly ill that I couldn't leave you to her mercies, but you're quite safe. What happened just now—well, it didn't mean anything.'

His eyes kindled. 'Didn't it?'

'Hey, it's been four years. How long can a woman live like a nun? You're an attractive man. OK, I was tempted. Haven't you ever been tempted even while one part of your mind was saying, Better not?'

'Oh, yes,' he said ironically. 'That just about describes

my state of mind since the day we met. You've had "better not" written all over you, but I like risks.'

'So you took one, and it was nice, but now we've both come to our senses—'

'Have we?' he asked raggedly.

'Well, unless you want to be marched up the aisle at the point of Netta's shotgun—' A thought seemed to occur to her. 'Oh, Luke, I'm sorry. Are you saying you *want* to marry me? I never thought—'

'Of course not,' he said quickly. 'That is—I don't mean to be rude but—'

'Neither do I, *but*!' she broke in quickly. 'That's the whole point, isn't it? *But!* Two people kiss and it doesn't mean anything. Let's keep it that way. I just hope—'

With a convincing air of sudden alarm she dashed to the window to check the curtains.

'Lucky they were drawn,' she said. 'Nobody can have looked in. Just a moment—'

She made a play of opening the front door and looking out on to the staircase.

'Nobody there,' she said, returning and locking the door. 'We've got away with it. Our secret is safe.'

She turned out her hands with a bright air, as if saying, You see?

'Well, thank goodness for that,' Luke said, rallying and matching her apparent mood. 'Thanks for warning me.'

Hell would freeze over before he let her suspect how far he felt from laughing.

After that they were both glad to bring the evening to an end. They smiled and assured each other that it was all a good joke, and escaped each other as soon as possible.

Luke sat up for a long time, brooding in the darkness, wondering if his pain-killers were to blame for what was happening. They were strong, and he sometimes felt that they caused his thoughts to go astray. What else could account for the sudden blazing moment of illumination that had come on him with the discovery of Netta's plan?

He didn't want to laugh. He wanted to say that Netta was the wisest woman in the world. He wanted to seize Minnie's hand and jump into the deep end with her at once.

But, as a sensible man, he would resist this craziness, and hope that a night's sleep would return him to normal.

When Netta learned that she was to have a new boiler the upshot was predictable. Overjoyed, she immediately announced a party.

'Why not wait until the boiler's installed?' Minnie asked.

'Silly girl, we'll have another party then,' Netta chided her.

'Of course, I should have thought of that.'

'Yes, you should,' Luke agreed. 'Even I could see that coming.'

Netta drew Minnie out on to the staircase, well out of earshot, to ask, 'How is everything going?'

'It isn't,' Minnie said, adding defiantly, 'we're like brother and sister.'

Netta was horrified. 'He hasn't—?'

'No, he hasn't.'

'Then you're not trying hard enough,' Netta declared, and departed in high dudgeon.

Minnie didn't immediately return inside. To have told Netta the truth would have been impossible. She was no green girl but a woman who'd experienced years of passionate love. Yet that one kiss had left her thunderstruck.

It might have been the first kiss of her life, so disorientated had it make her feel.

Everything about Luke that antagonised her at other times—his power, his determination and masculine forcefulness—had been transmuted into fierce excitement the moment his lips had touched hers. It was like dealing with two men, one who could drive her to a passion of anger and opposition, and one who could thrill her to the depths, making her yearn to become one with him.

But they weren't two men. They were one. And the confusion was driving her crazy.

In desperation she'd revealed Netta's plan so that they could laugh about it together. It had partly worked, but it did nothing to help the feelings that coursed through her at the thought of him, especially at night.

Darkness had fallen. All over the courtyard, lights glowed out of the windows on to the geraniums, illuminating flashes of colour. Looking up, she saw the building winding upward until it seemed to reach a disc of sky where stars wheeled and circled before vanishing into infinity.

How often, after Gianni's death, had she looked wistfully at that infinity? Now it merely seemed cold and bleak, and she hurried back inside to where Luke was waiting, maddening and impossible, but somehow comforting.

The party was the following evening, and the first hour went as she had expected, with Luke being hailed as everyone's saviour. He grinned at her.

'Try not to look as though you've swallowed a hedgehog,' he murmured.

'Don't be so unfair. You've earned this, and I don't grudge you a moment of your popularity.'

'Liar,' he murmured in her ear, his warm breath sending shivers down her neck.

But soon after this she began to realise that something was wrong with him. His mouth had grown tense and his forehead was wet. Moving quietly, she slid beside him, firmly dislodging the young female who was flirting with him.

'Time to go home,' she murmured.

'Nonsense, I'm fine.'

'You're not fine, you're in pain. And like a good mother hen I'm going to take you home.'

He nodded and didn't try to argue any more. Minnie said a word to Netta, then guided him firmly out of the room and down the stairs to home.

'You know what they're saying back there now, don't you?' he asked with grim humour.

'After seeing us leave early, you mean?'

'Yes. Netta will expect an announcement tomorrow. What will you say to her?'

'Nothing, I'll just smile enigmatically. It'll drive her mad.'

He gave a grunt of laughter and indicated his bandaged right hand and arm. 'Look at me. How does she imagine that I could—?'

'Like a hedgehog, very carefully.'

He laughed again and winced at the effort. When they were safely in the flat he collapsed on to the sofa.

'Why didn't you say you were in pain?' she demanded.

'Damn fool pride, I suppose. I've been practising exercises with my arm. I may have overdone it a bit.'

'More than a bit. Have you taken your pain-killers?'

'No, I thought it was time I tried to manage without them.'

'Damn fool pride is right. Let the doctors decide that.'

She brought him a glass of mineral water and two of his pills, which he swallowed gratefully.

'I think you should go to bed,' she said. 'Come on, I'll help you.'

He put an arm around her shoulders and together they went into the bedroom. With impersonal hands she undressed him down to his shorts, helped to ease him on to the pillows, and drew the duvet up over him.

'Sorry,' he said with a sigh.

'Don't be silly,' she said, sitting on the bed beside him. 'It's partly my fault. I shouldn't have let you go to that party.'

'Think you could have stopped me?'

'I could have knocked you out.'

'Nah! Never repeat yourself.'

She smiled at his game attempt at humour. 'Shall I go away and let you sleep?'

'No, stay and talk to me,' he whispered.

'What about?'

'Did you really say it?'

'Say what?' she asked, puzzled.

He was silent and she thought he must have fallen asleep, but then, still with his eyes closed, he said, 'Not again!'

'Luke—?'

He opened his eyes.

'You said, "Oh, God, not again!" Or did I dream that? I was pretty much out of it, but I thought I heard you.'

Now she knew what he meant. In the shock of seeing him lying on the floor, covered in blood, she'd gathered him in her arms and had felt herself wrenched back to that other time. For a terrible moment she hadn't known which of them she held.

Her throat constricted and she couldn't speak. She

dropped her head into her hands and stayed there, her eyes closed, in torment, until she felt his good hand brush her hair.

'Tell me.'

'I can't,' she said hoarsely.

'Minnie, you must tell someone, or you'll go mad. What is it that you've been hiding for so long? Why can't you speak of it?'

'Because I can't,' she said passionately. 'I just can't.'

'Trust me, *carissima*. You can tell me anything. Just trust me as a friend.'

He thought she would refuse again, but then a shudder went through her and she raised her head. Her eyes were full of tears, and he wasn't sure that she could see him. But after a moment she took a deep breath, and began to tell him everything.

CHAPTER NINE

'I LOVED Gianni,' she said softly. 'I loved him with all my heart and soul. We were close in every way a man and woman can be close. We laughed at the same jokes, saw the world through the same eyes, and when we made love, everything was perfect.

'But in the last year things started to go wrong. My career had suddenly taken off and I had to devote a lot more time to it. He'd never minded before but he began to mind about my being away from home so often. And even when I was here I had to do a lot of work. He resented it, and we began to quarrel.

'In the end we seemed to do almost nothing but bicker. We tried to set aside some time for ourselves, we planned a big meal—we were going to cook it together—it was going to make everything right. But at the last minute I was called out to see a client. We had a terrible fight. He said if I went out now we were finished, he never wanted to see me again. I said that suited me fine because I'd had enough of him.

'I ran out, to go to my client. He called after me, then ran down the stairs into the street. I heard him but I didn't even look behind, I was so angry. So I didn't hear what happened, I only heard the crash and people screaming.'

She stopped, shuddering. Silently Luke reached up to curve his arm around her and draw her down against him.

'Go on,' he said sombrely.

'When I heard that terrible noise, I did look back. Gianni was lying on the ground, blood pouring from his head. He'd been hit by a truck. I ran back. He was lying so still and his eyes were closed, but I wouldn't let myself believe he could be dead. I had so much to say to him that I *had* to make him hear. I knelt beside him and lifted him in my arms, telling him I was sorry, I hadn't meant what I said, I loved him. I kept screaming over and over again that I loved him, but he couldn't hear.'

Her words ended in a gasp. Tears were pouring down her face, and he tightened his arm, letting his lips rest on her hair, but saying nothing.

'I did love him,' she sobbed. 'I didn't mean any of those things I said, and I was going to say sorry when I came home. But when I tried to tell him, he couldn't hear me. The last thing he heard me say was that I'd had enough of him—that was the last thing—the last thing—'

An anguished wail broke from her as her control collapsed, letting misery break through in a fierce stream that blotted out the world. There were no words now, just a wail that went on and on, as endless as her grief.

'Minnie—' he whispered. 'Minnie—Minnie—'

'It was the last thing he heard,' she screamed. 'I told him I was sorry—I told him again and again but he couldn't hear—he was dead and now he'll never know—'

The wail came again, punctuated by violent sobs that shook her until Luke feared she would break apart. He held on to her, cursing his own helplessness, feeling her grief become his own agony.

'It wasn't your fault,' he said, knowing that the reasonable words were worse than useless. All he could do was hold her against him, letting the warmth of his body communicate comfort, and hoping it would somehow reach her.

He was a man of action, who took firm decisions and saw things through to the end. Now he was all at sea, floundering, trying to achieve something that wasn't in his power, desperate at his own uselessness.

He didn't speak again, just rested his cheek against her hair, waiting for the storm to pass. Gradually her sobs subsided into a soft moan.

'It was my fault,' she said at last.

'What do you mean? How can it be?'

'If I'd gone back when he first called me—it wouldn't have happened. I could have stopped it—he'd be alive now—'

'Minnie, don't think like that,' he begged. 'It's the way to madness.'

'I know. I've gone mad, and come back and gone mad. In my dreams it happens all over again, but this time I turn around and go back, and he's safe, and he stays alive. And then I wake and he's dead, and I go mad again.'

She was clutching his arm, her fingers digging in so tightly that he winced with pain, but he didn't try to pull away. Nothing would have made him move at this moment.

'I keep thinking that if only I could turn time back, and stop it in the right place—' she whispered.

'I know, I know—'

'I try and try, but it goes on without me, and there's nothing I can do.'

'There never is,' he said sadly. 'Finality is the hardest thing to accept. There's nothing to be done, and you can beat yourself senseless trying.'

'Yes,' she said. 'But being senseless would be a relief. It's remembering that's torture.'

'What do the others in the family say? Surely they don't blame you?'

'They don't know. Nobody knows.'

'Dear God!' he whispered, appalled by her isolation.

'Nobody else heard what we said. Several people saw him chase me down the stairs and out into the road, but they didn't know we were quarrelling. They think he was trying catch me up because I'd forgotten something, or he wanted to give me a final kiss. I've never been able to tell Netta the truth, not just for my own sake, I swear it, but because it would add to her pain. She can just about cope with thinking it was an accident—'

'It *was* an accident.'

'No, it wasn't,' she said with bitter self-condemnation. 'It happened because I was angry and cruel and—'

'Stop it!' he said fiercely. 'Stop it, don't talk like that. You're not to blame. It was just one of those terrible flips of the coin that happen without warning. It destroyed him, but it's come near to destroying you, too.'

'Yes,' she agreed bleakly. 'Sometimes I look at Netta and wonder what she'd think if she knew the truth. She's kind to me and I want to tell her that I don't deserve it.'

'But you do. You deserve kindness and love and everything that's good. How can I convince you?'

She didn't answer for a long time, and then she simply repeated, 'He'll never know,' in a broken whisper. 'I've tried to tell him so often since. Just before the funeral I saw him in his coffin and I told him that I loved him and I was sorry, but it was no use. It wasn't him. He was cold and grey like a waxwork and I couldn't see my Gianni because he'd gone somewhere I couldn't follow.'

A memory came back to him.

'That day when I saw you at his grave—'

'We go there on anniversaries, his birthday, the day he died—I'd rather go alone but Netta likes it to be a family party.'

'Yes, I remember, it almost looked like a party. The boys were telling him jokes.'

'That's how it is. Gianni's still one of the family. They talk as though he were there. They still love him, like they still love me, and I feel such a fraud.'

'And when you all went away, you turned to look back at him, and I saw your face. Everything you've just told me was there, only I didn't understand.'

'I knew you'd seen me, with the truth written all over me, and I hated you for it.'

'Don't hate me,' he begged. 'Minnie don't—don't, please—'

'How can I ever hate you? I've trusted you with something that nobody else in the world knows, and I still don't understand why.'

She spoke like a puzzled child and he knew a sudden surge of protectiveness.

'Because you know in your heart that you *can* trust me,' he said. 'I'm your friend, and I won't let you down. I'm here to take care of you.'

'It's supposed to be me looking after you,' she said, changing her position so that she could prop herself on her elbows and look directly at him.

Her face was still ravaged, and running with tears that she no longer seemed to notice. He stroked his fingers tentatively over her cheeks.

'We'll have to look after each other,' he said fondly, 'in different ways.'

'Can I get you anything before you settle down for the night?' she asked. She gave a little choke and tried to pull herself together.

'No, I'm all right. The pills are working now. But what about you? I don't think you're all right.'

'I'm fine, honestly. Sorry I made such a fuss.'

'You're not making a fuss. Your whole life is going to be ruined if we can't make this go away.'

'It'll never go away,' she said simply. 'It'll always be there, and the only way I can cope is to live with it.'

'But live with it how? By being overwhelmed with guilt? Minnie, you can't spend your life atoning for something that wasn't your fault.'

'Why not? His life was taken away from him because of me. What right do I have to a life?'

'Or to happiness?' he asked angrily. 'Or to love? His life was *his* life, and it's over. You can't prolong it by sacrificing the rest of yours.'

She shook her head and tried to pull away, but he held on to her.

'Minnie—'

'Let me go, I shouldn't have told you.'

'Yes, you should, because I'm the one person who can let the light of day into this. *Trust me, Minnie!*'

His voice was commanding and imploring at the same time, because something told him they were at a turning point and everything hung on this moment. She had turned to him but now she was turning away, and he knew he mustn't let it happen.

Suddenly she went limp, as though all the fight had gone out of her, and he was able to draw her against him again.

'Stay here,' he said, commanding now. 'You don't need to fetch me anything, so stay with me.'

'All right,' she said in a muffled voice. 'Just for a few minutes.'

He could feel her body relaxing against him, as though she'd just found something she was waiting for, and in another moment she was asleep.

For a while he listened to her steady breathing,

scarcely daring to hope that she had finally found a little peace. He wished he could see her face, but it was enough that she lay there, content and unafraid, in his arms.

He could almost have laughed to think how he'd yearned to have her in his bed, her body pressed against his. Now he had his wish, while at the same time being further away from it than ever. Yet he'd been granted something else, infinitely more sweet and precious, and full of hope.

His good arm ached from being trapped in one position, but nothing would have made him move and disturb her. So he stayed as he was, drifting slowly off to sleep, until he awoke in the small hours to find that the arm was numb, and she hadn't moved by so much as an inch.

Minnie's first sight on waking was the window of her bedroom, just as it had always been. But as memory came back she realised that she was in the wrong place. She should be sleeping in the spare room.

Only then did she become aware of Luke's body pressed against hers, his warmth reaching her through the thickness of the duvet that was between them, his good arm beneath her, his bad arm covering her protectively.

Moving carefully, she raised herself and turned, to find him regarding her from sleepy eyes, just as she'd last seen him before she'd fallen asleep. It was as though he hadn't slept at all, but had spent the night watching over her.

'Are you all right?' were his first words.

'Yes, I'm fine,' she said, realising that it was true. 'Goodness, is that the time?'

It was seven in the morning. Reluctantly, she disentangled herself and rose from the bed, wandering out of the room, too preoccupied to think where she was going. She realised that she was still fully dressed, and memories of the night before began to come back to her.

She had brought him home to look after him, but somehow he'd ended up looking after her. He'd done what nobody else could do, had drawn her agonising secret from her into the light of day, had given her a feeling of peace and strength that she hadn't known for four years.

But it was more than that. In his arms she'd slept like a baby, with no dreams, and this morning she felt well and strong. A healing had begun in her, and that it should be Luke, of all people, who'd brought it about, filled her with wonder.

Most wondrous of all was the fact that he'd held her all night without making a single move that couldn't have been made by a brother, or a nurse. She'd been deeply asleep, but instinct told her that she'd been safe and protected in his arms.

He didn't try to make love to me, she thought, smiling. *That's the best thing of all, but nobody else would understand.*

He'd said, 'Your whole life is going to be ruined if we can't make this go away.'

We! Not you, but we—the two of us, acting together as friends and allies.

She went to look out of the window on to the staircase where there were already signs of life. Behind her she could hear Luke moving about until he finally joined her. He was moving his left arm gingerly.

'I'm sorry. Did I keep it trapped all night?' she said fondly.

'Don't worry, I'll regain the use of it one day soon.'

They laughed together, and the warmth she felt was

quite different from the sensual excitement of kissing him. It was the warmth of safety, and it made her realise anew how long she'd been without it.

Over breakfast he said, 'I wish you didn't have to go out today.'

It was a casual friendly remark, but it carried a new meaning now. She, too, was reluctant to step outside the magic circle they had created.

'I wish I didn't, too. But I've got a big trial coming up. I'm defending someone in a case that should never have been brought in the first place. It's a try-on. They're hoping to scare him into paying them off, and I'm not going to let them.'

'So you're going into battle?' he said.

'That's right. And I may not be very good company when I'm here, so—'

'Minnie, it's all right,' he said quickly. 'You've promised to defend this man and you should give it all you've got.'

Her smile was full of relief, and it hurt him to see it.

He used her absence to make some urgent calls, several to the bank and one to a man the bank had found for him. His name was Eduardo Viccini. He called on Luke that afternoon, and they spent several hours going through papers and discussing tactics.

He had expected Minnie to be late following her day in court, but she was home for supper, and only just missed the visitor by minutes. Luke breathed a sigh of relief. He wasn't ready for Minnie to meet Eduardo Viccini.

She came in smiling, carrying a heavy bag, which she dumped on to the sofa, and followed it, bouncing up and down gleefully.

'You look like a kid let out of school,' he said with a grin.

'That's how I feel. Free! Free!'

'Your case can't be over already.'

'But it is. The other side backed down. They thought we were going to crack but we didn't, and they withdrew. I told you it was a try on. My client will get his costs, the other side gets a great big debt that they've run up with their lawyers, and it serves them right. And I get a holiday because I set aside time for a trial that isn't going to take place. *Free!*'

She threw her arms up in the air.

'Does that mean you can have a rest?' he asked.

'Well, I've got paperwork and stuff to catch up on, but I can relax a bit, yes. And do you know the best thing of all? Someone told me that they heard my legal opponent say they'd done a clever thing to back down rather than face me, because I was a Rottweiler. Isn't that wonderful?'

'Is it?' Luke asked blankly.

'Well, not normally of course, but in my job it's a great compliment.'

'I can see how it would be,' he said, amused. 'Then let's celebrate your freedom. I'll go out and buy some wine and a couple of ready-cooked pizzas. No cooking tonight, just relaxing—'

'And watching some stupid game show on TV?' she asked eagerly.

'The stupider the better,' he promised.

He returned a few minutes later, bearing food and wine, to find her changed out of her severe clothes into jeans and sweater, and looking like 'urchin' Minnie, the one he preferred.

It was a wonderful evening. Over pizza she entertained

him with vivid impressions of her courtroom opponents, which made him laugh.

'You should have been an actress,' he said. 'You have the gift.'

'Of course. That's what a lawyer needs. I can be anything in a courtroom—demure, respectful—'

'Or Avvocato Rottweiler,' he supplied.

She gave a reminiscent smile. 'The first time I was in an Italian court, it sounded so strange to hear the lawyers called *Avvocato*. I'd just returned here from England and it sounded like "avocado". I kept giggling and nearly got thrown out.'

'Things never sound so impressive in English,' he said. 'Take your noble ancestor, Pepino il Breve. You've got to admit that "Pepin the Short" lacks a certain something.'

'My noble ancestor!' she scoffed, then began to chuckle. 'Pepin the Short. I love it.'

Afterwards they sat on the sofa and hunted through the TV channels for the worst game shows they could find. There was plenty of choice and they bickered amiably, engaging in furious argument over the sillier questions.

Neither of them had mentioned their closeness of the night before, but when he laid his hand on her arm it seemed natural for her to lie down lengthways, with her feet over the end of the sofa, and her head resting on his leg.

'You got that last one wrong,' she said, taking a bite out of an apple.

'I did not,' he said hotly. 'There were three choices—'

'And you got the wrong one,' she insisted.

'You don't know what you're talking about. The first contestant said—'

'Oh, shut up and hand me another apple.'

He did so and she tucked into it until, a few minutes later, she began to laugh.

'Pepin the Short,' she said. 'What a name!'

'That's what you get for being English,' he said lazily.

'Half English.'

'How did that work out when you were a child?'

'Not well. I don't think my parents' marriage was very happy. My mother was a rather uptight person, while my father, as far as I remember him, was very—very *Italian*, emotional, with a big warm heart and a way of not letting himself be bothered by details. It drove Mamma mad, and I suppose she was right really, because it meant a lot of burdens fell on her. But I didn't see that. I just saw that he was wonderful, and she disapproved of all the things I thought nicest about him.

'When I was eight he died, and she took me back to England as fast as she could. But I could never be at home there. By that time I had an Italian heart and I hated the way she tried to make me completely English, as though she could wipe out my Italian side just by fighting it hard enough. I wasn't allowed to speak Italian or read Italian books, but I did anyway. I used to get them from the library and smuggle them into the house. I can be terribly stubborn.'

'Really? You?'

'Oh, don't be funny. Anyway, you haven't seen me at my worst.'

'Heaven help me!'

'I'll chuck something at you in a minute.'

'You wouldn't assault an invalid, would you?'

'I might if it was you.'

'Go on with your story while I'm still safe.'

'Luckily my mother married again when I was eighteen, and I was clearly in the way, so I could flee back to Italy without anyone trying to stop me. In fact—'

Suddenly a wry grin twisted her mouth.

'What did you do?' he asked, fascinated.

'I don't want to tell you; it's rather shocking,' she admitted.

'You never did anything shocking.'

'Don't you call blackmail shocking?'

'Blackmail?'

'Well, in a sort of way. Although I think bribery is probably a better word. My stepfather was very well-off and he let it be known that if I'd make myself scarce it would put him in a generous mood. I knew I'd need some help until I found my feet—'

Luke began to laugh. 'How much did you take him for?'

'Let's just say it covered my training.'

'Good for you!'

'Yes, I was quite pleased with myself in an insufferable sort of way.'

'Insufferable, nothing! You were smart. If you ever get tired of law I could use you in my business. Come to think of it, the business could use a good lawyer.'

'Ah, then I have to admit that I gave it all back.'

'Minnie, *please!*' he said in disgust. 'Just when I was admiring you! Now you've spoiled it.'

'I know. I tried not to. It was a fair bargain because we each gained from it, and I'd kept my side and never troubled them since. But when I was earning enough to repay it, I just had to. I was really cross with myself.'

He didn't speak for a while. He was fighting an inner battle, sensing the ghost hovering on the edge of their consciousness, unwilling to spoil the moment by inviting him in, yet knowing that he must do so, if he were to be any use to her.

At last he forced himself to say, 'What did Gianni think?'

CHAPTER TEN

HE WAITED to see if she flinched at Gianni's name, but she merely gave a fond, reminiscent smile.

'Gianni thought I was crazy but he didn't try to stop me. Come to think of it, that was always the way. He was very easygoing. He used to say, "You do it your way, *carissima*."' She gave a brief laugh. 'So I always did.'

'He sounds the ideal husband,' Luke observed, keeping his voice carefully light. 'You said, "Jump" and he jumped. What more could a woman ask?'

'Sure, it makes me sound like a domineering wife, but actually it was all a con trick. He pretended to be meek and helpless but it was just a way of pushing the boring jobs on to me. If there were forms to be filled in, phone calls to be made to officials, it was always, "You do it, *cara*. You're the clever one." And after a while it dawned on me that I'd been tricked into doing all the work.'

'Did you mind?'

'Not really. It made sense since I was a lawyer, and you know what bureaucracy is like in this country.'

'And if you hadn't been a lawyer?'

'He'd have found some other excuse, of course,' she said, smiling. 'He was just like my father. Anything not to fill in a form! But so what, as long as one of us could do it? We were a team, a partnership.'

'And you *were* the clever one, weren't you? Cleverer than him, I mean.'

'He used to laugh and say anyone was cleverer than him. Sometimes I'd rebel and say, "Come on, you can do that one yourself," and he'd grin and say, "It was worth a try, *cara*." But I didn't mind because he gave me so much in return, love and happiness. We had a marriage that—I don't know—I can't say.'

'Go on,' he said when she fell silent. 'Tell me how it was.'

She shook her head.

'Mind my own business?' he asked lightly.

'We were married for ten years. How can I tell you how "it" was? Which "it" are we talking about? The first year, when we were discovering each other, or the middle years when we settled into being an old married couple?'

'You mean when you were in your mid-twenties? That sort of old?'

'That's right. I didn't mind being "that sort of old" because I knew I'd come home and found the place I belonged. I wanted to stay there for ever.'

'But you can't. Life moves on.'

'I know,' she said with a sigh. 'At first we fitted together perfectly. I spent years going to law school and then serving an apprenticeship with a firm, not earning very much, and he didn't earn very much either.'

'What sort of job did he do?'

'He drove a truck for a local firm that buys a lot of stuff through Naples and Sicily.'

'So he was away a lot?'

'If it was Naples he could get back the same day, even if it was quite late. For Sicily he'd have to be away overnight, maybe two.'

'But that must have been handy if you were studying?'

'It was. He used to say that all the other drivers worried about leaving their wives, in case they were unfaithful, but he knew his only rival was my books.'

'What about children? Did you ever think of having any?'

Was it his imagination, or did she hesitate a moment?

'We talked about it, but there were always hurdles to clear first. I wanted to give him children. He had such a great heart; he'd have been a wonderful father.'

She didn't say any more and he left it there. Another show was coming up on television and they watched it for a while, making ribald comments about the quality of the contestants. She went into the kitchen to create a late night snack, then checked the curtains to make sure that they were completely closed.

'They weren't looking in, were they?' Luke asked.

'I wouldn't put it past them. Once Netta's set her heart on something, she doesn't give up.'

'Couldn't you just be strong, and tell her that nothing on earth would prevail on you to marry me?' he suggested.

'I've already done that. It didn't work. The way she sees it, our marriage would benefit everyone, so it's my duty to sacrifice myself.'

'Thanks!'

She grinned. 'I just thought I'd warn you of the forces ranged against you.'

'Think I can't manage for myself, huh?'

'Are you kidding? Between you and Netta I'd back her any day.'

'So would I,' he observed gloomily.

'Don't worry; I'll save you from that ghastly fate. I'll be strong for both of us.'

'Who's strong for you?' he asked impulsively. 'Who's ever done that?'

Her shrug seemed to imply that she had no need, but he was beginning to know better.

The game show was followed by a historical film, made about fifty years ago and set in the days of ancient chivalry. It concerned a knight escorting a lady to her wedding with a great lord. They fell in love but maintained perfect virtue, symbolised by the knight laying his sword on the ground between them as they slept side by side.

People said 'Gadzooks!' and 'Avaunt!' The lady swooned regularly. The colour was lurid and the film was truly terrible. They enjoyed it immensely.

'If you tried that sword trick in real life,' Luke observed, 'you'd be cut to pieces.'

'And they're all so clean,' Minnie objected. 'Days travelling through the countryside, and not a speck. Do you want anything else to eat?'

'No, thanks,' he said, yawning. 'I'm off to bed.'

'Me, too.'

In the doorway he paused and said lightly, 'I don't have a sword, but I do have a bad arm.'

'You don't have to reassure me,' she said quietly.

'I'll see you, then.'

When she appeared in his room a few minutes later he was in bed. He extended his good left arm and she tucked herself into the crook. He turned out the light, and for a while she was so still that he thought she'd fallen asleep. But then she said, 'Thank you, Luke.'

'Does it help?' he asked quietly.

'You'll never know how much.'

She fell asleep on the words. He waited, listening to her soft breathing in the darkness. At last, easy in his mind about her, he settled down.

Only once in the night did she stir and begin muttering

words that he could not discern. He stroked her hair with his bandaged hand, murmuring, 'It's all right. I'm here.'

She became content, and didn't move again.

Sometimes over the next few nights, lying in the darkness of that quiet room, Minnie had the feeling of being in a small boat that was drifting out into uncharted sea. Their destination was a mystery, but she knew there was nothing to fear.

She had no idea what deep instinct had made Luke so attuned to her needs, and so willing to subordinate everything else to her. This man whom she'd once thought harsh and insensitive, seemed to have the power to look into her heart, and be gentle with what he found there.

She lost track of time. By day they talked, or rather she talked while he listened, offering the odd word or question to bring forth more memories that always looked strangely different once she had voiced them. He had spoken of letting in the light of day, and it was true. At night there was the comfort of untroubled sleep.

It couldn't last. The passion that had briefly flared was still there, subdued but waiting. But, for now, this was the sweetest experience of her life.

She lost track of time. She only knew that one night his cellphone, which he kept beside the bed, shrilled until they woke. He fumbled for it, tried to press the right button with his left hand, and dropped it.

'Stay,' she said, motioning him back while she picked up the phone, pressed the button, and handed it to him.

He grunted his thanks. *'Pronto!'*

It was Toni, and Luke could hear at once that something was badly wrong. Minnie, watching, heard him say 'Mamma!' twice, and grow pale.

'I'll be there as fast as I can,' he said, and hung up.

'What's happened?'

'It's my mother,' he said, speaking with difficulty. 'She collapsed suddenly and had to be rushed to hospital. They think it's a heart attack and she might—I've got to get there, fast.'

'I'll call the airport,' Minnie said at once.

But the flight from Rome to Naples had just left, and there wasn't another until the following morning.

'It'll be midday before I land,' he groaned. 'That might be too late. I'll have to drive.'

'Not with that bandaged hand,' Minnie said. 'You'll never control a car.'

'Don't you understand? I have to get there!' he raged.

'Then I'll take you. The roads will be clear at this hour, and we'll be there in less than three hours.'

Without giving him a chance to answer, she went to her room and dressed quickly. When she came out he'd managed to scramble into some clothes and was standing by the door, his whole being expressive of tense urgency.

Her car was locked in a row of garages further down the street. As quickly as she could, she eased it out, and soon they were on their way out of Rome, on to the *autostrada* that led to Naples. Then she put her foot down, driving as fast as she dared.

Only once during the journey to Naples did he speak. 'Thank you. I don't know how I'd have managed but for you.'

'Anyone in that building would have done this for you,' she said. 'They all count you as their friend. But I wanted to be the one to do it.'

'Thank you,' he said again, and fell into brooding silence.

On the outskirts of Naples they came to a place where there had been an accident. Nobody had been hurt, but a truck lay on its side, blocking the road, save for one lane, and the traffic had slowed to a standstill.

Luke groaned and seized his cellphone. But his father's phone was switched off.

'Hospitals won't have them on,' Minnie said sympathetically. 'But we'll be there soon. The front of this queue is moving.'

He slumped down in his seat. 'It might be too late. *Why wasn't I there?*'

'Has she been ill before?'

'Not as far as I know.'

'Then how could you have been on the alert? You couldn't have known this was going to happen.'

'That's easy to say, but she might be dead right this minute, and I wouldn't know. I should have called her more often. She might have told me that she was feeling bad—'

'But maybe she wasn't. Luke, don't start creating "what ifs?" to torment yourself.'

'But you can't stop yourself creating them,' he said sombrely. 'You know that better than anyone. Suddenly I find myself saying all the things you said about Gianni.'

'But you didn't quarrel with her,' she said softly. 'She knows you love her.'

'I should have called her yesterday, but I didn't. If I had, I'd have said—' he sighed heavily '—probably nothing very much, but she'd have known I cared because I took the time to make the call.'

She longed to comfort him, as he had comforted her. The traffic was still for the moment, and, in her desperation to pierce his haze of misery, she took hold of him and gave him a little shake, forcing him to look at her.

'Luke, listen to me. How many years has she been your mother? More than thirty? Do you think she doesn't know by now how you feel about her? Do you think one incident counts against all those years?'

'Why not?' he asked her simply. 'Isn't that what you think about Gianni? All those years of loving him, and you can't forgive yourself for one incident.'

'But you've been telling me how wrong I was.'

'I know. And you *are* wrong, just as I'm wrong now. And we both know it, but it doesn't help, does it?'

'No,' she said, putting her arms right round him. 'It doesn't help, however hard we try to reason, because in the end reason has nothing to do with it. It's what you feel.'

'If she dies—'

'It's too soon to say that.'

'If she dies before I can speak to her—then I shall really understand what you've been going through, instead of just talking about it. Oh, Minnie, what an idiot you must have thought me! All talk, knowing nothing.'

'It wasn't like that. You gave me so much—more than you'll ever know. But it wasn't the words, it was that you were there, all the time. That was what I needed most. Now *I'm* here. Hold on to me.'

His grip was painful, but she was glad of it. It was all she could do for him, to offer back a little of what he had given, and pray that in the end he wouldn't need any of it.

'The line's moving again,' she said. 'We'll be there soon.'

She kissed him again and again. 'Just a little longer. Hold on.'

He nodded. She could see tears in his eyes, and it was with reluctance that he released her.

A policeman was waving them on. She started up and

began moving at a crawl until at last they were past the accident, the road widened and she was free to drive on.

'You'll have to guide me from here,' she said.

He gave her the name of the hospital and directed her until the huge building came into view.

'I'll drop you at the main door, then go and park the car,' she said. 'I'll find you afterwards.'

His answer was a tense smile, and she knew he was fearing to hear the worst. As she drew up outside the main door, she reached over and gave his left hand a squeeze.

'Good luck,' she said.

His answer was a return squeeze, then he got out quickly and hurried into the building.

At that time of night the parking lot was almost empty. She parked without trouble and followed him into the hospital, where the man on the night desk directed her to the third floor. Upstairs she found herself in a corridor of private rooms. Turning a corner, she stopped at the sight that met her eyes.

A crowd of young men were standing, sitting or lounging close to one door. Two were young and handsome, with a definite facial resemblance, one was older, with the same resemblance, but less marked. It was enough to tell her that these were the Rinuccis.

They all seemed to notice her at the same time, and moved quickly towards her in a way that could have been alarming if they hadn't been so clearly friendly.

'Signora Pepino—Luke told us—we have been expecting you—you brought our brother here—*grazie, grazie*—'

Hand after hand clasped hers with vigour. It was overwhelming, yet powerfully attractive.

'What's the news of your mother?' she asked quickly.

'It's good,' said one of the men. 'I am Primo Rinucci.'

'Good—how?' she asked. 'I understood it was a heart attack.'

One of the handsome boys spoke up. 'Mamma was breathless and then she fainted, so we got her here, fast. The doctor says it was only a dizzy spell, but she must take better care of herself in case the next time is more serious. So we're going to make sure that she does take care.'

'But still we thank you for what you have done.' This was the other good-looking boy.

There was a chorus of agreement and they all swarmed around her again, this time embracing and kissing her. Now it felt like coming home, she thought. Being embraced by Rinuccis was like being embraced by Pepinos—pleasant and comforting.

The door opened and a man in late middle age appeared. Over his shoulder Minnie could see Luke sitting by the bed, his mother's hands clasped in his. Then he was shut off from her sight. The young men called him Pappa, and rushed to introduce her. This was Toni Rinucci, whose face bore the marks of a night of strain and fear, although it was gradually clearing.

He, too, thanked her, almost fiercely, and answered her question about his wife's health with a passionate, 'The doctors say she will be well, thank God! And you must forgive me for dragging you on this long journey, but I am her husband—I panic because I love her.'

'How could you not panic?' she agreed, nodding.

'All of our sons will be here soon,' he told her. 'Justin is coming from England, Franco is in America and will be here later today. My wife will feel better for having her whole family around her. She will want to meet you, too, but in the meantime you'll be wanting to get some rest. Carlo and Ruggiero will take you to our home.'

'Can we see Mamma first?' Carlo said.

'No, she can't have too many people in there at once, and this is Luke's time. Be off now, and look after our guest.'

'Let Carlo take your car,' Ruggiero said as they left the hospital, 'and I'll drive you in mine. It's not far. You'll see the house before we've gone a mile.'

She did see it, high on the hill, gleaming with lights that seemed to reach down to them as they climbed. As they drew into the wide courtyard a middle-aged woman came out to wait for them.

'That's Greta, our housekeeper,' Ruggiero said. 'Pappa will have called ahead and she will have prepared a room for you.'

Inside the house they thanked her again for bringing Luke, and she followed Greta up the stairs to her room. She accepted the refreshments the housekeeper offered, but she was longing to be alone to sort out her thoughts. It had all happened so suddenly that she was almost dizzy.

She had a shower in the little bathroom. It washed off the worst of the night, but she still felt the need to lie down for a nap.

When she awoke the sun was high in the sky, and her window showed her a car gliding up the hill. When it drew to a halt below she saw Luke and his father get out. They were smiling in a way that confirmed the good news. For a moment her instinct told her to rush down into his arms, but then she saw the others hurry out to them, heard the cheering, saw them all clap each other on the back.

She wasn't needed there, she realised. Luke was back

with his family, where he belonged. His mother wasn't seriously ill after all, and the moments when they had clung to each other, full of intense, despairing emotion, seemed to come from another world.

She sat down on the bed, feeling a bleak sense of anti-climax.

Since her job sometimes called for her to travel at a moment's notice Minnie kept a bag always ready, containing clean clothes and toiletries. She'd snatched it up before leaving and was glad now that she could dress smartly.

Greta came with coffee and a message to say that lunch was being served below. Luke was waiting for her as she descended the stairs. He looked unshaven but happy, and he enfolded her in an exuberant hug.

'She's all right,' he whispered in her ear. 'She'll be home later today, and she's longing to meet you.'

'She must have got a shock when she saw your bandages.'

'Yes, but I played it down, and she could see I'm all right. She's mad at me for not telling her before, but I'll be forgiven. She'll probably try to pump you for more details—'

'I'll be the soul of discretion,' she promised.

Now she must be introduced to the others, including Primo, whom she had briefly seen in the corridor that morning. She remembered Luke saying, 'Primo had an Italian mother, so he calls me *Inglese*, as an insult.'

And there, with Primo, was Olympia, the black-haired woman of the photograph in Luke's wallet. Meeting her now, Minnie saw that she only had eyes for Primo, and she embraced her willingly.

Carlo was missing and Luke explained that he'd gone to the airport to meet Justin, his wife and son.

'I told you about him,' he reminded her.

'The child who was taken away from her at birth,' Minnie remembered. 'And she thought he was dead.'

'Yes. They were married here a few weeks ago, and now they're barely back from their honeymoon.'

'The house is going to get very crowded. I should be going soon.'

'No way, not until Mamma has met you. She—'

The shrill of his phone interrupted him. He answered impatiently and she heard him say, 'Eduardo? Sorry I had to leave unexpectedly. I can't talk now—I'll call you back.'

He hung up quickly. Minnie was about to ask who Eduardo was when a noise outside caused everyone to rush to the windows to see Justin and his family arrive.

They had to be reassured that Hope was well and would be home later that day, and Minnie stood back while Luke was once more sucked into his family.

It was a fascinating sight, she thought, like watching the missing piece that completed a jigsaw puzzle. Always before she had seen him as an outsider. Now she saw the niche where he fitted. Even so, she could see deep into him now, and tell that the fit wasn't perfect. In part he was still an outsider, from choice.

When she could escape she returned to her room and called Netta, who had been agog with curiosity at finding the two of them missing. She was all sympathy when she heard of Luke's trouble, but added anxiously, 'You will bring him back, won't you, *cara*? You won't let him stay there?'

'Of course not,' she said mechanically, and hung up quickly.

She felt winded. She should have seen this coming. And she hadn't.

It hadn't occurred to Minnie that Luke wouldn't return with her to Rome, but now she saw the danger. For him Rome might be no more than a passing mood, to be put behind him once a convenient opportunity presented itself.

The closeness that had seemed to unite them could turn out to be no more than a chimera now that he was back with his family. They would still correspond about legal matters, but essentially it was over.

CHAPTER ELEVEN

HOPE RINUCCI came home that afternoon. Toni went to collect her, insisting that nobody should come with him, as he wanted to be alone with his wife. When he handed her out of the car she looked well, smiling with pleasure at her family's attention. It was obvious now that it really had been a false alarm.

Watching from the sidelines, Minnie saw an elegant, beautiful woman in her fifties, a woman who would attract admiring attention wherever she went, no matter what her age. She couldn't help smiling as Hope's sons converged on her. It was like watching vassals do homage. She almost expected them to kiss her hand.

One by one she hugged everyone—Justin, her eldest son, Evie, his new wife, and Mark, his son by his first marriage. Then Primo and Olympia.

'We can really get down to planning your marriage,' she told them.

When she'd kissed her twins, Carlo and Ruggiero, she looked around hopefully.

'Franco?'

'Later today, Mamma,' Carlo said. 'It's a long way from Los Angeles.'

At last Hope's eyes sought out the young woman who held back, watching and silent.

'And you are Minnie?' she said.

'Yes, I'm Minnie.'

She came forward to be enveloped in a scented embrace. Hope gave her a genuinely warm hug, then drew back and looked at her.

'Luke has told me how you brought him here,' she said. 'And I thank you with all my heart.'

Minnie, normally so assured, found herself suddenly awkward.

'It was nothing—just a short drive.'

A sudden tension seemed to come over Hope. It was almost indefinable, an extra edge of alertness, a slight turn of her head so that her ear was closer to Minnie, the better to catch a familiar tone.

'Three hours is not a short drive,' she replied, 'especially when you've been torn from sleep. I don't think it was "nothing". Also, Luke has told me how you've been looking after him since the explosion. We must speak more of this later.'

'I'm glad you turned out to be all right, anyway,' Minnie said.

Hope smiled and said something gracious, then gave her attention to Luke, who had been standing by.

Hope refused their suggestion that she should go to bed, insisting that she felt well and wanted only to be among them. Half an hour later a car drew up outside and the missing son appeared. Franco had been in Los Angeles for the last few weeks and had just stepped off the plane after a thirteen hour flight. He and Hope ran straight into each other's arms.

'I always thought he was her favourite,' said Olympia, who was close to Minnie. 'Of course, she'd deny that she has any favourites, but with Franco there's just a little something extra—I think.' Seeing Minnie looking at her, she added, 'With Hope it's never wise to be sure.'

'I can see that she's a very unusual woman,' Minnie agreed.

'She sees everything, she hears everything, she knows everything,' Olympia said. 'And she plots in secret.'

'Plots?'

'She thinks it's time she had more daughters-in-law, and she's not the type to just sit back and cross her fingers. Justin and Evie actually broke up, but she went to England and got them on track again.'

'And you and Primo?'

Olympia chuckled. 'I must admit that it was Luke who played Cupid that time. You wouldn't think it to look at him, would you?'

'He doesn't look like Cupid, no,' Minnie said, regarding Luke with her head on one side, and considering the matter seriously. 'But then, Cupid comes in many shapes. Sometimes he can look like a good friend, until you're ready for more.'

'There's got to be a whole fascinating history behind that remark,' Olympia said.

'There is,' Minnie assured her.

There were more introductions, but Franco was clearly too full of jet lag to take in many details, and he wanted to talk to his mother.

Minnie found an unexpected ally in young Mark, Justin's thirteen year old son, who turned out to come from the same part of London where she'd once lived with her mother. They had a good time saying, 'Do you know that place where—?' until Evie, his step-mother, came to join in.

As soon as dinner was over Minnie said quietly to Luke, 'I'll say goodnight now.'

'So soon?'

'I don't mean to be impolite, but I'm really in the way here. Your mother wants to be with her family, and I should catch up with my emails. I brought my laptop.'

'Do you take work everywhere you go?' he asked, appalled.

'It's always useful.'

She said goodnight to Hope, excusing herself on the grounds of catching up on her lost sleep of the night before.

In her room she connected the laptop and tried to concentrate on work, but it was strangely hard. From below she could hear the hum of a happy family, and it increased the sense of isolation that had swept over her.

I don't belong here, she thought. *I should get back to Naples and 'my' family, who need me.*

Then she wondered at herself for feeling this way. Since Gianni's death she'd taught herself to be self-sufficient, as content alone as in a crowd, and it was natural that she should be an outsider here. But she felt as though she'd been separated from Luke at the very moment that her heart wanted to draw nearer to him.

Jealousy, she thought, mocking herself. Jealousy at this late date.

And fear lest she lose him, a feeling she'd known so little that it had taken her time to recognise it.

She worked for a couple of hours, subconsciously listening to the house grow quiet about her. Then she shut down the computer, showered and got ready for bed. When the light was out she went to the window and stood looking out over the garden, where coloured lights hung between the trees.

A few yards along from her she could see a staircase leading down to the garden, and suddenly she needed to be down there. There was nobody in the corridor when she looked out, and she hurried along to where a door led out on to a balcony, from where the stairs descended.

In a moment she'd run down on to the lawn, hurrying to get between the trees.

Here there was fresh sea air to be breathed in, and a sense of release. She stood looking down at the bay, taking deep breaths, feeling herself relax after the nervous strains of the last two days. Passionately she longed for Luke to be here with her, but strangely she also longed to get away from here, back to Rome, back to the life she knew and where she belonged, back to the time before she'd met Luke.

She wanted him, yet he threatened something in her, and part of her wanted to flee, all the more because she sensed that he was as wary of her as she was of him.

'Are you there?'

She whirled around to see him coming towards her between the trees, and her own flash of happiness was like a warning. *Get away from him now.*

'Yes, I'm here,' she called back softly.

He reached out and drew her into the shadows with him.

'I was afraid I wouldn't see you again tonight. Did you come out to find me?'

'No, I just—well, maybe I did—'

Hadn't that been in her mind all the time? she wondered.

'I wanted to talk to you all evening,' he murmured, 'but I couldn't get close to you. This place is too crowded. I wish I could come back to Rome with you, but I can't leave just yet.'

She made a wry grimace. 'The flat is going to feel awfully empty without you.'

'Yes, you won't have anyone to tell you the answers in the game shows,' he agreed.

'Or help me with the crossword puzzles.'

'You've got to admit, I have my uses,' he said with a wry attempt at humour.

'Oh, yes—Luke—Luke—'

Minnie reached up to take his face between her hands, looking at him intently, torn by two powerful emotions, full of confusion.

'What is it?' he asked. 'Which of us are you looking at?'

'Luke—don't—'

'Who is it, Minnie? Him or me?'

This time it was she who drew him close. 'Not now,' she whispered.

He wanted to protest that it mattered, but the sweet scent of her was in his nostrils. He'd been strong for her sake, but now it was she who wanted him to be weak and that was harder to fight.

When her lips brushed against his he knew that resisting her wasn't going to be hard, but impossible. The passion he'd thought under control welled up now, so that she was flame in his arms, burning and igniting him, driving him to kiss her with a kind of ruthlessness.

And at once he felt her response to that ruthlessness. She was no green girl but a woman who'd experienced passionate love, but had then lived celibate while desire built in her, waiting to be triggered by the right man. It was all there in the heated movements of her mouth, the sensuality that made her press closer to him, the hot breath that mingled with his.

She offered no resistance when his lips trailed down her neck to the base of her throat, then further to the swell of her breasts. He could feel the pounding of her heart, hear the soft groan that broke from her and everything in him urged him on to what could be a blissful conclusion.

Or disaster.

'Minnie—' He seemed to hear himself say her name as if from a distance. 'Minnie—wait—'

Using all the strength he could find, he drew away and held her at arm's length.

'Wait—' he said again. 'Not like this.'

'What?' she whispered.

'Look at me,' he said urgently. 'Look at me.'

Her face was upturned to him but he saw with alarm that her eyes were unfocused.

'Where are you, Minnie? You're not here with me. *Where are you?' And who's there with you?* he wanted to add.

'Why do you worry about things now?' she whispered.

'Because I want you too much to risk what we could have,' he said hoarsely. 'Or maybe I'm fooling myself and we could never have it—'

'No, you're not fooling yourself but... So much has happened. Luke—if you want me—'

'I do. I want you as much as any man has ever wanted any woman, *but not like this.*'

'What do you mean?'

'Where is Gianni? Can you tell me that?'

There was a stunned look in her eyes, as though she were pulling herself together with an effort.

'He's here, isn't he?' Luke raged. 'He's here because he's always here, but that's not good enough. I want you to come to me, *me*, not some fantasy figure that's half me and half the man you really love.'

He gave a little shake. 'Get rid him,' he growled. 'Or tell me how to get rid of him.'

'I don't know how.' It was a cry of pain.

'You must, if there's ever to be anything for us. I want

to make love to you. God knows how much I want that, but only when I come first with you. Until then—'

A tremor shook him, made up of thwarted desire and rage.

'Until then there's nothing between us,' he managed to say before thrusting her from him and walking away.

It felt brutal, but he had to do it while he still had the strength.

He got as far away from her as possible, but then turned back. He wanted to tire himself, even though he knew it was no cure for what was raging through him. There was only one cure for that, and he began to think he would never find it.

Looking up, he saw a light in Minnie's window. He longed to go up to her room, beg her to forget what had passed tonight, say he would accept anything if only he could find a home in her bed, in her heart.

But this was the most dangerous temptation of all. He ran from it, turning into a path that led away from the house, into the trees, then out again to where he knew there was a garden seat, overlooking the bay. There he could be safely alone.

But someone was there before him.

'Come and sit with me, my son,' Hope invited, patting the space beside her.

He did so, seating himself with a sigh, and running a hand through his hair. Hope watched him, silent but understanding.

'So now I've met your ''chambermaid''?' she said at last, with a twinkle.

'Chambermaid?'

'The one who answered the phone that morning. There now, don't I have a marvellous memory for an old woman?'

'You'll never be old, and I've sometimes wished that your memory was a little less marvellous.'

'I know that. It's quite disconcerting how well I remember certain things. You said she was the chambermaid.'

'Mamma, I didn't actually say that. You suggested it and I—'

'Saw a useful way out,' Hope teased. 'Admit it.'

She was laughing, and after a moment he joined in. 'All right, I'm a coward. No question about it.'

'You may also recall,' Hope said, 'that I heard in her voice that she had a passionate nature. Now I've heard that voice again, and I know I was right.'

'Yes,' he murmured, still trying to calm himself. 'Yes. But Mamma, it's not like that.'

'Perhaps it's time you told me what it *is* like.' Hope came to the point of real importance. 'Am I going to have another daughter-in-law, or not?'

'I don't know,' he admitted. 'It's complicated.'

'Then why not tell me about it?'

'What is this? The Inquisition?'

'Just a mother's curiosity.'

'Is there a difference?'

'Not much,' Hope admitted, patting his hand. 'So, give in and tell me everything without making me work harder.'

'Yes, that was always the easiest way,' he recalled. 'All right, she was in my hotel room, but I wasn't there with her.'

'Then where were you? Tell me.'

'Yes, tell us,' said a voice from the shadows, and they both looked up to see Olympia standing there with a glass of champagne in her hand. She strolled forward and settled herself on a fallen tree trunk that lay nearby, and looked at their faces.

'I'm all ears to hear where you were,' she said.

'The trouble with acquiring a sister,' Luke said with careful restraint, 'is that it's just one more female to put her nose into a man's private affairs.'

'Good, then I'm doing the right thing,' Olympia said gleefully. 'Come on, tell. Where were you?'

Luke took a deep breath. There was no putting this off any longer.

'I was in a police cell,' he said through gritted teeth.

If this disconcerted his mother she gave no sign of it, merely nodding her head as if to say that sooner or later every young man saw the inside of a police cell. Which was probably what she did actually believe. Olympia contented herself with a little choke of laughter.

'What were you doing there?' she asked mildly.

'I got involved in a brawl and was arrested. Charlie was brawling too—he's Minnie's brother-in-law.'

'And his name's Charlie?' Olympia asked.

'It short for Charlemagne, because the family name is Pepino, which was the name of Charlemagne's father—'

'And they're descended from him?' Hope said.

Luke grinned. 'You'd never get them to admit that they weren't. And one of the neighbours has a cat called Tiberius—'

'After the Emperor Tiberius?' Hope asked, her lips twitching.

'Of course. It's that sort of place.'

He began to laugh at the memory, unaware that his mother was looking at him with fascination.

'So you and Charlemagne were brawling,' she reminded him.

'And Minnie came to bail him out, and that's how we met. She ended up defending me in court as well.'

The two women burst into laughter.

'How I wish I'd been there to see,' Hope said at last. 'My sensible, businesslike son, in a drunken brawl!'

'I didn't say drunken—'

'Nonsense, of course it was!' Olympia said firmly.

'Oh, dear—'

They went off into more gales of laughter while Luke gritted his teeth. But after a moment he relaxed and grinned.

'I remember the day you left here,' Hope said, 'full of plans to confront her in a businesslike fashion, not standing for any nonsense—'

'And I did confront her, in a police cell, with my clothes torn. I didn't have my ID card so she had to go to the hotel to collect it, and my phone. That's how she came to answer it.'

'You've been keeping a lot to yourself. You told me that you'd moved into the Residenza, but you left out the best things.'

'Well, I wasn't going to boast about my criminal record to my mother,' he said defensively, but he was grinning again.

'But the two of you have made friends now, since she was the one you went to when Toni called.'

He hesitated. 'I didn't have to go to her, Mamma. She was right there with me—'

'In your bed?'

'Her bed. I've been staying with her so that she could nurse me, but it wasn't—as you think.'

'I think nothing, my son, since nothing in your relationship with this young woman seems to follow a normal course. Where do you stand with each other?'

'I only wish I knew. I feel closer to her than any other woman I've ever known, and I know that she needs me. But I'm not the man she loves.'

Hope's eyebrows rose. 'Loving another man, she shares your bed?'

'Not in the sense you mean. For the last week she's cuddled up to me at night as she might have cuddled up to an old dog. The man she loves is her late husband, Gianni Pepino. He's been dead for four years but it might be yesterday, she's still so tied to his memory. No, he's more than a memory, he's a ghost that she can't escape. He's in her thoughts, he's there with us all the time. At night I've held her in my arms while she spoke of him.'

'And that's really all?' Hope asked, incredulous and slightly scandalised at the same time.

'Yes, it makes me sound like a wimp, doesn't it? All right, I *am* a wimp, but it's what she needs. She must talk of him or go mad, and she can't tell the others, so it has to be me.'

'And that is all the use she has for you, my son?'

Luke gave a wry laugh. 'That is all the use she has for me. Tonight, I did briefly hope—but it wasn't me. Not really.'

'But why do you put up with it? There are many other women in the world.'

He said nothing for a moment, but at last he spoke as though with the words he had finally discovered the truth.

'No, Mamma, there aren't. There isn't another woman whose smile can wring my heart as hers can, or make me want to throw aside everything else if only I can make her happy.'

Hope regarded him quizzically. 'This is *you* talking—my son, whose life has been lived balancing the accounts, calculating what everyone and everything was worth to him, and taking the long view?'

He winced. 'I'm not as bad as that, am I?'

'You were. But not now, I think.' Then, as though there were some connection, which perhaps there was, she added, 'I passed on your message of thanks to Olympia, by the way.'

'And I'm beginning to understand it now,' Olympia said. 'At one time you'd never have said the things you're saying now.'

He nodded. 'At one time, if a woman didn't go my way, I went off in another direction,' he mused. 'You were the first one I stuck around for, although I knew I might be knocked back—and I was. So, when Minnie knocks me back, I'll have some experience to help me cope.'

Olympia's answer to this was to lean forward and kiss him lightly on the mouth.

'I don't think she'll knock you back,' she said. 'Although you may have to come to your big sister for some advice.'

'Now go on with the story,' Hope commanded. 'Tell us some more about this man she married.'

'She feels guilty about his death because they were quarrelling, he chased after her and was run over in the road. He died in her arms. As a man—' Luke shrugged. 'He seems to have been a good-natured fellow, kind and affectionate. He was a truck driver, so I doubt if he'd ever have set the world alight, but he made her feel loved.'

'Oh-ho!' Hope exclaimed, regarding him with slightly scornful irony. 'So a truck driver has thrown you into the shade! You, of course, know all about setting the world alight, but have you ever made a woman feel so deeply loved that she never recovered from your loss?'

'Never,' he growled. 'There's no need to labour the point, Mamma.'

'No, because you've seen it for yourself, haven't you? You spoke lightly of throwing everything else aside for her sake, but were they only words, or could you live up to them if you had to? You might make her love you in a way, but suppose you can't also drive his ghost away? Can you live with him there, too, for her sake?'

'That's the thought that torments me. Does she love me, or does she merely cling to me from need?'

'And, if it's the second, can you love her anyway? Love isn't like a book-keeping ledger, my son. You don't always get equal repayment in return for what you give. Do you love her enough to settle for less, as long as she is happy?'

'I wish I knew myself better. Tonight we were together out here, and there was a moment when I thought I could make love to her. But I didn't. Something stopped me, something in here—' He laid a hand over his heart.

'What was it that stopped you, my son?'

'He was there and I couldn't get rid of him, and if I can't, how can she? I told her I'd never make love to her until I came first, but—'

'But suppose you never do?' Olympia asked gently. 'What then?'

He was silent for a long moment, before saying wretchedly, 'I don't know. Heaven help me, *I don't know*!'

Minnie was packed and ready to go next morning.

'Of course you must attend to your work,' Hope told

her kindly, 'but you must return to us soon. Luke, I rely on you to arrange it.'

The others came to bid her goodbye, including Franco, who said, 'You must forgive me for not remembering your name. I was jet lagged out of my mind last night.'

'This is Signora Minerva Pepino,' Luke said.

Only the most astute observer would have noticed the sudden *frisson* that went through Franco. Minnie was too occupied with her troubled thoughts to sense anything.

Luke walked her to the car. 'I'll be in Rome in a day or two,' he said.

'Your mother may want you to stay longer.'

'I can't risk it,' he said lightly. 'Who knows what legal mischief you'll get up to in my absence? I'll be there soon. Count on it.'

'Let's hope they've finished renovating your flat,' she said lightly.

'Are you that anxious to throw me out?'

'Goodbye,' she said, extending her hand and giving him a smile. It contained no warmth, only finality.

'Goodbye,' he said, taking her hand, not knowing what else to say or do.

He watched as she drove away, then walked slowly back to the house.

Franco was on the steps, staring at the road down which Minnie had driven away. He looked puzzled.

'What is it?' Luke asked.

'Nothing, I—did you say her name was Pepino?'

'Yes.'

'Minerva Pepino?'

'That's right. Have you heard of her?'

'I might have. And her husband's name was—?'

'Gianni.'

Franco drew in a sharp breath.

'Whatever's the matter?' Luke asked. 'Did you know Gianni?'

'Not well, but yes, I met him a few times.'

'In Rome?'

'No, here in Naples. He used to come here often.'

'That's right, he collected things in his truck.'

'So he may have done, but he also came to see a woman.'

Luke's head jerked up. 'That's impossible. He was happily married until he died four years ago.'

Franco shrugged. 'Maybe he was, but I'm telling you that he had a woman here, and a son.'

CHAPTER TWELVE

'AND I tell you, you've got it wrong. You're confusing him with someone else.'

'The man I knew was called Gianni Pepino, he had a wife called Minerva and she was a lawyer in Rome.'

Luke poured himself a glass of brandy, and drained it in one gulp. Somewhere inside him an earthquake was taking place.

'I don't believe it,' he murmured. 'She adored him. She still does.'

'Well, he certainly managed to pull the wool over her eyes,' Franco said. 'The girl is called Elsa Alessio, and the child is called Sandro. He got her pregnant when he was down here one summer, fooling around. He was only eighteen, and there was never any talk of marriage. She was older, a divorcee, and she had some money of her own.

'From the way he talked, they weren't in love or anything. They just had a fling and stayed friends. He used to come here to see her and the boy, then go back to Rome. After he got married he just kept on visiting her, chiefly to see his son and give her money—'

'I thought you said she didn't need money.'

'She didn't need to marry him, but a decent man supports his child, and maybe a little extra as a present for her.'

'*Bastardo!*' Luke said softly.

'Why? Gianni loved his wife, and what happened before they married didn't concern her.'

'But he never told her.'

'Of course he didn't. Why hurt her for nothing?'

It was a point of view, Luke realised, with which a lot of men would sympathise. But he was conscious of a burning anger for Minnie's sake.

'How often did he visit her?' he demanded.

Franco shrugged. 'How do I know? But I had a friend who knew him better, and he said Gianni used to boast of those visits.'

'Boast? How?'

Franco shrugged. 'How do you think?'

'Perhaps you should tell us, my son,' Hope said quietly from the shadows.

Franco jumped. 'Mamma. I didn't know you were there.'

'Evidently, or you wouldn't be indulging in foolish, loose talk. Minnie was a guest under our roof. How dare you spread such stories?'

'I didn't invent it, Mamma. It's true.'

'How much is true? About the child? Perhaps.'

'And he boasted that he could have Elsa whenever he wanted,' Franco said.

'And do you know that he was telling the truth? Does one believe every word that a boastful young man says? I don't think so. Listen, my son, you are not to say another word of this matter. Rumours can hurt people, even when they are unfounded, and I would not have Minnie hurt for all the world. Please promise me that you'll forget this and never repeat it.'

'All right, Mamma. I promise.'

'And you'd better keep that promise,' Luke said, 'or I'll throttle you.'

'I've forgotten everything I ever heard, I swear it.'

Looking sheepish, Franco kissed his mother's cheek and departed, careful to avoid Luke's eye.

Luke didn't speak for a while after Franco left. He stood looking out over the terrace, brooding. 'It can't be true, can it?' he asked at last.

'He had the right names,' Hope said. 'It could be true about the child.'

'Bastardo!' Luke said again. 'She thinks he was so wonderful, and all the time—'

'But why are you angry?' she asked him. 'Surely this solves your problem?'

'How do you mean?'

'You wanted a way to drive him from her heart, and now you have it. Just tell her that the husband she idolised deceived her. Surely the simplest calculation should make that plain.'

'I don't like the word calculation,' he growled.

'It's the one you've always lived by. I was merely speaking your own language.'

'All right.' He swung round. 'Let's say I tell her about this woman and child because I've *calculated*—' he nearly spat the word '—that it will benefit me. But will it? It happened before he knew her, so where's the betrayal?'

'He went on seeing them when he came to Naples.'

'As any decent man would, rather than abandon his child. He kept quiet so as not to hurt her, but that still makes Minnie the one he truly loved. If I want to destroy him in her eyes, I'll need more than that.'

'But he went on sleeping with this woman,' Hope pointed out. 'There is the betrayal. Tell Minnie that. Make her accept the truth. Then the road should be clear for you.'

In silence he turned and looked at her.

* * *

Minnie's phone rang at exactly eleven o'clock.

'I waited until now so as not to interrupt your work,' Luke said.

'I might be asleep by now,' she pointed out.

'You never were. We were usually still talking nonsense at this hour. Then you'd make the cocoa.'

She laughed, and they fell silent.

'What are you doing now?' he asked.

'Just closing the books, then going to bed.'

Trying to put off the moment, she thought, *because it's so lonely without you.*

'You were supposed to be having some time off after that case collapsed,' he reminded her. 'You could have stayed here.'

'No, I—I don't think that would have been a good idea. There's too much... Things get confused.'

'Yes,' he said, and she knew that he, too, was remembering their last meeting alone, when he'd railed at Gianni's ghost.

'What about you?' she asked. 'What are you doing?'

'I went to the hospital with Mamma, for her to have a check-up. Everything's fine. And my bandages have been removed.'

'Is your arm better?'

'Looking good. I'll be back soon, driving you crazy.'

She thought, but didn't say, When?

'Franco's going back to Los Angeles at the end of the week.'

So it would be at least the end of the week before he would return. She forced her voice to be bright and cheerful, saying, 'I'm sure your mother wants him with her as much as possible before he vanishes again.'

'She was thrilled with the card you sent her, by the way.'

'She was so nice to me, I wanted to thank her, and wish her well.'

They talked for a few more minutes, saying nothing about the things that were really in their minds. When she had put the phone down the flat felt very quiet. It had always been quiet and lonely since Gianni died, but somehow this was different.

She took out his picture and settled down with it as she had done so often before.

'What do I do now?' she whispered. 'You were always a fast talker—go on, tell me.'

The smile in his eyes was as charming as ever, but now something was missing. There had always been a gleam, inviting her into the loving conspiracy they shared. Now it seemed to be gone. It was just a flat photograph. She tried again.

'I don't know whether I'm coming or going. No man ever did that to me before, not even you. You came on to me the very first evening, and I always knew what you were thinking. But now—'

She waited, hoping for what had happened before, that out of her memories would rise one that gave her the answer. But there was nothing, and she realised that Gianni couldn't help her with this.

In fact, there was no more help he could give her. The moment had been a long time coming, and she wasn't quite sure when he'd finally slipped away from her. Closing her eyes now, all she could feel was Luke's hand on her hair, and his whispered promise, 'I'm here.'

She opened her eyes again. Gianni's face was the same, unchanging, as it would always be now. She pressed her lips against the glass, realising finally how cold it was.

'Thank you for everything,' she whispered, 'all the years—thank you, thank you, my love. And goodbye.'

She put the picture away in her desk, and turned the key in the lock.

Luke called her every day. The calls were always the same—cheerful, non-committal, cautious. It was as though they were both waiting for something to happen.

Netta remained obstinately smiling, refusing to admit that her plans had suffered a setback. Minnie even found her going through a magazine full of wedding dresses.

'That one,' she said, pointing to a slender, elegant creation.

'I couldn't wear that,' Minnie said, outraged. 'It's bridal white, and I'm a widow.'

'So, there's a law against it?' Netta snorted. 'You wear what you like.'

'Only if I'm getting married, and I'm not. I wish I could make you understand that.'

'Pooh!' Netta said. 'It's written in your stars. You marry in Santa Maria in Trastevere—'

'Oh, so you've chosen the church as well as the dress! It's a pity we don't have a groom, but why be troubled by a detail?'

'I take care of the church and the dress,' Netta said. 'But I leave the groom to you.' She added, as a parting shot, 'You've gotta do *something* for yourself.'

Minnie glared but, since Netta took no notice whatever, she had no recourse but to depart and head back to her own home.

There was a man on the staircase, looking up and down and around, clearly lost.

'Can I help you?' Minnie asked.

He turned, smiling. Something in that smile sent a *fris-*

son of alarm through her, although she couldn't, at that moment, have said why.

Ten minutes later she knew the worst, and was running down the stairs to find her car and head out of Rome, hell-bent for Naples.

The family had been to see Franco off at the airport, and had enjoyed a good dinner on their return home. Now the Villa Rinucci was closing down for the night, and Luke and his mother were taking a last walk around the garden.

'It's been wonderful to see Franco,' Hope said wistfully, 'but it's probably a good thing if he's not around while you're sorting things out with Minnie.'

'Yes, he knows too much,' Luke agreed wryly.

'Have you decided yet what you're going to tell her?'

'No, I have no idea.'

'It's been nearly a week. I don't recall when I've seen you so indecisive.'

'I keep thinking it's simple. I'll tell her, because I can't live out the future keeping such a secret from her. But then I think what it will do to her, and I know I can never say anything.'

'Even if it means living with Saint Gianni for ever? Could you do that?'

'I don't know.' He added lightly, 'I suppose, if we're married, it's always possible that she might turn her thoughts to me occasionally. I'm not asking for miracles, but, hey—it might happen.'

She laughed and patted his arm. 'You're becoming a realist, my son.'

They had reached the front of the house and he stopped, looking down the hill to where he could see moving lights.

'What is it?' Hope asked.

'Someone's heading towards us at a great rate.'

They watched the fast moving lights winding up the hill until Luke said, 'Surely, that's Minnie's car?'

'I think it is,' Hope said, unable to keep the pleasure and excitement out of her voice.

The car came to a halt with a screech and Minnie was out in a moment, slamming the door behind her and advancing on Luke with a face of doom. The lamps showed tears glistening on her face.

'You!' she said, pointing at him. 'I knew it! *I knew it!* I should never have trusted you from the first moment, but you made me feel sorry for you and I swear I'll never feel sorry for anyone again as long as I live. I trusted you, more fool me!'

Luke finally got his breath. 'Minnie, will you please tell me what this is all about?'

'I'll tell you in two words,' she raged. *'Eduardo Viccini!'*

His groan and the way he closed his eyes in despair told her all she needed to know.

'You do know the man I'm talking about, don't you?' she snapped.

'Yes, I know. I gather you've met him.'

'Yes, I've met him. He came looking for you today and said some very interesting things. You should have been more careful, Luke. You should have warned him that I knew nothing about the interesting little scheme the two of you had cooked up. You lying, treacherous, two-faced—'

She broke off as more tears came, furiously brushing them away, trying to deny them, but unable to stop because she felt as though something was crushing her heart.

'Minnie—' He reached out to her but she flung his hand aside.

'Don't come near me.'

'Look, I'm sorry you met him like that—'

'You're sorry I met him at all. At least, you are if you've got any sense. I wasn't supposed to find out that you were planning to betray the lot of us until it was too late, was I?'

There was careful movement inside the house as the sounds of altercation brought the rest of the family to doors and windows, but silently. Nobody wanted to miss this, certainly not Primo and Olympia, who stood, arms entwined, watching the last act of a drama that was partly their own. Hope melted softly into the shadows.

'I have not betrayed you,' Luke said. 'Any of you.'

'Oh, I suppose it isn't betrayal to sell out to a development company—'

'I haven't—'

'Don't lie to me,' she cried. 'You'll be telling me next that you've never heard of Allerio Proprieta.'

'I've done more than heard of it. I formed it. Allerio Proprieta is me, with some backing from Eduardo Viccini. I'm the boss but I need his finance. What I'm planning is going to be expensive.'

'I'll bet it is, starting with clearing the whole lot of us out.'

'No, I swear it. Everyone who wants to stay is safe. You've said yourself that I can't force anyone out, and I'm not trying to. Offering them sweeteners is another matter.'

'You admit it?'

'I don't admit anything,' Luke said, 'because I've done nothing wrong. If a man has something I want I'll offer him a fair price for it. He's free to say no, and if he does he'll get no trouble from me. If he says yes, it's because he's gaining something, and that is fair exchange.'

'Some of them are leaving already. You must have worked damned hard to bring that about.'

'You mean Mario in number eight? He's been offered a good job on the other side of Rome and he wants to live close to it. It's a promotion, so he can afford a bigger home, which is fine because his wife is pregnant.'

'And I suppose it's coincidence that he was offered that job now?'

'Coincidence, nothing! Eduardo knows someone who's always looking for people with Mario's skills. Their meeting was a success, and now Mario has the job of his dreams. Do you think he feels ill-used? I promise you he doesn't.'

While she tried to find an answer to this, Luke went on, 'What about the couple in number twenty-three? They want to stop renting and buy, but they haven't got the deposit for the place they want. Or rather, they didn't have.'

'And you gave it to them?'

'No, I'm not Santa Claus, it's an interest free loan, and now they're happy as skylarks. If you don't believe me, ask them.

'I could give you a dozen other cases. They're not all attached to the Residenza as we are. For them it's just a place to live for a while, then pass on. I'm just making it easy for them to do that.'

'And what about my family?'

'They'll stay. Anyone who wants to can stay, but plenty will leave, willingly, and I can start work, making it a smart place to live.'

She was silent, confused and troubled. One thing he'd said was flashing in her mind.

'What do you mean, *we*?' she asked.

'We?'

'You said, "They're not all attached to the Residenza as *we* are." *We?*'

'Yes, I love it. I plan to live there. That's why Pietro is moving out of the flat next to mine, and into a small one lower down. Boy, did that cost me! I need both those flats so that I can knock them into one and have a place that's big enough for two people.'

'For—two?'

'Yes, I don't think that you and I can live in your present home. Better to make a fresh start in our own place.'

'Whoa, you're going too fast for me. Who said we were going to live together?'

Luke drew a deep breath. 'Well, people who marry usually do that.'

'And who said we were going to get married?'

'Netta said it. And Charlie said it, and Tomaso said it, and every single person in your family said it. But they only said it because Netta said it first. Now I'm saying it. It only needs you to say it, and everybody's said it.'

'Wait a minute!' She held up a hand to stop him. 'Are you proposing that we get married just because Netta's given her orders?'

'Why not? Your mother-in-law is exactly like my mother. People do what she says, sooner or later. Face it, Minnie! Netta had it sorted on the first day, so we may as well give in now.'

She stared at him, aghast.

'And that's a proposal is it? That's the great romantic proposal?'

'Well, I'm not at my best in front of an audience,' he said, jerking his head to include the crowd standing behind him, grinning now and relishing every moment.

'You—you've got a nerve—you dare—'

'I'm just doing as I'm told. You know I'm right about Netta. It wouldn't surprise me if she's actually decided on the church. She's probably even picked your wedding dress. What is it?'

Minnie had gasped and clapped her hands over her mouth.

'Minnie—what is it?'

She couldn't answer. The eerie accuracy of his prediction had taken her breath away. It was as though fate had tapped her on the shoulder and said, This way!

'Santa Maria in Trastevere,' she whispered.

'Is that the church where we're marrying?'

'Netta says so.'

'Has she fixed the date?'

'Probably—*Luke!*'

'Come here,' he said fiercely, and pulled her towards him.

In the long, long kiss that followed the rest of the Rinucci family emerged slowly and quietly, until they were standing on the porch, watching with pleasure the two who were embracing in the patch of light below. Only Hope stood a little apart, holding her breath for the issue that she knew was still to be resolved.

'How could you think I'd stoop so low?' he asked when he finally released her.

'I don't know, but it was the worst thing that ever happened to me. I trusted you.'

'That's not what you used to say,' he said wryly.

'Not to your face, maybe, but I always knew you were decent and honest, no matter how many insults I hurled at you. And then, when I thought you'd cheated us—it was as though the central pillar of the world had cracked. Until then, I didn't know how much I minded. Luke, don't you understand, it's the most terrible thing that can happen, to trust someone you love and then find out they were betraying you?'

'Yes,' he said softly. 'I do understand that. And that's why—' he was holding her hands tightly '—there's something I have to say to you, and I want you to listen well, because it's important.'

'Yes?' She was looking at him with shining eyes.

'I told you once that I'd never make love to you until I came first.'

'But you do come first—in my heart—in my whole life—'

'First among the living, but I wanted to drive out his ghost.'

'Luke—'

'It's all right; let me finish. I wanted to get rid of Gianni, but I was being selfish. I was jealous of him. He gave you ten years of happiness, and who knows if I can measure up to that? I guess I just didn't like the competition, so I wanted to deprive you of the sweetest memories you have, all to suit my convenience.

'Try to forgive me for that, because I see more clearly now. One love doesn't drive out another. Nor should it. Keep your ghost, my darling. Keep him and go right on loving him as he deserved. I dare say I can manage to live in a threesome.'

Every eye was fixed on them. Nobody noticed that Hope's face was transformed by a smile of pride in her son.

Minnie looked intently at Luke. 'Do you have anything else to say?'

'Nothing.'

'Does that mean you're not going to tell me?'

'Tell you what?'

'About Elsa Alessio,' she said simply.

He stared, truly shocked.

'What do you know about that?'

'I know that she's a woman in Naples who bore Gianni's son, years ago, before he met me. He used to see them when he drove his truck down here. He was a good father, but I was the one he loved.'

'He told you—everything?' he asked, hardly daring to believe.

'Of course he did. We loved each other. He wouldn't have deceived me. He told me everything that I needed to know,' she added with a slightly ambiguous phrasing that he didn't notice until later.

He could hardly believe that he'd been let off the hook. Or at least, almost. There was still one tiny hook.

It was on the tip of his tongue to ask if she believed Gianni had been faithful to her on those visits to Elsa. Did she know that he had boasted otherwise?

But the next moment he knew that this was a secret he must keep. Who could tell if such boasts had been true, or even if he'd said any such thing? And, without certainty, he had no right to speak.

And if the worst was true, and she had to learn it one day, he would prepare for that day by making her so happy in their marriage that nothing from the past could touch her.

That was the resolve he made to himself, that he would keep in secret and never speak of to her as long as they both lived.

'Would you really move to Rome, for me?' she asked in wonder.

'I can extend my business there, and become a sleeping partner in the Naples factories. I'll enjoy the challenge of new territories. You can't leave your practice. You've built it up in Rome.'

'And you're not jealous of it?' There was an old anxiety in her voice.

'I swear I'll never be jealous. Or at least, if I am,' he added with a touch of humour, 'I'll keep it decently to myself.'

She reached up and took his head between her hands, searching his face.

'When I thought I'd lost you, it was the end of the world for me. I love you so much; without you there's nothing.'

'Don't say it unless you're completely sure,' he said anxiously.

'Completely, totally, utterly sure. I thought I could never love any other man again, but I was only waiting for you. I didn't want to believe it—I got so mad at you—'

'Yes, I know that,' he said with a laugh that sounded shaky because relief and happiness were making him weak. 'I tried to get mad at you, but I could barely manage it, and I could never stay mad for five minutes. You used to look at me in that way you have, and then—I don't know—things happened to me.'

'I think it's time something happened now,' she murmured, tightening her hands on his head.

In the long kiss that followed they could hear the sound of soft cheering from the shadows.

'My family are just loving this,' he murmured.

Then he was silent, holding her fiercely against him, as though afraid to risk her slipping away, kissing her again and again.

'Do I hear applause?' she murmured.

'Probably. The Rinuccis are like the Pepinos. Love and marriage concern everyone. All those things they heard me say once, about keeping control of my life, being cautious, even in love—what a laugh I'm giving them now! But I don't care. Let them laugh, because I'm the winner. *Carissima,* I don't want to keep control of my life any longer. I want you to have it. Take it, and keep me safe.'

'There's something I want you to know,' she said earnestly.

'What is it, my love?'

'I said goodbye to Gianni yesterday, finally and for good. He understands.'

It was said afterwards that the meeting of Netta Pepino and Hope Rinucci was like the meeting of monarchs. An official visit was made from Naples to Rome, and the Rinuccis were ceremonially entertained.

Hope and Netta inspected the two flats that were being knocked into one and pronounced themselves satisfied.

'You have done the right thing in choosing to live in Rome,' Hope told him privately later. They were standing at the window in Netta's front room, eating her delicious home-made cake. 'Franco will be home soon, and it's best not to risk him saying a word out of turn.'

'I nearly said it myself,' he observed.

'Oh, no,' Hope said fondly. 'You were never going to tell her anything.'

'You can't be sure of that.'

'Certainly I'm sure. You love her far too much to hurt her. I always knew that. But I wasn't sure that *you* knew.'

'I didn't know, until I was faced with the choice. Then I realised there was no choice. There never had been. But you—all that stuff you were handing me about calculating how to get what I wanted—'

'My son, I knew you wouldn't actually do it. I know you better than you know yourself.'

Toni, who'd been standing behind them for the last minute, observed, 'Even so, I think he can still surprise you.'

'How do you mean, *caro*?'

'Tell her, Luke.'

'Years ago Toni offered me the chance to become a Rinucci, and I turned it down because there was still a lot about families that I didn't understand. An hour ago I asked him if the offer was still open.'

'And I told him it was,' Toni said.

He was right. Hope was taken utterly by surprise. Her eyes filled with tears of joy and she embraced the son who had finally decided to come in from the cold.

The only person not pleased by this arrangement was Netta.

'Better you change your name to Pepino,' she advised him. 'Then you'll be descended from an emperor.'

Laughing, Luke vetoed the idea, but Netta had her own way in everything else. Minnie wore the slim white dress and veil for her wedding in Santa Maria in Trastevere, and afterwards she and her groom went in a horse-drawn carriage through the streets to the Residenza, where the reception was to be held in the courtyard.

The carriage took the long way round, for the sake of all her neighbours who wanted to see her, and by the time it reached home the families had contrived to get there first, climbing the stairs, hung with fresh white flowers, until they lined the inner surface of the courtyard, almost to the sky.

Netta and Hope, two queens, led the cheers that broke

out as they appeared under the arch into the courtyard, and when hundreds of white petals showered down on the bride and groom as they stood gazing upwards in wonder, it was they who threw the first and the last, and they who cheered, laughed and wept the longest.

We're thrilled to bring you four bestselling collections that we know you'll love…

Bedroom Bargains of Revenge

Emma Darcy
Melanie Milburne
Trish Morey

featuring

BOUGHT FOR REVENGE, BEDDED FOR PLEASURE
by Emma Darcy

BEDDED AND WEDDED FOR REVENGE
by Melanie Milburne

THE ITALIAN BOSS'S MISTRESS OF REVENGE
by Trish Morey

One Passionate Night's Miracle

Susan Stephens
Carol Marinelli
Melissa James

featuring

ONE-NIGHT BABY
by Susan Stephens

THE SURGEON'S MIRACLE BABY
by Carol Marinelli

OUTBACK BABY MIRACLE
by Melissa James

3 in 1 ONLY £5.99

On sale from 17th December 2010

MILLS & BOON

By Request

...Make sure you don't miss out on these fabulous stories!

3 in 1 ONLY £5.99

featuring

RIDING THE STORM

JARED'S COUNTERFEIT FIANCÉE

THE CHASE IS ON

by Brenda Jackson

featuring

PRODIGAL SON
by Susan Mallery

THE BOSS AND MISS BAXTER
by Wendy Warren

THE BABY DEAL
by Victoria Pade

On sale from 1st January 2011

Available at WHSmith, Tesco, ASDA, Eason and all good bookshops

www.millsandboon.co.uk